Brinshore

The Watson Novels

ANN MYCHAL

To Gladys
In loving memory

What in the name of common sense is to recommend Brinshore? – a most insalubrious air – roads proverbially detestable – water brackish beyond example, impossible to get a good dish of tea within three miles of the place – and as for the soil – it is so cold and ungrateful that it can hardly be made to yield a cabbage…

Sanditon Jane Austen

CHAPTER ONE

Osborne Castle 1816

'Her head is full of emptiness!' said Mrs Turner.

'Indeed it is! Quite full of it,' agreed the Dowager Lady Osborne. 'Emma is just as she should be at nineteen. I cannot deny it — my granddaughter reminds me of myself at that very age.'

Mrs Turner sighed in fond remembrance of a happier time. 'Oh, to be nineteen again! To laugh and flirt and dance to one's heart's delight! If only Emma were more inclined to show herself to advantage...'

'Exactly my view,' interrupted the Dowager. 'The ball at Lowford Park is a case in point.'

Mrs Turner, determined to be heard, raised her voice and continued, 'Why, Lowford's nephew was obliged to enquire of his uncle whether *Miss Osborne* was out or not.' Vexed by the Dowager's insistence on interjecting at every turn, Mrs Turner quickly added, 'It was quite the other way in our day.'

'Indeed,' replied the Dowager. 'No one was left in any doubt about you, my dear Mrs Turner.'

Lady Osborne regarded her aunt and mother-in-law with amused complacency but said nothing. Instead, she set about mixing the tea leaves, and contented herself with thoughts of her own concerning certain practical matters of household management. When called upon some minutes later to proffer an opinion on a matter quite unrelated to the contents or otherwise of her daughter's head, Lady Osborne was lost for words.

'Forgive me,' said she. 'My mind was elsewhere.'

'Dear me,' said Mrs Turner, 'you are too young to suffer unsteadiness of mind. Such is my defence against tiresome society.' Glancing at the Dowager, Mrs Turner continued, 'I expect we two are rather wearisome company at times.'

'Oh no, dear Aunt,' said Lady Osborne. 'Wearisome is not the word.' Taxing might better have described the company of the two women who had first become acquainted half a century ago in the old rooms at Bath, and who graced Her Ladyship's drawing room with relentless frequency. The Dowager Lady Osborne and Mrs Turner's presence could be relied upon on every fine day of the year, every feast day, and on days when the ancient barouche at the Dower House was deemed fit for use in inclement weather. The Dowager, who was quick to assert and retain her independence over every sphere of her life, would accept no help from her son and his wife concerning matters pertaining to the maintenance of her conveyance. Her insistence on moving here and there at will, without the inconvenience of explaining her movements by sending to the Castle to beg the use of one of her son's carriages, would not be surrendered easily.

'Then what think you of our scheme?' said the Dowager.

'Scheme?' said Lady Osborne.

'Mrs Turner is to give up Delham Cottage,' her mother-in-law replied.

'Aunt?' Lady Osborne looked to Mrs Turner for an explanation.

'I am to move to the Dower House,' said she.

In a lofty tone, the Dowager added, 'I have invited your aunt to be my companion.'

Lady Osborne had, over the years, learned to expect a certain element of the unpredictable from her mother-in-law and bore it well, but this news was of a different order, and entirely unforeseen. Nevertheless, she endeavoured to maintain as steady a countenance as she was able in light of her mother-in-law's disclosure.

However questionable the plan seemed in the mind of the hearer, given the dispositions of the persons concerned, Lady Osborne was inclined to speak favourably of it, at least for the present. Objections could be safely left to her husband, who would have no hesitation in raising them once his amusement and incredulity at the prospect of such a proposal had been properly spent.

'So you approve, my dear?' said Mrs Turner.

'I do,' replied Lady Osborne with studied nonchalance.

'My dear Mrs Turner, one is not obliged to seek approval of one's family upon such matters,' said the Dowager. 'Indeed, one is not obliged to seek approval of one's family on any matter of import at all. It is quite enough simply to inform them of one's decision.'

Mrs Turner caught the look that passed between the Dowager and Lady Osborne, and gave up any thought of pursuing the subject further. For several moments the ladies sipped their tea in silence, avoiding each other's gaze. At length, as the clock in the hall chimed on the hour, and to ease an awkward breach in the proceedings, Mrs

Turner ventured to observe, 'How very agreeable it will be to have a carriage completely at one's disposal, having been so long without one.'

'The carriage will, of course, be at your disposal when I have no use of it,' said the Dowager.

Mrs Turner replied with a slight, acquiescent nod of the head.

A further silence ensued until once again she took the liberty to remark, 'I shall bring my servants with me, of course.'

'Oh no, my dear,' said the Dowager. 'There will be no room for your servants at the Dower House. Find them new positions, if you will, but do not foist them onto to me.'

'Foist them?' replied Mrs Turner, incredulous.

'Better still, send them to the Castle. Their need is greater than mine judging from the state of the morning room and the chimney in the great hall.'

Lady Osborne smiled with all the patient benevolence she could muster. 'Dear Mama, how very obliging of you to offer the services of those who are not in your employ.'

'I am ever willing to offer advice where it is needed,' her mother-in-law replied.

'And you offer such liberal amounts of it,' said Mrs Turner. 'Your generosity knows no bounds. I — '

'And when you have consulted my housekeeper,' interrupted the Dowager, 'you will agree to the wisdom of the plan.'

'But what about Hedges? Poor dear Hedges! She makes the most delicious rabbit fricassee! And she is so very attached to Delham Cottage, and to me. How will she bear it?' said Mrs Turner, contemplating the disagreeable prospect of losing her cook.

'With perfect ease, I should imagine,' said the Dowager. 'She will have the distinction of being in the employ of the Castle.'

'The Castle already has a cook,' replied Lady Osborne. 'And you know what they say about *too many* cooks.'

'Quite,' said Mrs Turner, in full agreement with her niece.

Seeing that the Dowager would not be moved, her daughter-in-law sighed, 'I will see what I can do.'

'Without delay if you please, my dear' continued the Dowager, 'or Mr Edwards will have Mrs Turner marching up the aisle before one can say — '

'Mr Edwards? Whatever do you mean?' said Lady Osborne. 'Aunt?'

Before Mrs Turner was able to open her mouth, the Dowager interjected, 'And if your aunt is to avoid Mr Edwards' advances, which are, I might add, wholly unwelcome, the Dower House is the perfect place for concealment. Were he to call, I should simply not receive him.'

'Is this true, Aunt?' asked Lady Osborne.

'And Mrs Edwards not yet a complete twelvemonth in her grave,' said the Dowager. 'It is scandalous how men get out of mourning their dear departed so much sooner than the rest of us!'

Mrs Turner shrugged. 'I expect Mr Edwards means well.'

'He is in want of company. His spirits are low, as they must be at so great a loss,' said Lady Osborne.

'One might describe Mr Edwards in many ways, but "grieving widower" is not, I fear, one of them,' replied the Dowager.

'If Mr Edwards seeks companionship,' said Lady Osborne, 'why should he not —'

'Mr Edwards is five and seventy if he is a day!' replied the Dowager.

'Five and seventy is indeed a great age for any gentleman to be contemplating matrimony. What can a gentleman mean by it?' said Mrs Turner.

'One can only imagine,' replied the Dowager. 'In your case, my dear, any consideration of material advantage must be ruled out. We can only conclude, therefore, that comfort of another kind is his aim.'

'Impossible!' said Mrs Turner, smoothing out the creases of her gown. 'I am outraged by such a suggestion.'

Lady Osborne suspected that neither her aunt nor her mother-in-law would appreciate even the gentlest of reminders that they too were nearer five and seventy than five and twenty.

'In his defence,' said Mrs Turner, 'Mr Edwards retains most of his teeth and more strands of hair up top than any other elderly gentleman of my acquaintance.'

'That may be, but he is, as you describe him, an old man. The application of the word 'gentleman' in this case is perhaps a degree too generous. Were he fifteen or even ten years younger — I cannot abide an old man who seeks to pass himself off as a younger one. Nor can I abide a man who eats gruel for supper!' said the Dowager.

The marriage of Miss Watson (a parson's daughter from the nearby parish of Stanton) to Lord Osborne, the Dowager's only son, had confounded the neighbourhood some twenty years earlier. The Dowager, who had reconciled herself to the alliance by degrees, finally condescended to bestow on her daughter-in-law the honour of addressing Her Ladyship as 'Mama' when a longed for, but quite unexpected, event at last took place.

When hope had been almost extinguished, the happy circumstance that brought about a change in relations between the two women was the arrival of an heir, the birth of Master Francis in the year thirteen. Since that time, the visit of the Dowager Lady Osborne and Mrs Turner to Osborne Castle had become an almost daily affair. The doting grandmother and great aunt had much to boast of and delight in. 'Little Frank' had 'saved Osborne Castle' and it was 'little Frank' who would 'save the line' for generations to come from the redoubtable threat of extinction.

There could be no greater gift, no treasure more precious, than the infant who at three had delivered an ancient and noble family from impending obscurity and ruin. The present Lady Osborne, the Dowager acknowledged, had played some small part in so fortuitous a turn of events, and was rewarded for her efforts by the bestowal of an abundance of advice, instruction and regular interference.

The Dowager occupied her days with the business of her grandson's upbringing, for the boy's mother alone could not be relied upon to supervise and nurture those aspects of his character that marked him out as a future peer of the realm. Nothing denied, and no effort too great, the Dowager saw to it that Master Francis was left in no doubt as to his proper place in the world.

The removal of the tea things was routinely followed by the appearance of the said heir. The prelude to his entrance was marked by a tussle in which he would endeavour to release himself from his nanny's grip; a shriek of joy then followed as he burst into the large drawing room. Once free of his captor, of the constraints of nursery governance, and of the elderly ladies who insisted on fluffing his hair and straightening his jacket, he proceeded to render his surroundings an imaginary world in which he, and he alone, held sway. All was tolerated, and all was forgiven; it was a world entirely fitting to the destiny that fate had bestowed upon him. The boy would climb on to the chaise longue and pretend to sail the ocean; and when once he had arrived on dry land, he would run and dance around the room beckoning his mama to chase him here and there, through a forest of chairs, and under the table into his cave. Drapes were his hiding place, and drawers a treasure chest in which to hide fruit, candlewax, and silk thread stolen from his mother's work basket. His fascination for precious vases, statues and trinkets, (immeasurably more appealing that the wooden play things in the nursery) was irrepressible, and more often than not led to calamity. The temptation to dislodge one or other of these fascinating objects from their proper place was too great for a lively boy of three; consequently, the item that had raised his curiosity often ended its days in pieces on the floor, and little Frank was accorded a mild reprimand and a prompt removal from the scene of his transgression. On such occasions he would climb on to his mama's knee for consolation and the immediate restoration of her good opinion. The boy's appeal was never denied, for the inability of Lady Osborne to scold severely, or to allow her displeasure to endure for more than two minutes together, was her greatest weakness. Powerless to refuse him, Lady Osborne would stretch out her arms and embrace her son until all was well again.

On this occasion the heir to Osborne Castle had a sore throat and a high temperature. His nanny had deemed it advisable for Master Francis to keep to his bed, and word was sent forthwith to Her Ladyship.

'Shall you send for Mr Granby's nephew? He is reputed to be a fine physician, and handsome too. And now that Osborne's man is gouty and takes to his bed five days out of seven, you could do no better, my dear, than to —'

'Dear Mama,' said Lady Osborne to the Dowager, 'it is but a chill. There is not the least need to send for a physician. Frank will be perfectly fine in a day or two. Bed rest and a little honey and lemon is all that is required for a complete recovery.'

'I quite agree,' said Mrs Turner. 'My dear, you must curb your impulse to send for a physician the minute anything appears amiss. It is folly to cosset and coddle the boy.'

'He is an Osborne,' said the Dowager with indignation. 'He is heir to Osborne Castle!'

'He is a little boy with a sore throat!' replied an equally indignant Mrs Turner.

'Dear Mama, dear Aunt,' said Lady Osborne, in an attempt to steer the conversation into calmer waters, 'let us not forget Emma. I fear that sometimes we overlook the fact that she is also part of this family.'

'If only she were as charming as Anne Musgrave,' said Mrs Turner. 'She speaks her mind far too freely for one so young.'

'Indeed she does,' agreed the Dowager. 'Just the other day she spoke to me — my own granddaughter — in a most forthright fashion. Your attire, said she, is old fashioned, Grandmamma, and your hair requires attention. I was quite put out, I can tell you. And there was more. Said she, I should dismiss any maid of mine who allowed me to appear in society in so sorry a state of *dishabille*. I was speechless. Quite speechless.'

'For two seconds together,' said Mrs Turner. 'You have spoken of it without pause every hour of every day since. Perhaps we might all do well to contemplate this: one might dismiss the messenger, but one should take great care not to dismiss the message.'

'You are correct, my dear Mrs Turner. Indeed you are. For Emma said much the same thing about you.' The Dowager, who enjoyed nothing more than to have the last word, regarded her prospective companion with glee, and raised a smile of triumphant complacency.

CHAPTER TWO

February had been an unusually mild month, and so, at the first sign of a change in the weather and frost on the ground, the Dowager called for the carriage. Before leaving the Castle, the matter was settled: Mrs Turner was to move to the Dower House on the first day of March, accompanied by her maid. Her manservant, cook, and scullery maid would be informed directly of their good fortune: Osborne Castle was to be their new abode until new positions were found for them in the neighbourhood.

Following their departure, Lord and Lady Osborne and their daughter, the Honourable Emma Osborne, sat down at eight to a simple meal of soup, fowls, hunter's pudding, boiled custard and fruit from the hothouse. The Dowager's invitation to Mrs Turner was the chief topic of conversation.

'Shall you seek a new occupant for Delham Cottage?' Lady Osborne enquired of her husband.

'Not immediately, my dear,' he replied.

'Is that because of the wager, Papa?' said Emma. At nineteen, Emma was as beautiful as her mother had been at that age; but, unlike her mother, whose fortune had been lost through her Aunt Turner's foolish alliance, Miss Emma Osborne was assured of every advantage that rank and fortune could bestow.

Lady Osborne put down her knife and fork and turned towards her husband in search of an explanation. By the expression on his wife's face, Lord Osborne perceived that nothing less than a full account of the matter would suffice.

'It is of little consequence, my dear,' said he.

'Papa and Uncle Musgrave have a wager. Uncle Musgrave declares that Great Aunt Turner will stay one month complete with Grandmamma in the Dower House. Papa insists that the arrangement will last no more than a week,' said Emma. 'Oh Papa! Was I sworn to silence?'

'There are no secrets in this house,' said her father, smiling awkwardly at his wife.

'Well then, Papa, I should like to wager that Grandmamma and Great Aunt Turner —'

'You will do nothing of the kind,' her mother replied.

'But I know I am right,' Emma pleaded. 'And I should like very much to own —'

Lord Osborne coughed. Emma perceived that her papa was most anxious to change the subject.

Lady Osborne, however, was not as eager as her husband to lay the matter to rest, and enquired of her daughter, 'And when did your papa hear of your grandmamma's plans?'

'On Sunday. After morning service. Mama, you were talking to Aunt Musgrave. Papa said it was of little consequence as it was bound to come to nothing.'

Lord Osborne glanced sheepishly at his wife.

'And what did your papa wager?'

Emma looked pleadingly at her father for an answer.

'An old cart horse. Little more than a donkey really,' said Lord Osborne, playfully.

'I see. Well, my dear,' said Lady Osborne to her husband, 'you won't raise any objections, I daresay, when I tell you that we are to have a new cook, manservant and scullery maid.'

'*What?*' replied Lord Osborne.

Lady Osborne smiled casually her husband. 'Your mama has kindly arranged it all.'

At that moment, Lord Osborne saw that it would serve no purpose to object to the plan; moreover, he judged that it was a concession worth making, and would provide some purchase next time his wife raised the matter of the wager.

'Grandmamma's dressmaker is expected tomorrow,' said Emma. 'I promised to be at hand to offer assistance. Have you seen the abominable cut of Grandmamma's new pelisse? I should not have worn it beyond the walls of my bedchamber – not for twenty pounds! Not even in the thickest fog and in the middle of an empty field —'

'Tread carefully, my dear, that your grandmamma does not mistake assistance for interference,' said Lady Osborne.

'I doubt your grandmother knows the difference, Emma,' her father replied.

'Emma, I shall visit the Musgraves tomorrow,' said Lady Osborne. 'Your Aunt Musgrave and I have in mind a plan to restore the assembly rooms in Delham to something of their former glory. Should you like to accompany me? We might walk there if the weather is fine.'

'Must I?'

'I thought you might like to visit Anne.'

'Not if I am expected to pay compliments to my cousin at every turn. Last time I was made to sit still one hour complete to admire sketches of dragon flies and spiders. There was not a single flower, hill, stream or portrait among them. You cannot imagine how very tedious it is to feign interest in something so tiresome.'

Lord and Lady Osborne looked at each other in amusement. They had spent many an hour over the years feigning interest in dull conversation.

'I remember saying something of the kind to your mother before we were married. She thought me quite ill-mannered, I recall. My manners in a ballroom were singled out for particular attention. I received the severest reprimand of anyone I know.'

'That cannot be, Papa! You are so very affable and obliging to everyone.'

'Indeed?' said he, with a hint of surprise in his voice. 'It was not always the case. But I wanted more than anything in the world to make a good impression on your mother. I knew that if I did not mend my ways, I would have no chance of succeeding.'

'And it is worthy to note, my dear,' said Lady Osborne, teasingly, 'that such efforts have just as much merit after marriage as they do before it. It is a notion that is sometimes forgot.'

'Well, I shall make no alteration of the kind. I have no wish to recommend myself to anyone,' said Emma.

There was but one person who in Emma's eyes was worthy of the exertion. She was, however, persuaded that the gentleman in question would neither expect nor require adjustment of any kind either in her character or her behaviour, for he was the most tolerant and most genial of men.

'Not now, perhaps,' said Lady Osborne. 'But there may come a time when your words and actions matter more than they appear to do now.'

A sudden, inexplicable change occurred in Emma's countenance. Her eyes welled with tears. Lord and Lady Osborne were at a loss to understand what had brought about the alteration in their daughter.

'Nothing I say or do matters to a soul. Do you not see, Mama? Papa?' Emma begged to be excused; the request was granted without question whereupon she fled to her room.

Lord and Lady Osborne were confounded by the sudden change in their daughter's disposition. It seemed so out of character, so unlike her. Nothing ever appeared to ail, frighten or distress her. If anything could be said of Emma, it would be that she showed little interest in the opinions of others. Her forthright views and fearless behaviour, which drew unwelcome attention at times from her social equals, never appeared to vex or concern her. Indeed, she was more inclined to savour controversy than avoid it. This sudden outburst, therefore, was as rare as it was perplexing.

'Emma?' said Lady Osborne, tapping on the door of her daughter's bedchamber some minutes later.

'Not now, Mama. I should like to be left alone.'

Impossible to accede to her daughter's request, Lady Osborne entered the room. 'And I shall not be at peace until I know what troubles you, my dear.'

Lady Osborne closed the door behind her and sat on the edge of the bed.

'I cannot say,' said Emma, 'for I hardly know myself.'

'Should you prefer to speak with your papa?'

'No, Mama. I shall be myself again. It is nothing. It will pass.'

Lady Osborne sensed that whatever the source of her daughter's misery, it was not nothing; but unable to discover the cause, after some time she went down, and found her husband seated by the fire in the drawing room awaiting her return. She sat down beside him without a look or a word. Lord Osborne took his wife's hand.

'Well?' said he softly.

'Our daughter wishes to be left alone.'

'That is all very well, but —'

'Let us respect her wishes for the time being,' said Lady Osborne. 'Let Emma decide the right moment.'

They sat quietly by the fire for some minutes, preoccupied with their own thoughts. It had been a day of surprises at Osborne Castle, and not entirely agreeable ones.

In due course, the silence was broken by Lord Osborne.

'The wager, my dear. Am I forgiven?'

'Sunday morning, directly after divine service, and in reach of the churchyard gate? To enter into a wager at such a moment!'

'It was foolhardy. I admit it,' said he. 'Quite inappropriate. But, my dear, you must concede that the notion of my mother and your aunt living agreeably for two minutes together would be nothing short of a miracle. And with a sermon to hand on the very topic, it put me in mind of —'

'Well, I hope it *is* a miracle. In which case I fully expect you to offer the proceeds of your wager to the Dower House.'

'Impossible! It's as fine a horse as — that is to say —'

'An old cart horse? A donkey? Ready to be put out to pasture?' Lady Osborne smiled at her husband. 'Have no anxiety on my part, my dear. I never believed it for a moment. And what did Tom Musgrave wager?'

'A curricle,' he replied. 'A fine one at that. New lamps, new set of wheels, fine leather interior —'

'Then there is every reason to ensure that Aunt Turner's removal to the Dower House is a success, for I doubt Elizabeth will be happy with Tom when she learns the truth of the matter.'

'No doubt your sister will be just as obliging as you, my dear. Did I ever tell you how beautiful you look when you are vexed with me?'

'Repeatedly,' replied Lady Osborne.

The next morning Emma was awakened by the entrance of Abigail, a young maid, with a breakfast tray, followed some minutes later by Lady Osborne herself.

'I should go down, Mama,' said Emma.

'Allow me to spoil you a little this morning,' she replied.

Lady Osborne sat on the bed and stroked her daughter's hair. 'When I was your age, I had my sister, Elizabeth, to talk to.'

'You do not expect me to talk to Anne as you talked to Aunt Musgrave, do you, Mama?'

Lady Osborne was disconcerted by her daughter's question.

'Are you truly not fond of your cousin?'

'We are so very different, Mama. But your temperament and interests are not dissimilar from those of Aunt Musgrave.'

'That may be so. And yet your Aunt Harding and I have little in common, but it does not alter my affection for *her*.'

'I do not think Anne's affection for me is so very strong.'

'She speaks of you in the warmest of terms, and she is the least artful young woman I know.'

'She clearly possesses all the qualities I lack. Great Aunt Turner reminds me of it constantly.'

'You are a fine young woman, Emma. I love you and I am proud of you.'

Emma looked away. Her eyes fixed on a miniature of the grandmother she had never known.

'Your mama died when you were very young.'

'Yes,' said Lady Osborne.

'What are your memories of her?' Emma replied.

'I have no true memory of my mother. I was but five years old when she died.'

For some moments, Emma was silent. She was sensible of the fact that every advantage a young woman could wish for, of birth, parentage, situation and fortune, was hers. Some among her Croydon relations would take the view that she had no cause, nor right, to succumb to low spirits. For one so fortunate in life, it was nothing less than wanton self-indulgence.

'I do not wish to visit Aunt Musgrave today,' said Emma.

Her mother replied, 'I shall not press you. Will you call at the Dower House?'

'I think not, Mama. I expect I should be in the way there.'

Lady Osborne was left to ponder the reason for her daughter's melancholy. No element of their conversation, nothing that her daughter had disclosed, afforded Lady Osborne any clearer understanding of the matter. Emma seemed to wish for nothing more than her own society; but with the promise secured of another conversation later in the day, with reluctance Lady Osborne left Emma to her breakfast.

As her mother left the room quietly closing the door behind her, Emma sighed and pushed her breakfast tray away. She slid under the bedcovers and remained there until the fire took away the chill in the air. An hour and a half later, the Honourable Emma Osborne, dressed in a dark green habit, entered the library to inform her papa that she was to spend the morning riding.

'I shall ride into Delham, Papa. Have no care. I shall be back before luncheon.'

'Very well,' said he, without a trace of anxiety, for Emma was as fine a horsewoman as her mother and her Aunt Beresford. Standing at the library window, Lord Osborne watched his daughter disappear from view; he observed with some curiosity the path she had taken was not the most direct route to Delham. Nor, he supposed, was Delham her intended destination.

When Emma, some ten minutes later, drew close to Osborne Cottage, she was pleased to discover that its occupant had no other morning callers. It had been almost a month since Mrs Blake, a long-standing friend of the family, had visited Osborne Castle. Of late, the mother of Captain Charles Blake had been much engaged with her sister-in-law, Mrs Howard, a woman whose notoriety within the neighbourhood and beyond had prevented her from being received in Delham by her father, Mr Edwards. Mrs Blake, ever a woman of kindness and understanding, had been disposed to look on her sister-in-law's plight with compassion, for Mrs Howard, stricken with remorse at the news of her estranged mother's death, had since been eager to make amends with both her father, and her husband.

At one time, Mr Howard had been Rector of Wickstead, a living in the gift of the Osborne family; the clergyman celebrated for his activity in the pulpit had also been tutor to Lord Osborne. When his marriage to Miss Edwards was announced, many were surprised by the news, for the general expectation was that Mr Howard would make an offer to the beautiful Miss Watson, Emma's mother.

All that could be said of the marriage between Mr Howard and Miss Edwards was that neither party had entered into it with the purest of motives. Miss Edwards had been eager to leave Delham for London in order to be closer in proximity to the real object of her affection; unfortunately for Mr Howard, the object of her affection was a redcoat by the name of Captain Hunter. Despite their marriage being, from the start, a loveless one, the alliance had its compensations for Mr Howard: on marrying Miss Edwards, Mr Howard had gained instant elevation to a position at Westminster through the influence of Mr Edwards' brother who was well-connected there. The movements of his wife, however, once known abroad, had brought shame and disgrace on the family; and when the full extent of the scandal reached Delham, it was said that the knowledge of Mrs Howard's misdemeanours had led to her mother's untimely demise. In truth, Mrs Edwards had contracted pneumonia; the illness, being of short duration, carried Mrs Edwards away before any prospect of a reconciliation with her daughter had presented itself.

Mrs Howard's penitence had been too late in coming: her father refused to receive her, and her husband, having been obliged to retire, ostensibly for reasons of indifferent health, to the obscurity of a quiet Somerset village, would give her no admittance.

Emma knew little of the story, except for the curious detail that her mother had once been in love with Mr Howard and was once a friend of Miss Edwards. Intriguing as the story of Mrs Howard might be, Emma's interest tended in quite another direction.

Emma Osborne met with no warmer a welcome than the one she received at Osborne Cottage. Mrs Blake's affection for Emma, as for her mother before her, was undeviating; and her connection with Osborne Castle had been of more than thirty years' duration. The years that had passed since then had served only to strengthen the bond on both sides. Mrs Blake was as dear to the Osborne family as any of their nearest relations.

'My dear Emma, you quite surprise me this morning! I could not have hoped for a more welcome visitor.' Mrs Blake sent to the kitchen for Emma's favourite apple tart.

'Is Mrs Howard gone?' asked Emma.

'She is. Mrs Howard is gone into Somerset, but I do not know what good it will do. She has taken lodgings quiet enough to avoid society and close enough to hear news of Mr Howard. He resides some fifteen miles south of Whitcombe.'

'Oh dear! I should not think Aunt and Uncle Beresford likely to receive Mrs Howard.'

'Nor I, my dear. And nor should I expect it.'

'Shall you see her again soon?'

'Mrs Howard? I think not. I think not. Indeed, I have news of my own. It surprises me to say it, but I am to spend the summer at the coast. By the sea. I am to visit Sanditon. By all accounts it is quite charming though I have never before set eyes on the place.'

'Sanditon? Let us hope that it proves more promising than its name.'

'Whatever do you mean, my dear?' replied Mrs Blake.

'A town build on sand? What would our earnest curate say about that?' said Emma.

'Oh, yes, of course,' said Mrs Blake, 'I see. I see. How droll! Sandy-town! How clever of you!'

'Though, I suppose a town that promises sand must be a fine thing. I defy anyone to find an inch of sand worth bothering about on the coast thereabouts. Aunt Margaret won't go to the sea unless it is to Cromer. The countryside is more to my taste, though I should like very much to go to Brighton. What takes you to Sanditon?'

'My dear Charles,' said Mrs Blake.

Emma was thrilled to hear mention of his name. 'Captain Blake? Dear Mrs Blake, is he expected?'

'I received a letter from Charles a week ago. A dose of sea air, said he, will do you the world of good. Indeed, I have had the very good fortune to be invited, and Charles also, as the guest of Mr Fitzroy for the entire summer. He is the brother of Charles' fellow officer, the late Captain Fitzroy, and has inherited one of the finest houses, indeed the finest house, on Waterloo Crescent. It is newly built, and almost complete, and by all accounts has a very fine prospect. A full view of the bay is assured. Poor Captain Fitzroy! He did not live to see the house in its full glory. Everyone was stunned by his loss.'

'I have heard Captain Blake speak of Captain Fitzroy. I believe they served together during the Trafalgar action.'

'Exactly so. Charles was but a midshipman then. And since Captain Fitzroy's untimely death last year, Charles has maintained a connection with one member of the family at least, Captain Fitzroy's younger brother. Therein lies a story which is not mine to tell. The house is now complete — the proceeds of prize money, you see — and never better deserved in my view. Having no son and no entail, Captain Fitzroy was at liberty to bequeath the house as he saw fit. And he saw fit to leave it to his younger brother, for he was disinclined, quite rightly in my view, to give it up to the elder one.'

The conversation was interrupted by the entrance of a maid bearing apple pie and cocoa. Emma, on seeing the inviting tray, found that her appetite, which had been poor at breakfast, was now restored.

'Riding always makes me hungry,' said she.

Mrs Blake cut Emma a generous portion of pie.

'Mama is gone to see Aunt Musgrave, for she has sprained her ankle.'

'I hope it is not serious.'

'It seems Anne learned a new dance at Lowford Park. A waltz. It is quite daring. Aunt Musgrave was eager to learn it too and stumbled over the steps. I have seen the steps. They do not appear complicated to me.'

Mrs Blake was amused by her young visitor's observations, and said, 'If only it were possible to stay young forever! Then no measure would be too difficult to master. I believe I should like to learn the new steps myself.'

'Perhaps you should introduce the waltz into Sanditon society while you are there!' said Emma, laughing at the prospect. 'You must promise to write to me every day. Will Captain Blake stay with you for the entire summer?'

'Indeed he will. But he has every intention of paying a visit to Osborne Castle first. He made a point of it in his letter.'

'I cannot tell you how happy I am to hear it,' Emma replied.

Emma's eyes wandered to the two miniatures that adorned the wall above the fireplace. Mrs Blake followed Emma's line of vision. The first was of her husband, the late Captain Blake, a handsome man of thirty or thereabouts; the second was a likeness of their son, Captain Charles Blake, who had attained the same rank as his father in the Navy.

'The similarity in countenance and stature of father and son is remarkable,' said Emma. 'Has Captain Blake taken charge of his new vessel?'

'He has. But he is to give up the Navy so the ship will not be long under his command. He is but bringing *her* home. At least those were his words. This very week he is expected to set sail from the West Indies.'

'I hope the *her* to which he refers is the vessel, and not —' said Emma, in an attempt to dispel any doubt of her own.

'Oh yes, indeed!' laughed Mrs Blake.

'How soon will Captain Blake be here?'

'Not very soon. He goes first to Cork before arriving in Portsmouth sometime in May. But it is a happy thought to know that he will be back in England by the end of spring, and on dry land.'

'Do you worry?' Emma enquired. 'Though the war is over, a prodigious number of ships are lost at sea. I can hardly sleep for thinking about it.'

Mrs Blake paused to compose her thoughts before making a reply. 'My dear Emma, it would diminish our contentment immeasurably if we thought only of the worst catastrophe possible every minute of every day. When my dear husband set sail to a distant shore, I own, I thought of nothing else. I never knew a moment's peace. The years that have gone by have taught me to live in hope, and only when adversity strikes, strive to meet its challenge.'

'Sometimes such dark thoughts overwhelm me,' Emma conceded.

'My dear child, unhappiness is sure to find each one of us at some time or other, but we must not spend our lives awaiting, indeed expecting, its arrival. We must strive not to place ourselves forever at its disposal,' said Mrs Blake. 'Do not let melancholic thoughts take up residence in your heart.'

'Mrs Blake,' said Emma, 'there is something I —'

Mrs Blake had known and loved Emma from the moment of her birth. No child could have been dearer to her than the daughter of the two people she esteemed above all others, Lord and Lady Osborne. Until the marriage of Mr Howard to Miss Edwards in the year ninety-six, Mrs Blake's home, and that of her son Charles, had been with her brother at Wickstead. When Mr Howard and his new bride moved to London and Mrs Blake was left homeless, without a moment's hesitation, Lord Osborne proposed that Osborne Cottage be placed at Mrs Blake's disposal for as long as she required it. The cottage was supplied unstintingly from the well-stocked kitchen and gardens of the Castle, and a tutor was employed for Charles so that he might continue his education at home. Since that time, Mrs Blake had lived at Osborne Cottage as happily as it was possible to be from the moment she had stepped over its threshold.

Mrs Blake had watched Emma grow into a beautiful young woman; and Charles had been to Emma everything that an elder brother could be, always protective of her, teasing and playful, and ever mindful of her welfare. Over time, Emma's affection for Charles had changed; it had grown into something of which she dare not speak. As a girl of fifteen, she delighted in the light-hearted raillery at her expense that often accompanied his name. As her feelings grew, however, her ability to endure the teasing ceased; Emma began to fancy herself in love with Charles Blake. Indeed, there could be no other feeling that explained the extraordinary interest in his situation. Emma had begun to search the newspapers daily for shipwrecks and dispatches and had memorized the names and characteristics of every naval vessel of the same rate as his. On hearing that gooseberry was Charles' favourite pie, Emma had considered making it hers too, but for the inconvenient fact that she detested gooseberries. Once she had spent a whole afternoon writing their names on scraps of paper — Captain and Mrs Blake — Mrs Emma Blake — Admiral and Mrs Charles Blake — Rear Admiral of the Blue and the Honourable Mrs Blake — Vice Admiral of the White and Mrs Blake — Admiral of the Fleet and Mrs Charles Blake — that were later found by her maid, Abigail, who, sworn to silence on the subject, tore up the scraps of paper and burned them on the fire.

After a pleasant hour spent with the mother of her future husband, Emma left Osborne Cottage with thoughts and feelings left unsaid, but with the gratifying prospect that Charles Blake would in all probability return to Delham before the end of spring.

When Lady Osborne called at Delham Hall, she found her sister recumbent on a sofa by the fire, her ankle resting on a cushion. Elizabeth explained that Tom had gone into Delham on horseback and was not expected back until three.

'He is gone to see the blacksmith about a spare wheel, or something of the kind. He would not commission another soul with the errand and insisted on doing everything himself. Anne has taken the old carriage. She is gone to visit the Forbes' girls at Lowford and begs your forgiveness. The engagement was of long-standing. It seems there is a rather fine collection of exotic birds in the long gallery there. Dead ones, of course. Stuffed. I have never seen the attraction of such things myself. Quite apt for Lowford Park. I spent such a dreary time of it on our last visit. Tom had no care, for he was deep in conversation with Lowford about a curricle he had just purchased from a new maker in town. Take me home before I die of boredom, said I, when Lowford was out of earshot. One hour and five and forty minutes later we were still there.'

'Dear Elizabeth,' said Lady Osborne, 'is there anything I can do to ease your present discomfort? A poultice for the pain?'

'Thank you, dear sister, I have all I need,' she replied. 'But, now I think of it, there is something. Would you ask Osborne to persuade Tom to dispose of the contraption?'

Lady Osborne smiled. 'Dispose of the curricle?'

'I have no notion why Tom purchased it in the first place,' said Elizabeth. 'And I shan't have a minute's peace until it is gone. It is quite unsteady. One can hardly get in or out of it. It caused me to sprain my ankle, you know. And my knee is just as badly affected.'

'Tom said you had sprained your ankle learning to waltz,' said Lady Osborne.

Elizabeth sighed. 'No indeed. That is what he would have you believe,' said she. 'I have become rather partial to the waltz. And now it will be some weeks before I have the opportunity of dancing it again! But that curricle! Every time I think of it —'

'Have no worry on that score,' replied Lady Osborne, unable to suppress a smile. 'I am sure a way will be found to relieve you of the curricle before long.'

The marriage of Mr Tom Musgrave to the elder Miss Watson was as much a surprise to the neighbourhood as the alliance between

Lord Osborne and her younger sister, and considerably more surprising than that of Mr Howard and Miss Edwards. Of the three, Tom Musgrave had known and loved Elizabeth Watson the longest. Whatever Elizabeth's feelings had been for Tom in her youth, at nine and twenty she was slower than most young women would have been on the verge of spinsterhood to welcome his advances. After refusing Tom Musgrave's proposal of marriage on two occasions, and crying off on the third, the eldest daughter of Mr Watson had expected to end her days caring for her father at Stanton Parsonage. When, therefore, Tom Musgrave proposed a fourth time, and proved himself beyond any shadow of a doubt to be in earnest, she promptly accepted him. In the year following their marriage, their daughter Anne was born. A young woman with many talents, Anne excelled at music, reading and drawing. Chief of all, however, was her passion for nature.

Miss Emma Osborne and Miss Anne Musgrave had lived in close proximity since their birth, Mr Musgrave's estate being but three miles from Osborne Park and not beyond walking distance in fine weather. The cousins, though of similar age, height and beauty, had few common interests. Emma liked to ride; Anne preferred to walk. Emma, who supposed that the main purpose of walking was fresh air and exercise, would stride at a brisk pace, stopping only to tie a shoe lace or catch her breath. Anne favoured a gentle saunter to take in the beauty of the countryside; flora and fauna, birds and insects, and curious rock formations provided hours of fascination and delight for Emma's cousin.

Anne was considered the better artist, taking her time to perfect every detail, each element of a drawing accurately observed. Emma, on the other hand, was content to work quickly and leave the outcome to chance. Consequently, poorly executed drawings were torn up by the latter and disposed of; only the less objectionable pieces were saved. Music complemented the two cousins perfectly: Anne had the better voice, while Emma was the more accomplished pianist.

As Lady Osborne's visit drew to a close after the matter of the renovation to Delham's old assembly rooms had been exhausted, the mail arrived.

On hearing that Elizabeth had received a letter from Mrs Penelope Harding, their sister in Chichester, Lady Osborne delayed her departure to hear their sister's news.

'Penelope has invited herself to stay,' sighed Elizabeth. 'She doesn't say why, but it seems she has some news to relate that won't wait. She is to arrive on Wednesday.'

'I wonder, should I invite her to stay for a few days with us — at least until you are a little better?'

'My dear, would you?'

'Of course.'

'But what if His Lordship should object?'

'Osborne will be most accommodating. At present he has every reason to oblige me,' said Lady Osborne.

'Then I shall write to Penelope directly,' Elizabeth replied.

CHAPTER THREE

The inhabitants of Osborne Castle expected the arrival of Mrs Penelope Harding at four o'clock on Wednesday afternoon. At five o'clock a messenger arrived with a note. Mrs Harding had been obliged, by unforeseen circumstances, to delay her visit by two days. No explanation, nor any information regarding the hour of her proposed arrival was given. In the event, Mrs Harding arrived shortly after four o'clock on Friday afternoon. Lady Osborne had kept watch every hour since noon while Lord Osborne had retreated to the confines of his library in anticipation of Mrs Harding's arrival. Emma had ridden into Delham in the hope of being the first to welcome Aunt Harding to Surrey after an absence of two years.

All was easily explained; Penelope had called to see the Musgraves on the way, having stayed the previous two nights with an old school friend in Horsham.

'The road from Chichester to Arundel was quite as bad as ever. The rest was not so very good either. I managed to rest my eyes for little more than half an hour before reaching Horsham. Travelling is a desperately tiring affair,' said she. 'My dear sister, you look quite pale. I do not wonder at it. I should not have wished for an infant at nine and thirty. It was work enough at four and twenty.'

'How is my nephew?' enquired Lady Osborne.

'Weak in the head. He is determined to have Mrs Shaw's youngest daughter, though they are quite ill-suited. I have nothing against the young woman, except that she is equally determined to have *him*. Two thousand pounds is all she can expect. Miss Wake has six — and she would have taken him in an instant! Mercifully, his ship is gone to the East Indies, and he with it. I do not know when I have wished him further away than I do now, except for the time he began to think of Mrs Shaw's niece. The East Indies will delay matters long enough for the youngest Miss Shaw to begin to set her cap at someone else. If you know of anyone who might do for her, then tell me at once.'

Lady Osborne placed Penelope's arm in hers. 'Penelope, come and rest a while by the fire and have a dish of tea.'

'Ah! A dish of tea. Well, thank heaven for that! Miss Shaw has consumed all mine. I've not a spoonful of tea leaves left in the chest, for she insists on calling every other day and making herself quite at home. She has taken too strong a liking to Dr Harding's residence (which was sensibly bequeathed to me). It is a rather fine town house, as you know. One of the best in Chichester. I have often observed that young woman in an idle moment eyeing up the Meissen and counting the windows. She is likely possessed of the notion that it will all one day be hers. Well I shall see to it that it is not.'

'I thought you once said that the youngest Miss Shaw was quite charming. Is Miss Wake just as charming, or does her six thousand pounds render her more so?'

'It is all very well for you. It is the easiest thing in the world to love a rich man.'

'Rich or not, Penelope, I married Osborne for love, as you well know. And I love him still.'

Penelope gave a sigh of exasperation. 'Love! I am glad all that nonsense is behind me!'

When at last the tray arrived, Lady Osborne presided over the tea. Not long afterwards, Emma entered the drawing room in her riding habit, her coat dishevelled and her hair a tangle, after having taken her horse at a gallop through the park.

'Aunt Harding!' said Emma. 'I went into Delham with the express intention of meeting you.'

'My dear Emma, you look quite wild! Whatever have you done to your hair?'

24

Emma shook her hair loose. 'That's better. Never mind me. Where have you been and how did you escape my notice?'

'I decided to call on your Aunt Musgrave on the way,' said Penelope. 'But come here, my dear. Let me tie up your hair.'

'There is no one here to care about it,' said Emma. 'Anyway, Frank will come down shortly, and he will pull at my hair whether it is dressed or not. I'm quite certain I will be bald by the summer. Yesterday he pulled out a handful of hair and was quite delighted with himself. Mama never scolds him the way she should.'

Penelope saw the uneasy look that passed between mother and daughter.

'Excuse me, Aunt Harding. I shall go and change.'

As the door closed and the two sisters were quite alone again, Penelope looked to Lady Osborne for an explanation.

'Emma is troubled. I do not know what it is that troubles her. I wish I knew.'

'Insist on an explanation. I should,' said Penelope.

'Until she is ready to provide one, I cannot —'

'Nonsense!'

'If she speaks to anyone, it will be to her father.'

Of the Watson sisters, Penelope had a superior understanding of the nature and foibles of family relations. It was Penelope who had first noticed the degree of affection between their elder sister, Elizabeth, and Tom Musgrave. And she had been quick to understand that her own situation required the practicality of thought that necessitated the triumph of reason over emotion. In marrying Dr Harding, an old but comfortably wealthy clergyman, Penelope had chosen practicality and necessity over love, and yet during the years of her marriage, which were more numerous than she had in the beginning anticipated, given her husband's age and infirmity, she had suffered few regrets. It was enough for her that two of her sisters had found themselves in the happy situation of marrying for love two of the wealthiest men in the neighbourhood. Penelope's life had been one without passion; and though not entirely without complaint, she was able to look back on her life with some measure of satisfaction that as a respectable woman of three and forty, she was happily and independently situated, and would likely continue in comfortable circumstances.

The evening passed without unease of any kind. Lord Osborne had little to do but appear congenial in the right places, while Lady Osborne attended to Penelope's news from Chichester and reports from Croydon of the families of their brother Robert and sister Margaret with whom Penelope had spent Christmas. The most longed for news — the purpose of Penelope's visit — remained a mystery.

'All being well, I expect to receive confirmation of the matter tomorrow afternoon in the mail,' said she. 'You must wait until then.'

As the weather looked promising, the following morning Penelope proposed a walk into Delham. Lady Osborne, preoccupied with letter-writing and with putting the housekeeper's mind at rest over the matter of the new cook's duties, encouraged Penelope to seek out Emma's company.

'Emma,' said Penelope to her niece, 'will you not accompany me? I shall call on Aunt Turner, for I know she will expect it. But I should first like to look in at Mason's in Delham on the way. It is an age since I bought a length of muslin or even a pair of wool stockings.'

'I shall come with you as far as Mason's, though there is hardly an item worth looking at, and nothing worth buying for more than sixpence,' said Emma. 'But I have no desire to enter Delham Cottage for it is in a terrible state of disorder. Trunks and boxes everywhere and nothing in its proper place! I doubt Grandmamma will have an inch of space left when Great Aunt Turner moves into the Dower House.'

'Then you *will* come with me. I shall brook no refusal. Aunt Turner shall profit from your help and mine, whether she likes it or not. I am the best manager of havoc and confusion in the world.'

Emma sighed, but made no further objection to the plan.

Aunt and niece set out for Delham with the prospect of buying nothing at Mason's and the intention of bringing about a transformation in the removal arrangements at Delham Cottage. On finding that Mrs Turner was not at home, there was little to be done, and so the pair returned to Mason's and spent a rewarding hour purchasing as many items as Aunt Harding's budget would allow. By the time they reached Osborne Castle, tired and hungry, the delivery from Mason's had already been made. Three shawls, four pairs of stockings, two pairs of gloves — one white, one brown — and two lengths each of muslin and silk, comprised the morning's purchases. Each article, its merits and serviceability explained, was displayed before Lady Osborne.

'Yes, the shawl is quite beautiful — I have no doubt it would cost a full two shillings more in London. But altogether, it amounts to a very costly morning's occupation,' said she.

'Mama! It is a bargain! Worth every penny. Truly. Feel the quality of the silk.'

'Nevertheless your Aunt Harding has paid out a lot of money,' said Lady Osborne.

'It is of little consequence,' said Penelope. 'Can I not treat my niece now and again? I rarely see her.'

'Of course. But this is a degree too generous,' replied Lady Osborne. 'Emma is well provided for and has an allowance of her own.'

Mrs Harding took her sister aside while Emma gathered up several of the items to show to her father. She waited until her niece had left the room before saying, 'You are right. Emma is well provided for. Yet I fear she is in need of something more. Little Frank is a dear boy, and every attention is rightly accorded him. But Emma has lost her place — she has been obliged to give way to Frank. Of course, she could never inherit, but I believe she feels that she has lost her place in your heart too.'

'That could never be. Emma is dearer to me than my own life,' said Lady Osborne.

'I know. But it is time for Emma to know it too,' replied Penelope. 'If you will not speak of the past, permit me to do so.'

Lady Osborne moved over to the window and surveyed the grounds of Osborne Park. 'Why should a child of mine be at once privileged and burdened with all this? Why should a daughter not have equal claim with that of a son? Osborne has no greater love for Frank than for Emma, of that I am certain. But of the two, Frank must come first for the sake of these walls, the land, the line, the title. And one day Emma will feel all the responsibility of bringing a child — a boy — into the world to fulfil a similar destiny. It is a very dear wish of mine that Emma should marry whomever she chooses, that it should not matter one whit that she is the daughter of a lord. Were she to choose Charles Blake, with whom I suspect she thinks herself a little in love, I should bless the union and welcome it with open arms.'

'But Lord Osborne would not?'

'Osborne would give his blessing. He would not stand in the way for he loves Charles as I do.'

'Then where is the difficulty?'

'The Dowager is determined that Emma should aim higher. She wishes to see her granddaughter a countess, a marchioness or even a duchess.'

'Then I am not surprised that Emma is troubled,' said Mrs Harding. 'I was going to wait until later, when we are all assembled, to tell you my news, but an idea has occurred to me, and I should like to know your view.'

Dinner was served a little after eight owing to the late arrival of the Dowager, Mrs Turner and Mrs Blake.

'I have never known a soul to take three and twenty minutes to put on a coat and bonnet. Mrs Blake can vouch for me. It is no exaggeration. If there had been no blanket in the coach, we should have died of frost bite waiting for Mrs Turner to make herself ready,' said the Dowager.

'May I remind you that your note stated a quarter to the hour, not a quarter past the previous one!' said Mrs Turner in reply.

'I expect we shall be in possession of a very fine curricle before long,' whispered Lord Osborne to his wife. 'Indeed, I have quite made up my mind to enjoy the evening.'

'It may not be quite so great a prize as you imagine,' said Lady Osborne.

Her husband was mystified by the comment but allowed the matter to rest as his attention was demanded by the Dowager over the pressing matter of the damp found in the breakfast room at the Dower House.

Mrs Blake and Mrs Harding complimented their hosts on the fine array of dishes placed before them. The Dowager, who had the ability to conduct one conversation while listening to several others, added, 'We would, nevertheless, be led to believe that a vast improvement in the table is to be anticipated when Mrs Turner's cook is installed at the Castle.'

'Come now, Mama, you may rue the day you did not employ Mrs Hedges yourself. I have had some very fine dinners at Delham Cottage,' said Lady Osborne.

'For a cook who learned her trade, not in Paris, but in some obscure town near Peterborough, one must make certain allowances. I expect she can make a decent pork pie when called upon to do so.'

'Hedges spent several months, nay almost a year complete, in the kitchens of Carlton House,' protested Mrs Turner.

'Ah, but one can only conjecture that her employment at that establishment had little to do with the boiling of an egg,' replied the Dowager.

'Come now, Mama,' said Lady Osborne, in an attempt to quell the mounting tumult. 'My sister has some news that is most pleasing. Are we not all eager to hear it?'

Neither the Dowager nor Mrs Turner could resist the prospect of securing a piece of news that was not generally known in the neighbourhood; and though news that was pleasing was in the main less diverting than scandal and speculation, there was so little of it to be had in Delham in February, that any news, agreeable or otherwise, would suffice.

Mrs Harding waited until all eyes were fixed on her. 'I am to give up the house in Chichester,' said she.

'For good?' asked Mrs Turner.

'For good,' Mrs Harding replied. 'It is sold.'

'Sold? How can that be? It is a fine house and pleasantly situated,' said Lord Osborne, with a note of concern in his voice. A disconcerting thought entered his head — that Mrs Harding might seek to take up residence at the Castle.

'Dr Harding purchased the Chichester house some years ago while he still retained the living. It was in anticipation that I would outlive him by a considerable number of years, given our difference in age. On my husband's death, our son received a substantial inheritance from his father's lucrative business interests in the West Indies. The house, however, was bequeathed to me in its entirety to do with as I saw fit. And I saw fit to sell it. This afternoon I have received confirmation that my new house is shortly to be ready. I may say that its position is without compare, for it is situated in the most heavenly spot on earth.'

The news was met with general astonishment.

'I hardly think Delham Cottage would be to your liking,' said the Dowager, looking anxiously at her son.

'Delham Cottage? Whatever would I want with Delham Cottage?' said Mrs Harding.

'How exciting! Dear Aunt, let us have a competition to guess the whereabouts of your new residence,' said Emma, with a spark of enthusiasm that had until that moment eluded her.

'Oh yes indeed!' said Mrs Turner.

The Dowager agreed at once.

'If Delham Cottage is not the place, are you to settle elsewhere in Delham?' asked Mrs Blake. 'There is a pretty house not far from Osborne Cottage, and not more than —'

'Delham? Certainly not!' replied Mrs Harding, almost indignant at the thought. 'My new house is to be by the sea.'

Lord Osborne breathed a sigh of relief.

'Margate!' said the Dowager. 'It must be Margate. Margate is eminently suitable for a widow in your situation.'

'It is not Margate,' Mrs Harding replied.

'Then it is sure to be Weymouth. My dear Penelope,' said Mrs Turner, 'I adore Weymouth. You could not have chosen a better place in the whole world!'

'Weymouth? I can do better than Weymouth.'

'The seaside? A heavenly place? Let me guess. Does it begin with a B?' asked Emma.

'It does,' said Mrs Harding, confounded by her niece's reply.

'And might the second letter be R?' she continued.

'Indeed it is!' Mrs Harding suspected that her news was not so very new after all. She looked at Lady Osborne for an explanation.

'I have said not a word,' Her Ladyship insisted.

Emma went on, 'Then the third letter must be I.'

'Well done, my dear. How clever you are!' said Mrs Harding.

'It is Brighton!' Emma exclaimed. 'Aunt Harding is to move to Brighton! What wonderful news! Aunt, I beg you, allow me to come and stay when you are quite settled. I should like it above anything.'

Her aunt replied, 'Brighton is *not* the place.'

'But surely there is no other —'

'Bristol!' Mrs Turner exclaimed.

'How could one possibly describe Bristol as the seaside?' said the Dowager.

Lord Osborne, relieved and amused by his sister-in-law's astonishing pronouncement, suggested, and indeed longed for, Bridlington to be the place.

'Bridlington? Where on earth is Bridlington, Papa?' asked Emma.

'If by "heavenly" you mean bracing winds, sea and sky several shades of grey, and cold tea, then you have settled upon the perfect spot,' said Mrs Turner.

'Brighton, Bristol, Bridlington! I am astonished at their very mention! You must see that the place on which my heart is set is by every measure superior to all three. Not one of them, nor all three together, should be named in the same day as Brinshore.'

'Brinshore?' said Emma in amazement. 'I have never once in my life heard of Brinshore.'

'I promise you, Emma. You shall know it and love it as I do,' replied her aunt.

'Its name is not very promising. Brin-shore. It puts me in mind of slimy sand and salty water. *Brine*-shore,' said Lord Osborne.

Emma, having inherited her father's sense of humour, laughed heartily at his remark, and was about to mention that other obscure seaside town, the place in which Mrs Blake was to spend the season, when Mrs Harding interrupted, issuing His Lordship with a firm rebuke.

'But it is sand that one can walk on! Brinshore is not in the least like those beaches, so called, that stretch for miles and consist of nothing but peebles, cockles, seaweed and driftwood. I have purchased a house — new in every aspect — I have yet to determine its name — it should express the splendour and distinction of its situation — for there is no house more sought after, none so spacious and bright in the whole of Brinshore — indeed, it is situated in the shelter of a cliff with a sea view incomparable to any other in England. Number one Trafalgar Terrace.'

The astonishment on hearing Mrs Harding's news was shared by all except Lady Osborne to whom the plan had been imparted earlier in the day. Further to the scheme, Mrs Harding had set forth a proposal to invite her niece to spend the season at her new house in Brinshore. Lady Osborne, though amenable to the idea, doubted that Emma would welcome it. Initially, Her Ladyship's doubts appeared to prove founded, for her daughter showed little desire at all to visit

Brinshore; and despite her aunt's attempts to persuade her niece of its merits, Emma would not be moved. It was not long, however, before Emma's disinclination for the place swiftly began to fade.

'My dear Mrs Harding,' said Mrs Blake to Penelope, 'I cannot imagine news more welcome than this, nor more surprising! Brinshore is but three miles from another beautiful spot, and one perhaps better known. Sanditon. Indeed, Brinshore is reckoned almost as prettily situated as Sanditon, or so I am told. There could be no circumstance more pleasing, for I am to stay the whole summer in Sanditon, and I should be most happy to receive you there, should you be tempted to venture beyond Brinshore's borders.'

'Mrs Blake, how very extraordinary!' replied Mrs Harding. 'I wish you had consulted me first. I should have recommended Brinshore over Sanditon in an instant. I have never heard Sanditon spoken of as boasting anything more than a tolerable shore and a clump of ill-constructed cottages. The nearest haberdasher of repute, to which the inhabitants of Sanditon flock, is Peacock's, and that establishment is in Brinshore.'

'You must be right,' said Mrs Blake, not wishing to cause disagreement of any kind at the Osbornes' table. 'Had I thought to secure a house myself, I should have been pleased to benefit from your superior knowledge. But, you see, my son and I are invited to Sanditon as guests of the brother of a dear late, and much lamented, friend of Charles.'

Mrs Harding was gentler in her reply. 'I see. So Sanditon will also have the pleasure of Captain Blake's presence over the summer. I understand he is to set sail shortly from the West Indies.'

'Charles is more eager than I to spend the season in Sanditon, for his heart is set on a particular project. He says nothing more in his letter, but it seems nowhere but Sanditon will do.'

'How very mysterious,' said Lady Osborne.

Emma had not anticipated a season spent in Brinshore as holding any attraction for her at all, but on hearing that Charles Blake was expected to spend the summer in Sanditon, the notion of staying with her aunt by the sea but three miles east of the town, increased in appeal by the moment.

The Dowager and Mrs Turner paid little attention to the competing merits of Sanditon and Brinshore, or of Mrs Harding's plan to invite Emma to stay; but when the matter of Mrs Blake's visit was made known, the subject of Sanditon created between them heightened curiosity and attentiveness.

'And is Mrs Howard to spend the summer there too?' said the Dowager, half in jest. 'It is hardly proper for a respectable woman to court the company of a disreputable one.'

'You forget, my dear,' said Mrs Turner, 'I was once considered disreputable.'

'Indeed you were,' said the Dowager. 'That imposter to whom you thought yourself married was never found out nor punished. It is a great shame that he did not suffer the same fate as that most engaging Comte with whom I danced at Lady Forbes' ball two seasons before the Revolution. Scandalous! Quite scandalous! Despicable, worthless man! What was his name?'

'Le Comte de —'

'No! No! No!' said the Dowager. 'The redcoat.'

'Ah. I suppose you refer to Captain O'Brien,' said Mrs Turner. 'And yet you have invited me, a woman once beset by scandal and disgrace, to share your home. Shall you withdraw your offer now?'

Lord and Lady Osborne exchanged amused glances. There was every probability, thought His Lordship, that Musgrave's curricle would soon be his. Her Ladyship, knowing her husband as thoroughly as she did, guessed the substance of his thoughts.

Despite her husband's shortcomings, which were happily few in her eyes, she loved him without limit or condition. Never had she entertained a moment's regret on becoming his wife, for she could have loved no other man as she loved him.

There were times when she longed for a more modest existence, unbounded by the society of those she was obliged to tolerate for his sake, those who prized rank and consequence above all else; but she rarely gave voice to such thoughts, and when she did, the acknowledgement of her good fortune in life swiftly gave way to gratitude and sincere appreciation.

'Mrs Howard is gone into Somerset. I doubt I shall have the pleasure of her company for some time to come,' said Mrs Blake in an attempt to ease an awkward moment.

'If only the same could be said of her father,' whispered the Dowager to her daughter-in-law. 'Mr Edwards has quite lost his senses. Fancying himself in love with your aunt at his age! What next,

33

I wonder! One day we may find him waltzing his way around the assembly room, and then there will be no escaping his clutches.'

At the close of the evening, the inhabitants of Osborne Castle were as well acquainted with the delights of Brinshore, its health benefits, geography and principal families, as the inhabitants of the said seaside town themselves. Its superior situation and the beauty of its rugged landscape, its spotless sandy beach, the purity of the air and sea water, marked Brinshore out as the place that would one day rival Eastbourne, or even Brighton. For Emma, its proximity to Sanditon proved to be its greatest merit and, by the end of the evening, she found that she could tolerate the thought of a season in Brinshore very happily indeed.

The next day brought a succession of visitors to the Castle, among them the Musgraves. Elizabeth, though still not fully recovered from her injury, discovered that her ankle had undergone a remarkable improvement overnight; as Tom Musgrave had every intention of calling on Lord Osborne that morning, and Anne had promised to visit her cousin Emma, Elizabeth made up her mind to accompany them.

The morning passed without a single utterance of the words 'Dower House', 'curricle' or 'ankle', for the news of the day was Penelope's removal to Brinshore. The virtues of Brinshore were once again rehearsed by its most fervent advocate, and when the clock struck two, the Musgraves were pressed to stay for luncheon.

'How very fortunate you are, dear cousin, to have before you the prospect of a summer by the shore. I love the sea beyond anything,' said Anne. 'Brinshore is the very best place in the world to collect sea shells of every description, and even fossils. I am so very fond of fossils though I have but few in my possession. Dear Aunt Harding, I am quite persuaded that Brinshore is the jewel of the south coast.'

'Indeed it is,' said Penelope. Anne's rapturous declaration in praise of Brinshore was greeted by her aunt with delight.

'It was our privilege to spend two hours there last autumn. Do you remember, Mama?' said she to Elizabeth. 'We stopped to change horses on our way to Hastings. The Red Lion serves the best dish of tea in the world. Do you know the inn of which I speak, Aunt?'

'I do indeed,' replied Mrs Harding. 'A most respectable establishment, and not five minutes' walk from the shore.'

'One cannot commend the beauties of Brinshore too highly,' replied Anne. 'Were we to spend the whole day recounting its worth, it would be a day well spent.'

'Indeed, a day is hardly long enough to do it justice,' agreed Penelope.

'Brinshore is without compare,' said Anne.

Penelope could not have been better pleased with her niece. 'Then you shall not be deprived of its splendours a moment longer. I shall brook no opposition. Not a word shall be said against it! Elizabeth, do you hear me? Anne will accompany Emma. Both my nieces shall stay the whole summer in Brinshore, and not a day less.'

Elizabeth raised not the slightest objection, and delight at the news filled the room. The greatest happiness, however, was felt by Anne, who, unable to express her appreciation in words, was filled with tears of joy.

Emma's pleasure at the news that she was to spend the summer with her cousin was less apparent. After luncheon, and when all the guests were gone, Lady Osborne went in search of her daughter, and finding her in the music room practicing on the pianoforte, she sat a while unobserved to listen to her daughter's execution of a pretty sonatina. On perceiving that her mother had entered the room, Emma left off and replaced the lid of the instrument.

'My dear, do not stop. Your proficiency on the pianoforte is truly a pleasure to hear.'

'I have practiced long enough today, Mama,' said Emma.

Lady Osborne looked out of the window. 'Then come and take a turn in the gallery with me. I thought perhaps we might walk in the park, but the sky is grey, and rain threatens.' She observed one of the gardeners at work in the distance by the lake. The scene stirred in her a memory. She recalled the day his father, who later became the head gardener, had urged her to seek shelter from the rain at Osborne Castle.

'Charles was a young boy then. He insisted on a walk by the lake in Osborne Park. If I recall, he wanted to collect feathers or horse chestnuts or some such thing. He was always collecting things – usually of the living variety. Frogs were a particular favourite of his.'

'Where was Papa?' asked Emma.

'Watching from the library window. There was so much rain that year, and mud everywhere. I had hoped to escape your papa's notice.'

'I don't understand,' said Emma.

'He was not your papa then. And I was no more than the daughter of a humble clergyman.'

'Dear Grandpapa! How I miss him.'

'Do you? Truly?'

'Yes, Mama. I did not miss him while he lived. But I miss him so terribly now.'

Lady Osborne embraced her daughter. 'Your grandpapa loved you very much.'

The long gallery was empty as Lady Osborne had expected it to be. Lord Osborne was always in his study at this hour; and Penelope had asked for a fire to be made up in the small drawing room where she was busy about the business of writing letters to her friends, informing them of her news.

'Mama, do you like your name?'

'What a strange question.'

'It is so very confusing at times. When Aunt Harding or Aunt Musgrave call you Emma, I sometimes think they address me.'

'Should you have liked a different name?'

Emma thought for a moment. 'Yes. I believe I should. I prefer longer names. Forgive me, Mama, but "Emma" is exceedingly short. A name of distinction should comprise three syllables at least: *Isabella*, *Marianne* or *Georgiana*. Even *Eleanor* or *Catherine* are not without charm. Still, I suppose it is not so plain a name as *Anne*.'

Lady Osborne hesitated for a moment. Emma had never been told why she bore the same name as her mother. Perhaps the time had come for the circumstances of her birth to be made known, thought she. But as Her Ladyship pondered what to say, the moment was lost, seized by her daughter whose concerns turned to the pressing matter of Brinshore.

'I do not mind that Anne is to come to Brinshore for the season, but I do not know how I shall tolerate her ceaseless enthusiasm for the place. She is so earnest, so determined to find pleasure at every turn. A little mild diversion now and again, and a comfortable room with a well-lit fire would be satisfaction enough for me. But I shall be expected to admire and approve every sea shell, every splinter of driftwood, every crab and barnacle that was ever offered up by the tide. It is too much to ask of me, Mama. You know it is not my disposition to be pleased with everything I see.'

'*Mild* diversion! My dear child, you are nineteen. Let me hear you speak instead of *wild* diversion.'

'You cannot mean it, Mama,' said Emma.

'I should like you to take pleasure in your surroundings, and the company of those who esteem and love you. You must strive not to disappoint either your aunt or your cousin. Let Anne's enthusiasm for the sea be your example. What joy it would bring to your Aunt Harding to know that her generosity and hospitality were appreciated. Your pleasure and approval would be the very best gift of all.'

CHAPTER FOUR

The day of Mrs Turner's removal to the Dower House arrived and passed with comparative ease. Every aspect of the task was managed with fastidious attention to detail. The Dowager took charge, giving instructions liberally and persistently to all in her path. Mrs Turner, perceiving that her presence as part of the proceedings was a greater hindrance than a help, had no difficulty placing herself outside the reach of her new companion. The Dowager's chair in the south-facing drawing room was vacant, and the fire lit; thus the inducement to occupy it was too tempting to resist. There Mrs Turner passed a pleasant hour, unperturbed by the chaos around her. She placed her feet on the Dowager's footstool and plunged her hand into the bowl of sugared almonds on the table beside her.

'Callers,' said the Dowager, on entering the room, 'and on such a day as this!'

Mrs Turner was afforded a clearer view of the scene from the Dowager's chair. 'It is only Osborne. I see Tom Musgrave is with him,' said Mrs Turner, making no attempt to vacate her present position.

The Dowager beheld the scene before her with wonder and determined that such behaviour required the strongest rebuke. *Only* Osborne? That any person of equal rank should take the liberty of describing her son as 'only' anything was shocking indeed; that Mrs Turner should feel at liberty to do so while consuming a dish of her finest sugared almonds, seated comfortably in *her* particular chair with her feet resting on *her* favourite footstool, was an outrage.

'My dear, I shall not encourage His *Lordship* or *Mr* Musgrave to stay long. I trust you will at least give the impression of diligence and employment. You might begin by finding a suitable alternative to your present comfortable arrangements.'

Before Mrs Turner had the opportunity to relinquish the Dowager's chair, the door opened to admit Osborne and Musgrave. On entering, the visitors' surprise at the scene before them caused Tom Musgrave to glance delightedly in Osborne's direction.

'Ah! What a happy sight I see before me!' said Musgrave. 'You look quite at home already, Mrs Turner. Is it not a happy sight, My Lord?'

'None happier,' replied he, persuaded that Musgrave's curricle would soon be his.

Mrs Turner stood to her feet, assisted by Musgrave. 'A very serviceable chair, I grant you. Where it lacks support, it makes up for in width. I defy you not to choose my chair over your own for the very best comfort of all,' said she, addressing the Dowager.

'My dear, you may place your chair at the opposite side of the fireplace if you will, and though it does not match the elegance of my interior, I shall, for your sake, tolerate it. But I am as certain as the day is long that I shall never be tempted to sit in it.'

'So generous an accommodation in Your Ladyship's domestic arrangements is an example to us all,' said Musgrave to the Dowager. 'I declare, I shall move my favourite card table into the drawing room as soon as I return home. And if Mrs Musgrave says one word against it, I shall set forth Your Ladyship's exemplary conduct as my defence.'

The Dowager indicated her approval with a haughty nod and a look of self-righteous complacency.

'Shall you indeed?' said Osborne. 'Did I not hear Mrs Musgrave say only yesterday that she intended to offer the very same article to her sister Mrs Harding as a gift for her new house in Brinshore?'

'Impossible!' said Musgrave, shocked at the very idea.

'It is a sturdy piece as I recall, and will be well used in Brinshore, though I daresay the salt air will do it no favours. But never mind that,' said Osborne, brushing the matter aside, 'I'm sure Mrs Harding will polish it from time to time.'

Mr Musgrave was left speechless. His attachment to that particular card table was great indeed; many a happy rubber had been played upon it, many a winning hand had been dealt there.

Turning to Mrs Turner, His Lordship continued, 'My dear madam, my purpose in coming here today is to assure you that, should your plans change in the next *day* or *two* —'

'Or indeed the next *month*,' added Musgrave.

'I have made provision for you to return to Delham Cottage. It shall remain empty until you are quite sure that you wish to give up the house entirely,' said Osborne.

The Dowager and Mrs Turner exchanged amused looks and at once burst into fits of laughter. Nonplussed, Osborne and Musgrave sat patiently until their laughter ceased, curious to know the cause of such mirth.

'We know your game!' said the Dowager.

'And we should like a part in it too,' Mrs Turner added.

'What game?' said Osborne.

'Why, the wager of course!' said his mother. 'Never mind how we know. Neither of your wives were forthcoming; they did not give you away. They are not the guilty ones.'

'Emma,' said Osborne. 'My daughter is the very worst keeper of secrets in the world.'

'And the very best gossip,' said the Dowager. 'You must not censure her.'

'Indeed you must not,' Mrs Turner agreed.

'Our proposal is this,' continued the Dowager. 'If Mrs Turner remains at the Dower House until Midsummer's Day —'

'We shall win the wager —'

'And the horse and cart shall be ours.'

'Horse and *cart*?' said Musgrave. 'It is as fine a curricle as you would find in the whole of England!'

'Cart? Curricle? There's little in it. The difference is slight. A cart is a degree more practical, but that is all,' said Osborne teasingly.

'The point is this,' said the Dowager. 'A curricle will not serve our purpose.'

'Not at all,' agreed Mrs Turner.

The Dowager continued, 'We cannot be seen to be taking rides in the park in a curricle.'

Mrs Turner nodded in agreement.

'Then what?' asked Osborne.

'A landau and a pair of greys is just the thing,' his mother replied.

'It will serve us very well, I think,' said Mrs Turner.

'Yes, very well indeed.' The Dowager nodded in agreement.

'A landau? Impossible!' Osborne and Musgrave were speechless at the proposal. When at last their initial astonishment was overcome, Osborne asked, 'But what of Musgrave's curricle?'

'Sell it,' said Mrs Turner. 'You will get a good price for it if you let it go to Mr Edwards. He has not the least clue in the world when it comes to the purchase of a conveyance.'

'Let him think his purchase is of assistance to Mrs Turner,' said the Dowager.

Musgrave and Osborne looked at each other in amazement.

'And I'm sure, my dear, that fine pair of greys you keep at your stables might easily be parted with,' the Dowager continued, addressing herself to her son.

'Easily parted with?' said Osborne.

There appeared to be no better incentive for domestic harmony than the prospect of acquiring a new landau and a pair of greys for the Dower House; consequently, the Dowager and Mrs Turner had not the slightest intention of giving up their new domestic arrangements, at least not for some time to come. As Osborne and Musgrave took their leave, the Dowager spotted the arrival of a familiar carriage.

'And now comes Mr Edwards with his old-fashioned equipage and amorous imaginings!' said she. 'Well, Osborne, you must tell him to go away. We are not at home to receive him. We are all at sixes and sevens today, as you see. But first Mr Musgrave, you must get him to take that curricle off your hands.'

CHAPTER FIVE

The spring came and went without any further event of note: the installation of the new inmate at the Dower House was made complete when excess furniture and empty trunks belonging to Mrs Turner were placed in storage; and there was little to perplex or occupy the inhabitants of Osborne Castle, or the neighbourhood, beyond the restoration of the assembly rooms in Delham and the question of the vacancy at Stanton. Of the former it was said that the rooms would be completed by October in readiness for the first assembly of the season, for Lady Osborne and Mrs Musgrave had taken a great interest in the management of the scheme; of the latter, little was known, but much was speculated upon, about the necessity to appoint a new incumbent by Michaelmas.

Since the death of Mr Watson in the year fourteen, Stanton Parsonage had been served by a willing curate whose evangelical zeal had compelled him to seek a higher calling: the eager young cleric was shortly to abandon his service to the godless of rural Surrey for the more spiritually profitable enterprise of preaching the gospel in foreign lands. Hence, Stanton was soon to be vacant again. Speculation as to the new incumbent was heightened when rumours began to circulate throughout the neighbourhood that the living was to be sold. Such was the situation that the uncertainty continued into late spring after the young curate had delivered his last sermon at Stanton Church.

'The matter should be settled without delay,' said the Dowager. 'A flock without a shepherd is apt to go astray and become wild and unruly. I expect our man at Wickstead would take it given half the chance.'

'Oh! I do hope not,' said Mrs Turner.

'Why so?' asked Lady Osborne. 'What objection have you to Mr Blackmore?'

'He is so earnest and so very decided in his opinions. Is it fair that Stanton should have more of the same? Let the new incumbent be a breath of fresh air,' replied Mrs Turner.

'Indeed. Let him be liberal and open-minded and good-humoured,' said the Dowager.

And so they continued.

'And tall if he possibly can be,' added Mrs Turner.

'And strong.'

'With kind eyes and good manners.'

'Blue eyes and roguish. And presentable.'

'He must be well connected too.'

'Loyal to his parish. Not one of these young clerics who is forever moving about here and there, and finding sin around every corner and fault with everything he sees.'

'And above all, he should be young and handsome,' said Emma.

'Well spoken, my dear,' said the Dowager. 'Yes, the most important attribute is that he be handsome. It is the only means by which to secure a full congregation.'

41

'Stanton is dear to me. I confess,' said Lady Osborne. 'I should like to see the matter settled soon. All these weeks of speculation add to the uncertainty. If Stanton is to be sold, I should like to know to whom, and on whom the living is to be bestowed.'

Lord Osborne folded his newspaper and set it aside. 'I see. Well, for my part, I pity the new incumbent, whoever he may prove to be. With such expectations of him, he is likely to disappoint before he opens his mouth to announce the first hymn.'

'Papa! How amusing you are! Perhaps we should set about writing a list of prospective candidates,' said Emma.

'Yes, indeed,' agreed the Dowager. 'Whom do we know among our acquaintance in town?'

'It is a fruitless enterprise for we do not know to whom the living now belongs, nor are we likely to exercise any influence over the appointment of the new incumbent,' said Lady Osborne.

Her Ladyship knew that her husband was usually consulted about matters of import and interest to the neighbourhood, and asked, 'Shall you not be among the first to know, my dear? Can you not make enquiries?'

Lord Osborne paused for a moment before making a reply. 'My dear,' he replied, 'I have no need to enquire, for I know that the living has been purchased and I know by whom.'

'Then why did you not say so?' said the Dowager to her son.

'Do tell us, Papa! Who has bought Stanton?' said Emma.

Lord Osborne got up and walked to the window. The eyes of all present followed him.

He turned and said, 'I have.'

'Oh Papa! How delightful! And to keep us all guessing!'

'You have purchased the living at Stanton?' said Lady Osborne with astonishment.

'Excellent!' said Mrs Turner.

The Dowager was astounded by the news. 'Whatever for?'

'I believe I know why you bought it, Papa. It is because Grandpapa Watson is buried there.'

'It was, I confess, a consideration,' said he. 'But there was another.' He fixed his eyes on Lady Osborne. 'Stanton was the very spot where I became the happiest of men.'

'Under the church porch! In the rain!' said Emma, looking at her mother.

'Yes, indeed,' said Lord Osborne. Taking his wife by the hand, he continued, 'It was the place where your mother consented to be my wife.'

Lady Osborne smiled at her husband. It was enough for him to search her countenance and ascertain her feelings on the matter, for she was incapable at that moment of expressing the sentiments that swelled in her heart.

'That being the case,' said the Dowager, 'we must set about the task of finding a suitable parson at once. Mrs Turner and I will do what we can to make enquiries. Emma, your Aunt Harding may know of a candidate among her circle. Was not your Uncle Harding a parson in Chichester?'

'Indeed he was,' replied Emma.

'There. You see.' The Dowager enjoyed nothing better than the management of some scheme or other, for it provided much needed occupation as well as the opportunity to issue instructions and make unreasonable demands of those around her.

'The difference between Chichester and Brinshore must be great indeed,' said Mrs Turner. 'The latter is more likely to yield a dissenter than a respectable man of the cloth.'

'And so Emma,' said the Dowager, recalling the purpose of her granddaughter's visit, 'you have come to take your leave. How long will you stay in Brinshore?'

'Two months at least.'

'I hear Anne Musgrave is to accompany you,' the Dowager went on.

Emma nodded. 'Uncle Musgrave will take us as far as Brighton. Aunt Harding is to send her carriage to meet us there. I daresay I should prefer to stay in Brighton the whole summer. But Brinshore is nearer Sanditon and so Mrs Blake will be close by. But I should like to see the new additions to the Regent's Pavilion at Brighton. It is so very strange and exotic, is it not?'

'Brighton is a place of danger as well as delight,' said the Dowager. 'At Brinshore, under the protection of your Aunt Harding, and in the company of your cousin, you will be protected from undesirable attentions.'

'Do I need protection?' said Emma.

'Mrs Turner is better acquainted than I with the consequences of male artifice and trickery when deployed successfully against an unsuspecting female, even an elderly one,' replied the Dowager. 'An heiress most particularly must take care never to fall under the spell of a fortune hunter. Make sure, my dear, that you heed my words, and that your cousin does likewise.'

'Anne has no interest in anything that does not flap, crawl, or sting. She has not the slightest desire to see Brighton or the Regent's palace.'

'Every soul must see Brighton! I recall a very fine ball at Marlborough House in the year eighty or thereabouts,' said the Dowager. 'Brighton is full of delights! And I can think of nothing more pleasing than a ride in a new landau —'

'Attached to a pair of greys —' said Mrs Turner.

'On a summer's day,' the Dowager added wistfully. 'Midsummer's Day.'

Mrs Turner joined the chorus. 'On the seafront. At Brighton.'

CHAPTER SIX

The journey from Delham was accomplished in good time; and the weather, being temperate and clear, increased the eager anticipation of the two young cousins as Brighton came into view. The town appeared radiant in the sunshine, the sights and sounds more brilliant and intense than ever. As the journey came to its end, whatever parting guidance and counsel was given, was forgotten in an instant. Mr Musgrave at once savoured the expressions of delight at the sight of the sea that enthralled his daughter and niece, and yet he felt apprehensive at the prospect of bidding them farewell. Every conceivable thought that ever entered the mind of an anxious guardian was expressed at that moment: they should protect and defend one another — seek guidance and direction from their Aunt Harding if ever in doubt — never withhold a secret that concerned the welfare of either cousin — never be induced to act in a manner at odds with their conscience — beware flirtatious, charming and unmannerly young men who seek to recommend themselves without respect for the rules of decorum.

Had Mrs Musgrave the opportunity to witness her husband's speech, her approval — and her amusement — would have been complete. Every piece of advice dispensed by Mr Musgrave was just as it should have been, though as a young man he had rarely heeded a word of it himself.

A cold luncheon was quickly followed by a short walk to the shore, and by the middle of the afternoon Anne and Emma were once again on their way. The shortness of their sojourn in Brighton was particularly irksome to Emma; Anne, however, was just as excited at the prospect of completing their journey and of their first glimpse of Brinshore in the evening light.

'We should have insisted on staying in Brighton for one night at least. Look at us! We shall not be fit to be seen when we arrive. We should aim to reach Brinshore under cover of night. My frock is full of creases from sitting and my hair is like hay. I look like Grandmamma,' said Emma.

'I do not care one whit how I appear. I care only to see Brinshore, to breathe its pure air, and gaze at the splendour of its situation,' Anne replied.

Emma sighed with frustration. She closed her eyes and dreamed of all she had seen that day, of all the pleasures that might have been hers had Aunt Harding chosen Brighton over Brinshore.

Some minutes later, Anne, overcome by sleep, slumped heavily onto Emma's shoulder. For a mile or two, Emma allowed Anne to rest her head until the weight of her cousin, despite her small frame, became too uncomfortable to bear. Rummaging through her reticule, she pulled out a handful of sugared almonds. 'Here you are,' said she, waking Anne. 'Grandmamma gave them to me for the journey.'

'Thank you, no. I think I shall be sick. How much further, Emma?' said Anne.

Emma stopped the coach. As Anne alighted for air, her cousin ascertained their exact whereabouts from the coachman.

'Sanditon?' said Anne.

'Yes, Miss.'

'Then we are almost there. It is but three miles to Brinshore, is it not?' Emma replied.

'Yes, Miss.'

Emma was more inclined to tarry a little while longer in Sanditon than her cousin. The thought that one day soon Charles Blake would walk the same stretch of sand, that his footsteps would follow where her feet had trod, was irresistible. She glanced at the terrace above, a row of fine new houses with an outlook over the sea. Soon Charles

45

Blake would stand at one of those very windows, his mind filled with thoughts of her, of declarations, engagements, love and weddings.

Emma was roused from her daydream by the sound of Anne being sick. She knew not how to assist her cousin in a practical way but gave every assurance that they would soon arrive at their destination and all would be well. 'You had better take one of these after all,' said she, placing a sugared almond into Anne's hand. 'It will take that horrid taste from your mouth.' Anne quietly acquiesced, and a few minutes later the cousins were once again on their way.

When at last they arrived in Brinshore, the sun had gone down. Unexpectedly, Emma found herself steeped in admiration and wonder at the scene that met her eyes: the moon was full, the night clear, and the sea still. The reflection of the moon on the sea was as pleasing to her as anything she had seen that day in the whole of Brighton.

Flustered and fretful, Aunt Harding had been waiting all evening for their arrival. 'I have kept watch every fifteen minutes since seven o'clock. Where have you been?'

As soon as Emma had explained the reason for their delay, Anne was taken up to her room and word was sent to the local physician, a Mr Fowle, to attend her directly.

'Really Aunt, I am sure it is nothing. Anne does not travel well. That is all. We had a fine ham luncheon in Brighton, and a very good game pie, most of which Anne deposited in Sanditon.'

'My dear Emma, one cannot be too careful. If anything were to happen to your cousin, your Aunt Musgrave would never forgive me.'

'I'm sure no one would mind if anything happened to me,' Emma replied.

'You know that is not true.'

'Oh yes it is. It is only Frank that Mama and Papa care about.'

'Come, my dear. You are fatigued after your journey. You too need some rest. I don't know why I didn't suggest that you stay in Brighton overnight.'

'I wish you had,' Emma replied.

The next day Emma woke to the sound of the waves on the seashore. Before the maid had entered to make up the fire, Emma got out of bed and opened the curtains. The vista before her was not as she had imagined it to be; the clear sky at night had given way to a thick covering of sea fret by day, and the view of the shore was completely obscured by it. Undeterred, and with every expectation that the mist would soon clear, Emma decided to go for an early morning walk before breakfast.

The geography of Brinshore, though having been described to her on several occasions by Aunt Harding, was unfamiliar, and was made even more strange and disconcerting by the quietude of the place and the encircling mist. Within minutes Emma was disorientated; but for the gentle rise and crash of the waves there was not a sound to be heard. The mist fell thicker and heavier until not even the faint outline of a building or rock was visible.

For some moments she stood fixed to the spot, unable to decide which way to turn. Some distance away she sensed the presence of a creature moving quickly towards her, the light patter of footsteps on sand. It was a young girl of about six or seven, expressionless, thin, barefooted and in rags. Emma instinctively took the girl's hand; and without a word, the girl led Emma back to her aunt's house.

'What is your name?' said Emma.

The girl gazed at the ground but said nothing.

'How did you —'

The young girl pointed to Aunt Harding's residence.

Of course, thought Emma. The girl must know that I am a stranger here. The whole of Brinshore must know of our arrival. 'Come with me. Let me find some milk for you.'

The girl refused and ran away as suddenly as she had appeared.

When Emma entered the house, a full explanation was demanded and given. Mrs Harding, unused to the unpredictability of young women and how to keep them in order, had been on the point of sending a party of servants to search for her niece.

'You gave me such a fright!' said she. 'You might have been set upon by highwaymen, thieves, or fishermen.'

'Aunt, really. No harm is done, as you see. I am perfectly well. How is Anne?'

'Mr Fowle has prescribed bed rest for two days. Your cousin is a little feverish. It is better, says our dependable physician, to exercise caution in these matters.'

'Then I shall go up to her by the by and make myself useful.'

'You must not stay long for she needs complete quiet. Indeed, you shall come with me when the mist clears, and I shall show you Brinshore.'

'But what about Anne?'

'Payne, my maid, will take care of her. You have no need to worry your head on that score. She is most efficient.'

Once the mist had cleared and Emma had sat for half an hour at Anne's bedside, Mrs Harding called for the carriage.

'A carriage, Aunt? Surely the market square is not beyond a walk. Brinshore is little more than a village.'

Mrs Harding chose to overlook the remark. The carriage, it seemed, was essential, not for the purpose of transportation, but as a means of parading her niece before Brinshore society. Accompanied by the Honourable Emma Osborne, Mrs Harding anticipated the very great pleasure of introducing her niece to the few notables of which Brinshore could boast.

'What a triumph!' said Mrs Harding. 'Only imagine, until your arrival, my dear, the very best Brinshore had to offer was the second son of a baronet and a retired Admiral of the Red. I have every expectation that Brinshore will, in a year or two, be as fashionable as Brighton. I should not be surprised if the Regent himself were to build a fine palace atop the south cliff.'

Emma looked about her; Brinshore was indeed more charming than she had imagined. As a pleasant place for sea bathing it might one day rival Lyme, and yet, a fashionable town by the sea it was not, nor would it ever be in her eyes.

'Dear Aunt,' said Emma, 'I should like so very much to walk. The mist is much improved. Shall we not take advantage of the fine weather while we can?'

'There is hardly a day when the weather is not fine in Brinshore. A little sea mist is neither here nor there,' her aunt replied. 'I daresay it rains almost every day in Sanditon. I should not wish to be without an umbrella in Sanditon.'

'I thought Sanditon quite charming when we passed through it yesterday.'

'I suppose Waterloo Crescent will afford Mrs Blake some measure of obscurity. Such is very easily achieved in Sanditon. And as one cannot be certain that Mrs Howard will stay safely settled in Somerset

— her word is not to be trusted — Mrs Blake should remain where she is. As long as Mrs Blake keeps Mrs Howard away from Brinshore, I shall be satisfied, for I should not wish to be obliged to acknowledge her.'

'Surely Mrs Howard cannot make herself the guest of Mrs Blake in a house that is not her own,' said Emma. 'Was Mrs Howard's behaviour so very wrong?'

'It was. It is. She should return to her husband, make amends and do what she can to restore some measure of respectability. What does she mean by putting Mrs Blake to so much inconvenience? Imposing upon her in so bold a fashion, visiting Osborne Cottage as though she were the Queen of Sheba calling upon King Solomon. I heard it all.'

'Perhaps Mrs Howard was unhappy in her marriage.'

'It was entirely of her making, though unhappiness in marriage is more common than not. One must make of it what one can. The very best marriage survives where there is love *and* money. But if one cannot have both, then one should choose money. For poverty, where there is no way out of it, will extinguish love in an instant. Mrs Howard has nothing left of her own — it is all gone to her husband. There is nothing to be done. She must return to him if he will have her, and endeavour to make herself useful.'

Mrs Harding indulged her niece by acceding to Emma's request for a walk, and within the hour the pair set out in the direction of the square. It was not long before Mrs Harding found greater pleasure in a walk than she had anticipated; for, during their progress towards the square, she was obliged to introduce her niece to no less than four families, and each one desirous of making the acquaintance of a viscount's daughter. As they strolled along the main street, Emma became separated from her aunt when a fine hat in the milliner's window caught her attention. Turning to find that her aunt had crossed the square, she hastened towards her without first looking to see if the way was clear. Startled by the sudden approach of a gig, she stepped out of the way and into a pool of muddy water, almost losing her balance. The sensation of stepping into mud was not new to her, but it was deeply unpleasant. She looked down in horror at her shoes and the hem of her new frock.

The gig came to an abrupt halt. Its occupant, a young gentleman of about five and twenty, alighted and approached her. He made an apology of a kind by putting it to her that had she looked about her to ensure the way was clear, the incident would not have occurred. Emma pointed out that it was his carelessness, not hers, that was the cause.

'Look at my frock!' said she.

'Charming, though a little too fancy for shopping. If I were you, I should choose something more serviceable in future.'

'But what am I to do? Just look at me!'

'It is only mud. It will wash,' said he.

'And what if I should have no means of washing it?'

'Your maid will know what to do.'

'Help me,' said Emma. He extended his hand to steady her as she stepped out of the mud. 'And if I should not have a maid?' she continued, brushing his hand aside when she had no further use of it.

'I'll warrant that beneath that very fine lace glove is an equally fine hand that has never seen a day's work in its life,' said he. 'Now, allow me to return you to your party.'

'That will not be necessary, sir.'

The scene attracted the curiosity of bystanders. Among them were those who had particular intelligence as to the personage of the young lady in question; and when the incident was drawn to her aunt's attention by one of the onlookers, Mrs Harding hurried to Emma's side to take charge. The young man made his apologies and placed the offending gig at their disposal. While Aunt Harding was disposed to accept the young man's offer, Emma was decidedly against it. The young man bowed graciously, took his leave, and continued on his way.

'We did not ask his name,' said her aunt.

'I have no desire of knowing it,' replied Emma.

'Such a handsome young man, amiable and unaffected. Elegant too — in an unstudied sort of way.'

'I think, Aunt, you mean ill-bred, casual to the point of off-hand, and carelessly outlandish in his behaviour. He was exceedingly uncivil to me.'

'Was he? Well, I do hope we come upon him again. Once we are properly introduced, you may give him a piece of your mind.'

To her surprise, the wishes of the aunt were granted the following morning when a stranger presented his card and was duly shown into the drawing room. Mrs Harding was delighted to discover that the name on the card was already familiar to her: when Mr Fitzroy entered the room, she recognised the very same young gentleman they had met in the square the previous day. On entering the drawing room a few minutes later, Emma, having completely dismissed the incident from her mind, was astounded to find the young man, seated quite comfortably upon the best chair in the house, conversing in an uncommonly casual fashion with her aunt.

Introductions were accomplished with little ceremony. There was some measure of unease and suspicion on Emma's part at his presence, for he seemed quite unlike the disagreeable and opinionated young man she had encountered in the market square. And so, when a sincere and fulsome apology was extended, she relented somewhat reluctantly and even managed half a smile.

'My dear Emma, what a happy chance this is! We shall make no further mention of yesterday's unfortunate incident — or perhaps I should say *fortuitous* incident. All is forgiven and forgotten! You see, Emma, Mr Fitzroy has been telling me how very determined he was to ascertain our whereabouts, making enquiries here and there, for he wished above all things to offer his apologies in a proper manner and in person. I do not believe there is anything to forgive! Indeed, I do not! It is such a happy coincidence, my dear Emma, for Mr Fitzroy is in fact no stranger to us at all.'

Emma was slower than her aunt to lower her guard. 'I am sure I have never seen Mr Fitzroy before in my life until yesterday.'

'Indeed, my dear, that is so. Nor had I. But our visitor is not any Mr Fitzroy. He is *the* Mr Fitzroy, the very good friend of a very good friend of ours. Can you not guess?' replied Mrs Harding. 'Captain Blake! Our very own Charles Blake, you see!'

Mr Fitzroy observed with fascination the remarkable transformation in Emma's countenance that occurred at the mention of Charles Blake; and although she made every effort to conceal it, the many enquiries that followed gave their new acquaintance reason to conclude that her interest in his friend was considerably greater than the relationship described by the aunt as 'almost brother and sister'.

'Then you must be the brother of the late Captain Fitzroy. Mrs Blake mentioned something of the circumstances that —' said Emma.

'Indeed,' said he, quickly. 'Captain Fitzroy was my brother. I wish you had known him.'

Her voice softened in reply. 'I am sorry for your loss,' said she.

'Thank you,' he replied.

The visitor showed little inclination to dwell on his brother's passing, the sad event that had brought him to Sanditon; nor did he have any desire to furnish them with the particulars of his brother's final hours, despite Mrs Harding's entreaty to do so.

The conversation continued in a more cheerful vein as their visitor delighted Mrs Harding by acknowledging the superiority of Brinshore and its attractions compared to other towns situated within the vicinity.

'Brinshore has as fine a prospect as I have ever seen,' said he.

His observation seemed wholly sincere, and Mrs Harding could not have been better pleased with their guest, for he could not have commended himself in any nobler way than this. Mr Fitzroy's praise of Brinshore singled him out as one of the finest and most sensible young men of Mrs Harding's acquaintance.

Emma was not so easily pleased with their visitor, believing him to be about the business of recommending himself too readily; for no one obliged to spend more than five minutes in Mrs Harding's company could fail to comprehend her enthusiasm for Brinshore, nor grasp the best means by which to ingratiate themselves.

The news, however, that Charles Blake was expected in Sanditon within the fortnight was the most pleasing of all to Emma. Mr Fitzroy explained that Waterloo Crescent was now ready to receive Mrs Blake and her son; everything that could have been done had been done to secure their comfort and convenience.

Their visitor sat for half an hour before taking his leave. In that time Emma was able to ascertain that Mrs Blake and her son were expected to take up residence in Sanditon within the fortnight, that Charles Blake was expected to remain in Sanditon for two months complete, and that Mr Fitzroy would urge his guests to frequent Brinshore at every possible opportunity.

'Excellent!' said Mrs Harding, after their visitor had left Trafalgar Terrace. 'What a fine young man! I shall insist on his being one of the party when I invite Mrs Blake to dine with us. Mr Fitzroy! A surname of distinction. It is a name that will grace my dining table very well indeed.'

'There is something in his manner that I do not —'

'Nonsense! He is perfectly amiable. A fine young man.'

'I thought his praise of Brinshore too fulsome to be trusted,' replied Emma.

Mrs Harding was astonished at her niece's remark. 'You know nothing of the matter, my dear. It gives me no pleasure to say it, but I fear Mrs Blake will be sorely disappointed in Sanditon. Five minutes in that forlorn and dreary little town is all she will need before she is longing for Brinshore instead. Indeed, I suspect, though Mr Fitzroy did not say so explicitly, it is a very great disappointment to him to have inherited a house in Sanditon. Unhappy the day that Captain Fitzroy built his house on Sanditon's sand, and not on the firmer foundation that is Brinshore!'

'Do you not wonder why Captain Blake continues the connection with Captain Fitzroy's brother? After all, Mr Fitzroy is not a naval man. In fact, he appears to be a man of no purpose. When Mrs Blake spoke to me of Mr Fitzroy, I paid little attention, but I believe there is some mystery surrounding him.'

'He has a fine face and a pleasant air. Such interesting young men must be few and far between in Sanditon.'

CHAPTER SEVEN

Anne Musgrave had, since her childhood, borne a striking resemblance to her mother; but, unlike her mother, she had not known any measure of the responsibilities that had befallen the beautiful Miss Elizabeth Watson as a young woman. Anne had led a life of ease and advantage, not dissimilar to that of her cousin. At nineteen, her mother, Elizabeth, had understood every particular required to discharge the duties and demands of a household bereft of a mother's influence, and being possessed of a distant and ailing father, quickly acquired those qualities of resilience, strength and courage that were to see her through the toughest of challenges. Anne had something of her mother's nature; always ready to please and be of service to any creature in need of succour, she thought little of her own needs. In Anne's eyes, happiness lay in making few demands of her own while graciously acceding to the demands of others.

Graceful in manner, practical rather than elegant in dress and air, and ready to be pleased with everything and everyone around her, Anne Musgrave was not expected to want for suitors. With a fortune of twelve thousand pounds and connections to the Osborne family, Anne was almost as interesting to the neighbourhood of Brinshore as her cousin. Restored to health after strict adherence to bed rest and thin gruel prescribed by Mr Fowle, Anne was impatient to explore Brinshore's countless rock pools and sea life. The view of the shore from her airless bedchamber was no substitute for a walk on the sand; and as soon as she was fit to leave her room, she wanted nothing more than to take in Brinshore's fresh sea air.

Emma was pleased to have Anne's company at last, for the society of her aunt had become less tolerable by the hour. Brinshore was charming; but wearied by her aunt's constant praise of it, together with the untold deficiencies of its rival, Emma began to form a curiously favourable view of Sanditon. Even the air which was reputedly stale, the damp climate, and the putrid effluence of the sea, began to acquire allure. Sanditon may turn out to be the worst place on earth, thought she, but I believe I should suffer it better for its shortcomings.

After breakfast, as Anne and Emma were about to set out for a walk, a letter arrived. Mrs Harding, eager to relate its contents, called them back into the breakfast room to convey the news concerning Captain Blake which Emma, most particularly, had been expecting.

'Mrs Blake has written to say that her plans have changed,' said Mrs Harding.

'For the better, I hope,' said Emma, anxious to ascertain that Mrs Blake's plans would still include spending the summer in Sanditon.

'Mrs Blake is to arrive earlier than planned for she is to travel in Mr Tomlinson's coach. The family are headed for Hastings and, it appears, the offer of a seat in a comfortable coach was too good an opportunity for Mrs Blake to miss. Hastings of all places! What is there to see in Hastings? Mr Tomlinson must be hard up indeed. But, as fortune would have it, Mrs Blake will be saved the expense and inconvenience of the stage. The journey will cost her nothing at all! And not a penny to pay when she reaches Sanditon, for Mr Fitzroy will shoulder every expense himself. Ah! Now here comes the interesting part. Mr Fitzroy, it seems, will not be there in person to welcome his guest for he has pressing business in London. So you see, she will have the house to herself. Mistress of all she surveys, at least for a day or two.'

'Oh, that is good news,' said Emma.

Their aunt perused the remainder of the letter. 'And there is more. What better news than this! There has been a reconciliation between Mr and Mrs Howard. A miracle indeed! Mrs Blake makes no mention of the instigator of the piece, though I expect she is responsible for it. No doubt she was as anxious as anyone to avoid any further visits by her brother's wife. I should not be in a hurry to see Mrs Howard, complete with trunk and valise standing on my doorstep. I can only wonder at the contrivances employed by Mrs Blake to bring her brother round. Perhaps Mr Howard has at last acquired a modicum of Christian charity.'

'Or perhaps Mrs Howard is truly penitent,' said Anne.

'Unlikely,' her aunt replied. 'But whatever the case, it is good news, for now I shall not be obliged to slight Mrs Blake.'

'I should not slight Mrs Blake for the world,' said Emma.

'It would have been impossible for me to invite her here had Mrs Howard taken up lodgings in Sanditon. Imagine what our neighbours would have said if Mrs Howard's circumstances had been made known to the world,' she replied. 'No. Let Mrs Howard return to her husband and stay there. I shall reply to Mrs Blake directly, and though the prospect of spending an hour in Sanditon grieves me greatly, I shall promise to call on her at the earliest opportunity.'

With the prospect of a trip to Sanditon, the two cousins set off with high hopes for a pleasant walk. They each had a particular view of what a walk by the shore ought to comprise, and those views were soon found to be widely divergent. Emma desired to go directly to the milliner's in the market square to try on bonnets, while Anne wanted only to explore Brinshore's fine coast. A compromise was settled upon, but the order in which both purposes were to be accomplished was not as easily agreed, as each cousin suspected that the other would likely spend an inordinate amount of time pursuing their preferred pastime to the detriment of the other.

Eventually, Anne gave way; the milliner's took precedence over the rock pools, and although Emma tried on almost every bonnet the shop had to offer, a purchase was completed within the hour. Every assistance was given, and every comfort extended by the owner on discovery that the Honourable Emma Osborne and her esteemed cousin, Miss Musgrave, had favoured them with a visit. Once news spread that Miss Osborne had purchased a bonnet, it was likely that every woman in Brinshore and beyond, young and old, would frequent the shop. There could be no better recommendation than the patronage of a viscount's daughter. Emma gave instructions for the bonnet to be delivered to her aunt's residence, and assurances were given repeatedly, that the said item would be delivered at once.

Emma, having little understanding of the world beyond the neighbourhood of Delham, of strangers and unfamiliar places, was surprised to discover the lengths to which the inhabitants of Brinshore would go to welcome the two newcomers. The market square appeared to be filled with friendly faces at every turn; the acknowledgement of strangers — a hat half-raised, a smile, a nod in their direction — left Emma with the impression that the neighbourhood of Brinshore was almost as genial as that of Delham. Anne was charmed by the cordiality of Brinshore society and required nothing more than to examine the rock pools and the longed for walk on the sand to declare Brinshore the most perfect place on earth.

Satisfied with her purchase, Emma agreed that they had spent enough time in the town square, and so, at Anne's request, they set out in the direction of the shore. A brisk walk found them minutes later on the seafront. Once the fine, powdery sand had been traversed, the wet firmness of the sand near the tide's edge made walking easier. Emma lagged behind, treading carefully to avoid getting sand in her shoes. Anne's delight was complete as she gazed in wonderment at the many rock pools that glistened with wet seaweed in the morning sunshine. She savoured the moment, taking in several deep breaths.

'Seaweed!' said she. 'More fragrant, more redolent, more prized than the finest perfume!'

'Have a care, Anne,' said Emma. 'You begin to sound like Aunt Harding.'

'Oh Emma, do come and look at this!' said she.

Emma's delicate shoes were hardly sufficient to withstand the slippery green algae that covered the rocks. She clung tightly to Anne's arm and peered at the pool of water in front of her.

'It is full of slime and brownness,' said Emma, singularly unimpressed.

'I have counted four different types of seaweed. Can you see the periwinkles and the tiny fishes? The crabs are a little harder to spot for they use camouflage,' said Anne. 'There's one! Watch it move! See!'

Anne looked at Emma more hopeful than expectant of an encouraging response. 'See,' she repeated.

Emma did not see. Nor did she see the point of standing on the edge of a slippery surface, some distance from the safety of the sand, gazing at seaweed and crabs while the tide edged ever closer towards them. For fifteen minutes or so Emma endeavoured to feign a modicum of interest in Anne's discoveries, but as her shoes started to let in moisture, she began to insist that it was time to go. Satisfied with the assurance that they would return to explore the rock pools the following day, Anne gave in to Emma's demands.

Despite the brevity of the expedition, Anne was pleased with her morning's enterprise. Bearing a handful of shells and four pieces of seaweed, she reached the edge of the shore where Emma was waiting, the hem of her frock covered in wet sand.

'Whatever will you do with them?' said Emma.

'I shall sketch them, of course,' replied Anne.

Emma sighed. 'I do not think Aunt Harding will take kindly to having seaweed in the house. It is quite the most unpleasant thing I have ever seen,' said Emma.

'Watercolour will serve my purpose best of all,' continued Anne, too preoccupied with her own plans to counter Emma's retort. 'If only it were within my power to capture the fragrant air and the refreshing sea breeze! Have you ever known such delight as this?'

Emma sighed again. 'I have never felt so hungry in my life.'

'Sea air. Isn't it wonderful?' said Anne, taking in another deep breath.

The days that followed were spent in similar fashion. When callers to the house were not expected, Anne and Emma passed their time in the town or by the shore. Anne was never happier; possessed of a pencil and paper, she was often to be found perched on her favourite rock sketching the bay. Emma had little interest in artistic pursuits beyond idly drawing circles in the sand with a stick. Occasionally, she would stop to admire the way the light fell at certain times of day on the cliffs, the swell of the tide, and the whiteness of the sea spray as the waves crashed against themselves.

When at last the day came to visit Mrs Blake, the clouds, almost by design, threatened rain. Not to be put off, Emma insisted, 'Dear Aunt Harding, what is there to fear from a few drops of rain? Your carriage is one of the sturdiest I have ever seen. Think of poor Mrs Blake, just arrived from Delham, alone in that friendless place which is Sanditon, with not a soul to call upon. Sanditon must surely be the worst place on earth for welcoming newcomers.'

'Never a truer word has been spoken,' said Aunt Harding. 'I expect Mrs Blake is even now full of regrets that she did not choose Brinshore over Sanditon.' Convincing as Emma's argument was, Mrs Harding was not persuaded of the wisdom of venturing out on such a day.

'The roads in Sanditon are the worst I have ever seen. Were they as stout and as serviceable as Brinshore's, I should have not the least reservation. But one cannot rely on the roads in Sanditon. I am told that the potholes have not been filled this last twelvemonth.'

'Perhaps we might postpone our outing to another day,' said Anne helpfully.

'Postpone it? There is no need for that,' replied Emma, putting on her bonnet. 'Consider, Aunt, the inferiority of Sanditon society, the drabness of its aspect, and the want of amusement of any kind. Would you wish Mrs Blake to spend a day, or even an hour, alone without a friend in such a place?'

Mrs Harding acknowledged that it was a bleak prospect indeed for poor Mrs Blake, and one she would neither wish on a friend, nor an adversary. At last the matter was settled and the carriage ordered.

'Umbrellas!' said she. 'We must not forget to take umbrellas. You can never rely on Sanditon for fine weather.'

By eleven o'clock the carriage was within a mile of its destination. A bend in the road to the right and a gentle decline towards the shore brought Sanditon into full view. The clouds lifted and the brilliancy of the sun on the sea made for a sparkling vista.

'Exquisite!' exclaimed Anne.

'We are fortunate indeed to see Sanditon on such a fine day as this. Enjoy it while you can, for it is likely to be the only fine day of which Sanditon may boast all season. Indeed, do not be fooled. The weather in Sanditon may change in an instant. I have it on good authority that it is not unusual to see sun, wind, thunderstorms, sleet and fog — and all in the same day — even within the same hour.'

The carriage came to a halt outside an elegant stucco fronted building, a short distance from what appeared to be a building site. Mrs Blake had kept watch at the window since breakfast, and on seeing the carriage approach came down to the front door to greet her most welcome of guests in person.

'Such dear friends — what a pleasure it is to see you!'

When every salutation and enquiry had been concluded, the party was ushered into a light and commodious drawing room and served with tea.

'It must be quite inconvenient to be situated so near to a building site,' said Mrs Harding. 'All that coming and going — labourers and masons with their chisels and hammers pounding and hammering all day long.'

'And yet,' said Mrs Blake, 'they are about their business at this very hour and there is not a sound to be heard. They are as quiet as the grave. I never notice them.'

Mrs Harding enquired further as to the purpose of the construction work.

'The foundations have been laid for a very grand house. A very grand house indeed. It is rumoured that the house is to be the summer residence of an elderly French comtesse who happily escaped the guillotine. By all accounts her husband was not so fortunate.'

'She should have visited Brinshore first,' Mrs Harding replied. 'It is sad to think that she has laid out a great deal of money for nothing.'

Mrs Blake continued, 'You may have observed that charming building opposite the hotel and assembly rooms. It is a rather fine circulating library, not long opened. Indeed, I have already placed my subscription. Mr Parker, a distinguished local personage, and one of Sanditon's greatest advocates, says it rivals any library or reading room that Bath or Buxton have to offer.'

Mrs Harding eyed Sanditon's newcomer with incredulity. Thought she, Mrs Blake installs herself at Waterloo Crescent while Mr Fitzroy is in town, she acts as though she owns the house, and even reckons herself intimately acquainted with the business of the neighbourhood! Emma had little trouble reading her aunt's thoughts from observing the expression on her countenance; happily for Emma, Mrs Harding was guarded in her reply, and her thoughts on the matter remained unspoken. 'Circulating libraries are full of worthless novels that fill young women's heads with nonsensical notions of love and romance,' said she. 'I should not wish to see the like in Brinshore.'

'Should you not, Aunt?' said Anne.

'Too much reading is a dangerous thing,' replied Mrs Harding.

'Sanditon's circulating library bears no comparison to Delham's paltry offering,' said Mrs Blake. 'It boasts a weekly raffle, and games of all kinds. There is a most comfortable room where coffee, tea and cocoa are served, not forgetting the famous Sanditon Bun. It is said to be superior in taste and with a slightly richer consistency than the Bath Bun. A reputable Guildford physician recently recommended it for his patients. He sends them all to Sanditon. Won't hear a word against the place.'

'I should like to visit the circulating library,' said Anne.

'I do not doubt it, my dear,' replied Mrs Blake, 'for I can say with the greatest certainty that it offers more than simply books and tea.'

'Oh, then I should like to go there too,' said Emma.

'Indeed, my dear Emma. You would love it above all things. One can purchase perfumes, hats, shawls, trinkets and all manners of articles there. And I had it from the postmistress who read it in the Sanditon Chronicle that a new Sanditon guide — an elegant little volume intended for visitors to the town — has this very week been published and can be purchased at the circulating library. Though,' she added, sensible of Mrs Harding's increasing discomposure and her strong views on the merits of Sanditon's rival, 'I am sure they do things in a far superior style in Brinshore.'

Mrs Harding was speechless, but her silence was of relatively short duration. 'Mrs Blake would, no doubt, have us believe that Sanditon has attractions enough to outshine Brighton, or will have, when the building work had been completed. It would be a great pity if the rush to build on every square inch that Sanditon has to offer spoils its current, moderately tolerable aspect.'

'What you say puts me in mind of a much-anticipated event. The circulating library is to extend its tea rooms and the opening is soon to take place. The new arrangements are said to be very elegant indeed,' said Mrs Blake.

It pained Mrs Harding to acknowledge that there was indeed much work to be done to enhance Brinshore's charms; and as the morning drew to a close it became equally clear to her that no one but she must have the direction of it. Mrs Harding sipped the rest of her tea in silence as she contemplated the improvements required to make Brinshore the envy of the south coast.

Mrs Blake had hardly begun to describe Sanditon's various attractions, and for some minutes continued forthwith recounting her arrival in Sandition, prompted by the enquiries of her two young listeners.

'What a warm welcome! Had I travelled the whole of England, I should not have found anywhere to compare to my beloved Delham, except Sanditon. Everyone is so very obliging. Since the moment I arrived, I can say, hand on heart, I have been made to feel quite at home, as though I had lived here all my life. And the house! Oh, the house! Where shall I begin? Modern, elegant, with every imaginable comfort! And what a prospect! Have you seen anything to compare to this?' said Mrs Blake, beckoning her young guests to the drawing room window. 'Every manner of thing that was needed to be done was done before my arrival. Mr Fitzroy saw to it all. What an obliging young man! I understand that he had the privilege of making your acquaintance, my dear Emma, quite accidentally. How does your frock fare?'

'Mr Fitzroy was only too ready to furnish me with an abundance of advice on the washing of it,' Emma replied. 'I did not like him at all. But I am now determined to like him a little better for your sake and for the sake of Captain Blake. With such a friend, he cannot be all bad. What news is there of your son, Mrs Blake?' said Emma.

'Dear Emma, how kind you are,' she replied. 'I wanted to keep the best news until last. I can hardly believe it myself. Charles will arrive in Sanditon within the week.'

Emma's delight at the news could not have been greater.

'I had, as you know, some reason to suspect that, given my sister-in-law's predicament, Mrs Howard might find her way to Waterloo Crescent. I raised the possibility with Mr Fitzroy, for these things must be made transparent. I should not wish to bring shame on his good name. Imagine! He was perfectly happy to secure lodgings on

Mrs Howard's behalf should the need arise. And he being intimately acquainted with all the facts. I find Mr Fitzroy slower than most to judge or condemn.' Mrs Blake continued, addressing herself primarily to Mrs Harding. 'But since I last wrote to you, my dear, there has been a development, one might say a decided improvement, in Mrs Howard's domestic arrangements. It is now quite certain: the longed-for reconciliation has taken place.'

'To the great relief of us all. Let us hope that the improvement is a lasting one,' said Mrs Harding. 'I suppose Mr Howard has taken her in, or, perhaps I should say, has been taken in by her.'

Mrs Blake was disinclined to pursue the subject of the Howards further. She returned instead to her current arrangements. 'I have rarely spent the summer by the sea these last twenty years. Mr Fitzroy has been so very obliging.'

'Does he have connections here?' asked Mrs Harding.

'The house belonged to his late brother, Captain Fitzroy, as you know. The good Captain, God rest his soul, was acquainted with Mr Parker. I believe you will hear much of him, for he is a most fervent advocate of the merits of Sanditon and a tireless promoter of its medicinal and health benefits. Mr Parker has made Sanditon his life's work.'

'A hopeless undertaking, I'm sure. Is Sanditon frequented by the entire Fitzroy family?'

'Not at all,' replied Mrs Blake. 'For our dear friend is somewhat at odds with his elder brother at present.'

'I must say, I am not in the least surprised,' said Emma.

'It grieves me to say it, but the present Lord Allersham, with his vast estate and influence, is a stranger to mercy. More than that I am not at liberty to say. Charles tells me that Mr Fitzroy's father was a good man, and our dear friend is very like him.'

'It is unfortunate then that he should be the third son,' replied Mrs Harding.

'Second,' replied Emma. 'For Captain Fitzroy is no more. A dead brother does not signify.'

'Emma!' said Anne, shocked that her cousin should speak so unfeelingly of the dead.

Mrs Blake worded her reply with care. 'Mr Fitzroy is at present estranged from his close family.'

'Ah,' said Emma. 'Then the present Lord Allersham must look out. For should he have cause to meet the grim reaper before his wife is safely delivered of an heir, his estranged brother will do him the greatest disservice by succeeding him.'

'The universe does not revolve around who is to inherit from whom,' said Anne.

'Certainly it does,' said Emma. 'You know little of the matter. It is all that is ever spoken of, I assure you.'

'Then it matters a great deal more than it should,' Anne replied.

'Lord Allersham is yet to marry. Mr Fitzroy has no wish to step into his brother's shoes, not even for a second,' said Mrs Blake. 'He is an extraordinary young man.'

'And likely a reckless one,' replied Emma.

'For a younger son, he is not without independent means,' said Mrs Blake. 'I should imagine any young woman would be fortunate to secure him.'

'He might do for Anne,' whispered Mrs Harding to Mrs Blake.

'What was the reason for Mr Fitzroy's estrangement from his family?' said Anne obligingly, curious to know more of the Fitzroys.

The hesitancy on Mrs Blake's part to supply further information about the young man had the effect of increasing rather than decreasing Emma's fascination. Her mind raced to all manner of conclusions, each of which seemed to her highly credible: a man trapped in a loveless engagement, a man whose offer of marriage had been rejected, or whose fiancée had cried off at the altar, a man secretly wedded to a bigamist, a murderer on the run. It seemed to Emma that any of the possible reasons that came to mind, or indeed any combination of them, were likely to be entirely of Mr Fitzroy's making.

In contrast, Anne's interest in the young man was almost immediately supplanted by the presence of a pamphlet lying on the table beside her. Detailing the times of high and low tides in Sanditon, it was a publication that she took up and began to peruse with the greatest of interest.

Mrs Blake had still to convey the most important information, information that Emma was most anxious to hear. 'Will Captain Blake go to Delham or travel directly to Sanditon from Portsmouth now that you are here?' she asked.

'I believe he will travel to Sanditon directly, my dear. But he intends to visit Delham one of these days,' replied Mrs Blake. 'Charles has business ashore that will keep him in Portsmouth a day or two. He would not say what it was. He is not ordinarily furtive, but in this matter he has shown that he can keep a secret as well as anyone. It is my belief that he means to make some kind of announcement.'

'I wonder what that could be,' said Emma apprehensively.

'It is quite plain to see,' said Mrs Harding. 'Captain Blake is to leave the Navy. He finds himself at liberty to marry, and he means to announce his engagement.'

'Impossible!' said Emma. 'Surely he would do no such thing without consulting Mrs Blake — or his friends — first.'

'A man may do as he pleases, as you well know, my dear. In such cases he requires only the consent of the young lady's father,' Mrs Harding replied.

'I cannot believe that Captain Blake would engage himself to any young woman without first speaking to Mrs Blake,' said Emma.

'Perhaps it is Captain Blake's intention to do so when he arrives in Sanditon,' said Anne. 'It is always better to convey important news in person.'

'I confess, the same thought had crossed my mind. Oh! But I cannot tell you how glad I shall be to see him. And,' she continued, 'very soon after his arrival, Mr Fitzroy insists that I make myself quite at home and give a dinner for my Brinshore friends. He has every hope of joining us if his business in town is concluded satisfactorily.'

The visit to Sanditon had been as pleasant as any visit might be, and when the hour to leave Waterloo Crescent arrived, even Mrs Harding was slow to vacate her seat. To Emma, however, the idea that Captain Blake might soon announce his engagement blighted an otherwise perfect morning. Despite her inability to proffer a more satisfactory explanation, Emma found it inconceivable that Charles Blake would attach himself to a stranger; the very thought of it would not only disrupt the intimacy between Osborne Cottage and the Castle, it would be felt just as keenly throughout the neighbourhood of Delham. The most troubling thought of all, however, was that Charles Blake should prefer anyone to her, for the possibility that he might, had not, until then, entered her head.

Her cousin's thoughts tended in a different direction. For Anne, a planned visit to the new circulating library provided the most pleasurable anticipation. Their aunt was less sanguine. Mrs Harding could not deny that Sanditon had attractions that Brinshore was completely without; she was, however, persuaded that Brinshore, when viewed from every angle, had by far the greater potential of the two. For the present, Brinshore's lack of a circulating library, a hotel, and a guide book for visitors and newcomers was uppermost in her thoughts and plans.

As a sailor anxious to leave a burning ship, Mrs Harding, little comforted by her visit, was eager to leave Sanditon. She had never been more restless to return to Brinshore, for her purpose was now firmly fixed: the task of transformation should not, indeed must not, suffer delay. Sanditon may soon boast a comtesse, thought she, but Brinshore would in due course be fit for an earl, or even a duke. For the time being, the daughter of a viscount was better than nothing; and, accordingly, Mrs Harding endeavoured to dismiss from her mind any regrets that her brother-in-law had not inherited a dukedom, and that her niece was only an honourable and not a lady.

CHAPTER EIGHT

In the days that followed, Mrs Harding set about plans for the institution of a new circulating library in Brinshore. The idea was at first opposed by the haberdasher, Peacock's, who kept a few shelves of books and raised a modest income from subscriptions. Assurances were given that existing merchants and their goods would take precedence over any new arrivals who wished to ply their trade within the premises of the new library.

'It is only right and proper that subscribers are encouraged to purchase goods from Brinshore's old established tradesmen. I am but a newcomer myself, and yet I understand the importance of loyalty in such matters,' said Mrs Harding.

The acquisition of books and journals received little mention in Mrs Harding's plans, an oversight that struck Anne as curious. To redress the situation, Anne set about devising a list of titles, books of popular and particular appeal, that no library should be without.

Emma had little interest in the circulating library beyond the possibility it served as a meeting place, or indeed a place of assignation. She employed her time less productively, dreaming of Captain Blake, making alterations to her best frock, and counting the hours to their first encounter after an interval of more than a year. Since their visit to Sanditon, Emma had conceived other reasons to explain the subject of Captain Blake's intended announcement. The opportunity, thought she, for a naval officer to make the acquaintance of a young woman at sea must be exceedingly limited. Surely he has some other scheme in mind: the purchase of a house or a carriage, a report from Somerset of Mr and Mrs Howard. The latter was entirely feasible; that Captain Blake should call upon his uncle at such a moment would show a family united once again. And, she mused, Portsmouth was no great distance from Mr Howard's Somerset residence.

The nearer the event, the more sanguine Emma became. To her amazement and delight, the hours to their first meeting were to pass sooner than expected, for three days after their visit to Sanditon, Mrs Blake returned the compliment and called on her Brinshore friends, accompanied by Charles, newly arrived from Portsmouth.

'My business in Portsmouth concluded early, and so I had no other thought but to make straight for Sanditon and surprise you all,' said he.

It was exactly as Emma had supposed, for his first thought was not of spending time in the company of some imaginary fiancée — unless, of course, the young woman's family resided in Portsmouth — but of renewing those important and intimate bonds with his family and friends. Emma sat on the edge of her chair in nervous anticipation.

'I could not have wished for anything better,' said Mrs Blake.

'We are all so very pleased to see you,' said Emma falteringly. She was conscious that her hair and dress were not as she should have wished them to be for her first encounter with Captain Blake.

'My dear Miss Osborne, I am so very —'

'Please do not stand on ceremony with me. I am Emma. I am just as I have always been,' said she.

'Indeed you are. Forgive me, my dear Emma,' said he.

'You are forgiven.' Nothing could be more pleasing to her ears. Nor could Emma's elation be suppressed. He had called her *my dear*. It carries such meaning when spoken in a tender tone, thought she. There is love in his every syllable.

'Miss Musgrave,' he continued, turning to Anne. 'And how might I address you? I do not wish to give offence. That is — Please overlook my clumsy speech.'

'You have always known me as Anne,' said she. 'What difference does a year make?'

'What difference indeed,' said Charles. His voice appeared to falter momentarily. 'Well,' said he, moving towards the window to look out. 'You must tell me all about Brinshore, for I am determined to be pleased with every aspect of it.'

'And so you shall,' replied Mrs Harding. 'You will find that no determination is required, for it is impossible not to be pleased with it.' She saw that such a fine advocate for the merits of Brinshore would be a most valuable ally if only were he to know the place better. 'Might I propose a walk? The weather looks promising and the sea calm. The beauty of Brinshore cannot be surveyed from this window alone, though it is indeed a fine prospect.'

Anne observed that the tide was out and suggested a walk along the sand.

'But there is more to see in the square,' said Emma. 'Let us walk into town.'

Unaware of the awkward predicament in which she had placed their visitor, Mrs Harding declared that Captain Blake, as their guest, should decide the matter. Charles listened to the young women's entreaties and protestations but hesitated to make his choice. Reluctant to give offence to either Emma or Anne, he heaped fulsome praise on each suggestion.

Mrs Blake knew too well her son's disposition; his nature was to please and be pleased by everything and everyone. She comprehended at once, as only a mother could, the fine line he must now tread, and said, 'My impression of Brinshore is that it has the proportions of a hamlet rather than a town. I am sure I am not beyond a walk both to the square and to the shore.'

Mrs Harding saw that Mrs Blake's delicate management of the situation averted an awkward moment, and in so doing she endeavoured to overcome her objection to Mrs Blake's description of Brinshore as a 'hamlet'.

There was naught to hinder their progress to the town: Charles walked on ahead with Emma and Anne, while Mrs Harding's slow pace afforded Mrs Blake ample opportunity to express her admiration for Brinshore's fine vista. On reaching the square, Mrs Harding was gratified to happen upon several of her neighbours, who might almost pass for quality, eager to obtain introductions to Mrs Blake and her son. The esteem and respect for Captain Blake as a naval captain, a man of honour who had served his king and country well, was pleasing to Emma. She had never been happier, prouder, nor more admiring of Charles Blake than she was at that moment.

Mrs Harding had made sure that his reputation had gone before him. No one among the notables of Brinshore was in any doubt that Captain Blake was a hero of the Trafalgar action, with a fortune in prize money that was understood to be something in the order of five and twenty thousand pounds. The presence of the Honourable Emma Osborne at the Captain's side did not go unobserved; indeed, Emma was convinced that the spectacle would so intrigue the neighbourhood that it would likely lead to the vastly pleasing speculation of a forthcoming alliance.

'Emma, my dear,' said her aunt, as they stood close to the spot where Mr Fitzroy had first become known to her, 'Is not this the very place you first came upon our friend?'

'It was,' said Emma in a disinterested tone. 'His careless hand at the reins of a horse and gig ruined my new frock.'

'Not ruined,' said Anne. 'There is not a speck of mud on it for it washed extremely well.'

'Even so,' said Emma, 'he should have taken more care.'

'And,' said Mrs Harding quickly, 'if you recall, my dear, he offered a most fulsome apology.'

'After some protracted deliberation,' said she.

'Poor Henry!' said Captain Blake. 'He is as fine a fellow as there is. He was mortified! He spoke of it to me with the greatest of regret.'

Emma laughed. 'Dear Captain Blake! I have never seen a man filled with so little regret. You should have heard him declare his belief that I had not seen a day's work in my life.'

'And have you?' asked her aunt.

'I have,' said she. 'Indeed I have. I sew and read. Sometimes. I visit the sick of the parish with Mama. Sometimes.'

'I doubt that was Mr Fitzroy's meaning,' her aunt replied.

'Your work is to be commended, Emma,' said Captain Blake. 'And I am sure that were you to know my friend better, and he you, your impression of him would bear improvement.'

'Captain Blake,' said Emma playfully, 'your determination to find goodness in everyone is a credit to your character, but I believe you are blind to your friend's flaws.'

'It is preferable by far to see the good in everyone and everything,' said Anne. 'If we look only for the bad, it contributes nothing to our peace of mind.'

'But we must surely exercise good judgement in all things,' said Emma, 'or we should easily be deceived by the corrupt and undeserving.'

'Mr Fitzroy strikes me as neither corrupt nor undeserving,' Anne replied.

'There is merit in both opinions,' said Captain Blake. 'Good judgement is as necessary as a liberal and tolerant heart.'

Emma smiled in triumph at her cousin, believing that her beloved Captain had settled the argument in her favour. Anne made no reply but was quietly and equally confident that Captain Blake had demonstrated his decided preference for her position.

After an agreeable promenade of the square, the party proceeded to the shore where the tide was inching its way closer inland, coating the firm sand with seaweed and foam. The dry, fine sand nearer the parade made the walk more arduous; in consequence of this, Mrs Blake and Mrs Harding decided to retreat to the comfort of the house, foregoing the pleasure of a stroll on the beach. Charles and Anne were content to continue along the sand, and though Emma would have gladly returned to Trafalgar Terrace, she was obliged to fall in with them for the sake of having Charles' company a little longer.

At the foot of the rugged cliff, Charles spotted a large stone, smooth and almost egg-shaped, which he picked up and beat against a rock until the object began to split in half. He prized it open to reveal at its centre an exquisite imprint of a fossil.

'Oh! How wonderful. Such a fine and flawless thing,' said Anne.

'A fossil?' sighed Emma, singularly unimpressed.

'An ammonite,' said Charles. 'A mollusc that once inhabited the ocean.'

'What a strange looking thing it is!' Emma continued.

'It is as though a sculptor has fashioned it from stone,' said Anne. 'May I have loan of it, Captain Blake? I should so like to sketch it if I may.'

'It is yours,' said he. 'I cannot lend something that is not mine to give. Please, take it and keep it.'

Anne was fascinated by the extraordinary object that Charles had placed in her hands. 'I shall treasure it above anything I have found on this shore.'

'Have you a collection?' said he with interest.

'Indeed I have,' she replied. 'I have a small collection of seashells which I have gathered from hereabouts,' Anne replied. 'Each day I find something of beauty to add to it. Though, I own, nothing I have found compares to this.'

'What a remarkable coincidence! I too have a collection of seashells. They have a curious charm, have they not?' said Charles.

Anne was in complete agreement. 'Oh yes! Indeed they have!'

'Fossils too,' continued Charles. 'I understand, though I have yet had no opportunity to discover for myself, that many fine examples have been found on the shore at Sanditon. I have even heard it said that Sanditon yields examples the quality of such rivals those found at Lyme.'

'Lyme Regis?' said Anne.

'The very place,' Charles replied. 'A thought occurs to me. We should organise a fossil-hunting expedition in Sanditon. What say you?'

'Oh, how I long for such an opportunity as this! Indeed we must!' Anne replied.

'Emma?' said Charles. 'Should you like to hunt for fossils too?'

Having had no part in the exchange between her two companions, Emma had begun to experience an unpleasant sensation, a feeling not unfamiliar to her of being overlooked, disregarded. Nonetheless, she endeavoured to quell her vexation even though her dissatisfaction with the course the conversation had caused her to wonder whether Anne had sought to monopolise their guest.

'What do you say, Emma?' said Charles, mindful that she appeared uncharacteristically silent and subdued.

Emma could do no other than agree to the plan, for resistance would appear churlish and unfriendly; and though she made every effort to maintain a tranquil countenance for the remainder of their walk, she was unable to banish completely the disappointment she felt at the outcome of her long-awaited encounter with Captain Blake.

As they approached Trafalgar Terrace, Charles insisted on searching for a fossil for Emma, one of similar dimensions to that which was now in Anne's possession. His quest, however, was in vain; and though he promised to secure as fine an example as Anne's specimen when next they met, it had little effect on Emma's lack of enthusiasm for their proposed expedition to Sanditon.

Emma succumbed to a feeling of discontent at Charles' apparent divided loyalty, but her displeasure towards Anne was much greater. Although she had expected to receive it, Charles had not given Emma his undivided attention. The scene of their first meeting that had been imprinted on her mind over weeks and months of waiting had borne no likeness to reality. The only similarity was the indisputable fact that Captain Blake was the most handsome and charming of men. No fault could be levelled at him: his conduct and address were entirely what they should have been. But in the scene that was fixed in her mind, the scene that raised and shaped her expectations, her cousin Anne was not present. Moreover, in all her musings, there was never a moment in which her hair was lank or required dressing, nor was she wearing her least becoming frock; fossils had no part in their tender discourse, and sea shells were as far from the substance of their intimate exchange as snow on a summer's day.

Mrs Blake and her son were persuaded to stay for luncheon at Trafalgar Terrace. Emma had little appetite; the misfortune of finding herself seated at the farthest end of the table, and often out of earshot of Captain Blake, was irksome and disappointing.

Pleasure at the prospect of meeting again very soon was pronounced by all; and though Emma had no inclination for Sanditon's fine fossils, she was disposed to hope for better things from her next encounter with Captain Blake. The fossil-hunting expedition, however, met with general approval; and though it entailed another trip to Sanditon so soon after the last, Mrs Harding raised no objection, for the addition of Captain Blake's society was as agreeable as any society could be.

Emma began to think that she should have been better pleased had Anne remained in Delham. She did not dislike Anne; indeed, her affection for her cousin had increased in some small measure during their short time together in Brinshore. Anne was not perverse, nor

71

did she demand her own way at every turn. This trait in her cousin's character rendered her a generally agreeable companion. And yet Emma had begun to wonder whether Anne's continued presence in Brinshore might pose something of an obstacle to her own happiness.

CHAPTER NINE

Mr Henry Fitzroy, handsome, sanguine, distinguished in gait, and with a natural, unpretentious air, had connections to an ancient family that had not served him well. The third son of a nobleman, Henry Fitzroy had erred in a manner wholly unforgiveable: he had declared his intention to marry a young woman, a Miss Barnes, who could boast neither birth nor fortune. The eldest of four sisters, her father had for some years served as chaplain in the private chapel at Allersham.

Miss Barnes' expectations on marriage were not likely to exceed forty pounds a year, a fact that was as immaterial to Mr Fitzroy as it was of the utmost consequence to his brother. Against the express wishes of Lord Allersham, who had demanded an immediate end to the matter on threat of estrangement, Henry had engaged himself to the young woman in the summer of fifteen. Separated from his family, and with no prospect of a reconciliation as long as his brother drew breath, Mr Fitzroy had made provision for his marriage to Miss Barnes to take place without delay.

Perceiving that the estrangement from her fiancé's family was, however, likely to endure, and that her father's interests were liable to be affected, Miss Barnes discovered that her interests and affections would be better served by attaching herself to an elderly baron of considerable means who suffered no such social impediment; happily for Miss Barnes, there was no one to object to the alliance, for the baron was without offspring.

Mr Fitzroy was not a man possessed of self-pity. He refused to dwell on Miss Barnes' duplicity, or his brother's want of clemency, and soon turned his attention to a matter more worthy: the fulfilment of a promise given to Captain Fitzroy on his death bed, the brother he had from childhood held in high regard, and whose loss he lamented greatly. The promise had been witnessed by Captain Blake who, without a moment's hesitation, had made a similar commitment to his dying friend. Indeed, as Captain Fitzroy breathed his last, his brother and his friend solemnly vowed to carry out his wishes, the money for which had been placed in trust until the appointed time. The remainder of Captain Fitzroy's fortune was bequeathed to Henry and with it the substantial new residence in Waterloo Crescent.

Mr Fitzroy's first impression of Emma Osborne was less than favourable. He perceived her to be little more than a young woman of high birth, used to the comforts of life, and accustomed to having her own way. On meeting Miss Osborne a second time, his curiosity was fostered by the change in her countenance at the mention of Captain Blake. Her demeanour betrayed an intriguing state of affairs that rendered her situation interesting. Miss Osborne, thought he, must be in love with his friend; and if that were the case, there could be no recipient more worthy of regard than Captain Blake, for he was indeed blessed with the best and most deserving disposition in the world. Consequently, Mr Fitzroy began to modify his opinion of Miss Osborne, for he could find no fault with her judgement: Charles Blake was an excellent fellow.

The opportunity to observe his friend in company with Miss Osborne came on the day of his return to Sanditon. Mr Fitzroy arrived at Waterloo Crescent, a house he was yet to call 'home', in time for dinner, to find Miss Osborne, together with her cousin and her aunt, about to sit down to a full table.

'It seems odd that we should be guests in your house, and you just arrived,' said Emma.

'This house is not my home. But to find it so pleasantly occupied makes it more so,' he replied.

The salutations complete, Mrs Blake continued, 'What a day of it we have had! Emma and Anne have been fossil-hunting along this beautiful stretch of shore. And what treasures they have found!'

'But for Captain Blake's assistance we should have returned empty-handed,' said Emma.

'No indeed!' said Charles. 'My dear Emma, you required no help from me. I was quite without employment all morning.'

'Anne has a better eye for finding fossils,' Emma conceded. 'I picked up a few sea shells, that is all.'

'Should you like to see our collection?' said Anne, directing her attention to Mr Fitzroy.

'I should indeed,' he replied with enthusiasm.

Anne showed him to the table in the corner of the room on which they had set out in rows sea shells and fossils of various shapes and sizes.

'A fine collection, Miss Musgrave' said he, picking up one of the exhibits and holding it up to the light. 'I particularly like this one.'

'That one is my favourite too!' replied Anne. 'See how complete, how perfectly it is formed.'

'Yes,' said Charles moving towards the table to join them. 'We were fortunate indeed to come upon that particular example.'

Mr Fitzroy observed how Miss Osborne's eyes followed Captain Blake as he moved towards the table where they were standing. After a few moments, Emma caught his gaze, and turned suddenly to look out of the window.

Despite her best efforts, she could find little to say about the collection of fossils and shells beyond their size, colour and who found them. Emma was neither curious to learn about the history of fossils, nor had she any desire to extend her knowledge (beyond its present level) to the life cycle of sea shells. A morning's expedition was quite enough. She had trudged through sand, searched the foot of cliffs, battled against a strong sea breeze, trodden in seaweed and feigned interest in the entire enterprise all for love of Captain Blake.

Therefore, when dinner was announced, Emma was relieved and delighted to find that she was able to secure Captain Blake's arm on entry into the dining room.

Mrs Harding looked about her to find fault with the arrangements but could not. 'One must neither skimp on candles nor use them to excess,' said Mrs Harding. 'I like to see what is on my plate, but too much light tends to illumine those aspects of one's countenance that benefit greatly from concealment.'

'Well said, Mrs Harding,' replied Mrs Blake. 'I too prefer the shadows for that very reason.'

'Indeed. Shadows are excellent for the concealment of a blush or a tear,' said Emma.

'I had in mind something else. I was thinking more of a line on the face,' said Mrs Harding.

'Or a grey hair out of place,' laughed Mrs Blake.

'Or a look?' said Anne.

'Most especially a look,' replied Mr Fitzroy, glancing at Emma.

The conversation, directed chiefly by Emma, took a turn towards the nature of truth and concealment between men and women, a pleasing respite from the marine life of Sanditon.

'Well,' Emma replied, 'I am not an admirer of concealment in any guise. Why should not all our dealings be honest and in the open?'

'That is not often possible,' replied Mr Fitzroy. 'Truth, whether it be expressed within one's family, or indeed among one's friends and acquaintances, has a tendency to cause more pain than pleasure.'

'I cannot agree,' Emma replied. 'It is falsehood that causes the greatest pain.'

All eyes were turned towards Emma. She continued, 'I speak of truth between men and women. A man may say what he chooses and choose when to say it. A woman has no such liberty.'

Mr Fitzroy put down his soup spoon. 'Surely a woman has just as much right to state her opinions as any man. Indeed, on first meeting you, Miss Osborne, I saw that you had no compunction whatsoever in doing so yourself.'

'You mistake my meaning, sir,' she replied. 'My words at that moment were entirely justified. I only marvel at my restraint and forbearance.'

Mr Fitzroy followed Emma's eyes as they rested on Charles Blake's face. She reflected, 'A woman is taught to conduct herself with indifference, never to make a parade of her true feelings.'

'Is it not also true of men? Do you believe that all men have at their disposal the power to steer their own course, like the captain of a ship?' Mr Fitzroy replied, with a nod towards his sea-faring friend.

'Men have it all their own way. They are captains both at sea and on dry land,' Emma replied.

'But a ship in turbulent seas is not guaranteed to reach its destination,' Mr Fitzroy maintained. 'It may be obliged to deviate from its course or retreat to a haven for shelter.'

'Forgive me,' said Emma, roused by the defect in Mr Fitzroy's argument, and directing her remarks solely to him. 'I had always supposed that the very purpose of a ship was to sail on rough seas, not to dwell within the safety of a harbour.'

'Bravo, Emma!' said Captain Blake. 'If it were in my power, I should appoint you first lieutenant on any ship of mine.'

'I do not think first lieutenant would do at all,' said Mr Fitzroy.

'No?' said Emma. 'And what *do* you think, Mr Fitzroy?'

'In your case, Miss Osborne, nothing less than Admiral of the Fleet would suffice,' said he.

As much as Emma fought to keep her countenance, she could not suppress a smile. The entire party was much amused by the course of the conversation and joined in the laughter; and as the ladies left the gentleman to their port, there was a general feeling of ease, good humour and friendliness in Waterloo Crescent.

Mr Fitzroy was somewhat confounded by his friend's reaction to Miss Osborne's discourse. For his part, he wholly comprehended its meaning and intent. There was no doubt in his mind that her aim had been to convey to the object of her affection her wish to speak openly of her love; but as a woman, bound by the constraints of convention, she was prevented from so doing. Indeed, her speech was almost a declaration; and yet Captain Blake appeared wholly to misapprehend her.

'I confess, Miss Osborne surprised me,' said Mr Fitzroy, once the ladies had departed.

Captain Blake agreed. 'Dear Emma is plain-spoken. I am sorry if her words offend you, but there is the greatest goodness in her heart.'

'I am not in the least offended. Intrigued, even surprised, but not offended,' he replied.

'I have known Miss Osborne my whole life. Had I been blessed with a sister, she should not have been dearer to me than Emma,' Charles continued.

'A sister?'

'The dearest of sisters.'

'A sister nevertheless,' replied Mr Fitzroy, puzzled by the deficiency in his friend's comprehension of the matter.

'There was a time, when Emma was three or thereabouts, she screamed and sobbed and threw down her doll — the finest china doll of its kind — I forget why. It shattered into tiny pieces, and was beyond repair, and Emma was sent forthwith to the nursery. The doll was not replaced except by one made of cloth. Even I had a hand in making it! Curiously, her mother once told me that Emma would not be parted from it. A doll made with old rags. She was never known to have thrown the doll on the floor in a fit of temper.' Charles smiled as another recollection occurred to him. 'I first met her mother at a ball in Delham in the year ninety-five. I was but twelve years old.

Lady Osborne, Miss Emma Watson as she was then, did me a great service. I have never forgotten it.'

'Indeed?'

'Do you wish to know what it was?' said he.

'It would be futile to guess,' said Mr Fitzroy, intrigued by Captain Blake's musings.

'She danced with me,' replied Charles.

CHAPTER TEN

Owing to a severe change in the weather, it was two days before Emma had the pleasure of the Blakes' society once again. A storm that had engulfed the south coast had caused several carriages to overturn on the road between Brinshore and Brighton. Accounts of injuries abounded, and much was made of them within the environs of Sanditon where several of the incidents occurred. When the matter was reported in the newspaper, however, the injuries recorded amounted to a sprain to the wrist, a blow to the head and four instances of minor cuts and bruises.

'Sanditon is as fine a place as one could wish for, but there is no surgeon at hand on whom to call at such a moment,' said Mrs Blake.

Mrs Harding was pleasantly surprised to discover that Sanditon was not the height of perfection after all. Delighted to find that Mrs Blake had uncovered a serious defect in Brinshore's rival, Mrs Harding set about exploiting it.

'A watering place worthy of the name should, at the very least, possess a surgeon, though I should settle for nothing less than a physician,' said Mrs Harding.

Mrs Blake replied, 'I wonder Mr Parker does not see to it with the greatest urgency, for he attends to all the important matters of the town.'

'Brinshore has a very fine physician,' said Mrs Harding. 'I understand Mr Fowle's reputation is second only to that of his uncle, the late Honourable Joseph Fowle. His uncle, Mrs Blake, was almost elected a fellow of the Royal Society, you know.'

'What better recommendation than this! The infirm are sure to be safe in Mr Fowle's hands,' said Mrs Blake. 'I wonder, might your Mr Fowle be persuaded to attend the sick of Sanditon?'

Astounded by Mrs Blake's presumption — that Mr Fowle might be prevailed upon to minister to Sanditon's ailing cohorts — Mrs Harding made her feelings perfectly plain. 'That would never do,' said she, 'never do at all! Mr Fowle is Brinshore's man. And he is constantly in demand. He would have neither the time nor the inclination to attend the infirm and afflicted of Sanditon.'

'I am sorry to hear it. Truly, I am. Brinshore must be a very sickly place indeed,' said Mrs Blake in an attempt to pacify her host.

'The sick flock to Brinshore, for in Brinshore alone they are assured of a cure. The pure air and the efficacious ministrations of Mr Fowle never fail.' Mrs Harding smiled complacently. She could not quite believe her good fortune: Sanditon had no physician!

'I am afraid it is so,' said Emma, hearing something of the conversation on entering the room. 'Brinshore is populated by invalids and, worst of all, those who imagine themselves ill.'

'I do not think people pretend to be ill,' said Anne, following Emma into the room.

'Oh yes they do. Grandpapa Watson was forever fancying himself ill,' Emma replied.

'Indeed! Your grandfather fancied himself ill until the day he died!' said Mrs Harding.

Emma caught the trace of a smile on the face of Captain Blake who was seated at the opposite end of the room quietly perusing Anne's fossil sketches. The smile was quickly brought into check as he moved towards the fireplace. In his hand was a sketch of the fossil he had found among the rocks at Brinshore.

'Forgive me,' said he to Anne. 'I should have sought your permission. Your aunt was most insistent. I —'

'I should be happy to hear your opinion, as long as it is not too severe,' Anne replied.

Captain Blake took the sketch to the window to examine it in the daylight. 'Light, shade, every detail captured to perfection,' said he. 'There could be no truer likeness. You have caught its properties most faithfully.'

'Praise indeed,' said Emma.

Pleased with Captain Blake's estimation of her artistic ability, Anne replied with unthinking enthusiasm, 'Then you must have it. I should be so very happy if you would accept it, as a gift.'

Surprised and confused by the offering, Captain Blake said that nothing would give him greater pleasure; and he gave every assurance that the drawing would remain safe in his hands. 'As soon as an opportunity presents itself, I shall go to Brighton to have the picture framed.'

'There is a man in Brinshore who charges half the price of any shop in Brighton,' said Mrs Harding, 'and only a fraction of Bond Street prices. His work is before you.' Mrs Harding pointed to a small landscape painting on the wall beside the fireplace.

No fault could be found with the picture frame, and there was general agreement that a frame of similar size and quality would serve Anne's sketch well.

'It is as charming a frame as any I have purchased,' said Mrs Blake. 'And, my dear Charles, a day spent in Brighton is a day away from your family and friends.'

Charles saw the wisdom of the argument and yielded immediately. 'Then it is settled,' said he. 'Might I therefore propose a walk to the square? There is no better time than the present to discharge the commission. Emma,' said he, 'what say you?'

Emma consented to Captain Blake's proposal, though her eagerness to walk to the square was greatly diminished by the purpose of the enterprise.

Anne, sensitive to her cousin's feelings, began to regret her gift to Captain Blake and wished she had held her tongue. She reproached herself for her lack of foresight; for the gift, though artless in its intent, was given without thought to the consequences. Retraction was impossible; and yet Anne had no wish to create ill feeling between herself and her cousin, nor did she wish to come between Emma and her affection for Captain Blake.

'Emma,' said she, 'I should be so very grateful to you if you would be good enough to choose the frame. You have an excellent eye for these things which I lack completely.'

Captain Blake added his support. 'My dear Emma, your choice will carry the day, for there could be no better view than yours.'

The offer of a walk was extended to Mrs Blake and Mrs Harding. Both, however, were comfortably settled and neither were inclined to move far from that comfort to face the bracing easterly sea breeze; consequently, both declined the invitation in favour of an additional dish of tea.

'And when you return from your outing,' said Mrs Harding, 'I have a treat for you. I have, with barely an ounce of assistance from my cook, devised a recipe for a new bun. Cook is executing it even as we speak. It is a bun that possesses certain attributes of the Bath Bun but is infinitely more wholesome than the Sanditon Bun. It is the combination of spices, which is a great secret, that makes my recipe superior to all others. It is, or will be, known as the Brinshore Bun.'

'What can I say?' said Captain Blake with delight. 'My dear Mrs Harding, I can hardly wait to sample its delights!'

As the three set out for their walk, Captain Blake remarked on the charms of Brinshore and how his fondness for the place was sure to increase the more he saw of it. Anne chatted uneasily about barnacles and rock pools, glancing awkwardly at her cousin from time to time. Emma walked on in silence, striving to effect an air of general cordiality despite her disappointment and growing discontent with her cousin.

'Mr Fitzroy has gone to London but has promised to return by the end of the week,' said Charles.

'Again? What business has he in town that takes him away from Sanditon with such regularity?' said Emma. 'Or does he flit here and there on a whim?'

'His brother's steward has summoned him,' said Captain Blake. 'Beyond that I have no information.'

'I suppose it is in his brother's power to do so, but I should not like to be summoned by my brother's nanny, or indeed anyone else for that matter,' said Emma.

'Perhaps his brother seeks a reconciliation and is willing to overlook his past indiscretion,' said Anne.

'I expect the price of reconciliation will be to find himself engaged to some heiress of his brother's choosing,' said Emma. 'It is usually how these things are managed.'

'I am sure his brother cannot be as bad as that,' said Anne.

'And I am sure he can if he so wishes,' said Emma. She turned to Captain Blake and said, 'What choice has your friend? If he concedes to his brother demands, he will cease to be a stranger to society. If he refuses, and continues in his wilful estrangement, he can never hope to marry well or be admitted to the first circles.'

Charles acknowledged Emma's point, but said, 'It is not in his character to act in a manner wholly to secure his own comfort.'

'I admire Mr Fitzroy's steadfastness. When everything is against him, he refuses to falter,' said Anne.

'It is folly to place steadfastness above every other virtue. Had I been born penniless, I should be foolish not to marry to secure my own advantage,' said Emma.

'Rich or poor, nothing but love would induce me to marry,' said Anne.

Before either Captain Blake or Emma had the opportunity to reply, they found themselves in front of a window displaying a framed painting of a familiar landscape. Emma led the way into a small gallery of watercolours and oils, snuff and trinket boxes, all decorated with scenes of Brinshore. The proprietor explained that such mementoes were the height of fashion in Brighton. 'Such an appealing souvenir,' said he, placing before them a small enamelled box for their perusal. 'It captures the true beauty of Brinshore, does it not? A visitor to Brinshore would feel incomplete without just such a keepsake. Last summer a person of the highest rank — discretion prevents me from naming the gentleman — purchased one such as this.'

Fascinated by the objects on display, Anne chose to purchase a small rosewood box. The lid, carved with shells and fishes, rendered the box perfect. 'Is it not a handsome box? Had I searched the whole of England, I should not have found such an example as this. It shall hold my collection of shells and fossils.'

'Your mama has one just like it,' said Emma.

'Mama's is plainer by far,' replied Anne. 'This one is so very finely carved. It is superior in every way to Mama's box.'

Charles showered fulsome praise on the box, but Emma could not help thinking that a box of such modest proportions would be of little use in a week or two as Anne's shell collection expanded by the day. Indeed, by the time the season was over, thought she, the purchase of a large trunk would better serve her cousin's purpose.

The purchase accomplished, Charles set about the business of the picture frame. Emma had little interest in the matter; but having agreed with reluctance to express a view on the choice of frame, she examined the examples placed before her. After perusing the options, she settled on a simple frame, a decision that took less than a minute, but which received universal approval. The sketch was placed with the proprietor, and assurances were given that, complete in its frame, the item would be delivered without delay the following day.

'Waterloo Crescent, you say? Surely you do not mean *Sanditon*?' said the proprietor, flattered by the notion that his reach and reputation extended beyond the confines of Brinshore.

The aroma of butter and sweet-smelling spices met the party on their return as soon as they were admitted into the hall, and all three professed an appetite for sampling the Brinshore Bun; but on entering the drawing room they found Mrs Harding in a state of heightened agitation. In her hand was a letter.

'What is it, Aunt?' said Emma. 'What news have you received?'

'Oh my dear, do sit down. You must all be seated. I do not wish to alarm you, my dear Emma, but you must prepare yourself.'

Captain Blake moved forward and led Emma to an empty chair. 'Courage,' said he, as he knelt by her side and held her hand in his.

'I have just received a letter from your mama,' said Mrs Harding.

'Has something happened to Grandmamma?' Emma asked urgently.

'Your grandmamma is well. Quite well. And Aunt Turner as you well know is never ill. It is little Frank. He has taken a tumble and has sustained a rather serious injury to the head.'

'He tripped on the staircase. It seems his nanny reached out to catch him but was too late,' added Mrs Blake. Then, looking at Captain Blake, she added, 'I was always in fear of the stairs at Osborne Castle. You were forever climbing them as a boy. I imagined that you, my dear Charles, would come to some harm on those very stairs one day.'

Captain Blake smiled indulgently at his mother but made no reply.

'What is required of me? What must I do?' said Emma. 'Am I to return to Delham? Am I to leave Brinshore? What does Mama say?'

'Your brother's condition is critical,' her aunt replied. 'Your mama and your papa need you.'

Little deliberation was required as every minute lost in debate meant further delay. The decision was made: Emma must return to Osborne Castle immediately. In an instant Captain Blake offered himself as Emma's protector for the journey and would brook no opposition to the plan. They would reach the Castle by nightfall if they set out at once. Without further discussion Mrs Harding ordered the coach to be made ready and sent instructions to the kitchen to prepare a basket of Brinshore Buns for the journey.

Emma had no time to pack her belongings but for a few essentials; her aunt promised to return the remainder of them should she receive further word from Osborne Castle in a day or two. Anne, however, proposed to stay in Brinshore with her aunt until more was known.

As Captain Blake handed Emma into the carriage, Mrs Harding came forward and whispered to her niece. 'Emma, promise me you will return to Brinshore the instant little Frank is out of danger.'

'But if he should —'

'My dear, little Frank is in the best hands. He is as strong and as determined as any little boy could be.'

Emma waved goodbye to her aunt and to Brinshore. Her consolation was Captain Blake's presence beside her. Quick to comfort, he did everything in his power to allay her fears. For her part, she could not have been better cared for; and the certainty of his undivided attention for several hours to come proffered the most pleasant consequence of the entire sorry business.

'Courage, my dear Emma,' said he, as he placed her hand in his.

Despite the anxiety she felt over her brother's fate, Emma delighted in the thought that she could not have secured a more advantageous situation in which to kindle feelings of intimacy and love in the heart of the object of her affection.

The first stage of the journey proceeded without impediment. They stopped only to change horses; neither professed any appetite to eat. A dish of tea and a Brinshore Bun was all that was needed to sustain them. As Surrey came into view in the half light, Emma attempted to gather her thoughts and apply them to the cheerless situation that was shortly to confront her; courage was needed at such a moment. She must prepare herself for the worst; and for the sake of her parents, she must not falter.

Mindful of her silence, and the fatigue of the journey, Captain Blake placed an extra blanket over his charge and said, 'Rest, my dear friend.'

Her eyes became heavy and she surrendered to sleep. Emma heard nothing of the rain that beat down on the roof as the carriage entered Delham; and when they neared the gates of Osborne Park, Captain Blake was obliged to shake her gently from her slumber.

'Courage,' said he.

The hall and drawing room were lit bright, and a dim light issued from the nursery. Within minutes Emma was by her brother's bedside where her mother and father had been stationed for much of the evening. Captain Blake, almost a member of the family, was admitted to the hushed, dimmed sick room to sit with them. Mr Granby's nephew was in attendance and had remained at the boy's side for the best part of the day; there he stood expressionless and silent but for a few directions given in a whisper to the child's nanny as she gently applied a cold compress.

'Poor dear child,' whispered Lady Osborne. 'Frank is concussed. The degree of severity is not yet known. There is a danger of apoplexy. And we are quite helpless as you see. We can do nothing but watch and wait.'

Lord Osborne comforted his wife. 'My dear, a child's head is more easily mended than any other. Come now, take some rest. Frank is in good hands. If any change should occur, however slight, you will be told of it immediately.'

Lady Osborne found little comfort in her husband's words but said nothing to the contrary for fear of causing any unnecessary disturbance in the sick room.

'Papa is right. You look weary, Mama. I shall sit with my brother a while. Indeed, I should prefer it,' said Emma, 'and I shall not be persuaded otherwise. Go Mama, Papa, and take Captain Blake with you. I shall rest here tonight.'

The night passed with little change in Frank's condition. Emma, having kept watch by Frank's bedside, mounted no resistance when, the following morning, her father bade her go to her room and rest. After breakfast, Lady Osborne was persuaded to take some air before returning to the nursery, and as the weather was fine, Captain Blake offered to accompany her.

They walked towards the lake, the scene of many cherished memories.

'I confess,' said Charles, 'I am beset by indecision. I neither wish to be a burden at such a moment, nor do I wish to depart too soon. Should I, by my presence, be of service to you —'

'Dear Charles,' said Lady Osborne, 'you have already performed the greatest service of all. I had hoped you would bring Emma home to us. Indeed, knowing you as I do, I felt certain that you would.'

Captain Blake smiled but made no reply, and they walked on in silence until they reached the lake.

'I know that you cannot stay long. And I know that you have obligations in Sanditon to your mother and to your friend,' said Lady Osborne. 'Please do not neglect them on any account. I ask only that you stay until Mr and Mrs Musgrave arrive. We expect them by noon. They may wish to send a message or a note to Anne.'

'Of course. Let me be of use in whatever way I can,' said he.

'Dear Charles, you have my word, and thank you,' said Lady Osborne. 'And now I must see my son, or I do not know what I shall do.'

It was settled that Captain Blake would return to Sanditon after luncheon; but Emma, disheartened by the news of his imminent departure, protested that the Castle was in greater need of Captain Blake than were Mrs Blake and Mr Fitzroy at that moment. 'Let him stay in London. What need is there for Mr Fitzroy to return to Sanditon so soon? Better still, let Mrs Blake stay with Aunt Harding in Brinshore until Captain Blake returns,' said she.

As the morning progressed, the condition of little Frank appeared to undergo a slight change for the better. His breathing stabilized, and his eyelids flickered momentarily. There was, however, general agreement that it was still too soon to be certain that the boy was out of danger.

The arrival of Mr and Mrs Musgrave proffered some distraction for Lady Osborne; the matter of the disposal of Mr Musgrave's curricle and the purchase of a new landau for the Dower House was talked of with some amusement by Mrs Musgrave and seemed to lighten the general mood. Similarly, Captain Blake and Emma endeavoured to entertain the party with stories of rivalry and discord among the inhabitants of Sanditon and Brinshore. The subject that was uppermost in their minds, however, the condition of little Frank, was circumvented entirely until the arrival of the next dispatch. Each report that issued from the nursery was eagerly scrutinized. The slightest hope for optimism was magnified ten times; even the notification that 'no change' had occurred in little Frank's condition was deemed to be confirmation of improvement.

85

As the time for Captain Blake's departure drew near, Mrs Musgrave scribbled a hasty note to her daughter and placed it in his hand; in return, assurances were given that Miss Musgrave would receive the note at the earliest possible opportunity. Emma, aggrieved at Captain Blake's untimely departure, gave every assurance that she would return to Brinshore the minute Frank was out of danger.

'Carry my good wishes to all our friends,' said Emma.

Captain Blake placed her hands in his. 'Whatever the future may hold, you have great courage. Look after your mama.'

'You have my word.' Emma watched as the carriage pulled away and disappeared from view. I cannot bear that he should be in Sanditon and I should be here, thought she. If only Frank would rally. He must rally.

On securing an assurance from Mr and Mrs Musgrave that they would delay their departure and stay for dinner, Lady Osborne went up to the nursery to visit her son after luncheon. Mrs Musgrave saw that her sister wished to be alone with her son and proposed a visit to the Dower House. 'Will you walk with me, Emma?'

'Is it advisable, Aunt, with your weak ankle?' Emma replied.

'Oh that,' said Mrs Musgrave. 'I find it is much improved. And anyway, your papa and uncle will likely spend the entire afternoon discussing carriages and horses and the purchase of landaus and I do not know what. All I know is that I do not wish to hear to it. A conveyance is a conveyance. Whether a gig, curricle, barouche or hay cart, each has seats, wheels and is pulled by horses. What else is there to be said? I am quite certain that I have nothing to say on the subject, except that I do not want any curricle or gig in our stable yard ever again, and I most certainly do not want your uncle to drive one. Your mama is gone up to sit with your brother and I do not wish to intrude on her time with him —not while he is in so delicate a state. So, will you accompany me?'

Emma assented to her aunt's request, though a little half-heartedly, and the two set out for the Dower House. Their unexpected visit proved to be a welcome diversion for the Dowager and Mrs Turner. The latter's removal to the Dower House had proceeded with ease, and with the promised arrival of the new landau, there was every reason for the two women to remain on the most affable of terms. The companionship between them occasionally suffered when a difference of opinion arose, but the temperament of the two was not dissimilar and disputes were soon put aside and forgotten about altogether. On this occasion, the matter at hand was Mr Edwards' unceasing advances towards Mrs Turner.

'He will not leave off! He will not! Despite receiving the strongest of hints that his attentions are unwelcome, he persists in this foolishness. Were it not for his skill as a card player, I should not receive him at all,' said the Dowager. 'Mrs Turner is too tolerant by half. Why is it that women gain greater command of their senses as they grow old and men lose theirs?'

'Surely, Grandmamma, you do not mean all men,' said Emma.

'Oh yes I do. What better example is there than your papa and your uncle. Forgive me for saying so Mrs Musgrave, but despite the considerable benefit to myself and Mrs Turner in this matter, my son and your husband have behaved like a pair of coxcombs. Wager indeed!' said the Dowager.

'Come Emma,' said Mrs Turner, who had a strong partiality for coxcombs and was desirous of knowing whether the seaside still yielded its fair share of them, 'do tell us all about the handsome young men in Brinshore.'

'Captain Blake is the only one,' Emma replied. 'And even though we have not yet had the pleasure of attending a ball, I know with absolute certainty that Brinshore is as deficient in handsome young men as Delham is in yielding up fossils.'

The Dowager and Mrs Turner laughed heartily at the analogy.

'Fossils?' said the Dowager. 'Why Delham is awash with them!'

'They can be found each Sunday gathered together in the parish church attending divine service!' said Mrs Turner.

Emma and Mrs Musgrave exchanged glances of incredulity as their hosts continued in similar vein. The ripostes endured for some time until they were brought to an abrupt end by the Dowager.

'Oh! And Mr Edwards must be Delham's arch fossil-hunter!' said she.

Mrs Turner was not amused, and immediately returned to the matter at hand. 'Almost three weeks in Brinshore without a ball, you say? Whatever is Mrs Harding thinking of? My dear, how do you spend your time?'

'We visit Mrs Blake in Sanditon,' Emma replied. 'Sanditon has many attractions.'

'It would appear so,' said Mrs Musgrave, who had received a full account from Anne. 'Am I correct in assuming that another handsome young man, a friend of Captain Blake, is also known to you?'

'I expect you mean Mr Fitzroy. He is handsome enough, I suppose, but his behaviour is quite the reverse. He splashed mud over my new dress when he drove his gig through Brinshore.'

'Did he indeed?' said Mrs Musgrave. 'There, you see. Whether a gig or curricle, young men or, I may say, men in general, are not to be trusted with such dangerous conveyances.'

'Mr Edwards is the worst offender of all,' said the Dowager. 'I should not like to ride an inch in any equipage handled by that gentleman. I recall, many years ago, his carriage overturned on the London road.'

'And Mr Howard brought him back to Delham,' said Mrs Musgrave. 'Who can forget Mrs Edwards' displeasure. God rest her soul.'

'You, my dear Elizabeth,' said Mrs Turner, 'were always reckoned an excellent hand at the reins.'

'I expect I had much practice, for I used to drive Papa's old chair,' said she. 'Penelope has taken it. A more serviceable chair, or a safer one, I cannot imagine.'

The Dowager had for some moments been inattentive to the course of the conversation. The direction of her own thoughts now became known. 'But what of the intriguing Mr Fitzroy?'

'Did you know that he is Lord Allersham's brother!' said Mrs Musgrave, delighted to be for once the source of information unknown to the Dowager. 'Anne spoke of him in her letter.'

'That being the case, I believe I was acquainted with his grandfather in the old days. Was it he who married that rather pious young woman. What was her name?'

'Miss Bradshaw,' said Mrs Turner.

'Exactly so,' replied the Dowager. 'And what a to do there was about that! His mother, God rest her soul, spoke not two words together to Miss Bradshaw, not even after they were married. As to fortune, I believe she had two or three thousand pounds or thereabouts. An additional ten might have made her daughter-in-law a little more agreeable.'

'My dear,' said Mrs Turner, 'need I remind you that my own niece was not to your liking at first. It was a matter that exercised you greatly at the time. And were we to venture further into the past, I recall a young woman before her of modest fortune who was lucky indeed to secure the affections of the late Lord Osborne.'

'That is quite a different matter,' said the Dowager.

'Anne speaks well of Mr Fitzroy. He is a principled young man, I believe,' said Mrs Musgrave.

'I should think that you, my dear Mrs Musgrave, would be happy at the thought of that young man paying his addresses to Anne,' said the Dowager. 'He might have done for Emma had he succeeded his father. Emma, my dear, be on your guard where that young man is concerned.'

'Grandmamma,' Emma replied, 'I can say without reservation that Mr Fitzroy is nothing to me. Indeed, I cannot think of anyone for whom I feel a greater degree of indifference.'

Mrs Turner held her tongue but mused on the notion that the flames of love are most often kindled in a young woman the moment she is urged to spurn the advances of a young man, for there is nothing more gratifying to the young than the exercise of perversity.

As Emma and Mrs Musgrave took their leave, assurances were given that a message would be sent directly to the Dower House should any change become apparent in Frank's condition.

News of Frank was not long in coming, for on the path leading to Osborne Castle, they were met by Mr Musgrave who had set out a few minutes earlier to carry the important information to the Dower House in person: Frank was out of danger. The child had stirred an hour ago, had uttered the word 'milk', and had been given a teaspoon of the same. Little more was said beyond the general sense of relief felt by all. Anxious to see her sister to procure a more detailed account of her nephew's progress than the one provided, Mrs Musgrave exchanged but few words with her husband beyond an entreaty to make his visit a brief one in case his presence was needed elsewhere.

On hearing the news, Emma experienced a host of emotions: her relief that Frank was out of danger was sincere, but the hour of his recovery was vexing indeed. Had he stirred but three hours earlier, she might have returned to Brinshore; and although she might now plan her departure from Osborne Castle, the journey would have to be made without Captain Blake as her companion.

As they entered the Castle, Emma felt a change in the air: the shadow that had fallen on the household had lifted, spirits were lighter, and there was a mood of celebration.

'My dear sister,' said Lady Osborne on greeting Mrs Musgrave, 'is this not the very best news of all? I had hardly dared to hope.'

The pressure of the last twenty-four hours had taken its toll on Lady Osborne; relieved of the burden of apprehension and suspense, she broke down. Whilst uncertainty reigned, Lady Osborne had endeavoured to hide her despair; for despite every word of assurance, she had prepared herself for the worst, indeed she had expected it. Comforted by her sister, Lady Osborne began to describe, minute by minute, every particular of Frank's recovery.

Emma left the room unnoticed; she saw that her presence was not required, nor would it be missed. Quietly, she went up to the nursery and peeped into the room unobserved. Frank was sitting up in bed fussed over by his nanny and nursery maid. By the window stood her father in conversation with Mr Granby's nephew, keen to comprehend the nature of the injury and the treatment required henceforth. All that could be done for Frank would be done. Whatever Frank needed would be provided. Not a minute would go by without the accomplishment of some action to aid his comfort or some word of encouragement to speed his recovery.

Unable to share fully in the general air of happiness and relief, Emma retreated to her bedchamber and lay on the bed. Thought she, I might as well be an animal in a glass case, like the stuffed fox in the long gallery, ignored and unnoticed, save as an object of curiosity when all other conversation is expended.

Exhausted by the events of the day, Emma drifted into a deep sleep and was roused sometime later — she knew not what time it was — by a knock at the door. The room was still light, but the entrance of her mother in evening dress, suggested the hour was late.

'Emma, my dear, why have you not dressed? Are you unwell?'

'No, Mama.'

'Where have you been?'

'Here. As you see,' replied Emma.

'I came to find you. We were to sit down to dinner fifteen minutes ago,' said Lady Osborne.

'Then do not delay any further on my account,' her daughter replied.

'You know I cannot do that. Shall we go down together?'

'Go, Mama. Do not keep Aunt and Uncle Musgrave waiting.'

Lady Osborne ignored Emma's entreaty. 'My dear, I wish you would speak to me. What is it? What troubles you?'

Emma looked away. 'I should like to return to Brinshore tomorrow. Would you arrange it with Papa?'

'Tomorrow? Will you not stay another day at least? Frank misses you greatly. He has asked for you several times this last hour.'

'Frank, Frank, Frank. He is in everyone's heart and thoughts. He can do no wrong.'

'I don't understand, my dear,' said her mother.

Emma sighed. 'I matter nothing. Only Frank is important. Will not all this be his one day? Every stone and stair, every item in this bedchamber, every piece of silver, every tree, and every blade of grass as far as the eye can see. What rejoicing there is at the news that Frank will mend! How could there not be?'

Lady Osborne placed Emma's hands in hers. 'Do you imagine that your Papa and I love you less than your brother?'

'I am of no consequence,' said she.

Lady Osborne was pained by her daughter's words. 'You know as well as I that in time your brother will inherit. He must inherit,' said she with gentleness. 'It cannot be contrived otherwise.'

'Do you not see how it is, Mama? In every possible way I am worth less than Frank. My brother alone is thought of and spoken of. The day Frank was born I ceased to exist.'

'My dearest child,' said Lady Osborne. 'What has come over you?'

'Can you not read my thoughts, Mama? No. I see you cannot. But there is more. Tell me, Mama, why I bear *your* name and not a name of my own. How am I to be myself? Though I have your name, I am not you. And all my life I have been compared to you in countenance, temperament and understanding.'

Lady Osborne wiped a tear from her daughter's cheek. Emma continued, 'My character — my disposition is mine, and mine alone.'

The bewilderment felt by Lady Osborne, on hearing her daughter express herself thus, was severe. Grieved by the strength of the feelings expressed, Lady Osborne reproached herself for her failure to apprehend the nature of her daughter's distress. She had not thought Emma as wretched as this. There was much for Lady Osborne to ponder, and even more to say. She paused to collect her thoughts.

At that moment, a maid knocked at the door to enquire whether dinner was to be delayed.

'Go, Mama. You are needed downstairs.'

Dinner was of the least concern to Lady Osborne, and had they been due to dine alone, a delay would have been of no consequence.

'You *must* go, Mama.'

Lady Osborne gave instructions that dinner should be served half past the usual hour.

When they were alone once again, Lady Osborne set about arranging her daughter's hair. 'We shall go down together, you and I. But I shall speak with you again in the morning.'

I have left it too long, thought she.

The following morning, after receiving a satisfactory account of Frank's progress, Lady Osborne came down at an early hour to find her daughter still at breakfast. Lord Osborne had business in Delham and had been gone an hour. The weather being fine, Lady Osborne proposed a visit to Stanton.

'Stanton?' said Emma. 'It is too far to walk.'

'I thought we might ride there,' said Lady Osborne.

'Very well, if you wish,' said she.

The ride to Stanton Woods was, in earlier years, a favourite route taken by Lady Osborne and her daughter. On occasion they would watch the hounds throw off there, and afterwards they would call at Stanton Parsonage to visit Emma's grandfather. Lady Osborne had been a frequent visitor there while her father had lived at the parsonage; and towards the end of his life, when he refused to move to the Castle or to the Musgrave residence, both sisters spent days and nights tending to his needs, listening to his complaints, taking up his tray, and reading to him.

'Shall we ride on?' said Lady Osborne. 'I should like to go as far as Stanton Parsonage.'

Emma assented to her mother's request.

A gentler trot slowed their progress, and as the house came into view, the familiar sight brought memories to the minds of both women. Lady Osborne and her daughter dismounted, tethered their horses and walked in the direction of the church yard.

She took her daughter's hand and led the way directly to the Watson family grave. Enwrapped in ivy, the wording on the gravestone had become obscured. Lady Osborne set about clearing it away. 'Your grandmother died on Christmas Eve in the winter of seventy-nine when I was but five years old. I should have had a younger brother, but he had no sooner entered this world than he left it.'

Emma turned away and was silent. Her mother continued to pull at the ivy, tearing it away from the stone.

'I should like to have had a younger brother,' said Lady Osborne.

'But you were sent away to live with Great Aunt Turner.'

Her mother nodded. 'I was too young to understand. Your Aunt Musgrave knows the facts better than I. Your grandmamma faced a difficult birth, the nature of which was not dissimilar to your entry into the world.'

'Oh,' said Emma, surprised by the disclosure.

'Your papa had been called to town on a matter of business that could not be delayed. Word reached him that he had a daughter, but that his wife was in danger and was not expected to survive the night. He returned immediately of course, and in what he believed to be my dying moments, he named you Emma. I recall nothing of the days that followed. One day passed, then another. Gradually, miraculously, I regained some strength. And when you were placed in my arms for the first time that I could remember, there was only a single thought in my mind. That thought I remember so very vividly. From that moment, and against all odds, I was determined to live. My dear Emma, the greatest joy I have ever known was the first time I heard you cry. It was strong and bold; and so are you.'

Emma looked with wonder at her mother. Lady Osborne understood well enough that, at times such as these, words did not flow easily; and sensible of her daughter's disposition, she comprehended her silence. Emma's countenance expressed what language could not; and her mother asked for nothing more.

The moments spent in Stanton churchyard left Emma with an unusual feeling of closeness and affection for her mother.

When next they spoke, it was on a new subject.

'I thought perhaps your low spirits had their origin in a matter of quite a different nature,' said Lady Osborne. 'Please do not misunderstand me. I do not wish to pry.'

Emma looked away, uncertain whether to speak openly on the subject or whether to remain silent. Lady Osborne led her daughter to a bench in the shadow of an ancient yew to shield them from the sun.

'Mama, I love Charles Blake,' said Emma, unable to keep her secret a moment longer. 'And I believe he may be attached to me.'

'I know he has the greatest affection for you. But has he given you any indication of the nature of his regard?' Lady Osborne enquired.

'Yes. Perhaps. Not exactly. No,' said Emma. 'I can't say so with any certainty. Captain Blake is universally affable and good-humoured. That is why it is so difficult to ascertain his true feelings. I have tried and failed. Sometimes I imagine one thing, and sometimes another.'

'Charles is entirely honourable. He would be the last person in the world to trifle with your affections, or give false hope,' said Lady Osborne.

'I know, Mama. But the delicacy of the situation may hold him back. Without Papa's approval, and yours, might he be prevented from declaring himself?'

'Dear Emma, any gentleman of Captain Blake's situation and understanding would apply to the father of the young woman he intended to marry. Charles understands this as well as any man. And were he to seek your father's blessing, I am certain that your father would give it.'

'Are you, Mama?'

'I am. Indeed, it would give me the greatest joy to see you both happily settled.'

'Grandmamma insists that I should marry higher.'

'It is not your grandmother's place to insist on anything of the kind. It is my wish that you marry the man you love.'

Emma hesitated. 'Mama, I do not know how to bring it about. Were Papa to make it known, in a general sort of way, that he would have no objection to an application from Charles — Captain Blake — or were you, Mama, to hint to Mrs Blake —'

'That would never do, my dear. Suppose — just suppose — that Captain Blake's affections were engaged elsewhere.'

'I am certain they are not, that is, I do not believe they are.'

'But suppose they were. If Charles knew of your regard for him, it would place him under a considerable obligation to make you an offer, perhaps even against his will. Were he to suspect that he had, by some oversight or error in his conduct towards you, engaged your affections, as a gentleman of honour he would seek no other course than this. For the sake of your own happiness and his, have patience, my dear. Conduct yourself in a seemly manner. Allow his affections to grow, if grow they will. And most of all, endeavour to remain the person you are, unaffected and artless in all your dealings. I have never known enduring love to be the consequence of contrivance and calculation.'

Emma pondered her mother's words but in her heart clung to the certainty that there could be no alliance more fitting nor more pleasing than the prospect of her union with Captain Blake; in time she trusted that even her grandmamma would be obliged to acknowledge the suitability of the match. For the present, however, she agreed that the exercise of patience in the matter was as wise as it was prudent.

'If only Anne had not —'

'Anne had not what, my dear?'

'Nothing, Mama. I should like to return to Brinshore. That is all.'

The hour of Emma's return was a subject on which she could not countenance postponement.

'Wait a day or two more and your papa will take you there himself.'

'Really, Mama?' Emma smiled. 'I cannot think of anything that would please Aunt Harding more.'

'What do you mean?' her mother asked.

'Aunt Harding will likely instruct Papa to drive up and down the shore all day long, with the coat of arms visible. And there had better be no fewer than two coachmen in livery or she will be quite put out. She is determined to make Brinshore more fashionable than Sanditon, or even Brighton, and is convinced that the way to do it is through the patronage of someone like Papa. But Papa does not care for that kind of thing. And he is the least fashionable of anyone I know.'

'You do your father a disservice. He was once reckoned very fashionable indeed.'

'That cannot be.'

'Your Uncle Musgrave was the first crop in Delham and your father was the second. All the young men followed his lead.'

'Papa a beau! That cannot be! He is so very moderate in his manner and appearance; though I can imagine it of Uncle Musgrave.'

As they rode back to Osborne Castle, Lady Osborne had a sense of unease, a consequence of her daughter's candid declaration. Charles Blake would indeed be welcomed and cherished as a son were such an alliance to take place; but Lady Osborne could not dismiss from her mind the notion that her daughter had in some way misconstrued the nature of Charles' affections for her. Curiously, as Emma had begun to speak of her love for Charles Blake, Lady Osborne was put in mind of his uncle, Mr Howard, the man with whom she has once fancied herself in love. As the Castle came into view, an idea entered Lady Osborne's head. She had a mind to observe Emma and Charles together; she would wait until little Frank was fully recovered; and as soon as she felt able to leave her son to the care of his nanny, she would go to Brinshore herself.

CHAPTER ELEVEN

A week passed by before a carriage bearing the Osborne coat of arms entered Brinshore, ending its journey at Trafalgar Terrace a little after five o'clock in the afternoon. Emma, in a state of heightened animation, was eager to hear all that had transpired in her absence and went on ahead to announce their arrival, leaving her father to inspect the horses and give directions to the coachman. Mrs Harding's delight at Emma's return, and more particularly the arrival of Lord Osborne, was almost as great as the sight of the Osborne barouche stationed in Trafalgar Terrace in full view of her neighbours. What a happy day for Brinshore! To be honoured by such a visit as this! thought she.

Emma, expecting Anne to be the only person present within, was pleasantly surprised to find the drawing room occupied by the very friends who were uppermost in her thoughts and of whom she was eager to hear news. The warmest of greetings met the weary traveller on entering the room; the pleasure expressed by Captain Blake and his mother at her return raised her spirits and dispelled her fatigue. Enquiries concerning the condition of little Frank soon followed and were answered in full — Frank was out of danger — no permanent injury had been sustained — bed rest had been prescribed for another week — Granby's nephew was to attend the patient thrice daily.

Emma had overlooked the presence of another guest; Mr Fitzroy, having stood aside until the general elation and the giving and receiving of greetings and enquiries had been accomplished, now came forward and enquired about the journey from Surrey.

'We made good progress as far as Brighton. The road was a little slow after —'

Her reply was curtailed by the entrance of her father. The party, except for the addition of Mr Fitzroy, required no introduction.

'Allow me to present to you my brother-in-law, Lord Osborne,' said Mrs Harding. Emma struggled to suppress a smile at the pretension in her aunt's voice as she made the introduction; she glanced at her father to observe his reaction and glimpsed the same amusement in his eyes. The phrase 'my brother-in-law' was repeated several times more by Mrs Harding until Emma was forced to looked away completely, knowing that restraint would have been impossible had her father caught her eye.

Lord Osborne, gracious in his greeting, expressed regret on hearing of the untimely death of his father, the late Earl of Allersham. 'I have a distinct recollection of your father some twenty years ago or more. He attended Lady Forbes' balls once or twice when he was in town. Indeed, I believe we met a time or two in the year ninety. He tried to sell me a rather fine spaniel. I don't recall why.'

Mr Fitzroy smiled. 'He kept rather a lot of them.'

Anne drew Emma aside to show her the latest addition to her fossil collection. 'It is the smallest and the most complete. I thought I might have it set in silver and fashioned into a broach. Or do you think it more suited to a necklace?'

Emma had no particular opinion either way and was less interested in the ancient relic and its decorative potential than in the conversation between the rest of the party concerning the expeditions planned for the days ahead. Mrs Harding was insistent that her brother-in-law stay a full week; Lord Osborne was equally determined to spend no more than a day in Brinshore before his departure.

'The benefits of Brinshore cannot be felt in one day alone. Brinshore has attractions enough to occupy a season complete.'

'I do not doubt it,' said Lord Osborne. 'But I am not at liberty to partake of them. I have pressing matters to attend to in Delham. Regrettably, however fine a place it is, I can spare no more than a day. The delights of Brinshore will have to wait.'

'Then we shall delay our excursion to Sanditon,' said Mrs Harding.

Mrs Blake looked anxiously at Emma and Anne. 'My dear Mrs Harding, no other day will do! Tomorrow sees the opening of the new extension to the tea rooms at the circulating library. Both Emma and Anne have expressed a great desire to be among the first guests.'

'We shall visit Sanditon another day. Tea rooms are much the same wherever one finds them. I should like my brother-in-law to spend the rest of his stay in Brinshore,' Mrs Harding replied.

It was impossible for Emma to remain silent. 'Dear Aunt Harding, ordinarily I should be happy to visit Sanditon on any day of the week, but having never had an opportunity such as this, I should like to attend the opening of the new tea rooms. And Papa, I assure you, has every intention of visiting Brinshore again very soon. It is his express desire to stay two weeks at least on his next visit.'

Emma looked anxiously at her father for his support and acquiescence.

'And when Brinshore has its own circulating library,' added Lord Osborne, 'I shall be its first subscriber.'

Emma was delighted to find her father so easily complicit in bringing Aunt Harding round. And for her part, Mrs Harding was persuaded that the promise of her brother-in-law's future patronage of Brinshore was worth the present sacrifice; patience would in time reap its rewards.

'What good fortune,' whispered Mr Fitzroy to Emma, 'to have such a father.'

'Whatever can you mean?' she replied.

'I suspect it is not the first time the two of you have contrived to get your own way,' said he.

'If you knew my grandmamma, you would understand the absolute necessity of it.'

The following day brought rain, and though Mrs Harding had hopes that it would dampen more than the ground beneath their feet, it did not. Emma and Anne were in high spirits.

Anne, on Captain Blake's recommendation, had in her possession a piece of paper on which he had written the title of a book, a certain illustrated guide to sea shells commonly found on English shores. Eager to discover whether such a copy might be purchased or borrowed from the circulating library at Sanditon, Anne took the greatest care to place the piece of paper inside her glove for safe keeping.

Less interested in the library as a place where books might be obtained and read, Emma thought only of the tea rooms and the society of her Sanditon friends that promised to make the day complete.

Nor had Mrs Harding any interest in books. For her part, the presence of Lord Osborne as one of the party added that measure of complacency needed to navigate the day with good grace. Sanditon society would be left in doubt as to His Lordship's connection with Brinshore, and the promise of Lord Osborne's patronage for Brinshore's own circulating library, an establishment that would, in time, rival some of the finest rooms in the country, was enough to render the day tolerable. More commodious than Scarborough or Harrogate, more comfortable than any example that Oxford could offer, and stock the scope of which was certain to equal the best in London, Brinshore's circulating library would bear no comparison to Sanditon's trifling endeavour.

'Dear Aunt,' said Emma, as they waited for refreshments to arrive, 'have you seen anything to compare to this? It is as elegant as any tea room in Brighton, I am sure. Look at the ceiling! Feel the comfortable chairs! I should be happy to spend an entire day here! Hot chocolate, coffee, tea, Sanditon Buns and much more besides. It is worth every penny.'

'And do you include books among the delights of this place?' said Mr Fitzroy.

'If any worthy of the time employed in reading them can be found here, I should be happy to include books among its delights. Gothic novels have little to recommend them, for the ending is plain to see before the first volume is read. I speak from my own knowledge, for I have read many such volumes. Every story is the same. I do not see the point of sitting for hours reading a second volume, and even less a third, to discover that wickedness is defeated and that every obstacle that stands in the way of the hero and heroine is, on the final page, inevitably overcome. It is quite clear to me that in life wickedness is not always vanquished and it is by no means certain that the heroine finds herself united to the object of her affection. Indeed, every woman thinks herself a heroine, and it is quite right that she should.'

Mr Fitzroy smiled. 'I cannot argue with that.'

Emma's gaze was drawn towards Anne who appeared to be in animated conversation with Captain Blake over the matter of a slim volume which she had in her hands. Without averting her gaze, Emma continued the point, 'Novels have a dangerous propensity to perpetuate untruths. Why is it that a woman has not the power to determine her own path to happiness? A man may choose his; but a woman must surrender hers to the vagaries of fortuity.'

'I do not dispute what you say,' replied Mr Fitzroy. 'But the liberty to choose a course of action is often regulated by its consequences. I know very few men who have the will to exercise complete freedom of choice. And that is as it should be, or we should all be libertines. But novels are meant to entertain, not to theorise,' said he. 'If you have no desire to read, a subscription to a library such as this is surely an unnecessary extravagance.'

'A guinea is not excessive,' she replied, 'and the surroundings are vastly more pleasurable than I expected them to be.'

'That may be,' said Mrs Harding, on hearing the mention of the word *subscription*. 'A guinea a year is little enough, but I fear it has the tendency to encourage the patronage of the less desirable and the undeserving. Visitors having neither rank nor connections — and there are many in Sanditon — on the payment of a fee will be disposed to think their entitlements extend beyond the borrowing of books. Brinshore cannot be too careful. I am persuaded by all that I have seen today that Brinshore should charge no less than two guineas a year, for Brinshore's own circulating library is to be an altogether more exclusive establishment.'

Anne returned clutching an illustrated volume of sea shells. It was not the precise volume she had asked for, but a brief examination of the contents marked it out as a most acceptable alternative. Captain Blake's opinion was immediately sought on the matter; and after a short inspection of the cover and the index of subjects, he pronounced his complete approval and applauded the excellence of Anne's choice. The volume was then passed to Mrs Blake who praised the quality and detail of the illustrations. Lord Osborne was similarly impressed; and Mr Fitzroy reckoned it to be an authoritative study, meticulously documented, substantial in the range of subject matter, and orderly in its arrangement. Anne was delighted that the volume, one of two recommended by the librarian, had received such high praise.

On observing the reactions of her party to Anne's chosen volume, Emma felt the want of a book more keenly than at any time since stepping over the library's threshold. On entering the building, the display of books had appeared to her as little more than ornamental: an enhancement, pleasing to the eye, adding character and ambience to the interior. She had quite overlooked the purpose of the library, a fact that was now painfully self-evident. Anne's unaffected joy at the discovery of a volume that had been severally described as 'scientific' and 'comprehensive', in Emma's eyes bore favourable comparison to her own lack of inclination to borrow, purchase or even read a book.

The number of subscribers that filled the tea rooms grew steadily during the course of the morning until the noise, squeeze and restriction of movement began to render the surroundings less pleasurable by the minute. Mrs Blake proposed a walk along the shore to escape the tumult, and the suggestion found general approval among the party. All were of the same mind: the morning had been agreeable beyond expectation, but the time to depart had arrived.

'This is precisely the situation that Brinshore must avoid,' said Mrs Harding, clinging tightly to Lord Osborne's arm. 'Full of nobodies and upstarts. That is what you get for a guinea a piece.'

'I found it quite refreshing,' he replied. 'Delham would benefit from just such a scheme.'

'Masons' has always managed things in Delham,' Mrs Harding replied.

'Indeed,' said Lord Osborne. 'But a few shelves of books in a haberdasher's is not what I had in mind.'

As their party reached the shore, Emma was gratified to find that Captain Blake made a particular point of seeking her out. As the rest of the party went on ahead, their pace slowed by degrees and eventually they found themselves out of earshot.

'How glad I am to see you again, my dear Emma,' said he. 'After the uncertainty of the last two weeks, it must be a great relief to you that all is well at Osborne Castle.'

'It is a relief to us all,' she replied. 'And it is a pleasure to be back in Brinshore. I doubt you have seen much of Aunt Harding and Anne during my absence.'

Captain Blake smiled. 'We had the pleasure of visiting Brinshore twice in your absence, but you were missed every second of every hour. Your cousin has taken a great interest in the sea. I must say, it is a joy to behold.'

'Nature is her passion,' said Emma.

'I believe so,' Captain Blake replied.

'Any creature that lives in a shell is of infinite fascination to Anne,' she went on.

'I had — have — just such a passion myself.' Charles hesitated. Emma sensed that he had not said all that he had wished to say, nor did he seem inclined to carry on in similar vein. In an instant his manner changed, and when he spoke again he made but a general observation. 'The sea looks perfectly still, does it not?'

'It does,' said she. 'Quite still.'

'But it is not,' he replied. 'Oh the sea! It is wonderful, powerful and terrifying in equal measure!'

Puzzled by the sudden change in his demeanour, Emma endeavoured to steer the conversation back to the more interesting subject of passion. 'And what is your passion?' said she.

'My passion? Life. Nature, the sea, fishing, reading, riding, dancing —'

'So many?'

'And more,' said he. 'There is much to be discovered, to wonder at, to comprehend. It seems odd, Emma. I have known you all my life, but I should be at a loss to guess passion.'

'You would? I take pleasure in riding, walking, playing the piano. But I do not think of them as passions.'

'One day, my dear Emma. One day,' said he.

Captain Blake's attention was claimed by Mrs Harding who was curious to enquire about a particular ship anchored near to the shore. Emma was content to release him; it suited her to linger behind the rest of the party and ponder in solitude the significance of their agreeable, yet perplexing, encounter. What could he possibly mean? One day, my dear Emma. His words echoed in her mind. Of what day did he speak? Was she meant to take hope or consolation from his words? Why should he seek to discover her passion? Had he attempted to draw her out? She neither knew what to think nor how to feel.

The ship anchored offshore was confirmed by Captain Blake to be a sloop of similar appearance to the first ship under the command of Mrs Harding's son. It was not the same ship, but Mrs Harding was nevertheless reminded of that aspect of her son's existence that did not give her pain; she fancied Captain Blake was a little like him, and for the rest of the walk was anxious to hear about the pleasures and perils of life on board a sloop.

Emma was heartened to observe Captain Blake's attentiveness to her aunt; and her father's courtesy to Mrs Blake was no less pleasing. Mrs Blake had been eager to point out the new buildings that would contribute to Sanditon's improvement, and it seemed that her father was genuinely interested in the matter. What pleased Emma more than anything, however, was Mr Fitzroy's attentions towards Anne, and her cousin's apparent preference for his company. She noticed his friendly manner towards her cousin and hers towards him; convinced that their demeanour bore signs of a growing intimacy, Emma found no better employment, nor any scheme more worthy or more urgent than the promotion of a match between them. Mr Fitzroy was, perhaps, not the most eligible man of her acquaintance, being estranged from his family, but as the brother of an earl, he was not without consequence of his own. If only he might be worked on to seek a full and lasting reconciliation with his family, the suitability of such a match would improve considerably. An alliance between Anne and Mr Fitzroy, thought she, would then be no bad thing. Indeed, the Fitzroy family could hardly object to Anne, an heiress with twelve thousand pounds, and from a family intimately connected to her own. The more the idea took root in her mind, the more persuaded she was that Anne would suit Mr Fitzroy perfectly.

CHAPTER TWELVE

Lord Osborne would not be prevailed upon to remain in Brinshore a moment longer than planned despite Mrs Harding's best efforts to persuade him to delay his departure for a day or two. His Lordship would not be moved or worked on. She comforted herself, however, with the thought that some measure of success had been achieved in securing assurances from Lord Osborne of his patronage, should the establishment of a circulating library meet with general approval. The neighbourhood, she was certain, would not oppose such a measure for it was in every aspect designed to bring vast improvements to the town. Only an irreversible undertaking to contribute to the new library was enough to obtain Mrs Harding's approval and secure his release.

His Lordship bid his daughter and niece goodbye and, entrusted with salutations, messages and missives, promised to deliver them to their intended recipients at the earliest opportunity.

'Do not forget, Papa,' said Emma.

'Have you ever known me to be tardy in any of your commissions?'

'Repeatedly,' said she.

Emma had anticipated a less than satisfactory day following her father's departure, for there were no plans to visit Sanditon, nor were there plans for the Blakes to visit Brinshore. Curious to gauge Anne's view of the matter, and more particularly to learn something more of her cousin's feelings in regard to Mr Fitzroy, Emma observed, 'I expect today will be very dull indeed.'

'Why so?' asked Anne.

'We shall not see our friends from Sanditon,' said Emma.

'I understand they are engaged today with the Parkers.'

'But do you not miss them, or one of them at least?' Emma enquired, hoping to draw Anne out.

Anne looked away. 'Not particularly,' said she.

Emma found her cousin's guarded response wholly unconvincing. It served only to proffer further evidence of a growing attachment between her cousin and Mr Fitzroy. All the signs pointed to it: there could be no other explanation.

'Do you not find Mr Fitzroy improves on acquaintance?' continued Emma, searching her cousin's countenance for a sign.

'My opinion of him was never bad. I think no more nor less of him than ever I did. He appears to be a respectable man, sensible and sincere.'

'He was very attentive to you yesterday,' Emma replied.

'No more than usual, I think,' said Anne.

Emma was intrigued by Anne's apparent unease, and though tempted to pry further, decided for the present to turn to a different topic.

'The book you have in your hand — is that the book you borrowed from the library yesterday? Mr Fitzroy spoke so eloquently of the excellence of your choice.'

Anne placed the book on the table and moved away. 'Shall we walk to the shore?' she replied.

Emma gave way to Anne's request and put on her cloak and bonnet, for Mrs Harding's maid had mentioned that there was a cool breeze in the air. As they entered the hall on their way out, they heard an unusual commotion in the morning room. Mrs Harding came out into the hall holding a card.

'I shall not delay you if you are determined to go out this minute but allow me to tell you the news. We have been invited to a ball! There is to be an assembly in Brinshore — yes, Brinshore — on this day week.'

'But where is it to be held?' said Emma.

'At the Angel. I wonder I did not think of it myself. Well, I shall accept the invitation directly,' said Mrs Harding. 'What an excellent thing for Brinshore! Any day, however dull, improves tenfold when there is good news to be had. And now my dears, go for your walk but be careful not to stay too long in the sun. One cannot be too careful. Crimson is most becoming on a strawberry, but it does nothing to enhance a young lady's complexion. Neither of you will leave this house without a parasol.'

Emma sighed. 'I shall share Anne's for I do not have one of my own.'

'No parasol?' said Mrs Harding.

'A parasol is a most inconvenient article to carry with one when shopping,' Emma replied.

'Nevertheless, you shall borrow mine,' her aunt insisted.

'I should prefer to share Anne's. See. It is large enough for the two of us, and I am sure Anne has no objection.'

Mrs Harding turned to Anne. 'My dear, as you are the more sensible of the two, I expect you to make sure that your cousin stays out of the sun. And if you hear any item of news about the ball, take note of it and tell me.'

'Yes, Aunt, I shall try,' said Anne.

'Shall you secure an invitation for Captain Blake?' said Emma.

'Indeed I shall!' said Mrs Harding. 'An excellent thought! I shall write to the Blakes at once.'

'And Mr Fitzroy?' continued Emma, glancing at Anne. 'He must be one of our party too.'

The cousins walked in the direction of the market square, each determined to purchase items for the ball. The morning passed more quickly than they had anticipated: Emma perused every shelf, drawer and counter to find the perfect accoutrement for her pale blue dress, while Anne considered the merits of each pair of gloves placed before her. After much deliberation, Emma purchased a fine white lace shawl.

'I cannot decide between them,' said Anne holding up two pairs of gloves for Emma's inspection.

'Then take them both,' Emma replied.

'But I have six pairs of gloves already.'

'Do you need another pair?'

Anne thought for a moment. 'Well,' said she, 'I suppose I do not. But are they not both very fine? Look at the needlework on this pair. Do you not think it complements the needlework perfectly on my yellow gown?'

The sound of a carriage drew Emma's attention away from the counter and towards the window. She caught only the briefest glance, and though she could not say with any certainty that the gig she saw belonged to Mr Fitzroy, the possibility that it did, gave her cause to bring their shopping excursion to a hasty conclusion. Emma looked briefly at the gloves and said hurriedly, 'Take both pairs. One can never have too many pairs of gloves.'

As the items were wrapped, Emma whispered, 'I think that was Mr Fitzroy's gig. We must go at once, for he may well have come to call on Aunt Harding.'

They walked briskly back towards Trafalgar Terrace. 'If we walk across the sand we will save two minutes complete,' said Emma.

'My parasol! I have left it behind,' said Anne.

'Oh, never mind the parasol. Send a note to Peacock's later,' said Emma. 'There is not a moment to be lost.'

Anne trailed two steps behind, unable to keep pace with her cousin. They were still some distance away from the house when a child ran towards them and, without a word, stood before her, blocking her path. Emma recognised the same young girl who had come to her assistance when, disorientated by the sea fret, she had lost her way on her first morning in Brinshore.

The young girl tugged at Emma's sleeve.

'Tell her to go away,' said Anne.

The girl pointed in the distance to a stretch of sand, cut off by the sea. There appeared a young boy, similar in age to Frank, who appeared to be stranded on a sand bank.

Emma looked about her for help but none was to hand as the incoming tide on that part of the shore had driven walkers away. 'We must go back,' said Emma. 'The tide has turned. Do you not see? He will have no means of escape if we do not act now.'

Emma grasped hold of the young girl's hand and all three ran towards the bank. The water that separated them from the boy appeared shallow enough. Anne looked down. 'Do not be deceived by the depth of the water, Emma,' said she. 'You must not attempt to wade through it at any cost.'

Emma told the young girl to stand beside Anne. 'Do not move!' said she.

In a panic, Anne exclaimed, 'Whatever are you doing?'

Emma tore open the parcel containing her new shawl.

'I'm going make it into a rope,' she replied, knotting the end.

The boy teetered on the edge of the bank and tried to catch hold of the shawl, but the breeze was too strong, and, after several attempts, Emma decided that something more was needed. 'If only you had not forgotten the parasol!' said she.

'Shall I go back to recover it?' Anne replied.

'No, Anne. It would take too long.'

Emma threw off her bonnet and drew up her frock.

'No, Emma! Think of the danger!' said Anne.

Emma stepped cautiously into the water. Her feet sank beneath the soft seabed as the tidal current made movement arduous and unstable. The water rose steadily above her knees as she waded further into the deep.

'Come back at once! Please do not be so foolish! The water is too deep!' said Anne.

In what seemed like an hour but was less than a minute, Emma reached the other side. She picked up the boy and lifted him to astraddle her hip. He was light, but she found that she could not move with ease as her wet frock clung to her body and her feet began to sink further beneath the sand.

Anne looked on in horror, helpless to intervene.

'Go and seek help!' said Emma.

'Where shall I go?' said Anne.

'The fishermen's cottages,' said she. 'And if you should happen to come upon Mr Fitzroy bring him here immediately, unless Captain Blake is with him, for he must not see me like this! My dress is ruined, and my hair is tangled!'

Anne set off directly, but the young girl stood quite still and fixed her gaze on Emma.

'Have no fear,' said Emma to the girl. 'All will be well.'

Then she turned to the boy and said, 'Dry your eyes and be brave. I have a brother like you. His name is Frank. He is a little taller, I suppose, but only by half an inch. When Frank gets himself into trouble, Nanny puts him to bed with nothing but bread and water for his supper. I cannot count the times I have taken hot milk and honey to the nursery when Nanny was not looking! I do not know what your mama will say when I tell her what you have done! Frank cares not one whit for anything or anyone. He climbs over furniture and breaks vases and cups and saucers all day long. He very nearly broke his head when he tumbled down the stairs.'

The boy seemed not to hear a word she said. His eyes were fixed on the fast-flowing current that surrounded them. The water now appeared deeper and wider than when Emma had first traversed it. There was no sign of Anne, and no time for further delay.

'Dear me! You must climb on to my shoulders and cling on tight,' said she. 'I used to carry Frank this way, but I am quite done with it for he wriggles far too much. Do you understand? I cannot abide wriggling.' Emma crouched awkwardly as the boy climbed on to her back, but the extra weight on her shoulders caused Emma's feet to sink further into the sand, making progress slow.

The boy hung on tight as Emma carefully lifted her skirt to her knees, struggling to maintain her balance. She looked about her to find the best place to cross and took a deep breath as they entered the water. Each movement, though unsteady and sluggish, brought them one step closer to safety. Her nerve faltered at first; but on she went, step by step, descending deeper into the tidal flow until the sea rose above her waist.

'Well, for a boy of three or thereabouts you say remarkably little,' said Emma. 'It is just as well, for I do not think I should have any patience at all for tears and tantrums at this moment.'

The boy made no reply.

Anxiety and dread must have caused him to lose his tongue, thought she. Their progress was steady as Emma found that she was able to withstand the current and the mire; but just as they were in reach of safety, Emma's foot hit a solid object. She could not determine what it was — a rock or a piece of bark from the hull of a sunken ship perhaps — it mattered little — for the object caused her to slip and lose her footing. In an instant the boy lost his grip and toppled over her head to safety, landing unharmed on the soft sand of the opposite bank.

Emma felt a sharp pain in her ankle as she tried to drag herself to her feet, the heaviness of her wet clothes making movement almost impossible. Dripping wet and covered in sand, she began to shiver uncontrollably.

'At last,' said Emma, as Anne hastened towards her accompanied by a ragged and weathered fisherwoman.

'Thank heaven you are safe!' said Anne, breathlessly.

Emma limped towards her to lean on her arm.

The fisherwoman knelt to examine Emma's foot and was pleased to confirm that her ankle was not broken but badly sprained.

'Well, I suppose is not the worst news of all,' said she. 'But it had better mend in time for the ball, for I have no desire to sit in a corner hemmed in by gossips and chaperones all evening. I should sooner stay at home.'

'Take my arm,' said Anne. 'I have sent word to Aunt Harding to bring the chair.'

'Grandpapa's old chair?'

'Yes.'

'I should not wish to be seen dead in that old thing.'

'I am sorry,' said Anne. 'It seemed the most practical solution, especially in light of your damp state.'

'Well, I must first return these two to their mama,' she replied. Turning to the young boy and girl, Emma asked, 'Where do you live? Are you brother and sister?'

'They have no mother,' the fisherwoman interposed, brushing the sand from the hem of Emma's cloak. Emma further learned that the children's mother had died some two years earlier and that their father had left Brinshore to look for work in one of the northern towns.

'A grim tale indeed,' Emma whispered to Anne.

'Oh Emma, think no more of it. The boy is safe. Let us go. Look! Aunt Harding is come.'

Anne placed a shilling in the fisherwoman's palm for her trouble. Word spread of the incident and onlookers began to assemble. Cold, wet and windswept, Emma limped towards her grandfather's old chair, her cousin at her side.

'I wish people would not stare so,' said she.

'Would we not do the same?' Anne replied. 'I should like everyone to know of your great courage.'

'And I should like to tell them to go away,' said Emma.

'You know as well as I that fanciful stories are inclined to circulate when the facts are not made known. An incident such as this can lead to all kinds of invention. Captain Blake told me of a young woman who fell down some steps on the cobb at Lyme not long ago and hurt her head. Everyone took her for dead.'

'Never mind that. How do I look?' enquired Emma.

'You are not fit to be seen,' said Anne. 'You had better let Aunt Harding take you home directly.'

Emma had little strength left to mount further resistance and with the greatest reluctance surrendered herself to the ministrations of her aunt.

'Oh, my dear! You might have drowned!' said Mrs Harding. 'Whatever were you thinking of, Emma? Look at you! Look at your dress! Look at your hair! Oh! What will His Lordship say? Your shoes are ruined! Ruined! They are quite beyond restoration! Come, my dear! Let me wrap you in this blanket for you will catch your death and then your papa will blame me and there will be no circulating library, nothing of note to speak of in Brinshore for years to come! If only Mr Fitzroy had stayed five minutes longer, but he would not! No, indeed. Mrs Harding, said he, I have a commission to fulfil and I must go now. Five minutes! Five minutes was all that was needed. Where are men when they are needed? And why do young men always have to be dashing about here and there making business for themselves that cannot be put off for five minutes complete? I expect he is gone back to Sanditon. I insisted he take with him invitations to the Brinshore Ball. Said he, I cannot speak for Mrs Blake, but I feel certain that Captain Blake will attend, and as I have no prior engagement myself, I should be happy to accept the invitation. There you have it. I expect Mrs Blake will not want to be left out. I'll wager she will make a point of attending if only to compare Brinshore's assembly with anything Sanditon has to offer. I suppose what Sanditon lacks in consequence, it makes up for in numbers. If their library subscriptions are anything to go by, assemblies at Sanditon are certain to lack refinement, for they will not be too particular about those to whom they give admittance.'

Mrs Harding hardly drew breath until they reached the house. 'Now do not fret, my dear,' said she. 'I have sent for Mr Fowle. We shall get you out of those clothes and into bed. What shall I say to your parents? We must first determine whether your foot is broken.'

'It is but a sprain,' said Emma.

'Mr Fowle will advise whether your foot is broken or not,' declared Mrs Harding.

The old chair, though large enough to carry two, was too small to accommodate three. Anne returned some twenty minutes later to Trafalgar Terrace to find that Mr Fowle had already arrived and had confirmed that Emma had sustained a sprain to her ankle. Bed rest was prescribed, and Emma was to be watched hourly for any sign of a chill, infection or fever.

'Should any change in your cousin's condition manifest itself, Mr Fowle is to be sent for directly,' said Mrs Harding.

'I shall not move from my cousin's side,' said Anne.

'Excellent! Excellent! I can see that Miss Osborne is in the safest of hands,' said Mr Fowle, taking his leave.

'You see, my dear,' said Mrs Harding as Mr Fowle was shown to the door, 'how fortunate it is that Brinshore should have to hand so able a physician in Mr Fowle. And to be so well connected. His uncle, you know, had the very great distinction of almost becoming a Fellow of the Royal Society.'

'Yes, Aunt, I believe you have mentioned it several —'

'Sanditon not only lacks the services of so reputable a physician as ours, it cannot boast one at all.'

'I have heard that the apothecary in Sandition is very good,' Anne replied.

'Apothecaries have their place. Indeed, Dr Harding was familiar with their practices through an acquaintance of his. But among them are quacks and charlatans, and it is often hard to distinguish between them. Unlike Sanditon, Brinshore is fortunate indeed to possess a physician of Mr Fowle's stature. Every respectable watering place should have a Mr Fowle. Mr Fowle is certainly Brinshore's man! You see, my dear, quackery is easily bred in places like Sanditon, for such a town attracts the weak and gullible, like pins to a magnet. I cannot begin to recount the stories I have heard of the old and infirm being parted from their money with the promise of miracle cures, potions and powders that in the end are found to have no beneficial effect whatsoever. Fortune hunters have much the same approach. They persuade unsuspecting young women to part with their fortune with the promise of lasting happiness and undeviating devotion. It is the way of the world. But be sure of this: I know an imposter when I see one. Brinshore is safe in Mr Fowle's hands.'

On the celebrated physician's next visit, Emma took heart from the news that she would soon be put to rights, but her joy was short-lived when Mr Fowle ruled out dancing for at least two weeks.

'We cannot be too careful,' said he. 'Miss Osborne has sustained a particularly injurious sprain. Her ankle is weak and needs rest and support.'

'Two weeks? Impossible!' Emma replied. 'What about the ball?'

'Attend the ball if you will,' replied Mr Fowle. Turning to Mrs Harding, he continued, 'I insist only that the patient comports herself with care. I daresay, I am often cast as the breaker of bad news. But I cannot make right what is wrong. Brinshore Ball or no — there will be no dancing for Miss Osborne.'

'Indeed, Mr Fowle. Excellent advice as ever,' said Mrs Harding. 'Emma, you may go to the ball and you may sit and watch and keep me company.'

The prospect of attending a ball for any reason other than to dance was unthinkable; indeed, the notion of spending the entire evening watching others dance was vexatious in the extreme; but to look on as Captain Blake danced with every young woman but her was utterly inconceivable. Emma was astounded at the injustice of it and was about to speak her mind when Mr Fowle interjected.

'Sit and watch? Sit and watch, my dear Mrs Harding?' said he. 'So very young of heart and light of step as you are — I had rather hoped that you might be persuaded to join me in a measure or two. I should consider it an honour.'

In the normal course of conversation, Mrs Harding was not a woman for whom the description 'taciturn' could be applied; never had Emma seen her aunt at a complete loss for words. But on this occasion Mr Fowle had rendered Mrs Harding speechless; and it was some moments before she was able to regain her composure. Intrigued by the scene that unfolded before her, Emma put aside her own indignation and disappointment; for, diverted by her aunt's patent confusion at Mr Fowle's clumsy but entertaining address, she was hardly able to keep her countenance.

The attentions of Mr Fowle had not been in Mrs Harding's sights, nor was she used to being surprised by anyone or anything.

'Well, Mr Fowle, I hardly know what to say,' said she, when at last she had command once again of her senses. 'I am flattered. Indeed I am. But I have not danced these past five or six years.'

'Dear Aunt Harding, Aunt Musgrave was not so very long ago learning to dance the waltz. And she is your elder. How could you refuse Mr Fowle's kind invitation?' said Emma.

Mrs Harding looked at Emma in horror. 'Precisely! My sister, Mr Fowle, sustained a very nasty injury to *her* foot — a consequence not to be wished for in my case.'

'Dear Aunt, you have it all wrong. The injury was caused by Uncle Musgrave's curricle.'

'Emma, my dear,' said Aunt Harding, in a firm whisper delivered through clenched teeth, 'My mind is quite made up. Mr Fowle and I will leave you now. Anne will look in on you when she returns from her walk.'

Emma persisted. 'Dear Aunt Harding, nothing in the world would give me greater pleasure than to see you dance! And as I am prevented from dancing myself, I must have something to cheer and delight in.'

'A very handsome speech, if I may say so, Miss Osborne,' said Mr Fowle. 'Mrs Harding can surely have no objection if you do not.'

'Mr Fowle,' said Mrs Harding, 'I must beg leave to decline your invitation. You do me a great honour, sir, but I am no dancer. My province is to chaperone, a duty that prohibits neglect.'

'Dear lady, I applaud the excellence of your principles. Your rectitude does you the greatest credit. The words "virtue" and "Mrs Harding" cannot be spoken except in one breath, for they are one and the same. Propitious the day Mrs Harding made Brinshore her home!'

For Emma, the notion that Aunt Harding had an admirer, and one absurd beyond reason, was a pleasing distraction from the limitations and frustrations of her own predicament. The confusion that had marked her aunt's response to Mr Fowle's application had been fascinating to observe, for it intimated that his attentions had not been entirely unwelcome. Emma had, until that moment, mistakenly supposed that the physician's eagerness to please had been due entirely to an excessive deference to rank and consequence. Not so, thought she. Mr Fowle must be in love.

Recumbent upon the bed and having nothing better to do than to while away the hours in idle repose, Emma began to occupy her time devising a plan to further Mr Fowle's interests.

When Anne returned from her walk before luncheon, on entering Emma's bedchamber, she was met by her cousin's reproach. 'Where have you been?' said she. 'I have looked for your return this past hour.'

'I have been to purchase this,' Anne replied. In her hand was a small green leather case. 'You may open it.'

Anne placed the object into Emma's hands. Inside was a silver spy glass, encased in ivory.

'I should like you to have the use of it. Is it not a fine object? Elegant and practical — powerful too. It is not too heavy, nor too cumbersome. And it was a bargain! Worth every penny!'

Emma raised the spyglass to her eye.

'On the way back,' continued Anne. 'I spied a brig and watched it turn almost on the spot. I thought it a pirate ship at first but was reassured when I observed — a clear as day — a rowing boat headed from the brig to the shore. I had no fear. Indeed, I was quite reassured, for through the spyglass I was able to ascertain that the sailors were perfectly respectable and did not look at all like pirates.'

Emma had little interest in pirates or sailing vessels in general, except those that carried Captain Blake. Of greater interest was Anne's news of the arrival of a bathing machine on Brinshore's sand.

'There are to be five in all. I had it from the proprietor of Peacock's.'

'Not before time,' said Emma. 'A dip in the sea is just the thing for a sprained ankle.'

'I do not think Aunt Harding, or Mr Fowle, would agree. A dip in the sea was the cause of your injury in the first place and I doubt it would be seen as its cure as well.'

'Then perhaps I should send for Mr Fowle to ask his opinion on the matter,' replied Emma.

'Send for Mr Fowle? Surely not,' said Anne. 'He has already attended you this morning.'

Emma smiled. 'Indeed he has. I have a secret, the nature of which you will never guess.'

Anne sat down on the edge of the bed.

'Mr Fowle and Aunt Harding,' whispered Emma.

'Is our aunt displeased with Mr Fowle for some reason?'

'Not in the least! Why should she be? No, indeed! You have it all wrong! Mr Fowle is violently in love with Aunt Harding. He almost made her an offer in my presence.'

'Impossible!' Anne exclaimed.

Emma related the particulars of the encounter that had caused Mrs Harding confusion and discomfiture, but Anne remained unconvinced.

'He is a respectable man. I cannot believe he would be so bold,' said Anne.

'His reputation as a physician and his connections must surely recommend him. But the speech he made this morning was quite ridiculous. Aunt Harding would have none of it, so I offered a little assistance of my own, for I could see that Mr Fowle had taken her quite by surprise.'

'You encouraged Mr Fowle?' said Anne.

'Certainly, I did. And you, my dear cousin, must teach Aunt Harding to waltz. If your mama is not beyond a waltz —'

'Mama would never dance a waltz at a public ball. It is hardly decent.'

'It is decent enough for Almack's. And poor Mr Fowle. Imagine! He will be sitting alone at his table at this very moment — with not a friend in the world — without a soupçon of hope — dejected — his soup untouched — and despair in his heart, contemplating the object of his affection —'

'Oh Emma, do be serious. Aunt Harding would never think of Mr Fowle. He is a physician. And she is far too old to think of matrimony.'

'The same might have been said of old Dr Harding. Why is it that old men see fit to marry whenever it pleases them? Mr Edwards would take Great Aunt Turner — five and seventy if she is a day — in an instant,' replied Emma. 'Promise me that you will teach Aunt Harding to waltz.'

'I will not. And even if I offered to do so, I doubt she would have any wish to learn it. Do you wish to make us all look ridiculous in the eyes of the world?'

'I care nothing for the eyes of the world. They may blink and stare, but they do not trouble me,' said Emma. 'If not the waltz, you might take her through the steps of a country dance or two, to refresh her memory. And the quadrille. Surely, if not the waltz, the quadrille will suffice.'

'I will not interfere, Emma. If Aunt Harding has a mind to dance at all, I am certain she will manage things her own way.'

CHAPTER THIRTEEN

Emma was more appreciative of Anne's spyglass than at first she had anticipated. A diversion to relieve the boredom, it afforded a uniquely entertaining prospect of the comings and goings on the sand at

Brinshore. To secure a more panoramic view of the shore, the next day Emma insisted on leaving the confines of her bedchamber for a seat in the drawing room. A chaise longue was hastily positioned by the window according to her instructions, and there she remained for the best part of the morning, absorbed in her new preoccupation. The sun and the retreating tide appeared to bring out the entire neighbourhood; fishermen with their nets, boatmen, bathing machines, donkeys, carriages and Bath chairs populated the firm sand that shimmered in the summer morning sun.

Amid her observations, more particularly the fascinating spectacle of what appeared to be a lovers' assignation at the rear of one of the bathing machines, she was completely unaware of the arrival of Mrs Blake. Roused from her musings by commotion on the stairs, Emma quickly hid the spyglass beneath a cushion and arranged her gown.

'Dear Emma,' said Mrs Blake on entering the room, 'I came as soon as I heard the news. How are you, my dear? Charles will follow shortly. He has business in Brinshore that cannot wait but wishes to assure you that he is not far behind.'

'Business in Brinshore? Whatever could that be?' said Emma, curious to know more.

'He is to call on a Mr Fowle, an eminent physician hereabouts.'

The lovers' assignation on the beach now paled into insignificance at the mention of Mr Fowle. 'Indeed, he is. An eminent physician and an excellent dancer. How very odd. Is Captain Blake ill?'

'No, my dear. Charles, as you know, is never ill, and even if he were, he would never admit to it.'

'It seems strange that he should call on Mr Fowle.' Emma could hardly curb her curiosity. 'Is this an attempt to poach Brinshore's celebrated physician to Sanditon's cause?'

Mrs Blake seemed restless, as though there was some news she wished to relate. 'I must hold my tongue. Charles is eager to tell you himself. I promised to keep his secret.' Gentle persuasion would have brought the matter out into the open, but Emma, preferring to hear it from Captain Blake's lips, curbed her curiosity and probed no further.

'All will be revealed shortly. Patience, my dear.'

There was no shortage of other news, but the most pressing was Mrs Blake's desire to procure a first-hand report of Emma's courageous rescue of the young boy. 'We are all astonished at your courage, my dear. It is known far and wide in Sanditon — how you saved that poor urchin from drowning — how you almost drowned yourself — how you cared nothing for your own life. Indeed, I should not be surprised to read of it in the Sanditon Gazette on Friday. Has news of your injury reached Osborne Castle?'

'If it has, it was not by my hand. I do not know if Aunt Harding has written to Mama. And it is of little matter now.'

'Not so, my dear Emma. Sanditon speaks of little else, and I'm sure Brinshore is just the same. You have done more for Brinshore's reputation than anything I know, for I am sure I have not heard the word *Brinshore* mentioned above five times all season in Sanditon, except by Mrs Harding, of course. But now, you see, it is on everybody's lips.'

Mrs Blake enquired after Mrs Harding and Anne.

Emma explained that they had gone for a walk. 'They would not have done so had they known of your visit. I am so very glad you are come.'

'We had to see you at once! Charles would brook no delay. Indeed, he brought forward his business with Mr Fowle by two days for the very purpose. We came to cheer you up, but I see that you are in excellent spirits already.'

Emma was animated by the imminent prospect of seeing Captain Blake; moreover, the nature of his visit to Mr Fowle was a matter of interest that served only to increase her anticipation. Three quarters of an hour passed before Captain Blake was announced, accompanied by Mr Fitzroy.

'What do you think?' said Mrs Harding, entering the room ahead of her visitors. 'We four met quite by accident in the square. Charles sent the coach on ahead, for Anne had no greater wish than to walk back to Trafalgar Terrace. And what a pleasant walk we had! Did we not, Anne? Accompanied by two fine young men, all eyes were upon us. Mrs Blake, what think you of Emma's escapade?'

Captain Blake came forward to secure a better view of the patient. 'My dear Emma,' said he, 'I cannot tell you how relieved I am to hear that you are safe and well. Anne has told me every detail of your act of courage. We are all in awe and full of admiration for you,' said he.

'Never mind that,' said Emma. 'Mrs Blake tells me that you have called upon our own Mr Fowle. How did you find him?' Glancing at her aunt, she continued, 'Did you know, Aunt, that Captain Blake called upon Mr Fowle? He had business there this morning.'

'And it should remain his business. It is not for us to pry,' replied Mrs Harding.

Captain Blake smiled broadly and stationed himself in front of the fireplace. 'Henry and I have, this very morning, been in discussion with Mr Fowle regarding an establishment for the convalescence of the weak and infirm. There are, for instance, many such naval men in need of our help, men who have lost limbs, men in poor health of body and mind. But more than this, if we might garner the healing properties of the sea, men and women, young and old, would reap the benefits.'

Emma was quite unprepared for Charles' announcement; although she had not known quite what to expect, no subject had been further from her mind.

'And you sought to steal Brinshore's own Mr Fowle, to recruit him to your cause and secure his removal to Sanditon?' said Mrs Harding.

'Mr Fowle's exertions in the medicinal properties of water are quite fascinating, and the work of his uncle, Mr Joseph Fowle, is well documented,' said Captain Blake.

'Water?' said Emma.

'Yes, indeed,' Captain Blake replied. 'For centuries, it seems, the restorative properties of water have been championed and utilised to great effect. We see examples of it in the many watering places that exist throughout this land of ours.'

'What Mr Fowle does not know about water,' said Mrs Harding, 'is not worth the time of day. Cold water, hot water, spring water, mineral water, sea water. The point is this: water correctly dispensed, whether purgative or calming, is the greatest curative of all.'

'Excellent! Mrs Harding,' said Captain Blake. 'You have encapsulated most dependably Mr Fowle's life's work, and the work of his esteemed uncle.'

'Though I say it myself, my superior understanding of Mr Fowle's endeavours serves me well. You see, Dr Harding was himself one of the greatest advocates of the emetic properties of water,' Mrs Harding replied, 'as am I. Mr Fowle's interest in such matters, being so closely aligned to my own, only adds to Brinshore's many attractions. And I should be sorry indeed to find that Mr Fowle had been persuaded to leave Brinshore for Sanditon, however worthy the cause.'

'Mrs Harding, that is not Captain Blake's intention, nor is it mine,' said Mr Fitzroy. 'None of the particulars have yet been settled. We seek nothing more than to fulfil a promise given to my late brother before his passing. Captain Blake and I have been entrusted with the responsibility of providing a place of respite and recuperation for the wounded and infirm,' replied Mr Fitzroy.

'And shall you have the running of it, sir?' Mrs Harding enquired.

'Neither I nor Captain Blake alone,' he replied. 'We have need of the expertise of others.'

'And you have Mr Fowle in your sights,' said Emma.

'If he can be persuaded to accept the commission,' Captain Blake replied.

Mrs Harding was vexed beyond measure. A weak and unsuspecting Mr Fowle might easily be persuaded by such an enticement, thought she.

'Are you not the very best candidate, Mr Fitzroy?' said she. 'Indeed, was it not *your* brother's wish? Should you not have full management of the scheme yourself?'

Captain Blake looked to his friend for an answer. Mr Fitzroy gave a nod of approval, allowing Captain Blake leave to say, 'When the task is complete, our dear friend is to take holy orders.'

The Brinshore women were astounded at the disclosure. 'The Church?' said Mrs Harding.

'Yes, madam,' replied Mr Fitzroy.

Whispered Emma to Anne, 'Now comes out the true reason Mr Fitzroy's intended threw him over.'

'Shush,' said Anne. 'He will hear you.'

On discovering Mr Fitzroy's intentions, Emma's matrimonial expectations for Anne seemed hopelessly doomed until her cousin's reply gave her renewed hope. 'I think it a noble profession. After all, Grandpapa was a clergyman.'

'Then you would not mind it?' said Emma.

'Mind what?' Anne replied.

'Mr Fitzroy sermonising.'

'Why should I mind it, Emma? What is it to me?'

Emma was pleased to find that Anne would not turn down an offer from a clergyman, but she was, nevertheless, persuaded that her cousin must yet be worked on, for though it was as clear as day that Mr Fitzroy was meant for her, Anne had still to make the same discovery.

'He is quite as handsome as Captain Blake,' she whispered, 'which can only be a good thing.'

'Why so?' Anne replied. 'Clergymen are not vain as other men are.'

'Indeed they are!' said Emma. 'Some are among the worst offenders, though I doubt our friend is one of them. Observe the singularly careless way he wears his neck tie. One would think he dresses himself. But his flock will be slow to complain, for, according to Grandmamma, if there is something worth looking at on Sunday morning all else might be forgiven. Even long sermons. The more I think of it, the more I see that there could be no better candidate for the Church.'

A thought struck Emma that was both intriguing and practical; there could be no better scheme, nor any proposal more beneficial, or pleasing to so many, as the one that now occurred to her. She would write to her father directly proposing Mr Fitzroy as the new incumbent of Stanton. The proposal should not be widely known; she would keep it from Anne, and Aunt Harding should not be told, nor indeed should any word of it reach Mr Fitzroy himself until the matter be finally settled. Only when Anne is happily installed at Stanton Parsonage, thought she, shall I take full credit for the successful completion of my labours!

For some minutes Emma was distracted by the brilliance of her plan to secure the living of Stanton for Mr Fitzroy. When at last her attention was sought, the conversation had taken an interesting turn.

'What is your opinion of Mr Fowle?' enquired Mrs Blake. 'My dear Emma, has he attended you well?'

'He has indeed,' Emma replied. 'I can find no fault with Mr Fowle's medicinal expertise.'

Mrs Harding rearranged a stray lock of hair on her forehead. 'And what impression did you receive of Mr Fowle's domestic arrangements?' said she to Captain Blake in an almost casual tone of voice.

'Exceedingly comfortable. It seems to me, and to my dear friend here, that Mr Fowle is a physician through choice rather than necessity. He had the good fortune to inherit a large estate from his uncle.'

Mrs Harding enquired further. 'Has he a housekeeper and a full complement of servants?'

'It did not occur to us to count them,' Mr Fitzroy replied. 'If you mean to ask whether his house is clean and well ordered, the reply must be *yes*. For a single man he seems as well provided for as a married one.'

'And so there is no Mrs Fowle to care about? I mean, no Mrs Fowle to care about *him*,' Emma continued, ignoring her aunt's severe look.

Captain Blake and Mr Fitzroy were puzzled by her remark.

'To what end does your question tend?' said Mr Fitzroy.

'I meant only to observe,' said Emma, 'that a single man in possession of a good fortune —'

'Must be in want of a wife,' replied Mr Fitzroy and Anne in unison.

'No indeed,' protested Emma. 'A single man in possession of a good fortune is ever in want of an even greater one. But that is not my point. A single man in possession of a good fortune will never be in want of any number of single women, young or old, willing to share it with him.'

'Mr Fowle is rather old to be thinking of marriage,' said Mrs Harding, whose interest in Brinshore's celebrated physician had grown by degrees during the course of the conversation.

Emma was tempted to point out that Dr Harding was an older man than Mr Fowle when her aunt consented to be his wife. For the present, however, it sufficed that Aunt Harding had shown interest enough to establish the fact that Mr Fowle's assets were considerably more than she had at first imagined.

For the remainder of the morning, the plans for the gentlemen's scheme were rehearsed and scrutinised. Mrs Harding's enthusiasm for the venture grew all the more as it became clear that there was some hope that Brinshore might prove to possess certain qualities that Sanditon was without. Captain Blake was able to report that Mr Fowle had spoken of his reluctance to place Brinshore's old and infirm at the mercy of a less able physician and was therefore loath to leave the neighbourhood.

'Why should he be obliged to leave Brinshore at all?' said Anne. 'Sanditon is but a stone's throw away. What is three miles when such benefits are to be had?'

'Three miles of indifferent road, impassable in inclement weather,' said Mrs Harding. 'No. Mr Fowle must stay where he is. And if he is vital to the success of our dear friends' endeavour, then the scheme must come to him and not he to it. There would be uproar in Brinshore over Mr Fowle's departure.'

Mr Fitzroy explained some of the new treatments of which Mr Fowle had spoken, efficacious treatments that would benefit the health of all Brinshore's inhabitants as well as those unfortunates wounded in action in the service of their country.

'Mr Fowle's uncle contributed vastly to this very sphere of medical understanding. If Mr Fowle would give an undertaking to oversee this important work, I am sure success would be assured,' said Captain Blake.

'Oh dear,' said Mrs Blake. 'Mr Parker would be grieved indeed to hear you speak so, my dear. He has long wished to rob Brinshore of its celebrated physician.'

'Well,' said Mrs Harding, 'let him be sorely disappointed. Mr Fowle will stay where he is, if I have to see to it myself!'

CHAPTER FOURTEEN

Mrs Harding made it her business to call upon the leading families of the neighbourhood in the days that followed; her object was to place before them a vision for Brinshore's future. It mattered little that her intervention proceeded without first securing Mr Fitzroy or Captain Blake's approval. Many and varied were the opinions on matters pertaining to Brinshore's proposed elevation in the world. A populous largely comprising the frail and infirm was not to the liking of some, while others hailed it a means of stealing Sanditon's thunder.

Mrs Harding was more proficient in the art of persuasion than most, having perfected her talent through many years' practice upon her husband. Her view was that persuasion was always possible as long as there was sufficient inducement; and there was no better inducement among the ranks of Brinshore society than the promise of admittance to the first circles.

'Oh yes, my dear,' said Mrs Harding to one of Brinshore's old families beset by certain misgivings concerning the proposals for the town. 'My brother-in-law, Lord Osborne, is quite set on it and has vowed to spend a great deal of money to bring it about. And I hardly need mention the generous accommodation made in Captain Fitzroy's legacy. His elder brother, you know, the Earl of Allersham, is —'

It was on one such morning, while Emma was still confined to a seat by the drawing room window, that Mr Fitzroy called. Disappointed that the caller was not Captain Blake, Emma soon found reason to welcome his visit, for to have her future cousin to herself for half an hour provided Emma with the perfect opportunity to further Anne's cause.

Mr Fitzroy was surprised, on entering the room, to find Emma alone.

'Forgive me for not getting up,' said she. 'I am under the strictest of instructions. Mr Fowle is insufferably cautious, and had I made my objections known, I should not have heard the last of it from Aunt Harding.'

'Poor Mrs Harding,' said he. 'I see she has in her charge a most reluctant patient.'

'I can tolerate anything but fuss and lectures,' said Emma.

Mr Fitzroy had in his hand three volumes which he placed on the table beside her. Emma afforded the volumes a cursory glance but showed no curiosity as to their content or purpose.

'I did not expect to find you alone,' said he.

'My aunt has taken it upon herself to rally support for Brinshore and Mr Fowle.'

'And you have certain misgivings,' said he.

'I am fond of Brinshore and I have no doubt that this scheme of yours, or indeed the plan for the new circulating library, would greatly enhance the town's appeal, but Aunt Harding's fervour is relentless. I am sure I should have no complaints whatsoever were I to procure one hour's rest in a day from the name *Brinshore*.'

'And does your cousin take the same view of the matter?' he asked.

Emma sat up smartly, encouraged by Mr Fitzroy's enquiry. It was proof indeed of his attachment to Anne.

'Dear Anne,' she replied. 'My cousin never complains. She has the sweetest temperament of anyone I know.' The interview, thought she, would likely be less uphill than anticipated.

'Please,' said she, pointing to an empty chair.

Mr Fitzroy made himself comfortable after removing an object from beneath a cushion.

'Ah,' said she. 'How remiss of me. It is Anne's. She has entrusted it to me for the time being. A spy glass is a useful object and provides hours of diversion.'

'I see,' said Mr Fitzroy.

'For what else is there to do all day? I must have some amusement,' Emma replied. 'It was so very kind of Anne to allow me the use of it.'

Mr Fitzroy smiled. 'And is Miss Musgrave in good health?'

Once again, Emma was heartened that his enquiry should be of her cousin. What surer sign could there be of a growing attachment on his part. 'Indeed she is. Dear, dear Anne. My cousin is quite remarkable. Anne is superior in every way to anyone I know. I wish I had her character and her constancy. Aunt Harding cannot do without her. As a niece, and I may say, as a cousin, she is the model of patience and kindness. Anne is excellence itself. Delham's loss is Brinshore's gain.'

'Praise indeed,' said he.

Emma's fulsome commendation of her cousin's qualities was immediately understood; Mr Fitzroy saw that he had been singled out by Emma as a suitor for Anne. He sat for some moments without uttering a word.

Satisfied that his silent musings were the surest sign yet of his affection for her cousin, Emma was content to allow the silence to express what words could not.

Presently, Mr Fitzroy picked up the spy glass to examine it more closely. Yes! Yes! thought Emma. What further evidence is needed! He must indeed love her, for he cannot put aside that which belongs to her!

Emma observed her visitor more closely as she allowed him time to contemplate her cousin's virtues: the cut of his coat and hair, his fine profile, the speck of dust on the sleeve of his jacket. But, eager as she might be to further her cousin's cause, Emma was also impatient to hear news of Captain Blake, and found it impossible to remain silent for long.

'Captain Blake regrets that he is unable to wait upon Mrs Harding this morning,' Mr Fitzroy replied. 'It appears that news has already reached Mr Parker of our proposed scheme. I understand that at this very moment Mr Parker is making as strong a case for Sanditon as his indifferent constitution will allow.'

'And why did you not accompany Captain Blake and make the case for Brinshore?'

'I make the case for neither. Both have merit,' he replied. 'Captain Blake took possession of the architect's plans late yesterday afternoon. Mr Fowle asked to see them at the earliest opportunity, hence the purpose of my visit to Brinshore. Your excellent friends insisted I call at Trafalgar Terrace to convey their good wishes. They are, as ever, anxious for news of you.'

It was not the answer Emma had wished for or anticipated. Still, thought she, a lover at first is often obliged by discretion and propriety to disguise the true nature of his actions and intentions.

'And so you called at Trafalgar Terrace for this purpose alone?' she continued.

'I had no desire to disoblige my friend,' said he.

'Well, now it seems you have fulfilled your obligation. Please inform Mrs Blake that I am quite well,' said Emma. 'And may I say, it is hardly gallant to describe one's visit as an *obligation*. Are you certain you no had other purpose in mind? What shall I say to Anne?' said she and, in haste, added, 'Or Mrs Harding?'

Mr Fitzroy chose not to reply. He took up one of the volumes he had placed on the table and offered it to her. 'You must require a little something more to do while you wait for your ankle to mend,' said he.

'You do not approve of idleness. You think it a sin, I suppose,' said she. Emma was taken by surprise and not entirely pleased by the offering. She perused the title on the cover of the first volume but made no attempt to open the book to ascertain its contents.

'*Pride and Prejudice?*' said she.

'Are you acquainted with it? Yesterday, at first I thought you had it in your sights when you alluded to single men of good fortune. I may have been mistaken there.'

Emma smiled. Yes, Mr Fitzroy! thought she. I comprehend your aim entirely. You foist such volumes upon me but in truth you mean them for Anne, for you know how she delights in drear, lofty tomes. Emma inspected the cover again before placing the volume aside. 'Thank you, Mr Fitzroy. It is the very thing to enthral and delight my cousin. There is no greater reader than Anne.'

'I have no doubt. Though I suspect Miss Musgrave is already familiar with the work,' said he. 'But tell me, Miss Osborne, how do you occupy your day?'

'If you mean do I embroider and darn — rarely. I am far more agreeably employed. I observe Brinshore through the lens of my cousin's spyglass. And how fascinating it is! The whole world in miniature is captured through the lens of a spyglass! And Brinshore is quite a revelation.'

Once again, Mr Fitzroy picked up the object in question and examined it.

Emma continued. 'Then, I take luncheon with my aunt and cousin and listen to the gossip of the day. On occasion I have the greatest good luck to receive callers of my own. At such times I spend the best part of the morning in idle conversation. So you see, I have no time for reading.'

He placed the spyglass on the table beside the discarded volumes of *Pride and Prejudice*.

'You disapprove,' said she, observing the look on his face.

'I neither approve nor disapprove,' said he.

'As a clergyman, will you not be required to spend your life approving and disapproving of everything and everyone you see? But your disapproval does not frighten me.'

Mr Fitzroy smiled. 'You have shown that you are fearless, and exercise little caution for your own sake. You speak your mind and care little what others think of you.'

'I cannot tell whether you mean to censure or to praise,' said Emma.

'To caution,' he continued. 'Your time might be spent more profitably than this. Spying on others, however innocent the intent, is a pursuit more likely to yield adverse, rather than beneficial, consequences.'

'I cannot agree, Mr Fitzroy. It is excessively entertaining.'

'For the present, perhaps. But one day you may, by accident, catch sight of that which you do not wish to see. Worse than this, you may mistakenly perceive something to be the case when it is not.'

Vexed by Mr Fitzroy's curious observation, Emma replied, 'That is a risk I am willing to take most happily. Why is it that men always seek to shield women from the world? Indeed, why should a woman's conduct be regulated by a man's notion of what is and is not good for her? Why should she not decide the matter herself? Churchmen are among the worst creatures of all for ordering the world according to their decrees.'

'Forgive me, Miss Osborne. You asked me to be candid. I took you at your word. But I see that you did not mean it, and I have upset you.'

'I am vexed by the world in which I live, Mr Fitzroy. As a man, you are but a part of that world.'

'I have no quarrel with you,' he replied. 'The case you put forward is, in my estimation at least, irrefutable.'

Mr Fitzroy got up to take his leave. Emma knew not what to make of his speech, and though he had indeed vexed her greatly, she could not remain angry with him for long.

She looked out of the window and sighed heavily. 'Then shall you take back your book of sermons?'

'Book of *sermons*?' said he, endeavouring to suppress a smile.

'Moral treatises then,' said she. Emma pointed to the volumes on the table.

He laughed and shook his head. 'I think not. Keep them. They may well be of use for pressing flowers or propping open a door. Do with them what you will.'

Mr Fitzroy's visit had left Emma perturbed and confused. He had irked her, it was true; but his curious reaction to her outburst was quite unexpected. He appeared neither affronted nor wounded by it. His demeanour was, for the most part, gracious; indeed, at the end, he even appeared to find some good-humoured amusement at her expense.

Mrs Harding and Anne returned within an hour of Mr Fitzroy's departure and both expressed regret that they had not been there to receive him. Emma relayed something of the conversation that had passed between them.

'How unfortunate that I should have missed him. Why did you not urge him to stay for half an hour longer?' said Mrs Harding.

'I expect he had more important things to attend to. Though, I suppose, I may have driven him away,' said she. 'I have no use for his sermonising. He left these,' said she, pointing to the volumes on the table.

'Oh!' replied Anne eagerly.

'A dreary discourse on the evils of pride and prejudice.'

'*Pride and Prejudice*?' said Anne. 'Are you sure?'

'You can, yourself, be a little prejudiced at times, my dear, where Mr Fitzroy is concerned,' said Mrs Harding. 'Do you recall when you first encountered him? You thought him quite uncivil.'

'And so he was,' Emma replied. 'And is still. He came to Brinshore, or so he says, with the express intention of visiting Mr Fowle. He had no scruple in admitting that it was Mrs Blake who had made a point of his calling at Trafalgar Terrace. And yet, he brought with him three volumes of sermons. He is of the opinion that I have nothing better to do than to benefit from their instruction while I sit committing the sin of idleness all day long.'

'Were those his precise words, my dear?' asked Mrs Harding.

'Not exactly, but that was his exact meaning. Quite honestly, I am not persuaded that Mr Fitzroy improves on better acquaintance. I cannot work him out at all.'

'I am sure he meant well,' continued Mrs Harding, half listening to Emma's reply. 'Is it Mr Fordyce's work?'

Emma shrugged her shoulders.

'I am not a stranger to Mr Fordyce, you know,' her aunt went on. 'Dr Harding was one of his greatest admirers. Though Mr Fitzroy seems to me something of a free spirit. I wonder if he has been beguiled by the Methodists. It would not be a surprise to me to find that those very volumes issue from the pen of one or other of the Wesleys. Dr Harding was once acquainted with a Methodist, and on one occasion invited him to dinner at the parsonage in Chichester,' said Mrs Harding.

At last, Anne, bemused by the conversation between her aunt and her cousin, said, '*Pride and Prejudice* is a novel. It is neither from the pen of Mr Fordyce nor one of the Wesleys. Have you not read *Sense and Sensibility*, Emma?'

'I have a vague recollection of something of the kind,' Emma replied falsely, unwilling to parade her ignorance before her cousin.

'*Pride and Prejudice* is by the very same author. Written by a lady,' said Anne. She opened the first volume and read, '*It is a truth universally acknowledged, that a single man in possession of a good fortune must be in want of a wife.*'

'Only a silly woman would write such nonsense,' Emma replied. 'And what of women? Is it not a universal truth that a single woman in possession of a good fortune must also be in want of a husband? I think not. She should better stay single and not give her fortune away. Therein lies the difference. For she can have no control of her husband's fortune, though he may take every penny of hers.'

'You mistake the author's intention completely,' said Anne. 'The statement is an irony. And were you to read on, you might find that the author is not so silly after all. I cannot believe you thought *Pride and Prejudice* a book of sermons! How diverting for Mr Fitzroy!'

Emma could not have been more painfully aware of her own ignorance. It mattered little that Mr Fitzroy should find her so patently ill-informed; it mattered greatly, however, that Captain Blake should think so. Her imagination ran to the likely course of the conversation in Waterloo Crescent that evening at dinner. Would all her friends find the episode as diverting as Anne professed it to be? Would Mr Fitzroy provide his own embellishments to the story to create even greater amusement? What would Captain Blake think of her?

Her sensibilities wounded, there was only one course of action open to her. After dinner, Emma took up the first volume and began to read.

Mrs Harding, seeing that Emma had claimed the volume for her private enjoyment, said, 'Emma, my dear, do not keep it to yourself. Anne and I have a great desire to hear *Pride and Prejudice*. For though I have not read it myself, Anne insists it is full of wit and charm. It promises to be superior in every particular to anything proceeding from the pen of Mr Fordyce. Shall you not read to us aloud?' said Mrs Harding. 'I should dearly like to hear it.'

'And I. Please do read to us, Emma,' said Anne.

A little put out that it would slow her progress, Emma sighed and started to read from the beginning. The evening passed more quickly and more pleasantly than she had anticipated. One chapter followed another; and never had her listeners been more attentive or more alert. By the end of chapter six the fatigue in her cousin's voice caused Anne to offer to read on. Another three chapters were completed before Mrs Harding suggested that it was time to leave Jane and Elizabeth Bennet at Netherfield Hall and ponder Mr Darcy's observation that a young lady's accomplishments must include the *improvement of her mind by extensive reading*.

With reluctance, Anne put the volume aside and bid goodnight to her aunt and cousin.

'I have something I wish to say to your cousin,' said Mrs Harding, placing a lighted candlestick into Anne's hand. 'Off with you,' said she. Curiously, Mrs Harding did not ring for Payne, but insisted on helping Emma to her room.

'If it is about the spyglass, Aunt,' said Emma, when they were quite alone, 'I have already received a reprimand from Mr Fitzroy.'

'Spyglass? What has a spyglass got to do with anything? No, my dear. I am grieved by what you tell me of Mr Parker,' said she. 'In truth, I have had not a moment's peace about it. The very thought of the man is enough to bring on one of my seizures.'

'I do not understand,' Emma replied.

'Should Mr Parker succeed in persuading our dear friends that Sanditon's claim is the greater, Brinshore might lose Mr Fowle altogether. I have no doubt that, despite his being a leading authority on the medicinal properties of water, Mr Fowle is as susceptible to persuasion as any man. Emma, I shall send for Mr Fowle tomorrow morning, for you will find on waking that your ankle is a little worse and in need of Mr Fowle's attention. Do not let me down, my dear.'

'Really, Aunt,' Emma replied. 'I expect Mr Fowle would attend you immediately without any pretence whatsoever, should you wish it.'

'No good comes of showing oneself too keen for the company of —' she broke off.

'Of the man you intend to marry?' Emma added playfully.

'What nonsense! My dear, I do not know where these notions of yours come from!'

Although the hour was later than usual, Emma was unable to sleep. Her mind was full of Mr Bingley and Jane Bennet. They are so clearly in love! But will Mr Bingley's sisters approve the match? And that obnoxious Mr Darcy! Jane is too mild; only Elizabeth Bennet has spirit and daring enough to put him in his place.

Her mind would not be quieted; and Emma, finding it impossible to sleep until she ascertained to her satisfaction that each character was accorded his or her just deserts, was determined to read on. She waited until the house fell silent and hobbled to the door.

A candle burned in the hall, providing just enough light for her to see her way to the stairs. She stood on the landing and, taking one step at a time, slowly and quietly descended the stairs. Having retrieved the volumes without a sound, she climbed the stairs in a similar manner until she reached the door of her bedchamber. As she opened the door, the volumes slipped out of her hands and tumbled down the top flight causing a clatter throughout the house. But for Payne, who had been wakened by the noise, the house did not stir.

'Would you bring me a candle or two?' whispered Emma, as Payne helped her back into bed. After several minutes, and with only a slight look of disapproval, Payne returned and lit a fresh candle. When Emma was quite alone again, she opened the volume at the place where Anne had left off, and read, '*Elizabeth passed the chief of the night in her sister's room…*'

CHAPTER FIFTEEN

The purchase of a new landau and pair of greys was anticipated with great delight by the women of the Dower House. Mr Musgrave, having parted with the curricle that had given Mrs Musgrave cause for constant unease each time he had been at the reins of it, was much impressed by the style and practicality of the carriage maker's model.

'Wind-down windows — convertible roof — finest leather — suitable for all weathers — winter — summer — solid perch — well sprung. I have a mind to purchase it myself. It is all very well having a fine conveyance such as this left to perish at the Dower House for want of use, but it far exceeds their needs. I am not persuaded that a landau will be made use of half as often as a smaller coach. I daresay a landaulet would be a perfectly acceptable alternative. Indeed, I doubt they would know the difference. A comfortable seat, upholstery to match their favourite apparel, safe, slow, and sprung to guarantee a smooth ride is all that ladies care about.'

Lord Osborne was similarly impressed by the design and sturdy construction. 'It is eminently practical. I purchased one in ninety-eight but let it go a year later. Lowford paid handsomely for it. Said he had seen nothing finer in the whole of Surrey. I believe he still has possession of it. I'm minded to take it off his hands for a fair price if I can persuade him to part with it.'

'I remember it. A first-rate contraption. Lowford would be a fool to part with it now.'

'The roof will likely require new leather,' Osborne mused. 'He may not want the trouble of replacing it.'

The conversation continued in the same manner for an additional hour as Osborne and Musgrave, convinced that nothing less than a full inspection of every vehicle in the carriage maker's possession was required, gazed approvingly at the collection on display.

Lady Osborne and Mrs Musgrave had been awaiting their return and had already taken their tea with the Dowager and Mrs Turner, for they could wait no longer.

When the pair at last made an appearance, Musgrave said in his defence, 'A purchase such as this cannot be rushed. It is often said, *Purchase in haste, repent at leisure.* There can be no truer saying.'

Mrs Musgrave cast a glance of playful exasperation at her husband. 'I believe you will find the exact rendition to be *marry in haste, repent at leisure.*'

'Well, my dear,' said he, 'You are the last person to whom that maxim can be reasonably applied.'

The Dowager and Mrs Turner were unable to suppress their mirth at so droll a retort, and laughed heartily at the pair until Mrs Musgrave replied, 'I hope the outcome of your morning's work meets with everyone's satisfaction, for it has taken long enough.'

'The choice of a conveyance is an important matter. I do not expect you to understand, my dear,' he replied. 'You may choose a yard of lace in an instant if you have a mind to — though I have never known such lengthy deliberations than those that take place at Mason's over a pair of wool stockings or a piece of ribbon. The purchase of a carriage is a considerable undertaking. It is not just the look of the thing that matters. Indeed,' said he, turning to the Dowager and Mrs Turner, 'after careful consideration, I am of the view, and I believe His Lordship concurs, that a landaulet is eminently more suitable for the purpose you have in mind than something as unwieldy as a landau. The moment I entered the place, a very handsome landaulet caught my eye, and I have talked of nothing else since. Smart, serviceable, elegant, convenient, adaptable, with red leather interior to match —'

'A landaulet?' cried the Dowager. 'I think not, sir! I have not seen fit to tolerate the company of Mrs Turner these past four months for such paltry recompense as this! No, indeed!'

'Nor I,' agreed Mrs Turner, joining the chorus of protest. 'I have endured a dinner table the like of which it is impossible to describe. My poor dear cook! Dear Hedges! I have, without complaint, swallowed every mouthful of every dish put in front of me. You know not how my digestion has suffered!'

'Indeed it has suffered, Mrs Turner. It has suffered from the number of additional portions to which you regularly help yourself,' replied the Dowager. Turning to her son, she went on, 'And what would our neighbours say?'

'Exactly so. It is known throughout the neighbourhood that we are to take possession of a landau,' said Mrs Turner.

'Lowford Park, Croydon, even Brinshore all know of it,' added the Dowager.

'To be seen riding about here and there in a, a —'

'— puny contraption half the size of a tea chest! It is unthinkable!'

Protests against the replacement of a landau for a less commodious landaulet continued for a full ten minutes until Mrs Musgrave succeeded in making her voice heard. 'A landaulet possesses four wheels, not two. Am I correct, my dear?'

'Indeed, you are,' Mr Musgrave replied, impressed by his wife's knowledge.

Mrs Musgrave smiled at her husband. 'Then if *your* heart is set on a landaulet, as you appear to profess, I should have no objection to owning one. My dear, from everything you have said, a landaulet would seem to be infinitely superior to a vehicle possessed of only two wheels. Buy the landaulet if you will, for it is much better suited to our needs.'

Mr Musgrave looked with alarm at Lord Osborne.

'But,' continued she, 'I am of the view that a promise is a promise. The Dower House was promised a landau, and a landau it should have.'

Lady Osborne agreed. 'Bravo, my dear sister! I am in complete agreement. There are conveyances here at the Castle that never see the light of day and might well be disposed of. I should be happy to have the use of a landaulet myself. But I too believe a landau will serve the Dower House perfectly.'

Lord Osborne returned Musgrave's look of alarm as all four women declared the case made and won.

'But, my dear,' said Lord Osborne, mounting a final challenge to the prevailing view, 'when a more advantageous solution presents itself, should we not consider its merits?'

'More advantageous to whom, my dear?' replied Lady Osborne.

The Dowager and Mrs Turner, triumphant for having succeeded in their undertaking, were wholly content to let the matter rest. The voices of Lady Osborne and Mrs Musgrave raised in support of their plea ensured that no more needed to be said on the subject. Consequently, the women of the Dower House had now only to await, with pleasant anticipation, the arrival of their new landau.

Mrs Musgrave was anxious to introduce a new subject, one of which she had been curious to hear more the moment she received news from Anne. 'What think you of Emma's courageous deed? I understand it is spoken of endlessly in Brinshore and beyond. Sanditon speaks of nothing else,' said she.

It was evident from the looks that passed between Lord and Lady Osborne that they had no knowledge of the incident to which Mrs Musgrave referred. 'Have I spoken out of turn? Perhaps you have not yet heard. I had it from Anne yesterday, in a letter in the afternoon post.'

'Emma?' said Lady Osborne, nonplussed.

'A courageous deed?' added Lord Osborne.

Mrs Musgrave related the facts — how Emma had rescued a small boy from drowning — as accurately as Anne had described them.

Shock, concern and pride were among the sensations felt by Lord and Lady Osborne on hearing of their daughter's act of courage. Even so, they were mystified by Emma's silence on the subject.

'A nasty sprain to the ankle you say? There was no mention of the incident three days ago,' said Lady Osborne.

'Perhaps Mrs Harding is preoccupied with other matters,' replied His Lordship.

'What matter could be of greater import to me? I worry about Emma constantly. My dear, I believe I should go to her.'

'She would not thank you for it,' her husband replied.

'It is not thanks that I seek. I want to see for myself. I want to know that my daughter is well. And now that Frank is much recovered I am quite content to leave him to the care of his nanny.'

The Dowager and Mrs Turner, and Mrs Musgrave all offered themselves as guardians of little Frank for the duration of his mother's absence.

'I do not doubt that Frank will have more attention than is good for him,' said Lady Osborne.

The conversation then turned once again to Brinshore and the scheme proposed by Mr Fitzroy and Captain Blake.

'I expect you are acquainted with the particulars of Captain Fitzroy's legacy,' said Mrs Musgrave, addressing herself to Lord and Lady Osborne. 'Anne writes of the tussles between Sanditon and Brinshore by the interested parties.'

'Is this the proposal for some kind of institution for the convalescence of the wounded and infirm?' said Lord Osborne.

'Dear Charles,' said Lady Osborne. 'He hinted as much when last we met. I believe Sanditon was in his sights, but it seems Brinshore has the added advantage of a physician.'

'Nothing yet is settled,' said Lord Osborne.

'I hear,' said the Dowager, looking at her son, 'that you have put yourself forward as one of the leading benefactors of Brinshore's new circulating library. Have you plans to improve Delham's offering?'

'I have given much thought to it,' he replied. 'Both are worthy, and both shall have the support of this estate.'

'Splendid,' said Mrs Turner. 'I once visited a circulating library in Bath on my late husband's recommendation. And I have no objection to visiting another.'

'Nor I,' said the Dowager, 'as long as one is not required to read a book. There are any number of books in Osborne's collection that have never seen the light of day. I daresay Brinshore's circulating library will enjoy an abundance of subscriptions, for there appears to be nothing else to do there but admire the sea. And when once one has admired it, what else is there to speak of.'

CHAPTER SIXTEEN

The day of the Brinshore Ball brought much excitement to Trafalgar Terrace. The morning was spent in tireless deliberation over the selection of gowns, accompanying accoutrements, and the best way to dress hair. Emma had chosen a pair of pale blue silk shoes to complement her gown, but quickly discarded them for a sturdier pair, her ankle being too weak to be left unsupported. The swelling had reduced to almost nothing, but her attempts to dance a step or two within the confines of her room brought her to the realisation that the weakness in her ankle might require more gradual rehabilitation. Still, she persevered; for standing up with Captain Blake for ten minutes was worth the sacrifice when faced with the prospect of an evening spent sitting down with widows, spinsters and chaperones.

When Payne had completed her work, Anne and Emma examined the results of her labours in the looking glass.

'I have a mind to dance one dance at least,' said Emma.

Agitated by Emma's declaration, Anne replied, 'Is it advisable? What does Mr Fowle say?'

'Mr Fowle may say what he pleases. He said a great deal to Aunt Harding yesterday when he attended me. And Aunt Harding said a great deal more back to him. It is all exceedingly tiresome. Mr Fowle will not dare to take himself off to Sanditon now. I should not be surprised if Aunt Harding dances with him, for she knows what she must do to get her own way.'

'Emma,' replied Anne, 'you must take care not to dance too soon and make your ankle worse.'

'One dance, I am sure, is not beyond me. Captain Blake will agree. I am certain of it.'

The change in Anne's countenance caused Emma to offer reassurance. 'I shall take every care. I promise.'

Anne looked anxiously at her cousin. 'Dear Emma, I am engaged to Captain Blake for the first two dances. Had I, or indeed had our friend, known of your intention to dance, I am certain he should not have applied to me.'

'Engaged to Captain Blake?' said Emma, taken aback by the disclosure.

'Mr Fowle was quite insistent two days ago that you should not dance. We understood that there was no prospect of your dancing at all.'

Crushed by Anne's news, Emma did all in her power to disguise her disappointment. 'I see,' said she. 'Of course. How stupid of me.'

Anne was not insensible of Emma's attachment to Captain Blake but had found it impossible to refuse him for fear of giving offence. Perceiving that the matter was certain to cause her cousin pain, she added quickly, 'I shall speak to him for I am sure it would give Captain Blake no greater pleasure than to stand up with you. I might dance with him later on, or perhaps on another occasion.'

'No,' replied Emma. 'I see how it is. You have given your word. It is perfectly reasonable that he should apply to you. I should not take pleasure in a dance that placed Captain Blake under an obligation to me. Indeed, on reflection, I do not believe I am quite ready to dance at all.'

'My mind is made up,' said Anne. 'I shall not stand up with him. Indeed, I shall not stand up at all. We shall have a famous time sitting out every dance, for there will be much to observe and laugh at.'

'That would never do,' replied Emma. 'There would be an outcry if you did such a thing, and my voice would be the loudest.'

Emma endeavoured to appear sanguine despite her disappointment. The pleasure of opening the ball with Charles Blake was not to be hers, and there was nothing more to be said or done about it.

There were reasons, perhaps not many, to raise her spirits. It was not unreasonable to suppose that Captain Blake would sit with her at some point during the course of the evening; thus, for a short while at least, she would have him entirely to herself.

Then there was the promising spectacle of Mr Fowle and his pursuit of Aunt Harding; the chance to watch the eager physician chase her aunt around the ballroom was a scene not to be missed. Indeed, Emma had reason to suppose that his advances would not be altogether unwelcome, for one afternoon, while Aunt Harding had thought her niece fast asleep, Emma had observed her aunt through the corner of her eye, practising the steps of a country dance.

Even the opportunity of a brief exchange with Mr Fitzroy during the course of the evening was not wholly displeasing to Emma. *Pride and Prejudice* was not the book of sermons she had supposed it to be, nor was it one of those gothic novels she had lately grown out of. None of the novels she had read previously had expressed half so well the very attitudes and preoccupations of the society she knew intimately, nor with such amusing observations.

Still, the matter of utmost concern was the fact that Captain Blake had engaged Anne for the first two dances; and though she could not quite say that they had purposely concealed it from her, she had been left wounded by it.

The Sanditon party was expected to arrive in time for dinner. Mrs Harding, on hearing the approach of a carriage, watched out of the window as the vehicle came to a halt outside Trafalgar Terrace.

'Impossible!' said she, as the passengers alighted.

'What is it, Aunt?' said Emma anxiously.

Moving towards the window to look out, Anne replied, 'Your mama is come!'

'That cannot be. She made no mention of it in her letter to me.' How very vexing! thought Emma. 'And is Papa among the party?'

'It does not appear so,' said Mrs Harding.

The presence of Lady Osborne among the Sanditon party astonished them all. Mrs Harding was delighted by her sister's appearance at that moment, for it proffered the perfect opportunity to flaunt her connections before the whole of Brinshore.

'Mama,' said Emma, 'why did you not say you were coming?'

'I wanted to surprise you,' her mother replied.

'And Papa did not travel with you?'

'Your papa could not be spared.'

'And what of Frank?'

'He is quite well. Have no care, Emma. Frank will be indulged and spoilt in my absence. Your grandmamma will see to it that nothing is spared on his account.'

'Will you stay long, Mama?'

'Long enough to see that my daughter is quite recovered from the injury she neglected to mention to me in her last letter.'

Any expectation that Emma had entertained for a pleasant ball now seemed unlikely. She would be obliged to spend the entire evening in the company of her mama; few young women, in anticipation of a ball, were inclined to regard such a prospect as anything but unfortunate.

Emma would not dance. The combined chorus of protest from Mrs Harding, Mr Fowle and her mother at any attempt to do so was sure to carry the day.

Captain Blake, with the greatest sincerity, expressed his disappointment at being denied the honour of dancing with Emma, and though it pleased her that he made a point of saying so, Emma knew that her own disappointment was the greater. He would dance with Anne; and he would dance with other young women to whom introductions were requested and made; consequently, in Emma's estimation, his enjoyment of the ball would not be much diminished.

For his part, Captain Blake was determined to enjoy the assembly, for his good humour never faltered; and though it was a quality that did him merit, it provided little indication as to the true state of his feelings. Emma pitied the young women who might throw themselves into his path; a young woman might easily be persuaded to believe him in love with her, for it was his nature to make everyone feel important.

The deference extended to the Trafalgar Terrace party was especially pleasing to Mrs Harding. By the time the master of ceremonies had seen the party to their seats, Mr Fowle had stationed himself by Mrs Harding's side looking every inch the gentleman in his new jacket and necktie. The physician bowed graciously as Mrs Harding introduced him to her sister.

Emma was disappointed to find herself separated from Captain Blake so early on due to Mr Fowle's interference. Having secured Mrs Harding for two dances, keen to please, the physician drew Captain Blake's attention to the presence of the family of a deceased naval officer who sought an introduction.

Mr Fitzroy seated himself beside Emma. Said he, 'Are you come to dance or to quiz?'

'Neither. I am expected to follow Mr Fowle's orders. He would not fuss over men in such a way. I am sure he thinks women's ailments slower to heal. It seems I am not to dance. Nor am I able to quiz my way through the evening for I do not possess a quizzing glass. Indeed, I dislike the practice.'

Mr Fitzroy smiled.

140

'What is it that you find so amusing?' Emma replied.

'I could not possibly say,' said he.

'Ah! I see. You think me contrary because I have no compunction in deriving pleasure by means of the quite innocent activity of observing the world through a spyglass.'

'We are all contrary creatures, Miss Osborne.'

'No one more so than my aunt, Mr Fitzroy!' Emma replied. 'I cannot make out whether Aunt Harding means to encourage or deter Mr Fowle. She protests that nothing is further from her mind, and yet look at her now!'

The opening bars of a country dance brought couples to the floor. Captain Blake led the way with Anne, while Mr Fowle followed with Mrs Harding.

'Come,' said Mr Fitzroy. 'You are not as weak as you imagine. Take my hand. I shall not let you come to harm.'

Emma looked at her mother and Mrs Blake. The two women were so deep in conversation that every movement around them seemed to escape their notice. Nothing but Emma's own misgivings could now prevent her from dancing.

'Very well. But if I *should* come to harm —'

'The greatest danger in a ballroom, Miss Osborne, is to one's feelings, not to one's feet.' Mr Fitzroy relented a little as Emma stood up unsteadily. 'Lean on my arm. You have nothing to fear.'

They waited until the set started by Mr Fowle and Mrs Harding was complete before taking to the floor. Emma was pleased to find that despite some initial discomfort, she was able to complete two dances before finding it necessary to sit down.

'Bravo, Emma!' said Captain Blake on seeing her dance down the set.

Anne was delighted to see the transformation in her cousin. 'Do not let Mr Fowle see you!'

'Mr Fowle is far too preoccupied at present to notice me,' replied Emma.

Lady Osborne and Mrs Blake at first seemed unconvinced of the wisdom of Emma's actions, but their fears were allayed when they saw that no harm had befallen her.

'You see, Miss Osborne,' said Mr Fitzroy, 'a little exercise is a fine thing for a sprained ankle. You quite forgot your discomfort on the floor.'

'Indeed I did. That is, until you trod on my good toe. May I ask? Is Mr Collins your model of behaviour in a ballroom?'

'Mr Collins? Ah. I see. The book of sermons.'

'I suppose you found my ignorance diverting.'

'Exceedingly so.'

'But to allow me to continue in my ignorance!' replied Emma. 'How could you do such a thing?'

'Can you forgive me?' he asked.

'I very much doubt it, Mr Fitzroy.'

'Nor should you,' said he. 'Have you completed all three volumes?'

'I have.'

'And have you formed an opinion of the piece?'

'I have,' said she. 'That Surrey, not Hertfordshire must be the neighbourhood the author describes. I can think of no less than three Mrs Bennets, a Mr Bennet or two, Jane Bennet — that would be Anne, two Mr Wickhams at least, and one Lady Catherine De Burgh. Lady Catherine reminds me of Grandmamma without high spirits. But we have yet to secure our own Mr Collins.'

'I wish you luck with that enterprise.'

'Do you?' said she. 'Luck always seems to elude me.'

'You have more luck than anyone I know,' he replied.

Emma was greatly puzzled by his comment. 'You do not know me.'

'Your situation in life is the greatest good luck,' said he.

'No, Mr Fitzroy. To find happiness is the greatest good luck.'

'It is not easily achieved, Miss Osborne. But to allow happiness to find you — that is something that requires patience, trust and acceptance.'

'Fine words,' Emma replied. 'But I cannot agree. Surely we must strive to create our own happiness.'

'But we often look for it in the wrong places. Happiness should not be our purpose in life.'

'Then what?' she asked.

'Service to others provides us with the best hope of achieving happiness in the end,' said he.

'You are right. We are all contrary creatures, Mr Fitzroy. And you are the best example. In one breath you speak of high ideals, in the other you find pleasure in laughing at me.'

'I cannot argue with you. I am flawed beyond compare,' said he, without artifice.

The dance ended. Emma, curious to understand his meaning, studied his face, but made no reply.

Mr Fitzroy led Emma back to her seat and into the care of Lady Osborne and Mrs Harding.

'Dancing? Against Mr Fowle's express orders?' said Mrs Harding, still breathless from her own exertion.

'Dear sister, no harm was done. Indeed, I think it did Emma good to stand up,' said Lady Osborne. Turning to her daughter, she added, 'You seemed to find that young man's conversation fascinating.'

'Have no fear, Mama,' Emma replied. 'He is not at all fascinating to me. Mr Fitzroy has a view on everything and is persuaded of the notion that everyone is eager to hear it. The Church will suit him very well if indeed he succeeds in conquering those defects in his own nature that show little promise at present. He teases me relentlessly, Mama. I am but an object of amusement to him!'

'My goodness!' said Lady Osborne, amused by her daughter's estimation of Mr Fitzroy. With a hint of irony in her voice, she continued, 'I have misjudged him completely. I thought him a rather fine, intriguing young man.'

Mrs Harding surveyed the room for sight of Mr Fowle. To her surprise, he was standing behind her, his face damp and scarlet from the heat. Eager to claim her hand once again, he offered his, and said, 'Madam, you do me the greatest honour.'

Emma looked on as a new set formed. It pleased her greatly to watch Anne partner Mr Fitzroy in the quadrille. Now, thought she, is the moment that destiny conspires with good sense to secure their mutual happiness! There could be no outcome more longed for, nor one designed to procure the approval of so many than an alliance between Miss Musgrave and Mr Fitzroy, thought she. The couple were all smiles, and anyone observing their demeanour must have arrived at the same conclusion: Anne Musgrave and Henry Fitzroy were almost half in love.

The second couple to join the set was Mr Fowle and Mrs Harding. Remarkably, Mr Fowle appeared to have acquired a more assured gait of which Mrs Harding seemed to approve. In turn, her aunt appeared to have lowered her guard; a strange mellow charm and affability, attributes that did not often characterise her aunt, gave Emma the impression that a match between the two was not quite as absurd as it appeared a week ago.

Captain Blake took his leave of a group of gentlemen with whom he had been conversing and moved towards Emma.

'My dear Emma, shall you dance again this evening, or are you quite done for?' said he.

'There is nothing in the world I should like more than to dance at this moment,' she replied.

In an instant, he helped Emma to her feet as the music commenced. 'Look at Mr Fitzroy and Anne! Anne has never looked happier! Let us stand by them for there is still room.'

Captain Blake was a little taken aback but duly agreed to Emma's request.

'I pity the person who takes no pleasure in a ball,' said Emma. 'I pity Papa. He dances rarely and only to please Mama. Poor Mama! She so loves to dance.'

'Then perhaps it is your Mama who deserves our pity,' said he.

In her eagerness to partner Captain Blake in the quadrille, Emma cast caution aside and hastened to where Mr Fitzroy and her cousin were standing. A step or two more would have brought her safely into position had it not been for an offending snuff box that had carelessly slipped out of its owner's hand and onto the floor. Emma inadvertently stood on it, causing her to slip and stumble, and her injured ankle to twist once again. Captain Blake acted swiftly; placing his arm around Emma's waist, he lifted her with ease and carried her back to her chair.

The dismay she felt on being deprived of dancing with Captain Blake was great indeed, and never more so than at that moment; and though there was little to quell the disappointment of an opportunity missed, she was comforted by the recollection of his gallant action. He had carried her in his arms! Her own dear Captain Blake! He had not carried her in his arms since she was ten years old when she fell off her horse!

Amid the confusion, Emma thought only of him. 'Mama, will you not dance? Captain Blake is in want of a partner. I shall sit here with Mrs Blake. You need not fuss. I am in no pain. Not much. Oh, do dance, Mama.'

Lady Osborne readily assented to her daughter's request. 'Very well,' said she. 'Then, I believe we should send for the carriage, my dear, for you look quite done for.'

'Oh no, Mama!' Emma replied. 'I shall go nowhere without a glass of negus.'

Solicitous of Emma's welfare, Mrs Blake was anxious to establish whether the further injury to her ankle had led to something more serious. 'In such cases, fractures are not uncommon. I salute you, I do, for standing up when you did, but time, my dear, time is the greatest healer. Let me see if I can catch Mr Fowle's attention. It is well he is present.'

'Have no anxiety on my account,' Emma replied. 'Please do not call for Mr Fowle. I should not wish to see the set broken up. What a glorious sight it is! Does not Anne and Mr Fitzroy look well together? And I have never seen Mr Fowle looking quite so complaisant, nor Aunt Harding quite so cheerful.'

After some moments, Mrs Blake observed, 'Your cousin Anne and Mr Fitzroy do indeed make a charming couple.'

'Quite charming!' Emma was delighted to find that Mrs Blake took a similar view of the matter. 'As to Mr Fowle, he is all smiles, and they are all directed at Aunt Harding.'

'He does seem well pleased with her.'

'And he seems no less pleased with himself,' said Emma. 'Do you think him a silly man?'

'A silly man? Not at all,' said Mrs Blake. 'Charles speaks highly of him. He is reckoned one of the most knowledgeable physicians in the whole of England.'

'It is unfortunate then that his considerable knowledge does not extend to other matters.'

'Whatever do you mean, Emma?'

'His sense of occasion is not what it should be. Mr Fowle practically declared himself to Aunt Harding in my presence.'

'I see,' replied Mrs Blake, with a smile. 'Not all men are equal to such things. Might you find it in your heart to overlook his indiscretion? I have often found that the lovesick act in curious ways. It puts me in mind of the first time I met your dear mama in the year ninety-five. Your papa's sister, Mrs Beresford — Miss Osborne as she was then, of course — was so in love with the Colonel that she broke her promise to Charles and stood up with dear Colonel

145

Beresford instead. Poor Charles was the picture of disappointment. Seeing how it was, your mama offered to dance with my little boy instead. What a happy meeting it was! How fortuitous! At the time, it was the general view that Miss Carr, your Aunt Beresford's particular friend, would become the new Lady Osborne. But when your papa set eyes on your mama, it was all over for Miss Carr. At first, Miss Carr would not be put off, but it was all to no avail. His Lordship preferred your mama and that was the end of the matter.'

'What happened to Miss Carr?'

'I believe she married a baronet. Your Aunt Beresford is familiar with the particulars,' said Mrs Blake.

'I have not seen Aunt and Uncle Beresford in six years, for they are both in such indifferent health they are quite unable to travel into Surrey. One day I shall surprise them and pay them a visit myself.'

'Are the Beresfords acquainted with the Fitzroy family, Emma?'

'Why should they be?'

'Did you not know? Allersham is not five miles from Whitcombe.'

'Aunt Beresford has never mentioned Allersham in her letters. I do not think my aunt and uncle are often seen in society.'

'If only the Beresfords had returned to Delham in the year six, before the Colonel began to suffer with his heart. Indeed, had they remained in Chatham, but a fraction of the distance from Delham, they might have enjoyed the society of their friends and all their family these past ten years,' said Mrs Blake. 'Dear Mrs Beresford was your mama's greatest supporter when objections were raised to the marriage. It was she who brought your grandmamma around in the end. There is a young woman in Sanditon who reminds me a little of your mama at that age. A Miss Clara Brereton. Lady Denham, Sanditon's great lady, summoned her to act as Her Ladyship's companion. Miss Brereton is a beauty but is never permitted to forget her lowly connections. A poor relation is always at the mercy of a rich one, and Miss Brereton is at the mercy of Lady Denham morning, noon and night. Her Ladyship is determined that she should marry well for it will save her the inconvenience of making provision for Miss Brereton in her will. We made their acquaintance last week at a dinner party given by Mr Parker. Miss Brereton is quite charming.'

'I do not like the sound of Lady Denham.'

'Her Ladyship is like many great ladies — your mama excepted — who expect to order the world according to their own peculiar decrees and requirements,' said Mrs Blake. 'Forgive me for speaking thus. What an ungrateful creature I am! Lady Denham has graciously issued Charles and I with an invitation to luncheon on Friday. It was not within my power to refuse her. Had I done so, she would have insisted on another day instead.'

'Has the famous Mr Parker recruited Lady Denham to his cause? Is it true that he is quite put out that Mr Fowle appears unwilling to give up Brinshore?'

'He is, I'm afraid to say. And Lady Denham is his chief ally,' said Mrs Blake. 'But I have no doubt that my son will set things to rights. When he sets his heart on a cause worthy of the fight he does not yield to any object less worthy.'

'And is Brinshore favoured above Sanditon?'

'I wish I knew. I hope the uncertainty will come to an end soon. There are still deliberations to be had,' said Mrs Blake. 'It is a delicate matter and must be managed carefully. I have never before in my life seen such rivalry as exists between Sanditon and Brinshore.'

Amid the press for refreshments Captain Blake had requested a small plate of plain cake and buttered bread from the table, to be set down beside Miss Osborne. A servant was also summoned to bring a footrest. Nothing was too much trouble; everything that might be done to secure Emma's comfort was done, and Captain Blake insisted on being himself the author of it. When all was accomplished to his satisfaction, he sat down beside her.

'I understand that Lady Denham has invited you to luncheon on Friday,' said Emma.

'An invitation I should happily have declined. But Lady Denham would not be gainsaid.'

'Perhaps Miss Brereton's presence will help assuage the situation,' said Emma.

The mention of Miss Brereton took Captain Blake by surprise. 'Are you acquainted with Lady Denham's niece?'

'No indeed. Until ten minutes ago, I did not know of her existence or of her great beauty.'

Charles smiled uneasily. 'Miss Brereton is considered a beauty. I cannot tell whether she is a great beauty.'

'Whatever do you mean?' said Emma.

'Great beauty, in my estimation, is not merely external. Acts of kindness, indeed artlessness, must also be the measure. I made Miss Brereton's acquaintance only the other day and exchanged but two words with her. I do not know Miss Brereton well enough to proffer an opinion.'

Emma found the temptation to inquire further too great to resist. 'Are there any young women among your acquaintance to whom —' Almost as soon as the words had left her lips, she regretted them. However artless her intention had been, even to her own ears it seemed as though she had sought to extract Captain Blake's approval. Retraction was impossible.

Captain Blake's good-humoured laughter did little to put Emma at ease. 'My dear Emma, what am I to say?'

'Forgive me,' Emma replied. 'I could never be considered a great beauty in your estimation for I do not have that measure of goodness in me that —'

'We are the best of friends, are we not?' said he cheerfully. 'In my eyes, you have goodness and kindness in abundance.'

Emma knew not whether to take hope or feel despair on hearing Captain Blake speak of that peculiar bond of friendship that existed between them. 'The best of friends' was at once as near and as far from a declaration of love as any expression could be.

The rest of the evening was spent as pleasantly as any ball where the joy of dancing is denied. Emma was gratified to have Captain Blake's full attention for half an hour longer, but when the music commenced once again, he begged leave to stand up with Anne. I expect he means to advance Mr Fitzroy's case, thought she. Her curiosity was at its height; and straining to secure a better view of the floor, she watched every movement as Anne and Captain Blake danced down the set. Presently, she turned her gaze towards Mr Fitzroy, who was standing close by the couple, and was pleased to find that he appeared to be quite as interested in their progress down the set as she.

Towards the end of the evening, Emma was further gratified to see her mother stand up with Captain Blake once again. Emma brought to mind what Mrs Blake had told her of that fortuitous moment in the year ninety-five when her mama, at nineteen, had first stood up with Master Charles Blake. Little did her mama know then what destiny had planned!

Save for the lack of a waltz, there was little else with which to find fault. Brinshore might have pretentions of becoming a fashionable watering place, but the tone of the evening, the ambience and arrangements seemed closer in character to Delham's modest affair than to the brilliance of Brighton's assemblies.

The evening would have progressed without incident had not Mrs Harding partaken a little too liberally of the Angel's excellent negus. A greater spectacle could not have been wished for by way of bestowing on the Brinshore Ball that air of fashion of which Brighton could customarily boast. The steady slippage of Mrs Harding's turban as she and Mr Fowle danced down every couple was a sight to be seen; for, giddy from an excess of wine, Mrs Harding appeared to throw off all the constraints of propriety and enter into the spirit of the dance with blissful abandon.

In spite of every objection posed by a pleasantly inebriated Mrs Harding, Lady Osborne insisted that the time had come to leave; she saw that there was danger in staying too long and of thereby increasing the degree of spectacle. Forced to act, Lady Osborne was in no doubt that, in the sober light of day, her sister's mortification would be complete. Hence, she ignored every protest and ordered the carriage. With assistance from Captain Blake and his mother, a merry Mrs Harding, affably expansive in her adieus, was escorted forthwith from the assembly.

Supported by Lady Osborne on one side and Mr Fitzroy on the other, Emma hopped delightedly through the corridor as fast as she was able.

'Slow down, my dear,' said Lady Osborne.

'If I slow down, Mama, we will not hear Aunt Harding bid the master of the inn a fond farewell! Poor Mr Fowle! He is left quite alone. I suppose he will not stay long now. I doubt Brinshore has ever seen the like. It adds a certain fashionable air to the proceedings. Aunt Harding will be the toast of Brinshore for weeks to come. Are you not amused, Mama?'

'Certainly not. Nor will be your aunt in the cold light of day,' said Lady Osborne.

Turning to Mr Fitzroy, Emma whispered, 'What must you think of our family? We have quite the same ability as any family to disgrace ourselves.'

'If this be your definition of disgrace, it is a very narrow one. I should imagine there is not a family in the land left unaffected. But look out. Here are three steps,' said he.

'Oh never mind me,' she replied. 'I am not so helpless. Mama will assist me. But Anne is left quite alone.'

Mr Fitzroy made no reply. With a nod of the head, in an instant he left her side and offered his arm to Anne.

'What do you think of Mr Fitzroy and Anne, Mama?' whispered Emma. 'Are they not perfect for one another?'

For a good part of the evening, Lady Osborne had been at leisure to observe those almost imperceptible gestures — looks, manners and conduct — that escape all but the keenest eye. She had begun to form an impression of some subtleties of demeanour among the party that had left her with a curious sense of unease. Her daughter's affection for Captain Blake was marked — no one could have failed to notice it — every look and smile on Emma's part confirmed it. And while Captain Blake's affection for Emma was undeniably sincere and unaffected, his manner towards her daughter did not appear to indicate any symptom of an alteration in his feelings. Lady Osborne received the impression that Captain Blake's look was that of a brother. It was most decidedly not the gaze of a lover.

In addition, Her Ladyship had seen nothing uncommon in the looks or behaviour of her niece to suggest that Anne had formed an attachment to Mr Fitzroy. And despite Emma's exertions on their behalf, Lady Osborne could detect in that gentleman's manner, no particular preference for Anne either. Of greater curiosity to Her Ladyship were the looks that passed between Anne and Captain Blake — of agitation, almost awkwardness, at times.

CHAPTER SEVENTEEN

The following morning brought a succession of visitors to Trafalgar Terrace curious to see how Mrs Harding had fared overnight. Accounts of the ballroom deportment of the town's self-appointed leading lady were guaranteed to furnish Brinshore's dining tables with conversation for weeks to come. Mrs Harding, however, was not at home to receive callers, and kept to her bed, owing to a severe headache and a strange stiffness in her arms and legs.

Lady Osborne took charge of the situation and saw to it that visitors were not denied. Accompanied by her daughter and her niece, she received them all with cordial equanimity. Such hospitality from the wife, daughter and niece of a viscount succeeded in its intended purpose; for Lady Osborne's charm, combined with Emma's carefree wit, and Anne's attentiveness, made for a pleasant morning, and surpassed in entertainment any speculation that might have ensued concerning the condition of Mrs Harding the morning after the ball.

The time for callers passed without incident until the arrival of a letter addressed to Mrs Harding. Lady Osborne ascertained from Mrs Harding's maid that the letter had been delivered by hand, by Mr Fowle's manservant.

Lady Osborne entered Mrs Harding's room and drew open the curtains.

'No light, please,' said Mrs Harding.

'A letter has arrived for you. It was delivered into Payne's hand by Mr Fowle's manservant. I thought it might be important.'

Mrs Harding eased herself upright. 'I have aches and pains the likes of which —'

'They will pass.'

'Do you recall, did I speak or act in any way I might regret?'

'I cannot tell.' Lady Osborne passed the letter to her sister.

'I blame Mr Fowle. Had he not insisted on my partaking of an additional glass of negus, I should not have suffered any ill effects at all. What an insufferable man he is!'

Lady Osborne laughed. 'I expect the proportion of port wine to hot water was not what it should have been.'

'That is my view entirely,' Mrs Harding agreed.

'Perhaps, on reflection, a second helping of port wine jelly was inadvisable. I daresay, I was little light-headed myself,' said Lady Osborne.

Mrs Harding sighed. 'Did I make a spectacle of myself? You know very well that it is not in my character to do such a thing! I blame the Angel. The inn-keeper, and he alone, is culpable. I have always said that one cannot expect anything remarkable from such a man. I suspect he directs a thoroughly disreputable establishment. But he has not heard the last of it from me!'

'My dear sister, the matter would be best left alone. I urge you not to fan the fire's flames. Save yourself from further reproof, if reproof you fear.'

'What if Mr Fowle should —'

'Should what?'

'Oh, I don't know. Did I in an unguarded moment say something amiss? I sincerely hope not. For then, you see, that annoying Mr Parker will have it all his own way. He will fill Mr Fowle's head with promises of this and that and persuade him to set up in Sanditon! And once Mr Parker gets his own way, he will strut here and there, all puffed up with notions of Sanditon's celebrity, and Brinshore will be left with nothing! I have not the will to read Mr Fowle's letter. You must open it for me.'

Lady Osborne did as her sister instructed. The letter was brief, the contents of which contained no unnecessary flourishes or introductory remarks. Her Ladyship folded the letter and placed it into her sister's hands.

'Mr Fowle makes you an offer,' said she. Her voice was calm and matter-of-fact, as though it was the commonest thing in the world to receive such a missive.

Mrs Harding quickly unfolded the letter. 'Pass me my spectacles. On the table. Over there. By the window.'

After re-reading the letter three times, Mrs Harding exclaimed, 'What am I to do?'

'What is it you wish to do?' asked Lady Osborne.

'It is a reasonable letter, not given to exaggerated sentimentality; and it seems to have been written during a moment of sobriety. The hand is steady and bold.'

'Oh Penelope! From what I have seen and heard since arriving in Brinshore, there is no doubt in my mind that Mr Fowle has formed an attachment to you. Charles says he is a perfectly respectable man.'

'Emma thinks him rather foolish,' Mrs Harding replied.

'The point is, do you? You speak of Brinshore as your first love. Is Mr Fowle a means to an end?'

'My dear sister, you know me well enough to suppose that an alliance must always be in some degree a means to an end. Dr Harding was hardly a man to excite one's passions. It was enough that I learned to tolerate his presence, and for a duration far greater than expected. I was utterly deceived there, you know. He was loath to breathe his last. Several times I was astounded by his determination to defeat the efforts of the grim reaper.'

'Do you love this man?'

'Love has nothing to do with it. The question is whether I can tolerate him. Mr Fowle must be willing to give up his house, for I shall not be persuaded to leave Trafalgar Terrace. I must have my view of the sea and the shore.'

Lady Osborne perused the letter once again. 'Mr Fowle does not seek an immediate reply. Take your time. Learn what you can about this man's character and former life. Has he children?'

'He is a widower of long-standing and has no children, no one to interfere or object to such an alliance.' Mrs Harding put the letter aside. 'I have much to do.'

'I thought you were unwell.'

'I am much better now, as you see.'

Mr Fitzroy's apparent disapprobation of Emma's daily pursuit did not prevent her from continuing to engage in the pleasurable activity of observing the world of Brinshore through a spyglass from the elevated position of the drawing room window in Trafalgar Terrace. An entertaining half hour was spent scrutinising that quarter of the shore that was dedicated entirely to gentlemen bathers. Indeed, the glimpse of a strong male form, unattired, and hair sodden with sea water, held the greatest fascination.

'Come Anne,' said Emma. 'You will never guess what I have seen. It is something eminently worthy of your attention.'

'Is it a seagull?' Anne replied.

'No.'

'A puffin? I do so enjoy the sight of a puffin.'

'No.'

'Are you sure?'

'I have never been more certain of anything in my whole life.'

Anne looked through the spyglass. 'Why, it is a rowing boat!'

'Look again.'

'Good heavens!' said Anne. 'It is the body of man half concealed beneath a shroud.'

'What?' said Emma, seizing the spyglass from her hand. 'It is nothing of the kind. You missed the interesting part. The man in question was a moment ago in a state of complete undress. He hides beneath a blanket to make himself decent, I suppose. Did you not see him move?'

Anne raised the spyglass to her eye once again. 'It is quite shocking,' said she, holding the instrument steady. 'How could you do such a thing!'

'Quite easily,' Emma replied. 'It is my turn.'

Anne reluctantly gave up the spyglass as the door opened to admit Lady Osborne.

'What has caught your attention?' said Her Ladyship.

Anne turned to Emma to proffer an explanation. 'We have been looking at a man in a complete state of undress, bathing in the sea. I was fortunate enough to spot him first. Anne had no such luck.'

Emma offered the spyglass to her mother. 'The far end of the bay, Mama. Point the glass towards that rowing boat over there!'

Lady Osborne took the spyglass from her daughter's hand and placed it on the table. 'Captain Blake is come to call upon us, and with him Mr Fitzroy,' she whispered, as the two gentlemen entered the room.

In that instant, the young women's confusion was not easily concealed.

'I see we have happened upon you at an inconvenient moment,' said Captain Blake.

'No. Not at all,' said Emma.

'No, indeed,' added Anne, blushing.

Lady Osborne endeavoured to suppress a smile. Looking pointedly at her daughter and niece, she said, 'On the contrary, gentlemen, I believe you have chosen your moment well.'

Captain Blake took a seat between Lady Osborne and Anne, while Mr Fitzroy sat by the window beside Emma.

'Mrs Harding will join us shortly.'

Captain Blake said to Lady Osborne, 'I hope your sister suffered no ill effects as a consequence of the ball.'

As the conversation continued at one end of the room, another was entered into by the window. Mr Fitzroy began in a low voice. 'I hope I find you in good spirits, Miss Osborne.'

'Tolerably so.'

'Did the famous Brinshore Ball meet with your expectations?'

'How could it? What is a ball if one has not the pleasure of dancing.'

'You danced with me, though I suspect that afforded little pleasure.'

'I danced very badly, as you well know.' Emma looked hesitantly at Mr Fitzroy. 'May I ask you a question?'

Puzzled by the request, he gave a slight nod of the head.

Unable to arrange the question to her complete satisfaction, at length she said, 'Never mind. It is of little matter.'

Mr Fitzroy smiled and said, 'I can vouch for Captain Blake. He heard none of the conversation that passed between you and your mother prior to entering the room.'

Emma was mortified.

'Nor, I might add, did I,' said he. 'Not a syllable.'

'Then how did you anticipate me?'

'Quite simply from the confusion expressed by your countenance,' said he. 'You looked as though you had something to hide.'

'Do not play games with me. Did you —'

'On my honour, I did not.'

Emma sighed with relief. 'Are you also invited to Lady Denham's for luncheon on Friday? Are you to have the pleasure of making Miss Brereton's acquaintance?'

'Two questions in one. The answer to both is *yes*. Are you acquainted with Miss Brereton, Miss Osborne?'

'I am not,' she replied. She raised her eyes to him and examined his profile. 'Anne was greatly admired last night.'

Mr Fitzroy's attention was drawn towards the other end of the room where Captain Blake and Miss Musgrave were in earnest conversation with Lady Osborne.

'I expect when at last you take holy orders, you will no doubt be in want of a wife,' she went on.

'Then you would be wrong, Miss Osborne,' he replied. 'I look not for a wife, but for a living.'

'Should you be willing to settle some distance from Brinshore, a living might easily be secured.'

'A living is not so easily come by these days.'

'My father has at least two in his gift. Wickstead is not vacant, nor will it be for some time unless Mr Blackmore takes ill and dies or receives a higher calling. But Stanton remains without an incumbent. Dear Papa purchased it after the last curate left for India. And Stanton has such treasured associations for my family. The parlour can be a little drafty in winter. My grandfather and my grandmother are buried there. And it is the very place where Mama accepted Papa. The Musgraves live but three miles from Stanton.'

Mr Fitzroy listened in silence, his head bowed in thought.

'Please do not imagine me ungrateful, Miss Osborne. I acknowledge your goodness in seeking to put me forward as a candidate, but it would be impossible for me to accept. Stanton is in your father's gift, and it is he who must decide to whom the living should be given.'

'But I can speak with my father. Indeed, I have already written to him and —'

Mr Fitzroy's serious look surprised Emma. 'I wish, Miss Osborne, you had not,' said he.

Very soon afterwards, the gentlemen took their leave at the insistence of Mr Fitzroy.

Despite his reluctance, Captain Blake agreed that the hour was late. 'We have much to do,' said he.

Ten minutes later, Mrs Harding entered the room, surprised to find that the visitors she had made every effort to receive had left.

Seeing the extent of her sister's malaise, Lady Osborne proposed a walk by the sea to take in the fresh air.

'You go,' said Mrs Harding. 'I shall sit quietly. Emma shall keep me company. You may take Anne with you. And if any among our acquaintance should enquire of me, inform them that I am in excellent health.'

The appearance of Mr Fowle on the doorstep of Trafalgar Terrace could not have been better orchestrated had it been contrived by the physician himself. At the very moment Lady Osborne and her niece appeared at the front door, there he stood, nervous, inarticulate, and red-faced. A brief salutation was exchanged between them before Mr Fowle was given entry to the house.

'Should we postpone our walk?' asked Anne anxiously. 'Aunt Harding is not herself today. She is quite unwell.'

'And Mr Fowle is a physician. What better visitor at such a moment?' replied Lady Osborne with a smile.

'Mr Fowle seems a little out of sorts himself. Did you notice how feverish he looked, Aunt?'

'I expect a cure is at hand,' replied Lady Osborne.

Anne delighted in the company of her aunt and, in turn, received every attention from Lady Osborne for she was Her Ladyship's goddaughter. As a child, she had spent many happy hours at Osborne Castle, investigating its countless rooms and passages, playing in the nursery with her cousin, exploring the grounds, and collecting crab apples, horse chestnuts and acorns. It was on one such occasion that Charles Blake, then a young midshipman, visited Osborne Castle. Returning from her morning's venture, Anne had set before him items garnered from the grounds of Osborne Park — a collection of horse chestnuts — ordered and assembled according to size and shape. He knew not how his fulsome approbation of her endeavours that morning had fostered her interest and fascination for the natural world.

Aunt and niece took the path that bordered the bay, stopping occasionally to admire the hue of the sea and the beauty of the sunlit cliffs. They talked of Anne's mother, of family and friends in Delham, and of the Brinshore Ball. Confidences were neither sought by the aunt nor tendered by the niece but, on their return to Trafalgar Terrace, Lady Osborne seemed convinced that she had acquired a clearer understanding of her niece's predicament, clearer, it seemed, than Anne herself.

'What do you think?' said Emma, on their return. 'While you were gone, Mr Fowle called on Aunt Harding. He stayed an entire half hour, for I watched the clock. But I had no part in it, for he was marched forthwith into the dining room and the door was full shut behind him! And I was left quite alone to wonder what I had done to deserve it.'

'Where is Aunt Harding now?' said Anne.

'She is gone to her room to lie down, for her headache is quite as bad as ever it was.'

Lady Osborne said, 'I shall go up to her.'

'No, Mama,' Emma replied. 'Aunt Harding says she does not wish to be disturbed. I cannot imagine what Mr Fowle has said to cause this relapse. He is supposed to cure people, not make their condition decidedly worse.'

'Never mind Mr Fowle,' said her mother. 'I think it is about time you, my dear, began to take some exercise. A little movement would not go amiss. Indeed, a little movement away from that window would please me greatly.'

Lady Osborne left the drawing room and went up to her sister's bedchamber. Despite her instructions to the contrary, Mrs Harding had expected her sister to look in on her, and almost hauled her into the room at the first knock.

'Well?' said Lady Osborne.

'At first, I resolved to accept him. Indeed, even as he made himself comfortable in Dr Harding's old chair, it was my express intention to do so,' said Mrs Harding. 'But when he eventually came to the point (I was obliged to hear him out a full ten minutes before he declared himself properly — I've never known anyone to make such a piece of work of it) I could not make up my mind to accept him.'

'And so you refused him?'

'I told him that I must have time to consider his proposal,' said she.

'And?' enquired Lady Osborne.

'He was good enough to grant my request, almost gracious, which I suspect was not easy for a man so little acquainted with eloquent declarations.'

'What changed your mind?'

Mrs Harding paced the room, wringing her hands in agitation. 'An alliance between us would be just the thing for Brinshore. Together, Mr Fowle and I might advance Brinshore's cause.'

'Of that I have no doubt,' said Lady Osborne. 'But that was not my question.'

Mrs Harding sighed. 'I am not willing to give away every penny to a man I hardly know and who may do with it as he pleases once we are married, and without reference to me. I need to consult our brother Robert in Croydon. The capital must be tied up by whatever means possible so that Mr Fowle does not have the direction of it.'

'I take it this is not the moment to speak of love or regard?'

'I can tolerate the man and that is enough for me. Indeed, at times I find him almost pleasing. And were he to limit his conversation to those subjects on which he is an expert, I should have no objections at all to his character. We should do very well together. It is his ardour that makes him ridiculous. Dr Harding was just as ardent, but he had the advantage of being a clergyman and kept his passion under good regulation.'

Lady Osborne was at a loss to understand her sister.

Mrs Harding explained further, 'Dr Harding was used to making speeches. He understood the importance of delivery. Do you not see? Eloquence goes a long way in matters of seduction.'

'Then surely once you are married you have only to wait a year or so for Mr Fowle's ardour to wane to be entirely at ease.'

'That is true. But the question of money remains.' Mrs Harding sat down beside her sister. 'I must go to Croydon without delay. It must be done. How I shall miss Brinshore! Sister, promise me you will stay. See to everything while I am gone. I shall not be gone above a week, but I must speak with Robert. He will advise me, for you know that he is very particular about money and is never happier than when he has the direction of it himself.'

'Impossible!' said Lady Osborne. 'What about little Frank?'

'Frank is very well where he is. He is out of danger and will have more attention than is good for him. The Dowager is never happier than when she is at the reins,' said Mrs Harding. 'And, my dear sister, I believe Emma is more in need of her mother at this moment.'

Lady Osborne stood up and moved to the window. 'Is there some aspect of Emma's present condition about which I am unware?'

'Are you indeed unaware? Have you not seen with your own eyes that which must only lead to heartbreak whatever may be the outcome?'

Lady Osborne acknowledged some measure of understanding but was disinclined to speak further for fear of breaking her daughter's confidence. 'Perhaps it is better for Emma to leave Brinshore. Perhaps I should take her home with me.'

'Leave Brinshore? No, sister, that would never do,' said Mrs Harding. 'Anne might more easily be spared and would proffer the least objection, for she is the more obliging of the two.'

'Let us understand one another plainly,' replied Lady Osborne. 'Have you reason to suppose that Anne has formed an attachment to Charles Blake?'

'I very much suspect so. And, I believe Captain Blake —'

'— is in love with Anne?'

CHAPTER EIGHTEEN

Mrs Harding's carriage arrived at the Musgraves' residence a quarter past five the following day. Mrs Musgrave was surprised to see her sister alight from the carriage unaccompanied; her first thought was that something dreadful had happened to Anne. Mrs Harding, however, was quick to put her sister's mind at rest and allay any fear she might have as to her daughter's welfare.

'Lord Osborne was not entirely happy with the arrangement, for I looked in on him on my way,' said Mrs Harding. 'He is of the opinion that Frank's needs are the greater. Men never understand these things.'

Mrs Musgrave was at first of Lord Osborne's view until her sister related in detail the circumstances that had necessitated her immediate visit to Croydon.

'I have heard something of Mr Fowle's late uncle, a physician and scientist of some renown. But I know nothing of the nephew.'

'He is just the man to take charge of Brinshore's establishment as the first among watering places, if only Mr Fitzroy and Captain Blake would exercise proper judgement on that score. Mr Parker and that dreadful Lady Denham still clamber to get their own way. And, oh, how it would be trumpeted in the Sanditon Gazette. But when Brinshore has its own newspaper —'

'Dear Penelope,' said Mrs Musgrave to her sister, 'tell me, how does my daughter fare? Does she send any message to her poor dear mother?'

'Anne fares very well indeed. Never a day goes by without a word of praise for Brinshore. She is quite content there, you know. But I am afraid that if someone does not act, hearts are likely to be broken.'

'Whatever do you mean?' asked Mrs Musgrave.

'It is not for me to say,' said Mrs Harding, 'but I will say this —' Without pause or hesitation Mrs Harding set before her sister the facts as she understood them. 'Anne has formed an attachment to Captain Blake, and he for her,' said she. 'As far as it is possible to ascertain, no preference has been openly expressed by either party for the other, nor has any understanding between them been acknowledged.'

'I confess, what you say surprises me, for I had always thought that Charles' affection for Emma was the stronger. Are you quite sure?'

'Not wholly, not absolutely,' said Mrs Harding. 'I cannot put hand on heart, but I am not alone in my conjecture. Our sister noticed it almost immediately — at the Brinshore Ball.'

'What was it that gave rise to such speculation?'

Mrs Harding hesitated for a moment. Avoiding her sister's eye, she smoothed out the folds of her dress. 'The detail escapes me, for I was not quite myself that evening. I had the misfortune to partake of a rather inferior cordial that did not quite agree with me.'

'Negus always goes straight to my head too,' said Mrs Musgrave.

'You mistake my meaning. I am not one to — Sobriety is Brinshore's maxim.'

'Admirable, I'm sure,' said Mrs Musgrave. 'Our newly refurbished assembly rooms in Delham are to serve only tea and lemonade with plain cake and buttered bread. Musgrave seems to think it the fashion, though the Dowager vehemently rails against the notion. I confess, I hate to be exposed to the sort of behaviour that demeans a perfectly respectable man when he places himself in a state of intoxication. I never drink more than half a glass of negus at a ball.'

Anxious to lay the matter to rest, Mrs Harding guided the conversation back to Captain Blake. 'It seems Emma has set her heart on him. What is to be done?'

'Nothing is to be done,' replied Mrs Musgrave. 'What can be done? Love must run its course.'

'Is Captain Blake what you want for Anne?' said Mrs Harding.

'I want what Anne wants, and so does her father,' replied Mrs Musgrave. 'Indeed, I doubt Captain Blake is the Osbornes' first choice for Emma. Our sister would not mind it, nor I suspect would His Lordship; but the Dowager would oppose it and I expect Aunt Turner would too.'

'Nevertheless, should Captain Blake suspect that he had, through some defect in his own conduct, engaged Emma's affections — misled and given her hope — he would likely feel obliged to make her an offer.'

'I do not doubt it. He is an honourable man.'

'One way or another, such a situation is liable to cause pain. Better that Anne is removed from Brinshore and away from Captain Blake's society altogether.'

Mrs Musgrave was astounded by her sister's recommendation. 'Perhaps something should be done, but not this. How cruel it would be to separate a young couple who are attached to one another!'

'It is less cruel than the alternative. Anne is better able to adapt her feelings and make of the situation what she will. Emma is not. If

Anne were to return to Delham, Captain Blake might be worked on in a gentle sort of way. Indeed, if given the chance, I believe his wishes and affections might alter before the season is out.'

'Emma is a dear girl, almost as dear to me as Anne. I could not bear to cause pain to either one of them. But if by some act of manipulation you endeavour to persuade Charles Blake to make an offer to Emma, when he is in love with Anne, you will do a grave disservice to all three. And I should never forgive you.'

'Charles Blake would have little difficulty transferring his affections from Anne to Emma. He is blessed with a disposition so affable and accommodating that he is bound to be pleased with either one of them. And surely you cannot wish Anne to marry a man fourteen years her senior.'

Mrs Musgrave looked at her sister in disbelief. 'And this from the woman who at three and twenty married a man forty years *her* senior? I wish Charles Blake every happiness, but he is not my concern. If he has had the good fortune to succeed in securing Anne's affection, I shall do all in my power to make sure that no obstacle stands in their way.'

'And if Emma should be the obstacle? Will you destroy her hope of happiness? Has she not a right to happiness? Elizabeth, are you not in danger of doing just the same as that of which you accuse me?'

After Mrs Harding had departed for Croydon the following morning, Mrs Musgrave went in search of her husband and found him in the library reading *The Times*.

'Well, well. Snow in summer. Have you ever heard of such a thing? It is quite extraordinary. I expect Brinshore has suffered none of the poor weather the rest of the world has. Forgive me, my dear, but had your sister remained here a minute longer, I believe I should have petitioned parliament to have Brinshore removed from every map, road and signpost that ever bore the name!' said he, lowering his newspaper. 'I am quite determined, Elizabeth. If I cannot have my way beyond the gates of this estate, I insist on having my way within the grounds of my own home. Brinshore shall not be mentioned in this house again!'

'I'm afraid, my dear, it must,' said Mrs Musgrave to her husband. 'For I should very much like to visit Brinshore.'

'*What?*' said he.

'And I should like you to accompany me,' his wife continued. 'We shall stay with Lady Forbes. I need hardly remind you that she complained most bitterly when she heard of your visit to Brighton. She was most put out that you did not call upon her, for you know how she likes to make a fuss of you. And she was sorely disappointed not to see Anne and Emma.'

'But she had not been long in Brighton. I did not wish to inconvenience her. Let Anne and Emma stay with her a day or two on their way back to Delham. I expect it will be a welcome relief, and infinitely superior to Brinshore.'

When asked why his wife had quite suddenly set her heart on a visit to the coast when all these weeks she had shown not the slightest interest in doing so, Mrs Musgrave replied, 'That dangerous contraption that you were so proud of had quite set me against travel of any kind.'

Mr Musgrave sighed. 'Well, I expect a dip in Brighton's restorative seawater would do you no harm. And when your sister Penelope returns to Brinshore, I shall not mind calling on her. I shall not mind it at all. I should like to see how far she inflates Brinshore's merits. Indeed, I can hardly contain my eagerness to hear her furnish us all with some grand scheme or other for its improvement. I almost choked on my soup at dinner last night on hearing of her plans for Brinshore's own pavilion: a tower of Pisa's proportions but wholly vertical! No doubt there will be a scheme or two to excavate the pyramids of Egypt and place them atop Brinshore's white cliffs before the season is over.'

'Think of the advantage to yourself, my dear. With such schemes to hand, Penelope will have little time to visit Delham. You may spend the rest of your days in peace and tranquillity, without disturbance or vexation of any kind.'

'Without disturbance or vexation, you say? Have you a mind to leave me too?'

Mrs Musgrave moved closer to the chair where her husband was seated and stroked his hair. 'Do I vex you greatly, my dear?'

'Utterly. And I should be in a pitiful state if you did not. You vex me at every turn and I have never been happier in my life, my dear Elizabeth.'

'Nor I,' she replied.

The matter of most concern was Anne. At that moment, Mrs Musgrave was unusually irresolute in determining whether to relate the facts of the matter to her husband. In those few moments of indecision, the opportunity was lost, for Mr Musgrave promptly stood to his feet and said, 'Well, I expect I should call at the Dower House to oversee the delivery of that deuced landau. Osborne should like me to be there. I expect I shall ride there unless, of course, you wish to accompany me, my dear. I can have the landaulet sent for.'

'Landaulet?' asked Mrs Musgrave, astonished by her husband's casual comment.

'Should you like to see it?'

'Indeed I should! Dear Tom,' said she, 'I do not deserve you! Allow me but ten minutes, for I should like to write a note to Lady Forbes.'

CHAPTER NINETEEN

The arrival of the new landau was eagerly awaited at the Dower House. Seated by the breakfast room window that proffered the finest view of the sweep, the appearance of the smart carriage and pair of greys did not disappoint the occupants of the Dower House; nor did the greyness of the sky, the coolness of the wind, or the threat of rain, dampen the thrill of anticipation. Mrs Turner sat restlessly on the edge of her seat, while the Dowager pounded the floor with her walking stick as the carriage came fully into view. The sight of a new landaulet, however, a short distance behind, caused Mrs Turner and the Dowager to exchange looks of puzzlement and apprehension.

'What is the meaning of this?' said the Dowager.

Lord Osborne, who had arrived a few minutes earlier to take delivery of the carriage in person, inspect the stables, and see that every particular was in order, was summoned to the breakfast room to explain the matter. But before His Lordship had time to open his mouth, all was settled to the Dowager's satisfaction when Mrs Turner observed Mr Musgrave assisting his wife out of the landaulet.

The superiority of the landau beside its smaller cousin was made much of by the Dowager. 'The springs are so evidently superior. I fear I should be thrown this way and that in a landaulet. So that the landau may be seen to full advantage, Mrs Turner and I shall take a ride in it.'

'It is hardly the weather for an open carriage,' said Mr Musgrave, bristling at the sound of the wind.

'A day or two's delay will do no harm, at least until the weather changes for the better,' said Lord Osborne.

'The Dowager has quite set her heart on it. I see no point in refusing her now,' whispered Mrs Musgrave to her husband. Turning to the new owners of the landau, she said, 'A winter travelling cloak and blanket is advisable. It is bitterly cold today.'

At length, as the sky darkened further, and the rain began to fall, they were persuaded to give up the idea altogether and wait for a better day. The invitation to an early luncheon at the Dower House was, therefore, greeted with welcome relief by Lord Osborne and the Musgraves. A fire was lit in the dining room and the table was laden with fine ham and cheeses, and produce from the gardens at Osborne Park.

Once the subject of the new landau was exhausted, conversation turned to the news from Brinshore. The Dowager insisted on having a full account of the Brinshore Ball; and although Mrs Harding's report of the proceedings was immediately to hand, Mrs Musgrave spoke briefly and made no mention of the matter that had caused contention between herself and Mrs Harding the day before.

'And what of the famous Mr Fowle?' enquired Mrs Turner. 'It is no secret. Penelope wrote to me about him. She would be a fool to take him without making quite certain that she has the direction of her own money. She should have spoken to me, for I know all about such matters.'

'Perhaps Mr Fowle is an imposter and will bring about Mrs Harding's downfall, just as Captain O'Brien achieved yours, my dear Mrs Turner,' said the Dowager.

'Do not mention that man's name!' she replied.

'If I recall, he had several names and used them all to great advantage,' continued the Dowager.

'Unspeakable wretch!' sighed Mrs Turner. Said she to Mrs Musgrave, 'And so Penelope is gone to Croydon. Well. Your brother Robert's talent for interference in such matters will cost her dearly. He will see to it that he is admirably reimbursed for his trouble. I should know. Indeed I should. Your brother will do very well out of this sorry business.'

The recollection of the loss of a considerable fortune at the hands of an imposter still at times awakened feelings of anger and resentment in Mrs Turner. Robert Watson had managed the recovery of what little fortune had been left untouched by Captain O'Brien; but, even after twenty years, Mrs Turner continued to take exception to the extent of the remuneration demanded by her nephew for his efforts on her behalf.

'Penelope will rue the day she ever set eyes on Mr Fowle. She had better remain as she is,' said she.

Mrs Musgrave looked to her husband for assistance. A distraction, a change in the course of the conversation was demanded. Sensible of his wife's silent entreaty, Mr Musgrave said brightly, 'And what news is there of Mr Edwards?'

The Dowager and Mrs Turner looked at one another in wonder.

'Surely you have heard the news!' said the Dowager. 'It is all over Delham. Mr Edwards is to visit Mr — '

' — and Mrs Howard!' said Mrs Turner. 'I cannot tell you what a relief it is — '

'Mrs Turner cannot wait to see the back of him,' interrupted the Dowager. 'I shall, of course, be obliged to invite old Mr Tomlinson to make up a card table.'

'Dear Mr Edwards,' said Mrs Musgrave. 'My father was so fond of him. My sisters and I used to dress and dine at the Edwardes on the day of each assembly of the season. I do not wish to speak ill of the departed, but he had a lot to put up with from Mrs Edwards.'

'And he has put up with a great deal more from his daughter!' said Mrs Turner.

'If there is to be a reconciliation between Mr Edwards and his daughter, it will not be a bad thing,' said Mrs Musgrave.

As the wind strengthened and the rain intensified, Mrs Musgrave glanced at her husband with concern.

'Let us hope that Mr Edwards has not set out to visit Somerset in this weather,' said he.

'No, indeed,' replied Mrs Musgrave, looking at her husband. 'We may be obliged to postpone our journey to Brighton a day or two.'

'Brighton?' asked the Dowager. 'What takes you to Brighton?'

'Lady Forbes has invited Tom and I to stay at her summer residence,' said Mrs Musgrave.

'Ah!' said the Dowager. 'It is no longer Lady Forbes' *summer* residence. She intends to remain there permanently. Lady Forbes is too tired and too arthritic for all the to-ing and fro-ing to London and Lowford and back. So she is to give up her London house altogether.'

'In that case, I wonder if it is reasonable to impose on her,' said Mrs Musgrave to her husband.

'She has servants enough to fill the Regent's Pavilion. She refused to settle at Lowford, you know,' said the Dowager. 'Go to Brighton, my dear. Lady Forbes will sit in her bedchamber all day long and make a great deal of fuss. You will hardly see her at all until it is time for dinner.'

CHAPTER TWENTY

The promise of a morning's sea bathing was inducement enough for Emma to declare her ankle almost mended; and there could be no treatment more beneficial than sea water to aid complete and speedy recovery. She had spent longer in languid repose than was justifiable for any young woman fortunate enough to spend the summer beside the sea.

With little to occupy her daughter but idle daydreams and the lens of a spyglass, Lady Osborne decided that it was time Emma spent her days more productively. Emma, for her part, was not disinclined to do so, but had different notions to those of her mother of what should comprise a productive day. Sea bathing, however, was a pastime on which they were happy to agree.

After a night of rain and gales, the sea and sky looked tranquil. Anne, preferring to take advantage of the morning light, declined the invitation to go sea bathing, and set off towards her favourite spot on the cliff from where she proposed to sketch the bay.

Lady Osborne and her daughter walked towards the shore where the services of a dipper were graciously declined. 'We shall manage things ourselves, thank you,' said she.

The sea water, though cold at first, was tolerable and brought a glow to Emma's cheeks. Lady Osborne looked on as her daughter met the waves and sea spray with delightful abandon, restricted only by the cumbersome garment that clung to her frame. Twenty minutes in the sea seemed to Emma like twenty seconds; another five minutes was called for and granted. After half an hour complete in the water, Emma was persuaded to leave it.

'Shall we make it a daily event, Mama? I am sure Anne will want to bathe too when she discovers what she has missed,' said Emma. 'I feel quite refreshed, and my ankle does not hurt at all. Did you see, Mama, how I floated on the sea like a water lily? It is quite safe. I had no fear of drowning at all. But my hair is in knots and I do not know how I shall make myself fit to be seen.'

Lady Osborne proposed that they return to Trafalgar Terrace and postpone their walk until the afternoon.

'I wish Abigail were here, for she would know how to untangle my hair gently. Payne is a little fierce at times and I do not like to cross her. The younger maid, Alice, is sweet-tempered, but looks after Anne.'

'Then allow me to brush your hair today,' said Lady Osborne.

'Very well, Mama,' Emma replied. 'Should you mind terribly if I became a crop? I think it would become me rather well.'

'I *should* mind terribly.'

Emma looked out of the window of her bedchamber as her mother gently untangled and smoothed out her hair. They spoke of home, of little Frank and his antics, and of the goings on at the Dower House. Lady Osborne observed that her daughter, though anxious to hear news of home, did not pine for its familiar comforts and society.

'Your papa told me that you had written to him with a request.'

'Yes, Mama,' Emma replied. 'Mr Fitzroy wishes to take holy orders. I thought he might do very well for Stanton. And I expect that Grandmamma would agree for he is handsome enough. And he is not wholly unconnected. If only he would make amends with his family. Can it be quite right that he should enter the Church and still be at odds with them?'

'But why single out Mr Fitzroy? Has he petitioned you to speak on his behalf? How came he to know that Stanton was vacant?'

'I told him so myself,' said Emma. 'But when I spoke to him about it he dismissed the idea entirely. I believe he saw it as interference. He did not welcome my assistance at all.'

Lady Osborne perceived from her daughter's demeanour that she had not been entirely transparent. 'Emma, my dear,' said she, 'had you some scheme in mind, some plan for Mr Fitzroy?'

At that moment a knock on the door came as a welcome distraction, for Lady Osborne was called away to settle a matter about the dinner menu, and Emma was spared the need to give an account of herself.

To pass the time until her mother's return, she reached for the spyglass and held it to her eye. The sea was calm. There was hardly a breaker in sight. Three young couples, a family of four, two men on horseback, two bathing machines, and a group of fishermen with a rowing boat and nets, populated the sand. Emma trained the spyglass on one young couple and was intrigued to observe the remarkable resemblance of the young woman to Anne. Curiously, the young woman who had provoked such interest had Anne's height and posture; her spencer and bonnet were precisely the colour and style of those her cousin had worn that morning. How peculiar! She is the very picture of Anne! My cousin has a twin! All that is needed to make the scene complete is Anne's sketchbook and pencils!'

Curiously, the gentleman of the pair was carrying just such a sketchbook and pencils. Emma moved closer to the window and directed the spyglass to the young woman's companion, a man who was as familiar to her as her own cousin.

Immediately, she left her room and rushed down the stairs to the drawing room to secure a better view; there, painfully, despairingly, through the lens of the spyglass, she beheld her cousin and her friend. The pair stopped momentarily to look at a sloop anchored some distance from the shore. Then, as the ribbons of her cousin's bonnet took flight in the breeze, Anne turned towards Captain Blake and looked into his eyes. Words, it seemed, were exchanged — the pair were enlivened by the dialogue — a hand reached out to prevent her cousin's departure. Anne paused. A debate ensued. At last Captain Blake placed the sketchbook and pencils into Anne's outstretched hands. The one to whom she had given her heart and soul appeared to stand, deflated and forlorn, as Anne walked away.

'Wretched, wretched device!' said Emma, throwing the spyglass on the floor, as Lady Osborne entered the room.

'Emma, my dear,' said she, 'whatever are you doing? What is wrong?' Her mother picked up the offending spyglass. 'Have a care. It is not your property to do with as you wish. It belongs to Anne.'

'So it does, Mama,' said Emma bitterly. 'Take it away. I have no use for it now!'

With little warning, and no time for preparation, Mr Fowle was shown into the drawing room. No one could have been less welcome in Emma's eyes at such a moment. 'Mama,' she whispered, 'tell him we are shortly to go out.'

Mr Fowle entered the room with a look of nervous apprehension.

'Your Ladyship,' said he, glancing briefly at Emma, 'I beg forgiveness for imposing on you at such a moment. I request only a few minutes of your time on a matter most delicate.'

Lady Osborne gestured to Mr Fowle to be seated. 'Emma,' said she, 'would you be kind enough to see where Anne is and inform the kitchen that luncheon will be delayed for half an hour.'

'My dear madam,' said Mr Fowle, 'I need only a minute or two of your precious time. Please do not alter your arrangements for my sake.'

Angry and upset, Emma sat at the top of the stairs to await Anne's return and Mr Fowle's departure. It was not long before the door to the drawing room was opened and Mr Fowle was shown to the front door. When Lady Osborne emerged from the room, she observed her daughter sitting on the stairs.

'Well, my dear,' said she, 'never a day goes by without something to surprise and entertain.'

'What did he want?' Emma replied.

'Mr Fowle wanted me to convey a message to your aunt,' said Lady Osborne.

'What message?'

'The message was intended for your aunt. I was not given leave by Mr Fowle to broadcast it far and wide. Come, the sea air has given me quite an appetite. Where is Anne?'

'I am here, Aunt,' said she, calmly placing her sketchbook and pencils on the table in the inner hallway.

Neither Emma nor Anne hardly touched the ham and pork pie. Anne, averting Emma's gaze, picked at a strawberry or two, while Emma seethed inwardly at her cousin's treachery.

'Did you spend a pleasant morning, my dear?' said Lady Osborne to her niece.

'Quite pleasant, thank you,' said Anne.

'Were you happy with your morning's work?' said Emma. 'Shall you show us the fruits of your labour after luncheon.'

Anne was agitated by Emma's request but, in reply, said simply, 'Yes.'

'You missed our visitor. He had a mysterious look about him,' said Emma.

Anne glanced fleetingly at her cousin with a look of alarm.

'Indeed, such clandestine behaviour makes one wonder what there is to hide,' Emma continued.

Anne looked away and said nothing.

'Emma,' her mother replied, 'let us say no more of the matter.'

Emma observed Anne's increasing nervousness but was so unfavourably disposed towards her cousin at that moment, that she did little to assist in easing her discomfort.

'You know how I dislike secrecy and concealment,' said Emma.

'Indeed, I do,' replied Lady Osborne. 'But forgive me, my dear. Had I leave to do so, which I have not, I should not reveal Mr Fowle's business to you or to anyone but the person for whom it was intended, however eagerly you desire to hear it.'

Emma gazed at her cousin, willing her to speak up.

'How was the sea bathing?' said Anne weakly.

'I felt enlivened by it,' Emma replied. 'Indeed, it was infinitely preferable to spending a full morning sitting alone, without a soul to speak to, sketching the bay. I shall make sea bathing my daily occupation. And you are welcome to join me if you have nothing better to do.'

Lady Osborne sensed a tone of resentment in Emma's address and gazed questioningly at her daughter. Emma felt her mother's eyes upon her and looked away. I shall not be induced by Mama or anyone to speak of the matter, thought she. If there be nothing irregular or underhand in my cousin's behaviour, Anne will speak of her encounter with Captain Blake and not conceal it from us. How strange, thought she, that he should deny his friends at Trafalgar Terrace the pleasure of his company!

For the remainder of the meal, Emma sat in silence. Had she courted a self-deception so great that she had dismissed every sign that contradicted her hopes for Captain Blake? There were times when she was ill disposed towards Anne, times when Anne had succeeded in securing Captain Blake's attention where she had failed. Interests shared by her cousin and friend — reading — fossils — shells — seaweed — such trivialities as these had on occasion left Emma feeling overlooked and in the way. The engagement to dance at the Brinshore Ball, requested and accepted, happened without her knowledge. An occasional look of approval — a blush — a sigh — gestures so commonplace, she had persuaded herself that they were of little matter. How, thought she, could he prefer Anne above her? Had she not the greater claim? Was she not of equal beauty? Had she not been blessed with superior fortune and connections? Was not this reason enough to tempt him?

Anne asked to be excused from the table having suddenly acquired a headache. The request was granted, and Anne withdrew in haste to her room. Emma breathed sharply to stifle a tear and pushed her plate aside.

'I too feel unwell, Mama.'

'I am surprised to hear it in light of your earlier declaration. An hour ago you had no such complaint,' said her mother.

'It came on quite suddenly. I must lie down too, Mama.'

'Then I had better send for Mr Fowle,' said Lady Osborne.

'Mr Fowle would be useless in this matter —'

'Has something occurred that you and your cousin are at pains to conceal from me?' her mother replied.

'You must ask Anne,' said Emma.

'You look quite wretched, my dear. I am asking you.'

Emma shook as tears welled in her eyes.

'Whatever is the matter, Emma?'

'Nothing, Mama. Nothing of any importance.'

Lady Osborne met with no resistance when she embraced her daughter but was unable to obtain an account of the matter that distressed her.

'Mrs Blake has requested the pleasure of our company for luncheon tomorrow. What reply am I to give?' said Lady Osborne, suspecting the cause of her misery.

'Go if it please you, Mama, and take Anne with you. I shall stay in Brinshore.'

Lady Osborne had fallen behind with her correspondence and was obliged to spend the rest of the afternoon writing letters. The letter to her husband was the most extensive and spread over two pages. She felt his absence keenly, and the absence of her son, Frank. It now seemed clear to her, however, that her presence in Brinshore was more essential than ever. Something must be done to alleviate her daughter's suffering. For the present she would stay in Brinshore and endeavour to persuade Emma to return with her to Osborne Castle as soon as Mrs Harding had completed her business in Croydon.

The entrance of the tea things into the drawing room at four was accompanied by the arrival of a letter in the afternoon post. Lady Osborne was anxious to hear news of Delham. Instead, it brought news that could not have been more welcome. Shortly afterwards, Anne came into the drawing room, holding a similar note.

'I see you have also heard the news,' said Lady Osborne.

'Dear Aunt, I should like to go to Brighton to be with my parents,' Anne replied.

'Of course you would, my dear,' said she.

'And I should like to stay with them if Lady Forbes will have me. Do I ask too much? I think it is for the best. If it can be arranged, I should very much like to leave tomorrow.'

'I am sure it can be arranged. Anne, my dear, is there something you wish to tell me?'

'No, Aunt. My headache is a little better, but I fear I have stayed too long in Brinshore.'

'I suspect the same is true of your cousin,' said Lady Osborne.

'Oh no. Emma must stay. Indeed, she must. I should not —'

'Should not?'

'Why do words desert me when I am most in need them?' said Anne. 'I — I should not have imposed myself — that is, I should never have come to Brinshore. Emma should have had the pleasure of Brinshore — of Sanditon society — without my —'

'My dear Anne, I am quite at a loss to comprehend your meaning.'

'Oh, Aunt, what can I say that will mend what has been broken?' said she. 'A situation exists — a situation made impossible by its very nature. And I am its author. I must strive in some small way to make amends. Nothing can be done except by me. Only my removal from Brinshore will suffice. Please, please do not press me further on the subject. I know my own mind and it is quite made up.'

However desirous of pursuing the matter, Lady Osborne assented to Anne's request. Said she, 'Does Emma know of your decision?'

'No, Aunt,' replied Anne. 'I shall —'

'What decision?' said Emma, entering the drawing room at that moment. 'Am I to be left in the dark about everything that happens in Brinshore?'

'Dear cousin,' said Anne, recovering her countenance, 'I have had the best news of all.'

Emma walked over to the window to look at the incoming tide. 'I'm sure you have,' she replied. The place on the sand where Anne had earlier spoken to Captain Blake was now immersed by waves crashing towards the shore.

'Mama and Papa are come to Brighton. They are guests of Lady Forbes. I know not for how long, but I hope to join them there. Tomorrow. That is my hope, at least.'

'Brighton?' replied Emma. 'If I recall, you were never keen on Brighton. What has changed your mind?'

The arrangements for Anne's removal to Brighton took an extra day to complete but were happily concluded to the satisfaction of all parties. Lady Osborne accompanied her niece as far as Waterloo Crescent where they were met by the Musgraves.

'It does me good to see all my friends again,' said Mrs Blake. 'But I am sorry to say that Charles is called away today on business. He was so very disappointed when he heard that he would not have the pleasure of meeting with all his dear friends. Mr Fitzroy is similarly called away. It seems they are occupied every hour of the day the Almighty sends. But it is all for the greater good and so we must not complain. But the uproar it has caused in Sanditon is quite without compare! Everything comes at a price and everything can be bought at a price. Lady Denham wrested from me a solemn promise to purchase asses' milk for the remainder of my stay in Sanditon. But what am I to do with it? We are all in perfect health. Indeed, we are quite free of every kind of infection and digestive disorder imaginable, and there are no infants that I know of for whom asses' milk might be prescribed. Poor Mr Fitzroy! He was obliged to make a similar pledge. Lady Denham has but two milch asses, though I daresay, when she is quite done, an entire herd will hardly suffice. If only Sanditon had its own physician! Then perhaps he might be worked on to recommend asses' milk to his patients.'

Eager to see her sister again, Lady Osborne proposed a short walk by the sea before luncheon. Mr Musgrave expressed a preference for seeing the library, having heard much about it from Anne.

'A walk to the library is what I had hoped for,' said Anne. 'There is a particular book about which I should like to enquire.'

'Then I might join you, if I may,' said Mrs Blake. 'Mr Parker is most insistent that patronage of the library is maintained. Every patron, says he, should frequent the library at least once a week. When I confessed that I had not put a foot inside the door for almost a fortnight he was quite unable to forgive my neglect.'

'Mr Parker seems to be just the type of individual of which every neighbourhood boasts and of which every neighbourhood could happily do without,' said Mr Musgrave. 'Perhaps we may happen upon him, if we are very unlucky.'

'Papa!' said Anne, 'if such be the case, you must promise to curb your tongue! From what I have heard, Mr Parker is a serious man. He is not possessed of much wit. He may likely take offence at your droll humour.'

'Mr Parker is not the only personage I have encountered without a sense of humour.'

Lady Osborne and Mrs Musgrave set out to walk in the opposite direction along a stretch of the shore that was almost deserted but for a solitary walker and an elderly couple.

'I have missed you, Elizabeth,' said Lady Osborne.

'And I you, Emma,' said Mrs Musgrave to her sister.

'How does Lady Forbes fare? Does Brighton suit her?'

'She is a little frail and hard of hearing, but her mind is as sharp as a needle. Nothing gets past her. Indeed, she is better acquainted with our business than we are ourselves.'

'I am sure she is,' laughed Lady Osborne. 'Whatever it may be, I have no doubt Lady Forbes has had some version of events from the Dower House.'

'Lady Forbes was exceedingly diverted by Aunt Turner's account of the new landau, an account which I understand was possessed of as much invention as fact. Indeed, the whole business has given Lady Forbes something to do. She has set about devising other wagers for our dear husbands. Her price is a new bath chair, and though she may buy a dozen if she so chooses, there is nothing more satisfying, says she, than winning a bet.'

'Osborne is not likely to take on Lady Forbes. He was quite put out after losing to his mother. I believe, indeed I hope, he has learned his lesson there.'

'I only hope the same is true of Tom,' said Elizabeth.

Lady Osborne smiled. 'My dear sister,' said she, 'how kind the years have been to us!'

'They have, indeed,' she replied.

'What will become of our girls? They have every possible advantage but —'

'To own the truth, it is Anne who brings me to Brighton,' interjected Elizabeth. 'Penelope suspects an attachment —'

'A complication concerning Emma and Anne?' said Lady Osborne.

'I believe so.'

'And Charles at the centre of it?' continued Lady Osborne.

Mrs Musgrave nodded. 'You suspected as much yourself? My dear sister, what is to be done?'

'Poor Charles. He will tear himself apart in order to do the honourable thing.'

'But what is the honourable thing in such a case?' Mrs Musgrave replied. 'Should he walk away altogether and risk becoming a stranger to both our families? Or should he choose one of our girls and risk estrangement from the family of the other?'

'Estrangement? What talk is this? Charles would never be a stranger to Osborne Castle. My dear sister, if Anne has had the good fortune to secure Charles' affection and he hers, then they must marry. No one should stand in their way. I can speak for Osborne. He would have it no other way. Charles is his godson.'

'But what of Emma? What of her feelings? Emma is as dear to me as any niece could be.'

'I know,' said Lady Osborne. 'And I bless you for saying it.'

They stopped to admire the serenity of shore and sky, shades of blue and sea green in perfect harmony.

'What trick of fate is this? That you, my dear sister, should break your heart over the uncle, and your daughter should break hers over his nephew.'

'Emma's heart will mend,' said Lady Osborne, 'as her mother's heart did before her.'

CHAPTER TWENTY-ONE

Emma's disinclination to accompany her cousin to Sanditon was more easily comprehended by her mother than she had supposed. The complaint of a severe headache was accepted unquestioningly, and though Lady Osborne had suspected that the pain in her daughter's head was not the true cause of her affliction, it had served to account for her absence from the party.

Adieus had been brief and civil, as both cousins had been impatient to conclude the business of parting. Emma had placed the spyglass into Anne's hand. The object that had provided hours of amusement and delight, and in an instant had caused untold anguish, was easily parted with. Love — or the idea of it — that inextricable union of pain and pleasure, had entranced, thrilled and deceived her. Emma had stood by the window and had watched with mixed emotions as the carriage bearing her mother and her cousin had departed for Sanditon.

With little to occupy her but her restless imaginings, by eleven o'clock she found the prospect of spending a day of solitude in Trafalgar Terrace too dreary to contemplate. I need employment, thought she. Is not idleness my greatest enemy? The words of the former curate of Stanton came to mind; and while it was quite impossible to offer herself for missionary work in some far-flung corner of the globe, she might find some less consequential service to occupy her for at least a day in Brinshore.

Emma went down to the kitchen and requested a basket of Brinshore Buns.

'Buns, Miss?' said the kitchen maid.

'Half a dozen will suffice. Surely there are some to hand. Aunt Harding is never without them.'

Some minutes later, Emma set out in the direction of the fishermen's cottages with a basket of buns. The day, being neither hot nor cold, and without a cloud in the sky, was perfect for walking. The cottages were easily reached before noon. Emma wondered at the atmosphere of industry and good humour among the fisherfolk, despite the sweat, toil and the pungent smell of fish that clung to the air. The women carried baskets full of mackerel and black bream, and among them were the brother and sister she had most especially come to see. She recognised the old fisherwoman who had come to her aid the day she sprained her ankle. As she approached the scene, silence fell as, one by one, each ceased their work, and Emma became the sole object of their attention. Embarrassed by looks of curiosity and awkwardness on the faces of the onlookers, Emma apologised for the intrusion.

'Please, take this,' said she, offering the basket of buns to the fisherwoman. 'Forgive me for such a tardy expression of appreciation. They are for you and for my two young friends over there. Had I known, I should have brought enough for everyone.'

The fisherwoman smiled nervously and wiped her hands on the edge of her apron before accepting the basket. She beckoned the children to her side and gestured to the others to resume their work. The girl took hold of her brother's hand and led him to Emma. They stood, silent and motionless before her.

'I trust no further mishap has befallen the boy since our last encounter,' said Emma. She observed the children's bare feet, their damp rags and sore hands.

'No, Miss.'

'What news of their papa?' Emma replied.

'No news, Miss.'

The fisherwoman thanked Emma for the basket of buns and went back to work.

As Emma walked back to Trafalgar Terrace, she wondered at the scene she had witnessed. The children, isolated and alone in the world, now occupied her thoughts. She compared her own situation of safety and abundance, to that of the children whose father had left them destitute and unprotected. Though disappointed in love, she had the good fortune to be possessed not only of family and friends who cared for her, but of every material advantage necessary for a life of comfort and ease.

On entering Trafalgar Terrace, Emma was met with the news that Mrs Harding had returned from Croydon.

'I return a day early to surprise you all, and what do I find?' said she. 'An empty house. Not a soul to greet me or with whom to pass the time of day. And not a Brinshore Bun in the house. I have thought of little else since leaving Croydon! They have nothing in Croydon but hard pastry and bread so indigestible one is forced to go hungry. It is the flour. As coarse as —'

'Dear Aunt, I am so glad you are come,' replied Emma. 'Mama is expected at six. She is gone to Sanditon with Anne. I do not know the particulars, except that Aunt and Uncle Musgrave are guests of Lady Forbes and Anne is to join them in Brighton.'

'The Musgraves will find nothing to please them in Brighton, least of all the society of Lady Forbes. I have no desire to take myself to Brighton. I shall not call on them there. I shall save my horses and my carriage.'

Lady Osborne returned at the expected hour with news of the Musgraves and the Blakes. 'The Musgraves stayed in Sanditon only until luncheon was ended, for they were anxious to set out for Brighton. Lady Forbes is to give a dinner in their honour.'

'And what of Captain Blake and Mr Fitzroy?' said Mrs Harding. 'Had you not the pleasure of their company?'

'They are gone to town to discuss the business of architects and builders and I know not what,' said Lady Osborne. 'I believe the conflicting proposals for the site of the edifice continues to cause much speculation. Mrs Blake is to leave Waterloo Crescent next month. I confess, I shall be happy to see her in Delham again. Charles' plans are uncertain, but it appears that Mr Fitzroy is to let Waterloo Crescent. He will look for a living nearby and manage things from there, I believe.'

'And what of Mr Fowle?'

'Mr Fowle's name was not mentioned.'

'While you were gone, Aunt, Mr Fowle visited Mama,' said Emma. 'It is all a great secret. I was afforded no part in the conversation.'

Mrs Harding and Lady Osborne exchanged glances.

'I see I am left out again,' said Emma.

'There is no further need for concealment. I know it all,' Mrs Harding replied. 'I have written to Mr Fowle and I have accepted him, but I shall not give up Trafalgar Terrace. Fortunately, Mr Fowle takes my view of the matter. It is a pleasing concession and is no less an indication of the way matters will likely be managed after we are married.'

The wedding was to be a quiet affair. The Croydon set would not be present, nor would Mrs Harding's son. 'His ship is due to reach the Cape of Good Hope in October. Osborne shall give me away. Perhaps you will mention it to him, my dear,' said Mrs Harding to her sister. 'The Musgraves and the Blakes will be invited. And Mr Fitzroy will not be forgotten. I do not enjoy that degree of acquaintance with the Dowager to issue her with an invitation, nor I suspect would she be disposed to travel so great a distance. It is just as well, for I should not like Aunt Turner to be possessed of the notion that she is invited too. I shall inform her after the event.'

'Aunt Turner must be told. Surely you would not wish to offend her,' said Lady Osborne.

'There is nothing she likes better than a wedding,' said Emma.

'I have seen Aunt Turner at a wedding. When the elder Tomlinson girl married that local farmer.'

'But that was five years ago,' replied Lady Osborne.

'It takes but two sips of wine to loosen her tongue, as you well know. Oh, how she kept half the neighbourhood entertained with stories of her wedding to that imposter O'Brien and what she would do to him were she ever again to set eyes on the brute! Reckless, reckless woman! I shall not have any of it! Brinshore shall be safe from Aunt Turner! She will not attend my wedding!'

CHAPTER TWENTY-TWO

The sense of pleasure and relief felt on receiving Her Ladyship's letter in the afternoon post could not have been greater: Lord Osborne was now impatient for his wife's return.

'I shall leave Brinshore tomorrow,' she wrote, 'and return to Surrey one day hence. Lady Forbes would have me break my journey and spend one night in Brighton with Tom and Elizabeth.'

Emma, despite her mother's entreaty to come home, insisted on remaining in Brinshore until after the wedding. In Brinshore she was certain to be spared the pain of her cousin's society; there she might learn to bear the disappointment of a broken heart; there her days were certain to be full, for she would have purpose and occupation.

'I should have been better pleased had you chosen to return to Delham with me. Your papa will be disappointed. And Frank asks for you daily,' said Lady Osborne. 'Indeed, Lady Forbes has expressed a great desire to see you. And is not Brighton a favourite place of yours? Will you not change your mind, my dear, and return with me to Surrey?'

'Not now, Mama. I need employment. I must have something to do. Please do not seek to change my mind, for it is quite made up. I am determined to stay in Brinshore for the present.'

Lady Osborne studied her daughter. 'Is there anything you desire to tell me?'

Emma shook her head and forced a smile. 'Imagine the stories I shall have to tell of Aunt Harding's wedding when I return to Delham in the autumn. Brinshore's celebrated bride and groom are certain to yield tales to see us through the winter! Papa will be amused.'

'Well,' said Lady Osborne, 'if you are quite certain, then I shall not press you further.'

Emma placed a letter into her mother's hand. 'See that Grandmamma receives this. She complains so very bitterly of my neglect, though I have already written two letters to the Dower House this month.'

'Your grandmamma complains when she is not the sole recipient.'

'But why should I write two letters when one will do. It doubles the cost and the time spent in writing when the news I have to convey is exactly the same. Great Aunt Turner does not complain.'

The carriage that conveyed Lady Osborne to Brighton appeared on the Steine shortly after three. With little time to brush away the dust of the road or make any adjustment to her dress, Lady Osborne was shown up to Lady Forbes' private rooms. There she was received by Her Ladyship who, regal in her powdering gown and slippers, sat impatiently awaiting the appearance of the tea tray.

'Excellent! I shall have you all to myself, which is exactly how I planned it. Elizabeth is gone to purchase a wool shawl at my bidding.

Ordinarily, I should not trust a soul with such a commission. But your sister values economy, and that can only be a good thing. Anne has gone for a walk with her father. They left an hour ago and I do not expect them back very soon. Tom's pace is too brisk for my liking. I expect they will be half way to Eastbourne by now if he has anything to do with it. I prefer to take your sister's arm for she does not march me about as Tom does, like a redcoat on parade.'

'Dear Lady Forbes, how Brighton suits you! I had not expected to see you as well as this. I was given to understand that you were in quite indifferent health,' said Lady Osborne.

'Old age is a wonderful thing' said she. 'One can do as one pleases — be as stout or frail as the moment dictates without giving offence to anyone in the world. Last week I had little inclination to attend Lady Clifton's card party — the last one was a very dull affair — and so I sent a note declining the invitation on the grounds of poor health. I was but a little out of sorts. It was not wholly invention — for I had suffered a slight bilious attack the previous morning. Burton will vouch for me. I find that I cannot do without her. She is as thick as thieves with one of my neighbour's footmen. Consequently, I know everything that goes on over there, you see, with the famous, or should I say, infamous Mrs F.'

Lady Forbes directed her gaze to the house visible from the window; Lady Osborne followed the line of her gaze.

'Lady Clifton threatens to invite me to another card party next month. But I shall not go. You see, my dear, infirmity is expected, indeed it is looked for, in the old. And I am not so naïve as to suppose that Lady Clifton will mind it one whit if I decline the invitation. No indeed. I consider myself under no obligation to tolerate the society of those who find the old burdensome. Nor does one wish to be taken pity of. But, I must say, Lady Clifton managed things very handsomely indeed. This morning I received a fine basket of fruit from the hothouse at Clifton Hall,' said Lady Forbes.

'Oh dear,' said Lady Osborne with good humour. 'If you should decline an invitation to Osborne Castle this autumn, what am I to make of it?'

'Nothing, my dear. You understand me. I know you do. Does my disclosure shock you?'

'Of course not. You forget — I have daily dealings with your friends at the Dower House. Nothing offends or surprises me.'

'Marvellous! Quite marvellous! I have always said that Osborne was a very lucky fellow indeed to get you. And I told his mother so at the time. Would you be good enough to mix the tea, my dear? My hand is a little unsteady today.'

'A little unsteady? Truly?'

The two women laughed heartily.

'A little rum in milk is all the medicine I have need of,' continued Lady Forbes. 'Brighton is my remedy. It is immeasurably more fascinating than Lowford Park. With the comings and goings on the Steine one is never without diversion. And I have such a fine view of it all, as you see. I enjoy the occasional outing, of course. Indeed, I have even considered engaging the services of a dipper.'

Lady Osborne smiled. It appeared that the account she had received of Lady Forbes' infirmities had been grossly exaggerated. 'I understood you to be quite unwell, quite unable to leave your room. Whatever will your friends at the Dower House say?'

'You must urge them to come to Brighton. I should be happy to receive them at any time. Indeed, I have a mind to insist on it.'

Delighted with Lady Osborne's company, Lady Forbes made herself comfortable as her visitor rearranged her cushions and placed a dish of tea into her hands.

'Now,' said she. 'Tell me, what aspect of this marriage business has been concealed from me?'

Said Lady Osborne, 'There is little to tell, though I am astonished that you know anything of it at all. My sister is to marry Brinshore's esteemed local physician, Mr Fowle, at Michaelmas.'

'Is she quite sound in the head?' said Lady Forbes.

'Penelope has made a detailed calculation of the benefits, I assure you, and they are believed to outweigh the manifest disadvantages.'

'If that be the case, let her make a fool of herself. She must be five and forty if she is a day. Surely she has no wish to become a nursemaid. What age is the groom?'

'They are of similar age, and have one object in mind: the promotion of Brinshore.'

'I had never in my life heard of Brinshore until last week. Well. Every day one hears of a new watering place. They spring up all over the place like dandelions in a meadow, and in the blink of an eye they are gone to seed. But that is not my concern. I speak of the business between Anne and the Blake boy. Osborne's godson. Why in heaven's name has she refused him?'

Astounded by Lady Forbes revelation, Lady Osborne was lost for words. 'What?'

'I got it out of her, of course — I insisted she tell me all — for she was behaving as though she had been sentenced to the scaffold. And though I gave my word that I would not reveal any part of the matter to her parents, I do not consider myself under any greater obligation than that. I made no promise to conceal the matter from her aunt. Now, why has Anne refused him?'

Lady Osborne selected her words with care. 'You are better informed than I. Until this moment, I had no knowledge of Captain Blake's offer. But, I confess, I did suspect an attachment.'

'Then why does she not take him?'

'Perhaps she is not sure of her own affection,' said Lady Osborne.

'I have not lived to this great age without learning something of those feelings and passions that are so very hard to suppress, especially in the young. Tell me. Are there any objections as to the Blake boy's family or reputation? Is he a spendthrift? A profligate? I understand he has made a considerable fortune at sea and is now eager to settle down. Anne might perhaps do a little better in London, but then again she might not. Disreputable men are two a penny in town. If she were utterly set against the Blake boy, she would not have been heard crying in her room at three o'clock in the morning.'

'Captain Blake is hardly a boy.'

'Oh, never mind that. At my age, everyone looks as though they are not long out of the nursery. I do not believe I have seen the Blake boy since before your wedding — in the year ninety-six or thereabouts.'

'I can vouch for Captain Blake. He is a fine, upstanding officer and a loyal friend to the family. Perhaps,' said Lady Osborne, thinking aloud, 'I should speak to Anne.'

'Yes, do, my dear!' replied Lady Forbes. 'That is just what I had hoped for. I do so hate to see young people crossed in love. If one has the means to bring about a satisfactory outcome, it is unpardonable not to attempt it. And I must say, it is wholly disagreeable to have an excess of emotion going on under one's own roof. It is something akin to living on the stage of a Shakespearian tragedy, and it makes my excellent cook's cuisine quite indigestible. Now, tell me all about Emma. Let me hear how she goes on in that little-known backwater that goes by the name of Brinshore. I expect to see her on the Steine before the season is out or I shall want to know why. Has that pretty daughter of yours made any conquests of her own this season?'

CHAPTER TWENTY-THREE

No morning's activity could have been more agreeable to Emma than sea bathing. The services of a dipper had been secured for every fine morning for the next complete month excluding Sundays and Wednesdays. The beneficial effects of sea bathing had been exhaustively rehearsed by Mr Fowle, who was now received at Trafalgar Terrace with enduring regularity. The most beneficial aspect to sea bathing in Emma's estimation, however, was the release it afforded from the physician's daily society.

To complement Emma's morning routine, a walk to the fishermen's cottages provided a purpose beyond her own amusement. A parcel of victuals discreetly obtained from the kitchen at Trafalgar Terrace and the occasional purchase of candles were all gratefully received.

Plans for the wedding provided varied employment during the afternoons; and Emma, rarely devoid of occupation of one kind or another, succeeded in some small part to dislodge Captain Blake from her thoughts and designs. He was never far away; but as fond recollections of him drifted back into her mind from time to time, she sought to meet them and use them to prepare herself for their next encounter. And while his absence from Trafalgar Terrace was painful, it was not unendurable.

Mr Fitzroy called periodically and stayed for ten or fifteen minutes; but when Mr Fowle was present discussion naturally tended towards loftier matters. One Wednesday morning towards the end of July, Mrs Harding was not at home, being engaged with Brinshore's leading seamstress, a woman commissioned on the recommendation of Peacock's, with the making of Mrs Harding's wedding dress. Having little expectation of morning callers, Emma was astonished to find Captain Blake waiting downstairs.

With seconds to collect her thoughts and straighten her frock, Emma struggled to calm herself.

'My dear Emma,' said he, coming forward to greet her. 'I trust I find you well.'

'You do, indeed,' she replied with trembling in her voice.

'We have not met since the Brinshore Ball.'

Emma motioned to Captain Blake to be seated.

'No, indeed,' she replied.

An awkward silence ensued as both parties were at pains to think of something to say.

'I trust Mrs Harding is well,' said he.

'Quite well and much occupied with the wedding,' Emma replied.

'Of course,' said he.

'I understand you were in Delham recently.'

'I dined at Osborne Castle two nights ago at your parents' kind invitation,' said he, with uncommon hesitation in his voice. 'They are well. They miss you, Emma. You were much in all our thoughts.'

Emma had not seen Captain Blake quite so ill at ease as this; she observed his uncertain demeanour and the mildness of his voice. The man who now appeared by her side was unfamiliar, almost a stranger to her. Indeed, the man she had known and loved, ever sanguine, abounding with enthusiasm, and full of confident optimism, now sat before her a little subdued and dispirited.

'I daresay, in a day or two, you will likely receive some news that may cause you to wonder. It was my express intention to conceal it as long as possible to avoid any awkwardness that might follow. Please understand that my wish was to protect the parties most affected by it. But some more colourful, intriguing narrative —'

'Tendered by the Dower House?' asked Emma.

Captain Blake smiled but was disinclined to confirm Emma's supposition.

'The narrative to which I refer has prompted me to act. I insisted that you hear it from my lips. Dear Emma, would you allow me to lay before you the facts?'

Emma made no objection. She had little desire to hear what he had to say, yet to flee from the truth was impossible. However disagreeable, she must hear that which was likely to confirm her worst fears. Had she not expected it? Had she not prepared herself?

Had she not already suffered greatly? The sooner the situation was made plain, the sooner she would be obliged to accept it.

'Before Miss Musgrave left Brinshore to join her parents in Brighton,' said he, 'I made your cousin an offer of marriage. My dear Emma, Miss Musgrave, rightly and decisively, declined my offer. Those are the facts.'

'Anne rejected you?' replied Emma, shocked by his disclosure. 'I cannot believe it.'

'It was a foolish act on my part. I see that now. I had no right to — I believe I have given pain to all your family.'

Agitation, vexation, hope, every possible contrary emotion, added to Emma's confusion.

'I see I have given *you* pain. My dear Emma, can you forgive me?'

'What shall you do now?' said she, weakly.

'I — I shall, of course, assist Mr Fitzroy until the promise I made to my late friend has been executed in full.'

'But are you quite certain about Anne? Perhaps there has been some misunderstanding on my cousin's part.'

'The misunderstanding was mine — is mine — and mine alone. Can you forgive me, Emma? My thoughtlessness and my utter lack of courtesy and consideration for — I deserve nothing but censure.'

Despite Emma's plea, Captain Blake's disinclination to disclose more than necessity dictated, resulted in a prolonged lull in the conversation. Uncommonly taciturn, some minutes later he took his leave. Emma reproached herself for having sought too eagerly to ascertain every detail of the discourse that had passed between him and her cousin — most particularly, the expression of his declaration and the manner of Anne's refusal — but no further word from him was forthcoming. The facts were recounted without embellishment, explanation or justification.

Emma was deeply puzzled by the turn of events. What had prompted Anne to reject him? She had welcomed his society; his was the opinion that seemed to matter to her the most. Indeed, on reflection, Emma was certain that her own displeasure with Anne was entirely due to her cousin's dealings with Captain Blake; for there was a degree of companionable understanding in their communication that Emma was forced to concede demonstrated compatibility beyond the normal course of conversation.

Had Anne failed to secure her father's blessing? Had she been obliged to reject him? Had Aunt Musgrave persuaded Anne to decline his offer for some other reason? None of the questions that issued back and forth in Emma's mind yielded satisfactory answers.

Anne must not be in love with him after all, thought she. No other explanation seemed as dependable as the possibility that Captain Blake had failed to secure Anne's affections. And yet, how could it be so? Had he mistaken amiability for love? It was not beyond possibility. Indeed, his own behaviour — his affable good-humour, his readiness to please and be pleased — might easily have given hope to any young woman unfamiliar with his character and temperament.

Another thought occurred to her — that perhaps her cousin's affections were already engaged elsewhere. Was Mr Fitzroy her object after all? Had he succeeded where his friend had failed? It did not seem likely; for Anne appeared to show no particular preference for Captain Blake's friend, despite Emma's hopes to the contrary.

Could it be that all the while her cousin had been at Brinshore, her thoughts had been fixed on Lowford Park? Had Anne not first waltzed at Lowford? Had she not remarked on the pleasure of twice standing up with Lowford's heir at the same ball? Lowford Park might reasonably be her aim. And though Emma did not much care for any of the Lowford men, Anne might have the estate and fine grounds in her sights. Perhaps this explained her eagerness to visit Lady Forbes in Brighton.

Emma was roused from her musings by the unexpected arrival of another visitor shortly after Captain Blake's departure. No other callers were expected, and so when Mr Fitzroy was announced, Emma was taken quite by surprise.

'Ah,' said he, coming into the room in a great hurry. 'I expected to find Captain Blake here.'

'And so you should have done had you called ten minutes ago,' said she. 'I know not where he is gone, whether to Sanditon or elsewhere. Have you urgent need to find him?'

'There is no very great urgency. We shall meet at Lady Denham's this evening.'

'What is the occasion?'

'We are summoned to make up a card table.'

'Is she a tolerable player?'

'She might show more promise were she to pay more thought to her hand and spend five minutes out of every ten in silent contemplation of it,' said he.

'Perhaps you might mention to Lady Denham that I should like to purchase some of her asses' milk. A little every Thursday would do. She need have no fear. I shall pay her every week from my allowance.'

'It is curious indeed, but I should, of course, be happy to convey the message to Her Ladyship.'

'I am much obliged to you,' said Emma.

'May I ask what prompts such an unusual request?'

'You may ask whatever you will, though I cannot guarantee a satisfactory answer,' she replied. 'For the present, allow me to say only that I have need of it. Will it be a small party?'

'The Parkers are invited. Miss Brereton will be present, of course. Sir Edward Denham, a Miss Heywood, and Mr Sydney Parker are also expected.'

'Oh,' said she. 'Card players aplenty!'

'I'm told Mrs Parker and Miss Heywood have little inclination for cards,' replied Mr Fitzroy. His look altered as the tone of his voice became more serious. 'I expect you have heard the news.'

'If you mean the news that Captain Blake has made an offer to Anne and she has refused him, yes, I have.'

Mr Fitzroy nodded slightly but made no comment.

'Have you no view of the matter?' Emma enquired. 'No opinion to offer?'

'Captain Blake is my friend. I am very sorry for him.'

'But what think you of my cousin's behaviour? Do you think her foolish?'

'No thought was further from my mind,' said he.

Mr Fitzroy moved towards the window where she was standing. 'Miss Osborne, would you allow me to speak with the same frankness more commonly reserved for flesh and blood? In so doing I should betray no confidence.'

Emma straightened the cuff of her sleeve and looked away to stifle a tear. Her voice faltered. 'Did my cousin refuse Captain Blake for my sake because she did not wish to cause me pain, Mr Fitzroy? Am I the impediment to their happiness?'

'Had you within your power the ability to relieve another's suffering but, in so doing, increase your own, what course would you —' He broke off. 'No. I ask too much. Forgive me, Miss Osborne. Forgive me.'

'You had better speak plainly,' said she.

Emma moved to the opposite corner of the room. She stood still, arms by her side, with a calm intensity in her eyes.

'Rarely have I had the good fortune to encounter someone whose artless good nature and courage have impressed me more,' said he.

'I know. Captain Blake is all these things and more,' said she.

'I do not speak of Captain Blake.'

Emma sighed. 'Of course. My cousin is highly regarded wherever she goes. We are so very dissimilar.'

Mr Fitzroy moved towards the mirror that hung over the fireplace. 'Come,' said he, beckoning her to draw closer. 'What do you see in the looking glass?'

'What is your point?' she asked.

'I am puzzled by your failure to recognise that the qualities of which I speak are those which you possess. It is of Miss Osborne I speak — not Captain Blake, not Miss Musgrave.'

Emma smiled weakly. 'You will make a fine clergyman.'

'I speak as a friend,' he replied. 'Your resilience, your generosity of spirit makes you strong.'

Drawing closer to the looking glass, Emma felt strangely heartened by his words. He took her hand and placed it in his.

'Have I misjudged matters entirely?' said she.

'Partiality for someone or something is oft inclined to blight clear-sightedness,' he replied. 'It is not a crime.'

'I suppose you mean that when we greatly desire something, we begin to believe it to be already in our possession,' said Emma.

A tear ran down her cheek. Blotting it out with the edge of her cuff, she replied, 'I fancied myself in love. No. I was in love. I believed that Captain Blake returned my affections. I was mistaken. Tell me, did Anne refuse him on my account? Is it I that stands between them?'

Mr Fitzroy spoke with care. 'Were you to suspect it to be the case, how might you act? What would you do?'

'I — I don't know. I suppose —'

190

Before Emma had the opportunity to answer in full, there was a knock at the door.

'Excuse me, Miss. A woman has left a basket of fish at the kitchen door. She refuses to take payment. My mistress is not here. What am I to do?'

'Please supply her with a basket of provisions from the store cupboard.'

'Yes, Miss,' said she, quietly closing the door behind her.

Turning to Mr Fitzroy, Emma continued, 'May I rely on your discretion?'

'You may,' he replied.

'I seek some information,' said she. 'I am anxious to ascertain the whereabouts, or indeed, the fate of an individual?'

Mr Fitzroy replied, 'I would need as many particulars as possible before I could determine —'

'Exactly,' said she. 'I can supply what I have.'

'It is a peculiar request,' said he, puzzled by her appeal for assistance.

'Even so, I should be much obliged to you if you would make enquiries concerning the person in question.'

CHAPTER TWENTY-FOUR

Several days passed during which Emma attempted to write to her cousin; five letters were composed of varying length and tone, and five letters were discarded. The delicacy of the situation, and the feelings and wishes of each party, rendered it all but impossible for Emma to commit words to paper. When, therefore, a letter unexpectedly arrived from Brighton, Emma was presented with the perfect opportunity to speak to her cousin in person. The letter, which was brief, was written in Lady Forbes' unsteady hand.

'My dear Emma, I make no bones about the matter. There you are in that dreary place that goes by the name of Brinshore when you should be in Brighton. It is a full twelvemonth since I have seen you. Tell Mrs H that she must spare you a day or two. My neighbour, the famous Mrs F, is to give a small dinner — no more than ten are invited. I thought you of all people should like to see the rooms at Steine House. Anne has positively declined the invitation on the pretence of indisposition. She refuses to see a physician. But your society, my dear Emma, will be the best cure. Look out your finest gown. I will send my carriage two days hence. Yours etc... PS My dear, say nothing of Mrs F to Mrs H. It is not within my power to secure an invitation for your aunt — whether I had a mind to or not — and I have not.'

The matter was settled with relative ease. Mrs Harding showed neither the inclination for Brighton herself, nor any great curiosity as to the object of Lady Forbes' request. 'Go,' said she. 'Lady Forbes is not a woman who likes to be crossed. She has not the forbearance, the temper, nor the generous spirit that I possess. I should find Brighton too florid, too tawdry, and too full of people. I have been spoilt by the tranquil elegance of Brinshore. One cannot be sure of a quiet spot to sit in Brighton, or a healthy dish of tea, for all the tea has been tampered with.'

Two days later, as Brighton came into view Emma found much to marvel at and excite. The carriage, which had taken a road that passed through an exceedingly pretty grove, was unfamiliar to its occupant. Perhaps I have stayed in Brinshore too long, thought she.

The contrast was marked; and though she should not have owned it to her aunt, Brighton was more stylish and more enterprising than Brinshore and Sanditon combined. Emma had become too accustomed to Brinshore and its parochial sensibilities. The possibility that a watering place such as Brinshore might one day surpass that of Brighton in prestige and importance seemed but a dream, for Brighton exuded an air of sophistication that Brinshore was completely without. Its buildings were taller, the terraces that lined its seafront were grander, and its inhabitants were attired in the very latest fashions.

On reaching Lady Forbes's residence, Emma was received by her Aunt Musgrave. 'Emma, my dear, I am so very glad you are come. I should not have been easy in my mind had I not seen you before our departure. We are bound for Surrey, you see. I insisted on waiting a day for I wanted to carry news of you to Osborne Park.'

'Leaving Brighton so soon? But why?'

'Anne is anxious to return to Delham, and to own the truth, I take the same view. Your cousin is not herself and I am persuaded that home is the best place for her.'

'Where is she? May I go to her?'

'Lady Forbes is waiting for you.'

'When do you leave?' asked Emma.

'We leave within the hour, for we are expected in Shoreham by eight. Robert has had business there this past week. He neglects to say what it is. I should like to know what business takes your uncle to Shoreham and never to Delham,' said Mrs Musgrave. 'But more than that, I should like to hear news of Croydon. I expect I shall have much to tell your mama when I see her.'

'I must see Anne,' replied Emma.

'And so you shall, my dear. We shall not leave without a proper farewell, I assure you.'

'No, Aunt. That will not do,' said she. 'I must speak with my cousin alone.'

'Lady Forbes does not like to be kept waiting.'

'Tell her that I must make adjustments to my dress. I shall wait upon her shortly.'

'Very well. On your head be it,' said Mrs Musgrave. 'Come with me.'

Anne was in her bedchamber sitting by the window, looking out onto the Steine. Dressed in travelling cloak and bonnet, she had in her hand a letter. As Emma entered the room, Anne quickly slipped the letter into her reticule. Emma saw that her cousin looked tired and drawn. The circles under her eyes were a dark shade of purple, and it was apparent from her cousin's reaction that she had not expected Emma to seek her out.

'Forgive me for not receiving you properly,' said she. 'I am not myself today.'

'I am shocked. I did not expect to see you as bad as this. Have you seen a physician?'

'I have no wish to — Delham is all I need. If only Mama had not promised to call at Shoreham on the way —'

Emma took a seat opposite her cousin. 'You look quite ill. Stay. You are not fit to make the journey home.'

Anne looked away. 'I shall go. I must go.'

Emma was less perplexed by her cousin's refusal to accept succour than by the sickly pallor of her countenance that seemed to suggest a disorder of a more serious nature.

'There is little time and I must speak with you on a subject of mutual importance,' said Emma. 'Forgive me for any intrusion into your privacy that might appear to you impertinent. No object could be further from my mind.'

Anne glanced briefly at Emma, as though anticipating bad news.

'It is, I am afraid to say, common knowledge that an offer of marriage has been made to you,' Emma continued.

'I have no wish to speak of it,' said Anne. 'Please do not press me on the subject.'

'But one word will suffice, and you shall hear nothing more from me.'

The weakness of Anne's voice rendered it almost inaudible. 'The answer is yes,' said Anne. 'Allow me to wish you joy, my dear cousin.'

'Wish me joy? What is this? Why do you wish *me* joy?'

'I am glad that everything is settled between you. Now I shall be content.'

It was evident to Emma, as it was not to Anne, that they were at cross purposes. 'You anticipated my question.'

Anne nodded.

'May I ask, what you imagined my question to be?'

'You wish me to be your bridesmaid,' said Anne.

'Then you have misunderstood me completely! Let us begin again,' said Emma. 'Do you love Captain Blake?'

'That I cannot answer, and you must not ask it of me,' replied Anne.

'Then I shall answer the question for you. I believe you love Captain Blake, but you declined his offer for my sake. If I am wrong, please, for all our sakes, deny it.'

Anne glanced at her cousin; her eyes began to well. 'I deserve neither kindness nor forbearance. When you know the full extent of my culpability, you will never speak to me again.'

'Whatever can you mean?' said Emma. 'Now I *must* know the whole of it.'

'Yes, you must. I see that now,' said Anne, glancing nervously at her cousin. 'Prepare yourself for the worst kind of betrayal imaginable.'

'Betrayal is a harsh word,' Emma replied.

'Early on I suspected a partiality on Captain Blake's side.' Anne continued, 'The day we visited the circulating library in Sanditon I perceived something in his manner — a look, a word — nothing very extraordinary. When Frank broke his head, and Captain Blake travelled with you to Osborne Castle I began to doubt my suspicions. I must say, I was relieved, for I had also begun to think myself a little in love, and I knew too well the hopelessness of my situation. You see, I was never in any doubt about your attachment to Captain Blake.'

'Oh,' said Emma.

Anne went on. 'Captain Blake stayed but two days in Delham. I had expected him to stay a full week. Shortly after his return, he came to Trafalgar Terrace, and I must own the truth to you, I made no effort to discourage him. Nothing was said between us. There was no declaration. Nothing at all. Then you returned to Brinshore. That was when I knew that I had been foolish. I had had it within my power to deter him, but I did not. On the evening of the Brinshore Ball, I suspected he would make me an offer, for he asked to see me. By then, my feelings for Captain Blake were, were — I loved him. Your mama, I believe, suspected an attachment.'

'Mama?'

'Yes,' said Anne. 'Captain Blake and I met by design the morning I begged to be excused from sea bathing. It was imprudent of me to insist on an interview that can only be described as clandestine. In Captain Blake's defence, he wanted to call at Trafalgar Terrace; the secrecy of the encounter was not of his choosing but mine. I suspected from your demeanour that same afternoon that you had witnessed some part of it.'

'I shall never pick up a spyglass again,' said Emma.

'Of course,' Anne replied. 'The spyglass.'

'Please, go on.' Emma fixed her full attention on Anne.

'On receiving Captain Blake's declaration, I knew that I had rendered you the greatest disservice. Could there be such treachery among cousins? By then I thought only of leaving Brinshore.'

'Everything now falls into place. But perhaps had I been a rational being, had I not yielded to my own imaginings, I might have understood what must have been plain for all to see. But then the truth is often more painful than a lie. And though I wish with all my heart it were otherwise, I thank you for your candour.'

Anne's eyes filled with tears. 'The worst of it is still to come. I beg your forgiveness though I am utterly undeserving of it. You see, I spoke both falsely and out of turn to Captain Blake. While I cannot lament the former, I deeply regret the latter.'

'Tell me,' said Emma. 'I must know it all.'

Anne looked down, unable to meet Emma's gaze. 'I denied my true feelings for Captain Blake. That I lament. Truly, I do. But greater than that, I regret — I regret — In seeking to explain myself, I revealed your true regard for him. I gave him to understand that he had, through his genial nature and affability, secured your affection. I urged him to do the honourable thing and make you an offer. There can be no excuse for the utter imprudence of my actions, but my intentions, dear Emma, please believe me, were sincere. I have managed things very badly. Very badly indeed. I alone am to blame. My dear cousin, truly my unforgiveable thoughtlessness grieves me constantly. I have been utterly foolish.'

'Thoughtless? Foolish? Yes, indeed! How could you do such a thing? You urged Captain Blake — begged him — to make me an offer? I cannot believe it! I cannot believe you could be so stupid. The humiliation! How could I possibly accept him now?'

'I am thoroughly ashamed of my behaviour,' said Anne.

'And so you should be. You welcomed his advances — enticed him — gave him hope — and then prevailed upon him to transfer his affections to me! You have not only treated me shamefully, you have treated the man you profess to love with contempt! You do not deserve him!'

'Tell me what I am to do — tell me how to act — tell me how I might make amends,' replied Anne.

'Your own conscience should tell you — should have told you from the outset. But no. You chose, instead, to seek refuge from the world, and the upset that is of your own making, by returning to Delham. And you cause anxiety to your mama and papa and all your family! They begin to fear for your health! Do not look to me for sympathy for there is no sympathy in me for what you have done.'

'Your words are harsh indeed!' said Anne, gaining some measure of resistance to her cousin's rebuke. 'But perhaps you should examine your behaviour! Had you not constantly laid before the world the desires of your heart, had your own partiality not affected your judgement, you might have been more discerning. Your perception was flawed, Emma. When all around you, including your mama, comprehended the state of affairs, you closed your eyes and your ears. Even now, your grievance with me rests on the assertion that I have destroyed forever your chances of securing Captain Blake. *How could I possibly accept him now?* Those were your words. You do not love him. Not truly. If you did, you would seek *his* happiness above your own. But you seek only to gratify your own desires.'

'You are wrong. I am come to Brighton to put right what is presently amiss. You have no comprehension of the sacrifice I make.'

'Indeed I have.'

Anne had no wish to prolong the quarrel that was so disagreeable to her. 'Emma,' said she, 'it seems we shall not meet again for some time. Let us part as friends. We are not, and could never be enemies. I should not like our parting words to cause regret on either side. And I am sincere when I say that I wish you every possible happiness.'

'What will you do?' replied Emma.

'I'm bound for Delham. The Lowford family are expected on Thursday. As you can imagine, they are anxious to hear news of Lady Forbes.'

'Are *all* the family expected?'

'I believe so.'

Emma glanced at the mantelpiece clock. 'I must go. Lady Forbes has been kept waiting long enough.'

The cousins embraced, and although their wounds were still raw, they endeavoured to part with good grace.

'Love is a curious business. I expect in years to come we will wonder at the absurdity of it all,' said Anne.

Lady Forbes was less put out by Emma's tardy appearance, than by a communication received from Steine House some fifteen minutes earlier.

'I am not used to having my tea so late in the day. What took you so long? A seamstress might have made up a new gown in the time it has taken you to adjust yours. Well, never mind that now. I have just received this from the mistress of Steine House. The famous Mrs F is laid low with influenza. The house, it seems, is full of it and so dinner is postponed a week.'

'A week? Then it will not be within my power to attend,' said Emma. 'I have been spared but two days. Aunt Harding cannot do without me with the wedding so close at hand.'

'All that wedding nonsense! It is nauseating! I suppose your aunt is determined to go through with it.'

'Quite determined, I assure you,' said Emma.

'It is enough to bring on one of my bilious attacks,' replied Lady Forbes. 'I have enjoyed excellent health these last forty years. Indeed, it was in no small part due to Lord Forbes.'

'Has he not been dead these forty years or more?'

'Precisely,' Lady Forbes replied. 'You may pass me a dish of tea, if you will.'

Emma acceded to Lady Forbes request. 'Without spilling half of it on my precious rug, my dear. Have you seen Anne? She has quite lost her bloom, and I have little hope that she will regain it. Your Aunt Musgrave is beside herself with worry. Emma, my dear, we shall be but two for dinner. I have no desire to sit in state in the dining room. Should you be willing to join me, I shall send to the kitchen for a tray by and by. We shall be snug just as we are, and you shall tell me all the news from Brinshore that does not concern Mrs Harding and her beau. I am particularly eager to hear news of Captain Blake.'

The evening passed more speedily than Emma had anticipated in the comfort of Lady Forbes private rooms.

'And so Mr Fitzroy is determined to carry out his brother's wishes. He is under no obligation to do so, you know. The money left to him must be substantial, and to my knowledge it was not irreversibly tied up. You see, I know rather more of the matter than you might imagine.'

'How so?' said Emma.

'Lowford's steward is the uncle of the steward to the present Earl — an unpleasant, disagreeable man. Lord Allersham, that is. Anyone in his employ requires the forbearance of a saint. It seems Miss Barnes, the young lady to whom Mr Fitzroy was engaged and who threw him over for another, did so, in part, because he would not be persuaded to break his word to his dying brother. She had the money in her sights. Curiously, the Earl had the same view of matter, though he despised the very sight of Miss Barnes. It led to some awkwardness with Allersham's chaplain too, Miss Barnes being his daughter. I expect the Earl would like to get his hands on part of the money at least, for he has lost a vast deal of his own at cards. And although the objection to Miss Barnes no longer exists, it seems Mr Fitzroy will not be moved. He will not pay Lord Allersham's debts and, therefore, he remains a stranger to his family. He is not admitted to Allersham.'

'He has chosen to carry out the wishes of Captain Fitzroy,' said Emma. 'I applaud his tenacity.'

'Do you, my dear? While the Earl remains single, Mr Fitzroy remains the heir. If anything should happen to the scoundrel, your friend will be saddled with a great deal of debt. I believe he should set aside some part of the bequest for just such an eventuality.'

'Would it not be better to find the Earl a bride as swiftly as possible?'

'What a life she would have of it! I should not wish it on any woman of my acquaintance. These days young women are less particular, I suppose, than once they were. War has claimed so many of our fine young men. Nowadays a pretty young thing will marry a title without a second thought. It matters not whether he has teeth or hair of his own, or even a penny to his name. Lord Forbes was greatly admired, you know, and he was agreeably possessed of a full head of hair, most of his teeth and all his faculties, as well as a considerable fortune.'

Stories of the old rooms at Bath — some new, some familiar — followed; but it was the narratives that bore the greatest similarity to tales told at the Dower House that held the most fascination for Emma. How differently facts are perceived when stories are remembered and retold from different sides! Intrigues and scandals were recalled in vivid detail; and the modifications and discrepancies that served to entertain and delight the hearer were savoured in equal measure by the narrator.

'Oh yes, my dear! I never saw a man so utterly forlorn and desolate as Mr Edwards! He refused to stand up with any other woman the rest of the season! But your great aunt had set her cap at Mr Turner. Poor Mr Edwards was left out in the cold, and Mr Edwards by far being the better dancer of the two.'

It was half past eleven before Lady Forbes, heady from the wine and the exertion of story-telling, fell fast asleep; Emma summoned Her Ladyship's maid to attend her, and returned to her room exhausted from all the events of the day.

The weather, being mild and fine the following morning, was the best climate for walking; and Emma, despite having no companion with whom to promenade, had a great desire to see more of

Brighton. Lady Forbes was unlikely to appear before noon, and so Emma set out on her walk soon after breakfast. The solitude it afforded was not only opportune but wished for; as she walked on, she pondered the previous day's events, more particularly, the exchange that had taken place between herself and her cousin.

The mortification that Emma felt on hearing Anne's full confession was intensified by the knowledge that her affections for Captain Blake were not, nor ever could be, reciprocated. How could she meet him again? How could she look him in the eye? What must he have thought of her when last they met in Brinshore, knowing as he did the true nature of her regard for him?

I could never be happy with Captain Blake now, she thought. It is clear what I must do. I must strive to forget him. I must put him completely out of my mind. In time, he shall once again be to me as a friend. In that respect I have a choice. But Anne will always be my cousin. It cannot be avoided. It cannot be otherwise. Nevertheless, I shall not seek Anne's society, not for some duration. No. It is said that time is a healer. In time all will be well, but it is not well now.

By the time Emma had completed her walk, her mind was made up. It was not enough to eschew their society; more had to be done. But as she entered the house the news that a visitor awaited her in the drawing room put all thought of Anne Musgrave and Captain Blake out of her mind. The visitor was Mr Robert Watson.

'Uncle Watson!' said Emma. 'Is something amiss? Has some accident befallen the Musgraves?'

'Do not be alarmed. All is well. The Musgraves set off for Delham at first light. Madness, in my view!'

'Why are you here? Have you news of Mama and Papa? Has something happened to Frank?'

'I have no news from Osborne Castle to tell though I am minded to call there briefly on my return to Croydon.'

'What brings you to Brighton? Will you stay for luncheon?' said Emma, still at a loss to understand the reason for her uncle's visit.

'Luncheon? I believe I shall. Lady Forbes is known to put on a good spread,' said he. 'Emma, the reason for my visit is this: I should like your assistance. I seek information from Captain Blake who I understand is at present residing in Sanditon. Did he or did he not return earlier this summer from the West Indies?'

'He did.'

'Then I should like to know the whereabouts of a Mr Hood, a gentleman who I believe had passage on his ship.'

'Why?'

'At present I am not at liberty to disclose my reasons for wanting to find this man. I seek only confirmation of the fact. When do you return to Brinshore? The Musgraves thought you would not be long in Brighton.'

'Tomorrow.'

'Excellent. Then I should be much obliged if you would break your journey and call on Captain Blake. Discover what you can. I am bound for Croydon in a day or two when I have finished my business in Shoreham. Direct any correspondence there.'

'Might I know the reason for the enquiry?' said Emma, with dread in her heart. Could any undertaking be more onerous than this, thought she. And at such a moment!

'It is better that you know as little as possible. All will become clear in time.'

'But what reason am I to give to Captain Blake? What if he should be unwilling to disclose — '

'Tell him justice would be served by it. That is all he needs to know.'

'I am sure a letter from *you* would do more good. Captain Blake may not wish to be drawn in, and certainly not by me.'

'Nonsense. Captain Blake will surely oblige you, Emma. Find out what you can for all our sakes.'

CHAPTER TWENTY-FIVE

The prospect of meeting with Captain Blake caused Emma great consternation; but having, of her own volition, made a promise to her uncle, she was now obliged to do what he had asked of her. On entering Sanditon, a state of anxious dread increased Emma's agitation; she wished above all things that she had declined her uncle's request. Moreover, she wished Captain Blake anywhere in the world but Waterloo Crescent. With little ceremony, she was admitted to the house amid a state of chaos and confusion, for Mrs Blake was making preparations to leave Sanditon.

'I shall miss this beautiful house. I shall miss the sea and the air, and I shall miss Sanditon. It has become so very dear to me,' said Mrs

Blake. 'How did Shakespeare have it? *Like as the waves make towards the pebbl'd shore, so do our minutes hasten to their end.*'

'I expect he was speaking of death,' said Emma. 'And surely, Mrs Blake, you are at liberty to frequent Sanditon at any time.'

'I am torn, my dear,' said Mrs Blake. 'When I am in Sanditon I miss the society of my dear friends in Delham. And I expect that when I return to Delham, I shall miss the society of the friends I have made in Sanditon. What a perverse creature I am!'

'No more than I or anyone else in the world,' said Emma. 'Mrs Blake, I hardly know how to begin. I am commissioned by my uncle, Mr Robert Watson, with whom I believe you are acquainted or were, to seek Captain Blake's assistance on a matter of some importance.'

Mrs Blake was puzzled by the request but curbed the impulse to enquire further. 'Of course, my dear. I remember Mr Robert Watson. I once had dealings with him. I shall fetch Charles directly.'

Emma awaited Captain Blake in nervous anticipation of their encounter. She was afforded little time to compose herself, as he answered her call without delay and strode urgently into the drawing room.

'Emma, what is it? What might I do? How might I assist you?' His look was kind and consoling, unlike his uncharacteristic unease during their last encounter. There appeared to be no awkwardness or resentment on his side. He was still the friend he had always been, the friend she had always known and loved.

She began to speak with unusual timidity. 'I am sent by my uncle to ask if you recall a gentleman who had passage on your ship from the West Indies. A Mr Hood.'

'Mr Hood? I do, indeed. A man of few words and considerable fortune. Softly spoken. A serious fellow.'

'Do you know where my uncle might find him?'

Captain Blake shook his head. 'It was a curious thing, though I made nothing of it at the time. He was disinclined to speak of his family or connections. He would not be drawn out. May I ask the reason for your uncle's enquiry, Emma?'

'He said only that justice would be served were he to discover Mr Hood's whereabouts.'

'There is a family of West Indians who have come to Sanditon for the summer. I wonder, should I make enquiries there? They may be able to furnish me with some particular or other. I should, of course, make no mention of your uncle's enquiry. A general remark will suffice.'

'Indeed,' said Emma. 'You might mention in a casual way that a Mr Hood had passage on your ship and that a friend should like to renew his acquaintance but has no means of tracing him.'

'I shall see what I can do,' said Captain Blake.

'Thank you,' she replied. 'If your enquiry yields results, would you inform my uncle directly?' Emma presented him with piece of paper on which the address of Mr Robert Watson's Croydon office was written.

'Of course,' said he. 'Will you stay, Emma? Will you rest a while?'

'Thank you, no. I must leave now. Aunt Harding is expecting me.'

'Emma —'

'Before I go,' said she, 'allow me a few more moments of your time.'

'You could never trespass on my time,' said he. 'You are a dear friend to me.'

'And we shall always remain friends,' Emma replied.

'Indeed we shall,' said he.

'Then as a friend, allow me to speak plainly. Forget what transpired between you and Anne when last you met, and renew your offer to her. If you delay, my cousin may, through some sense of well-meaning but misplaced loyalty, accept another.'

'If Miss Musgrave has had the good fortune to secure the affections of —'

'Of my cousin I am certain of this: her heart is yours. She made an error of judgement, but her intentions were honourable. Are we not all guilty of poor judgement at some time in our lives? Do not delay, my friend. The Lowford set are to dine with the Musgraves on Thursday. I can say no more for the present.'

However difficult the speech, however grim the duty to abandon every last hope, when once the words had been uttered, Emma found some consolation in the knowledge that she had acted honourably. I shall be forever reminded of this day, for we are to be bound inextricably by the ties of family, thought she. Captain Blake shall be my cousin, and that is the end of the matter, and I shall live to accept it, as I must.

The thought of Anne as the new Mrs Blake was as painful as it was inevitable. There was no denying the fact that the match was eminently suitable on both sides. Theirs was a union of minds, of tastes and principles; and thereby it accorded the greatest promise of marital harmony. I should be happy, thought she, but I am not. Until I have learned true acceptance I shall not seek their society. It is better that we should be settled some distance apart.

The warmth of her parting words to her friends on leaving Waterloo Crescent betrayed nothing of Emma's inner turmoil. My parents would not know me, thought she; indeed, I hardly know myself.

'I expect we shall not meet again until the wedding,' said Emma.

'The wedding?' asked Mrs Blake.

'Aunt Harding and Mr Fowle. It would give them the greatest pleasure to count you among their guests.'

When, at last, Emma reached her destination, Mrs Harding was in a sorry state due to some news she had received from her fiancé. 'It seems Mr Fowle is laid low. At first it was nothing more than a mild cold. He has since developed an infection of the lungs. A physician from Eastbourne was called to attend him yesterday. He is waited on hand and foot, for he has taken to his bed, and it will likely be a week or even two before he is fit to be seen.'

'That is unfortunate,' said Emma.

'It is much worse than that,' replied her aunt. 'There is much to be done, much to be decided upon.'

'The wedding is not so imminent that Mr Fowle's state of health would necessitate a postponement.'

'A postponement? No, indeed. For I should wheel him to the altar in your grandpapa's old chair before I would sanction a postponement.'

'But why the urgency? Surely you would enjoy the occasion more readily were Mr Fowle in good health.'

'But should he develop pneumonia and die before we are properly wed, I should have no claim on his estate. I shall not allow Mr Fowle to meet his Maker until I am bound by the ties that make me his widow.'

'Aunt Harding! What an extraordinary thing to say! Poor Mr Fowle! Why are you not at his side providing comfort in his hour of need?'

'It is not seemly, as you well know.'

'This is Mr Fowle of whom we speak, the man to whom you have given your heart,' said Emma.

'The man to whom I have given my *consent*. That is a very different matter.'

'Forgive me, Aunt, for being so bold. Have you any regard for Mr Fowle or his present situation?'

'I have the very greatest regard for his situation, but I have no intention of becoming Mr Fowle's nursemaid,' said Mrs Harding. 'Mr Fitzroy called in your absence. He left a note. There you see, it is on the mantelpiece.'

After the dust of the day's travel had been washed away, Emma sat alone in her bedchamber until the hour for dinner arrived. The note from Mr Fitzroy lay unopened on the table. She picked it up and examined the hand of its author. It was bold and elegant, but its style was not grandiose which, in her view, was often present in the writing of the vain and pretentious. The tone of the note matched perfectly the hand that wrote it. Absent from the letter was any narrative of the time or trouble spent in obtaining the information, a feature which often prefaced missives by those who sought praise for their endeavours. Mr Fitzroy stated simply that he had had some degree of success securing the information she had requested, but that the news was grave: the individual in question had committed a capital offence, and the punishment had already been carried out.

When next they met, Mr Fitzroy stayed but ten minutes to furnish her aunt with an account of Mr Fowle's condition. Mrs Harding claimed his full attention, as well as the larger share of the conversation, and Emma was left pondering how to contrive a brief moment alone with him. At last, as Mr Fitzroy took his leave, Emma insisted on seeing their visitor to the door.

'Machine-breaking?' said Emma. 'I cannot believe it. It seems so paltry an offence for so harsh a sentence. I am grieved indeed, not for myself but for —'

'Shall you disclose this information to whomever is affected by it?'

'What is your opinion?' said she.

'Listen to your conscience,' he replied. 'Your instincts serve you well.'

'Do they, Mr Fitzroy? Lately, my instincts have not served me at all well.'

The departure of Mr Fitzroy from Trafalgar Terrace left Emma with a curious feeling of regret. Should she have pressed him to sit down with them longer? He might have stayed for luncheon. Had she been remiss? Oddly, his society would have been a welcome addition, as welcome as any friend could have been at such a moment.

I shall never marry, thought she. I must learn to be content as I am. And when I grow old, I shall live with Mama in the Dower House and cause as much trouble as I can, just like Grandmamma and Great Aunt Turner. I shall visit the Castle at least twice a day and indulge my nieces and nephews until they become quite spoilt and unruly. And I shall disregard every complaint issued by their poor parents. When Captain and Mrs Blake come to call with their many children, when they quarrel and complain as married couples often do, I shall observe how very fortunate I have been — what a lucky escape I have had!

Two weeks passed before Mr Fowle's condition showed any sign of improvement. The news was carried by Mr Fitzroy, who called again at Trafalgar Terrace one morning in late August. Due to a sudden downpour, Emma had postponed her walk and was at home with Mrs Harding in the drawing room.

'Well,' said Mrs Harding, 'I am pleased to hear that Mr Fowle is a little better. Such performances as these are as familiar to me as an old pair of wool stockings. My late husband, Dr Harding, made a habit of the same. One day he would be at death's door, the next he would rally. I cannot count the times I was obliged to disappoint Mr Wake. But he managed things admirably at the last, and I do not know of a better undertaker in the whole of England.'

Emma and Mr Fitzroy exchanged amused glances.

'I bring a message from Mr Fowle. He wishes me to say that he should be honoured to receive you, should you be willing to call upon him. He knows you to be scrupulous over matters of propriety, and to that end he has asked if I might accompany you to Fowle

House. I am, of course, happy to oblige, should you agree to his request.'

'I see,' said Mrs Harding. 'Well, as the saying has it, let us strike while the iron is hot. I shall make myself ready if you will but excuse me for five minutes. Emma may sit with you.'

Mr Fitzroy replied, 'I have no other plan. The present is therefore as good a time as any to call upon Mr Fowle.'

It was some minutes before Mrs Harding reappeared; and Emma was grateful for the opportunity of a private conversation with Mr Fitzroy.

'I must thank you for your recent exertions on my behalf.'

'I regret being the bearer of bad news. And there is, I fear, more. Or rather, it is generally thought to be good news. It may not strike you in quite the same way. Has the post arrived from Delham?'

'Not yet. The last communication I received was from Mama. She wrote to me three days ago.'

'And you received nothing in yesterday's post?' enquired Mr Fitzroy.

'No,' said she.

'That is curious,' he replied.

'If you are in receipt of information that you believe may be of interest to me, I should be grateful to hear it.'

Mr Fitzroy's look unnerved Emma.

'If there is something I should know, please do not keep it from me. However unpleasant it might be, I should prefer to hear it.'

'Very well,' said he. 'The news concerns Captain Blake.'

'Of course it does,' Emma sighed. 'I can guess the rest, but I should prefer to hear it confirmed. Has my cousin accepted him? Are they engaged?'

Mr Fitzroy nodded. It was all the confirmation Emma required. Everything was now over for her; Captain Blake was lost forever.

'When was the engagement announced?'

'I received a letter from Captain Blake yesterday, in the afternoon post.'

'My cousin is not known to be tardy. I expect some other explanation —' Emma broke off, too shaken to continue. She stood up and paced the room.

'Did Mrs Blake reach Delham safely? I had hoped to call on her before her departure from Sanditon, but I was prevented from doing so. There has been much to do here, you see.'

'What changed your cousin's mind?' said he.

'It is of little matter now. The thing is done. There is nothing more to be said.'

'Nothing more but this: two people have been made very happy by your act of generosity,' said Mr Fitzroy. 'You must love your cousin and your friend very much indeed.'

'There was nothing generous about it. I merely acknowledged what was already the case, though I wish with all my heart it was otherwise. There, you see. I have made my feelings plain, though decorum dictates that I should conceal them and appear politely complacent. My humiliation is now complete.'

'You are mistaken,' said he. 'I have hardly seen a greater or a nobler act of love. I sense the depth of your despair, though I cannot share it.'

'How did Cowper have it? *Fierce passions discompose the mind, As tempests vex the sea...*'

'Are you familiar with Cowper, Miss Osborne?'

'As familiar as anyone I know. Cowper is a favourite of my father.'

'Then heed the words of the poet, and let contentment find you once again.'

The sound of commotion in the hall announced Mrs Harding's return; suitably attired in pea green and puce, and not a black ribbon in sight, she entered the drawing room in state, eager to be on her way.

'Emma, my dear,' said she, putting on her gloves, 'I shall sit with Mr Fowle for fifteen minutes complete; a moment longer and he is likely to consider himself a great deal worse than in fact he is. Nor should I like him to receive the impression that I have suffered for want of his society. I am not a great one for visiting the sick. Let us get it over with without delay.'

Emma watched from the window as Mr Fitzroy and Mrs Harding left Trafalgar Terrace.

And so it is done, thought she. Anne Musgrave and Captain Blake are happy then, and everything is as it should be. She felt nothing; it was as though a numbness had come over her. Her spirit was vanquished, her senses exhausted. I can sink no lower than this. She turned towards the door as a maid entered with not one, but three letters that had just arrived in the post. One was addressed to Mrs Harding; the remaining two were for her. The first was from her mother, the second she recognised as Anne's hand.

Breaking open Anne's letter first, she read her cousin's account of Captain Blake's proposal. Both wished for a short engagement and a quiet wedding to be attended only by their dearest friends and family. The wedding would take place at Wickstead as soon as the banns had been read. The Howards were unlikely to make the journey from Somerset; Mr Edwards was deemed too frail to travel. 'It would give me no greater pleasure, my dear cousin, than to see you as happily settled as I shall be. Charles is of the same view. I should be delighted if you would consent to be my bridesmaid, though should you deem it beyond your power to accede to such a request, I should, of course, understand. As to the date, the wedding will not take place before Michaelmas for we are as one on this point: Aunt Harding must have her day. Until we meet again in Brinshore on that happy day, yours affectionately etc...'

Lady Osborne expressed fear and concern for her daughter on hearing the news of Anne's engagement. 'It may suit you best to stay where you are for the present. There is much talk here of the engagement. I am, of course, delighted for Charles and Anne, as we all are, but I wish with all my heart that their joy had not come at so great a cost to my own beautiful daughter. You need only say the word and your papa and I shall come to you. Your loving mother... PS Frank asks for you daily. Yesterday he slipped out of the nursery while Nanny was busy and got as far as the stable yard before the alarm was raised. He had taken it into his head to go in search of you, my dear. Lady Forbes complains bitterly of the brevity of your recent visit. Go to Brighton if that suits you better. You will receive a warm welcome there. The celebrated Mrs F is apparently much recovered.'

Emma found little to comfort or to cheer in Anne's letter. Had she not understood her cousin's character and temper half so well, she would have supposed her request cruel and callous. No, it is not in my power to be a bridesmaid — to simper and smile and show myself full of joy for the happy couple. Their intentions are surely meant to be kind but they not; they are thoughtless and unfeeling. I did not deserve this. Let them wed in Delham before their family and all their friends. Let it be a joyous occasion. Let the sun shine upon them. I shall not be a part of it.

Her mother's words brought some measure of consolation; the knowledge that no constraints or obligations were to be placed upon her, that she may do as she pleased for the present, was a great comfort. She would remain where she was, for it was but a short time until her aunt's wedding; then all the family would descend upon Brinshore, and there would be little time to indulge her low spirits. And if little Frank should come too, it would be enough; for she would have no time to call her own.

There was still sufficient left of the day for sea bathing, and the weather was warm. She required little inducement, for the sea was the perfect corrective for unpleasant thoughts. The bathing machine was but moments away; the prospect of plunging into the water and floating on the swell was tempting indeed. As she stepped lightly down towards the shore, she thought of her conversation with Mr Fitzroy and began to reproach herself for having said too much. If it be not in my power to remedy my present distress, how am I to find contentment? No. I shall not be crushed, thought she. I shall rally. I shall face the world again.

She took a sharp intake of breath before submerging her head beneath the surface of the sea. The water was cold, but as she sank deeper, the coldness disappeared. Several times she repeated the exercise until, feeling quite restored by it, she returned flushed and refreshed to Trafalgar Terrace.

'I have been watching for you,' said Aunt Harding, anxiously pacing the room. 'My dear, prepare yourself. There is some news that will astonish you. You had better be seated. I hardly know how to begin. My dear Emma, Charles Blake has made an offer of marriage to your cousin, Anne, and she has accepted him.'

'Yes,' replied Emma. 'I know.'

'You know? But I have just heard. How long have you known, and why did you keep it to yourself?' said Mrs Harding.

'I knew nothing of it until today.'

Mrs Harding sighed. 'And to think that I might have prevented it.'

'Prevented it? How?'

'I saw it coming. Had I left Anne in Delham, had — Are you dreadfully cast down, my dear? If I were you, I should not be. You can do much better. With your fortune and connections you will never want for suitors. When once Brinshore is established, quality will follow. It is but a matter of time. In the meantime, perhaps your papa might take you to London or Bath. There is no shortage of —'

'Aunt Harding, I thank you for your concern. I must first reconcile myself to the news. I own, I had long cherished a different dream, but that dream has now come to an end.'

'Perhaps you might think of Lowford's heir by and by for —'

'Please do not concern yourself with such matters,' said Emma. 'I must be allowed to manage things my own way.'

CHAPTER TWENTY-SIX

The news of the engagement between Captain Blake and Miss Musgrave was welcomed at the Dower House. The Dowager looked upon the match favourably, gratified and relieved that it was Miss Musgrave and not Miss Osborne to whom she was obliged to express her joy. 'Charles will do admirably for Anne. Did I not predict this very outcome several months ago?'

'I do not recall any prediction of the kind,' said Mrs Turner. 'Is not your satisfaction at the turn of events due entirely to the fact that Emma is now quite out of reach of poor dear Charles?'

The Dowager reached into the bowl of sugared almonds beside her chair. She took one, examined it, and placed it back in the bowl. 'Emma is safe,' said she. 'It is a happy coincidence that the outcome is just as I had hoped it would be.'

'And you had no hand in it?' said Mrs Turner.

'The matter was managed splendidly without any great assistance from me.'

'Emma will not want to be a bridesmaid,' Mrs Turner observed.

'It would look very odd indeed were she to refuse. She must swallow her pride and do the right thing,' said the Dowager. 'Show the world that she approves the match, that she cares nothing for —'

'I cannot agree,' interrupted Mrs Turner. 'Emma must not be prevailed upon to —'

A firm knock at the front door caused a disturbance which was heard in the small morning room where they were seated. Some minutes later, a footman entered bearing the card of a gentleman, a stranger by the name of Mr Hood.

'The name is not familiar to me. I have never heard a Mr Hood spoken of in these parts,' said the Dowager.

'I understand the gentleman's business is with Mrs Turner, ma'am,' said he. Then, directing his attention to the Dowager's companion, he said, 'The gentleman seeks but five minutes of your time, ma'am. In private.'

'Well,' said the Dowager, 'be good enough to show him in. It is most intriguing. I wonder what he wants.'

'The request was for a private audience,' Mrs Turner replied.

'We know nothing of him. He might be a murderer or a highwayman.'

'I do not imagine it is common practice among murderers or highwaymen to present calling cards. The element of surprise, notwithstanding the need for anonymity, would be lost in an instant,' said she. Turning to the footman, she said, 'I shall see Mr Hood in the drawing room. What manner of man is he?'

'A young man, ma'am. A gentleman. He appears to be a man of means.'

'Even better,' said Mrs Turner to the Dowager. 'Excuse me, my dear. I must see what business this young man has with me.'

'If he be agreeable, do not send him away. He must stay and take tea. Make sure you bring him to me when your interview is concluded, for I too must know the nature of his business.'

Mrs Turner entered the room where Mr Hood had been waiting. The young man stood before her and bowed; he had an air about him of modest gentility despite the fine cut of his apparel.

'Mr Hood, I cannot imagine what business you have with me,' said she.

As he raised his eyes to meet hers, she saw something almost familiar in his look.

'I thank you for receiving me. I have no right to impose on you in this manner a moment longer than is necessary. Allow me to discharge my undertaking as swiftly as possible.'

'Then please be seated,' Mrs Turner replied, 'and state your business.'

'The business concerns my father,' said he. 'Mrs Turner, my father died suddenly a year ago after a short illness in the West Indies. As his only surviving son and heir, I was left to settle his affairs. In so doing, I found that aspects of his past dealings, of which I had previously been unaware, came to light; and it is this information that has brought me to England. Until three days ago, I believed my time here had been in vain. It was, however, my good fortune to receive, through my father's former man of business in London, information that your nephew, a Mr Robert Watson, had made enquiries as to my whereabouts. This happy coincidence was, in fact, no coincidence at all. Among the information I had in my possession was the address of a London tailor with whom a Captain O'Brien once had dealings. Forgive me. I do not wish to cause you pain.'

'Go on, if you please,' said Mrs Turner.

'Following his death, I discovered the existence, shall we say, of certain irregularities in my father's affairs. The name O'Brien was unfamiliar to me, but I have since learned that it was one of a number of names that had been used, disreputably, by my father in former years. Within days of arriving in England, I paid a visit to the aforementioned tailor, an elderly man whose powers of recall were second to none. I was grieved indeed to discover the extent of my father's profligacy. Foolishly, I left no forwarding address. However, following my visit, and unknown to me, the tailor had the good fortune to come upon some old correspondence pertinent to my enquiry. A Mr Robert Watson was named as the attorney acting on behalf of a Mrs Turner in the year ninety-six, an innocent who had been grossly ill-used, duped into a false marriage and subsequently abandoned. It is Mrs Turner I seek.'

'Then you have found her,' said she.

'I am relieved indeed. Thankful and relieved,' Mr Hood replied. 'Mrs Turner, I regret deeply the pain my father caused you. I can find nothing in his behaviour that warrants either justification or forgiveness. My father was a selfish and cruel man. I wish I could tell you that on his deathbed he repented his sins. But he did not.'

'Was I the only unsuspecting victim of your father's duplicity?' Mrs Turner asked.

'No, Mrs Turner. You were not,' said he. 'The difference, in your case, was that my father benefitted substantially — materially — when he separated you from your fortune and, I understand, the fortune of your niece. My father's actions were unconscionable. Mrs Turner, I am come to make reparations for his wickedness. You shall be repaid in full, with interest, an amount equal to that of which you were defrauded by him. You see, my father amassed great wealth in his later years.'

After Mr Hood's departure, the astonishing news left Mrs Turner in so fragile a state of mind that she was obliged to seek the solitude of her bedchamber. Irked to find that Mrs Turner had taken to her bed without a word of explanation as to the purpose of Mr Hood's visit, the Dowager began to think herself ill used.

Restless to know something of what had transpired, the Dowager ordered the landau with the intention of paying a visit to her son, if not to discover something more of the mysterious Mr Hood, then at least to be the first to report that the visit had taken place.

Unaccustomed to waiting, the Dowager entered her daughter-in-law's morning room unannounced and found Lady Osborne at her writing desk. Due to the early hour, the latter was taken by surprise. Her first thought was for her aunt.

'Dear Mama,' said Lady Osborne, 'what brings you here at this hour? Has my aunt been taken ill?'

'No, indeed. Your aunt will outlive us all.'

The Dowager looked at the fire burning in the grate. 'A fire? In summer?'

'Do you not find there is a chill in the air, this morning?' Lady Osborne replied.

'There is certainly a chill in the air at the Dower House. Your aunt is never better pleased than when she has some air of mystery about her. This morning, Mrs Turner received a visit from a stranger, a Mr Hood, and I should like to know why.'

'Dear Mama, are you quite comfortable?' said Lady Osborne, as the Dowager pointed to a footstool.

'I shall be when I have the means to rest my leg,' she replied.

Lady Osborne obliged and placed the footstool at her feet.

'Thank you, my dear. Now tell me what you know of the matter, for I have had not a word from Mrs Turner since Mr Hood took his leave. Your aunt has taken to her room and will not come out.'

'My aunt will, I am sure, furnish you with the particulars of the matter when she is ready. What manner of man is Mr Hood? An attorney, perhaps?'

'A seemingly respectable young man, if a little exotic. I caught a glimpse of him through the window as he disappeared. It will not do.

I cannot abide secrecy. I desire to know Mr Hood's business. Mrs Turner resides in *my* house and her business is *my* business.'

'Then you must wait, Mama, like the rest of us, until Aunt Turner is prepared to lay the facts before you,' said Lady Osborne.

The Dowager sighed in annoyance. 'To whom are you writing,' said she at length, glancing at the unfinished letter on the writing desk.

'To your granddaughter,' Lady Osborne replied. 'Emma has immersed herself in the affairs of a poor fisherman's family. It seems the mother died some years ago and the father recently met a tragic end. Emma wishes to do something for the children.'

'What nonsense is this?' replied the Dowager. 'Send for her immediately! Emma must not interfere in such matters. It will not do!'

Lady Osborne smiled and replied, 'Emma is not the first Osborne to interfere in the affairs of others. She is happy to remain where she is for the present. Your granddaughter seeks occupation, and I cannot think of anything better than this.'

'She would be better occupied in Delham helping her cousin prepare for the wedding.'

'No, Mama,' said Lady Osborne. 'That would never do.'

'And why not, indeed?' the Dowager replied.

Lady Osborne was disinclined to speak further on the subject of the wedding. 'Frank is eager to ride in his grandmamma's new landau,' said she, perceiving that a change in the subject was required. 'There is nothing more interesting to him at present than a horse and carriage.'

'Dear boy!' said the Dowager. 'Of course I shall grant his wish!'

'Please make sure that Frank refrains from climbing onto the perch,' Lady Osborne replied. 'Perhaps I should accompany him.'

'There is no need for that! I am eminently able to manage my own grandson,' said the Dowager. 'It is Mrs Turner who is unruly. Perhaps, my dear, you might ask Hedges to send some of her famous rabbit fricassee to the Dower House. If nothing else, a liberal portion of the concoction should tempt Mrs Turner out of her room, for I certainly shall not have it sent up to her on a tray!'

'Hedges has proved her worth. You may be interested to hear that she is to be employed by Captain and Mrs Blake after the wedding,' said Lady Osborne.

'Is she indeed? And does Mrs Turner approve?'

'The point is that Hedges approves. For the time being, Charles is to rent the house belonging to Mr Fitzroy, the house in Waterloo Crescent left to him in his brother's will.'

'Is Delham not good enough for them?'

'I expect, in time, they will purchase somewhere hereabouts.'

'Does Mr Fitzroy not have use for it himself?' enquired the Dowager.

'It is a new house; its associations with his brother are but slight. And, as Mr Fitzroy is to take holy orders, he has no need of Waterloo Crescent himself. Besides, it seems he has a house of his own in London.'

'And what of his scheme for Sanditon?' said the Dowager.

'There has been a surprising turn of events. Sanditon is not to be the place! I understand there is great rejoicing in Brinshore.'

'Great rejoicing in Brinshore?' said the Dowager. 'Has Mrs Harding announced her imminent departure?'

'Dear Mama,' sighed Lady Osborne, 'You may yet be greatly impressed. It seems those poor orphan children, to whom Emma has become so attached, led her to a hidden spring when she requested water to wash a graze to her hand. It has lain undiscovered, perhaps for decades, even centuries. Emma informs me that Mr Fowle considers it an important discovery and is quite certain that the spring possesses certain beneficial properties. And so, you see, Mr Fitzroy is to fulfil his promise to his late brother by building a spa where all — young, old, weak, strong, frail and infirm — can take the waters. And those patients under the care of Mr Fowle will, in time, be conveyed there and afforded all manner of new and efficacious water treatments.'

'There are any number of spa towns these days,' replied the Dowager, 'and too many to choose from. Brinshore will be but one among many. Mrs Turner will likely demand a month or two by the sea once the building is complete, though she is the least likely of any of us to benefit from it for she is never ill. And you, my dear, will receive the bill, for she claims to have not a penny to her name.'

The announcement, some minutes later, that Mrs Turner had arrived and was in need of a private audience with her niece, brought some sense of an impending resolution to the matter of Mr Hood that had quite possessed the Dowager. 'Let her come in. I am sure she cannot object to my presence,' said she.

'Mama, my aunt seeks the favour of a private conversation. Please allow me to grant her request,' said Lady Osborne, as she swept out of the morning room before the Dowager had the opportunity to rise to her feet.

On entering the library, Lady Osborne was at first alarmed to find Mrs Turner in a heightened state of confusion. The stupor that had come upon her on hearing of her good fortune was almost too great to comprehend. Mr Hood's visit had shaken her to the core; it had yielded such a varying array of emotions that she was powerless to make sense of them. Mrs Turner felt no less a sense of anger and injustice at the news as of joy, relief and satisfaction that, at long last, amends were to be made and justice was to be done. But redress had come too late. The life of ease she had, in former years, expected would ensue for the duration of the latter, had been a cruel deprivation; she had been divested of almost all she possessed, by a man who, through the exercise of duplicity, had invented a history as improbable as it was compelling, and whose declaration of love was a malicious falsehood. For years Mrs Turner had endeavoured to treat lightly the mistakes of the past with seemingly imperturbable and studied disregard; but as Mr Hood's story unfolded, Mrs Turner was reminded of the bitter suffering that was visited upon her by his father.

'My dear,' said Mrs Turner, 'I am quite at a loss to know where to begin. In short, it would appear that I am once again a rich woman! What am I to do? After all these years, my dear, years in which I have led a life of destitution and ruin.'

'A life of destitution? Surely, not, my dear Aunt Turner. Under Osborne's protection you have wanted for nothing. Naught has been denied you.'

'All the same, I —' Mrs Turner quivered uncontrollably as she began to relate the astonishing news that Mr Hood had imparted to her earlier that morning.

'Calm yourself, Aunt,' replied Lady Osborne. 'Come. I shall sit by you.'

As Lady Osborne established the particulars of the story, pausing occasionally to ascertain accurately the important facts of the matter, the full account of Mr Hood's disclosure became known.

At length, Her Ladyship conceded, 'I am as shocked as you! What an extraordinary young man! And you say that it is Mr Hood's *desire* to make reparation? Perhaps the reparations are in some way covered by a clause in the will?'

'That was not my impression. No. I believe Mr Hood has gone to a great deal of trouble to find me. He came to England with this aim in mind,' said Mrs Turner, recovering something of her former composure.

The main aspects of Mr Hood's disclosure were subsequently related to Lord Osborne and the Dowager who were equally astounded to hear the news of Mrs Turner's good fortune.

'I suppose you will have a mind to purchase Leverton Lodge now that the means to do so has come your way,' said the Dowager.

'I have always admired Leverton Lodge,' said Mrs Turner. 'And it would be quite within my power to buy the property at a fair price.'

'Should you be happy there?' Lady Osborne enquired.

'Lowford Park is little more than five miles away,' said Mrs Turner.

'But its grounds are extensive and will need prudent management,' said Lord Osborne.

'I shall appoint a steward to oversee all that,' replied Mrs Turner. 'In fact, you might help me find one, if you will.'

'It seems to me that a smaller house, conveniently situated in the neighbourhood would be more practical,' said Lady Osborne.

'Perhaps Mr Edwards will oblige and sell you his! Now that his house empty, he may be persuaded to part with it,' said the Dowager.

A disturbing thought occurred to Lady Osborne. 'Did Mr Hood indicate how his father came by his vast fortune?'

'Through deception and fraudulent means, I expect,' replied Mrs Turner.

'Your fortune, perhaps,' said Lady Osborne. 'But did not Mr Hood intimate that his father had made the greater part of his fortune in the West Indies?' Her Ladyship looked worryingly at her husband, who at once comprehended her concern.

'How are fortunes made? If not by good investment, they must be the product of fraud and treachery,' said Mrs Turner.

Lord Osborne replied with a question of his own. 'The point is, how are fortunes made in the West Indies?'

'Oh,' said Mrs Turner. 'I suppose you mean the trade.'

Lord and Lady Osborne exchanged glances.

'Allow me, if you will, to ascertain the means by which the money was made before entering into any formal transaction,' said His Lordship.

'Surely no such enquiry is necessary,' said the Dowager. 'Mrs Turner seeks only to recover that which is rightfully hers.'

'Indeed!' agreed Mrs Turner.

'Were the money found to be tainted might you be minded to refuse Mr Hood's offer?' said the Dowager. 'Under such circumstances, I suppose you could remain at the Dower House now that you have made yourself very much at home there.'

'I might take Hedges with me to Leverton Lodge,' said Mrs Turner, 'though I expect a house by the sea is more to Hedges' liking. And she is very fond of Anne. Indeed, when I think of it, Leverton Lodge is perhaps a little too large to be quite comfortable.'

'And the stairs are exceedingly steep. They offer little relief against an arthritic knee,' added the Dowager. 'They are quite unlike the stairs in the Dower House.'

'I had given no thought to the stairs,' replied Mrs Turner. 'You are quite right, my dear. Nothing compares to the gentle ease and, I may say, simple elegance, of the main staircase at the Dower House. I have climbed the stairs of many great houses in my time, and know of none so handsome nor so shallow.'

The Dowager turned to her son and daughter-in-law and declared, 'Let us have no more talk of Leverton Lodge. It is quite unsuitable. Mrs Turner will remain where she is. It is impossible for her to do otherwise. Your aunt is, I may say, somewhat perverse and obstinate at times, but I am the most patient and the most tolerant creature in the world. You will receive no objection from me to Mrs Turner remaining at the Dower House, for the foreseeable future at least. I shall bear it as best I can.'

Had the recovery of Mrs Turner's fortune been settled as effortlessly as the place of her abode, Osborne Castle might have been spared the arrival of Lady Osborne's brother, Mr Robert Watson, several days after Mr Hood's business with her aunt had been made known.

'Refuse it? What? All of it?' said Robert, infuriated by the very notion that Mrs Turner, or indeed any individual of sound mind, would willingly relinquish their rightful entitlement to so substantial a sum as the one tendered by Mr Hood. 'Has she taken leave of her senses? Once again I find myself drawn into that perverse woman's personal affairs, and at great cost to myself. You may be sure that I have spared no expense in my quest to ascertain the whereabouts of Mr Hood. Indeed, are we quite certain that Hood is who he purports to be? I should not be surprised if he inherited more than a large sum of money from the villain whom he claims was his father. Perhaps there is some character trait common to both.'

Lady Osborne, with whom the interview was conducted in private, made every effort to keep her composure, and spoke gently in reply. 'My dear brother, Mr Hood went to great lengths to find Aunt Turner.'

'And he went to great lengths to evade me,' Robert replied.

'Or perhaps your search led you in the wrong direction. It is entirely understandable that Mr Hood should have acted on the Shropshire connection. It was all the information he had to hand. He acted as any rational being would have acted. I should have acted likewise. But let us not argue, brother. The point is that Aunt Turner is happily settled where she is. The money would only complicate matters for she has no need of it now.'

'She may not have need of it, but allow me to remind you that Turner intended a substantial portion of his fortune to be placed at your disposal. Much of it must reasonably be assumed to be your inheritance. If Mrs Turner persists in this foolhardiness, you do not need to follow where she leads. I shall draw up documents before I meet with Mr Hood. If Mrs Turner will not of her free will exercise good sense in this matter, you will be obliged to make her do so.'

'Dear Robert,' Lady Osborne replied, 'It is impossible for me to do what you ask. Osborne has no need of the money, nor has he any wish to profit by it. Consider the manner in which it was likely obtained.'

'Nonsense! Where there is money to be had, I suspect there are some who call themselves abolitionists who would entertain few scruples in accepting it.'

'All I can say is that Osborne would be against the very idea of it, as am I.'

Robert paced the floor of the library in a pique. 'Then tell me, how am I to be recompensed for my time and efforts?'

'It is my understanding that you chose to act of your own accord in this matter — quite unknown to Aunt Turner, and wholly without her instruction. What manner of attorney would in the normal course of their business do such a thing?' said Lady Osborne, who began to relent the tone and manner of her expression the moment her words had been spoken. The recollection of a similar encounter with Robert concerning Aunt Turner had revived feelings that had lain dormant for some twenty years, and as such caused so uncharacteristic an upsurge of emotion on her part that she was surprised and overwhelmed by their intensity.

The strained silence that ensued between brother and sister was not easily broken. Robert, racked by incredulity at his sister's senseless obstinacy, was speechless with rage. Lady Osborne sought refuge in employment; a piece of embroidery that had lain untouched for some months now claimed her undivided attention.

At length, the silence was broken by Robert who muttered words barely audible to Lady Osborne. 'Folly. Utter folly.'

Despite the good fortune of an advantageous marriage, Robert had worked without pause to secure and maintain his place in the world. He had neither shirked his responsibilities, nor had he ever failed to discharge his duty on behalf of those with whom he was intimately connected; whether called upon to perform a service, settle a dispute or interpret a legal undertaking, Robert had acted both to protect and to advance the interests of all his family. In reply, his sister's tone was conciliatory. 'Your actions are well intentioned, for you endeavour, quite properly, to right a wrong. Osborne will see to it that you are reimbursed in full for your time and efforts.'

Mr Robert Watson took his leave of Osborne Castle on better terms than he had that day anticipated; and though his anger had not wholly subsided, by the time his carriage passed through the gates of Osborne Park and turned in the direction of the Reigate road, the resentment he harboured towards his sister had been in part placated by the full and handsome reimbursement he had received from Lord Osborne for his trouble. By the time he reached the inn at Redhill, where a change of horses and a pleasant meal saw him comfortably on the road to Croydon, Robert Watson reckoned that, all things considered, he was less than five and thirty pounds the poorer than he might have been had he assumed the direction of his aunt's estate.

As it is, thought he, a substantial sum has come my way without the necessity of much exertion. What is five and thirty pounds when measured against the strife and vexation that must follow any dealings that concern the affairs of Mrs Turner? By the time the outskirts of Croydon had been reached, the brother of Lady Osborne found that he was quite content with his day's work and was even inclined to lay to rest, if not dismiss from his mind completely, any remaining sense of exasperation caused by his sister's obduracy or his aunt's folly.

On securing a few private moments with her husband following the departure of Robert Watson, Lady Osborne was astonished to discover the sum His Lordship had laid out to bring the matter to an end. 'I believe I should not have managed it for less. Your brother is as shrewd an attorney as I have ever encountered.'

'Well, I should not have been half so generous,' Lady Osborne replied. 'Robert will surely find little to complain about for, I daresay, he could hardly have anticipated as satisfactory an outcome as this. But what of Mr Hood?'

'I shall write to him on Mrs Turner's behalf.'

'And my aunt has given you leave to do so?'

'She has.'

'Was Mr Hood's offer genuine?'

'It was. And though it is of little matter now, I was able to ascertain that Captain O'Brien was one among several names by which Mr Hood's father was known. His parentage and place of origin, though indeterminate, seem to suggest some foreign shore. I doubt his son will give up his quest to discover the truth of the matter though, had I been placed in such an invidious position, I should have had little inclination to engage in that quest myself. Mr Hood should have a care as to the unforeseen consequences of his worthy endeavour. Were he to seek my counsel, I should advise him not to dig too deep. And now, my dear,' said he, placing an arm around his wife's shoulder, 'I have some news that will please you. Mr Fitzroy is to call and bring news of our daughter.'

'Mr Fitzroy? What brings him to Delham?'

'He has business with Charles Blake.'

Lady Osborne smiled. 'Of course,' said she. 'I shall be pleased to renew the acquaintance.'

CHAPTER TWENTY-SEVEN

The wedding of Mr Fowle and Mrs Harding took place early on Michaelmas morn in the parish church at Brinshore, and in the presence of those members of the bride's family that gave consequence to the occasion. The groom's party was but slight, and comprised a handful of Mr Fowle's most notable London associates.

But on the eve of the long-awaited wedding and at a late hour, owing to a report from Somerset concerning the sudden and serious state of Mr Howard's health, Mrs Blake and her son were obliged to forego the event and exchange the delights of Mr and Mrs Fowle's wedding breakfast for the bedside of the ailing cleric and his wayward wife. Regret was expressed by many at the absence of the Blakes, and though Lady Osborne was among those who lamented the loss of their society, her anxiety was in some measure alleviated that it happened so, for her daughter was made the easier by it.

Emma greeted the news with relief, for the knowledge that Captain Blake would not be present removed the possibility of embarrassment that an awkward encounter might provoke. She had, in anticipation of the event, rehearsed more times than she cared to remember, the speech she had composed should she be called upon to wish them joy.

'Mama,' said Emma, putting on her gloves, 'I am relieved that I shall not be obliged to see them together. Anne will hardly speak of the wedding in my hearing. Indeed, I expect I know most of my cousin's plans already, for Grandmamma has been at pains to acquaint me with all the facts since the hour the engagement was made known. She applauds my lucky escape, you know. But why should Grandmamma think only of such inconsequential things as rank? She loves Captain Blake as well as anyone. I know she does. Mama, I should have taken him in an instant if he had —'

'My dear child, do not distress yourself. Strive to put him out of your mind and let this day be a happy one,' said Lady Osborne. 'Your time is yet to come.'

'You cannot know how I feel, Mama,' Emma replied.

'I can, and I do,' said her mother. 'At one time my feelings for Charles' uncle were much the same as those you profess for his nephew. It is a curious thing that it should happen so. Like you, I too was inconsolable. I gave no thought to your father — I barely acknowledged his presence — though we had been acquainted for many months. But, hand on heart, I can say, my dear Emma, that your father has made me truly happy.'

The wedding provided the neighbourhood of Brinshore with a spectacle quite unlike anything the town had ever beheld, and though the ceremony took place at an early hour, the market square was besieged by spectators, and enterprising proprietors eager to secure their custom. The union of two people, with fewer years before them than most who enter the married state, was an extraordinary sight, and one that provoked disapproval and delight in equal measure. Some disparaged the alliance of the pair and deemed matrimony a scandalous act among persons of advancing years and increasing decrepitude; others applauded their audacity to flout convention and afford little consequence to the narrow-minded and intolerant.

Mrs Harding eyed her new spouse with apprehension; he had regained something of his former vigour, but the frequency with which he had coughed and wheezed his way through the service had not gone unnoticed. Thought she, even Dr Harding, ten years his senior, was blessed with a stouter constitution on their wedding day. It occurred to her that the physician to whom she had vowed to remain faithful *in sickness and in health* might have need of a nursemaid sooner than anticipated. The restoration of Mr Fowle to full health was, therefore, a matter of the greatest urgency. The future of Brinshore depended on it; indeed, the establishment of the spa and all the new treatments it promised to deliver now rested on her power to make Mr Fowle flourish.

The fascination that surrounded the bride and groom was extended to the Osbornes, and even to the Musgraves. Nor did the curious composition of guests escape the prying eyes of Brinshore society; the easy familiarity exhibited between those accustomed to moving in the first circles, and the genteel of lower rank and consequence, confounded some onlookers.

Emma had expected to find herself seated beside Anne, but discovered that she was more pleasantly positioned between her mother and Mr Fitzroy, thereby being spared any new particulars of the forthcoming wedding in Delham and the adjustments proposed to Waterloo Crescent.

'I trust your plans for the spa proceed well,' said Emma to Mr Fitzroy.

'They do,' he replied. 'And there is no one to whom I am more greatly indebted than you.'

'I am pleased that you should be in my debt, and not I in yours, for there is something about which I must speak with you.'

'Ah,' said he. 'There can be no better time than the present.'

'That is my view entirely, for my feelings and opinions on weddings and matrimony are quite exhausted. I have nothing more to say about the parson's address, the bride's gown or the groom's manners.'

'You shall find no complaint from me,' said he.

'It is my belief that your debt of gratitude should be to my two young friends, and not to me.' Emma raised her eyes to meet his and was pleased to discover that his look carried no trace of opposition. 'Your plans would not have come to fruition in this interesting way had it not been for their part in the piece.'

'That is unquestionably so,' he replied. 'Have you in mind some means by which I might settle that debt?'

'I have,' said Emma. 'If you will, I should like you to provide them with schooling and guarantee them employment, with sufficient — I may say, liberal — renumeration for their labours at the end of it. In time, you might see fit to find them occupation about the spa.' She hesitated momentarily before adding, 'I feel certain that your brother would have desired it, for I believe he was a generous man with a good heart. Do you consider my request unreasonable?'

'Quite the opposite,' said he, struck by the force of her argument. 'I can think of nothing more worthy. I shall see to it myself.'

Satisfied with the outcome of her appeal, Emma looked away and smiled to herself. The pleasure she felt at the success of her petition caused her to observe to her mother, 'But for Mr Fitzroy's refusal to make amends with his brother, which must be due to some flaw in his character — obstinacy being the likely culprit — I should find little fault with him, except for his determination to take holy orders.'

Lady Osborne struggled to suppress a smile, and said, 'And so Mr Fitzroy is not the height of perfection.'

'Indeed he is not,' said Emma.

'I am greatly relieved to hear it,' her mother replied.

Having been obliged to listen to the views of one of the local notables on the fortunes of Brinshore's nearest rival, Mr Fitzroy's attention had slipped momentarily; he had inadvertently caught something of the conversation that transpired between Lady Osborne and her daughter and was greatly amused by the exchange.

'There is no doubt about it, sir,' the speaker continued. 'Before too long, Sanditon will unearth a spring of its own. Mr Parker has been much occupied of late in searching for one. Lady Denham is not quite so keen and reckons that such an edifice would obstruct her view. Sanditon is become so full of buildings, you see, that much of the natural landscape is obscured by them. A blade of grass is a rare sight in Sanditon.'

Mr Fitzroy gave only a nod in reply before the speaker continued, 'Sanditon is much aggrieved by the developments in Brinshore. I daresay it will all blow over, as these things often do. With three miles of road between the two, those who fancy themselves ill will think nothing of travelling to Brinshore for the sake of a cure. I have even heard it said that Mr Parker's own brother made much the same observation himself, for he is ever attentive to the state of own his health. Mr Parker was appalled by the remark and refused to give his brother the time of day for one week complete.'

The gentleman's attention was sought by another of the guests, to the satisfaction of Mr Fitzroy who once again turned his attention to Emma.

'Captain Blake will be obliged to tread carefully when he takes possession of Waterloo Crescent,' whispered Emma.

'Charles will think nothing of it,' he replied. 'We anticipated some reaction of the sort. Fifty years hence, Miss Osborne, there is certain to be construction the like of which has not been seen before. Three miles will be of little consequence, for Sanditon and Brinshore will meld into one.'

'What an extraordinary thought!' Emma replied. She looked at him in wonder. She had never given thought to the world as it might appear in five years' time, let alone fifty.

'Shall we see you in Delham soon? Shall you attend the wedding?' said she.

'It is my hope,' he replied. 'Presently, I am called away. Bound for Allersham. Miss Osborne, I have no means of knowing how long the situation that claims my attention will endure.'

'Allersham?,' said she. 'Goodness me! Surely you cannot abandon us? Not now. Not in this way! Think of your friends,' said she, surprised by the curious feeling of disappointment at the imminent loss of Mr Fitzroy's society. 'Can the matter be postponed?'

'If it were within my power to do so, the matter would be given up, relinquished altogether. But it cannot,' said he.

'I see,' said she. 'I suppose Captain Blake and Mr Fowle will manage things in your absence if their respective brides can spare them. But what is more important than the society of your friends at this interesting point? Have you had the good fortune to secure a living? Is it that which drives you away from us?'

'Forgive me, Miss Osborne. It is not within my power to disclose the nature of the business that demands my attention, however much I should wish to make it known to you.'

'Well then,' said she. 'I am bound for Delham in a day or two. I expect our paths are unlikely to cross for some time,' said she. 'Promise me that you will do all in your power to attend the wedding. How can you deny Captain Blake? He would be so very disappointed if you were not present.'

Mr Fitzroy remained silent. The temptation, in an unguarded moment, to say more than discretion allowed, was not easily overcome.

Emma was intrigued both by the warmth of his expression and his uncommon lack of coherence.

At length he replied, 'The business that takes me away from the society I have been privileged to enjoy these past months is unlikely to be concluded for some time.'

'When do you leave?' said she.

'At midday,' he replied.

'So soon?'

Emma found the news of Mr Fitzroy's departure and the uncertain prospect of his return exceedingly vexing. What could possibly require his immediate attention, and at such a moment?

As the wedding breakfast concluded, and the usual salutations and good wishes for the happiness and prosperity of the newly married couple were expressed, Emma speculated on the likely reasons for Mr Fitzroy's sudden departure. She had observed on leaving the church the peculiar spectacle of Anne Musgrave and Mr Fitzroy engaged in a private conversation. Had his feelings for Anne been as she had once imagined them to be? What other reason than this could there be to abandon Captain Blake at such a moment? And yet, had she not longed to do the same — to absent herself from a scene assured to cause pain?

Contrary to her conjecture, there appeared little in the manner of Mr Fitzroy's farewell to suggest a particular attachment towards Anne. Perhaps the business about which he was not at liberty to speak concerned the terms of the legacy. Was it not feasible that his elder brother might challenge the validity of the will and the soundness of mind of its originator? Might the cherished hopes for Brinshore's spa, entertained by so many, come to nought after all? And of the promises made and the services of many engaged to bring it about, what would suffice to quell the ensuing discontent should those dreams be shattered? Sanditon would rejoice at Brinshore's expense! How Mr Parker would crow!

When the morning's deliberations were concluded, the Osbornes and the Musgraves set out for Brighton with the expectation that they should arrive on the Steine just in time for dinner.

Mr and Mrs Fowle had no other plan than to spend the wedding night at Trafalgar Terrace, where a modest dinner of white fish and fried potatoes was served with the least possible fuss on the stroke of seven.

Mr Fitzroy left Brinshore an hour after midday. Apprehensive and dispirited, the news that had disturbed his peace came in the form of a letter from a distant relation, the widow of his father's second cousin, a woman who had long resided in the county of Somerset. Lady Russell's plea was urgent. Henry Fitzroy must return without a moment's delay to Allersham.

When the Osbornes and the Musgraves arrived in Brighton Emma found that she was obliged to share a bedchamber with Anne. A shortage of rooms was the cause, owing to the arrival of two further visitors, the identity of whom their hostess was at pains to conceal. Emma found that she was less disquieted by the arrangements than she had anticipated, for Anne said little about the wedding, preferring to speak almost entirely of the one that had taken place earlier that day.

'I suppose we must speak of Aunt Fowle now, and not Aunt Harding,' said Anne. 'Does it not sound strange?'

'It does indeed,' said Emma. 'Uncle Fowle sounds stranger still. Perhaps Aunt Hard — that is to say, perhaps Aunt and Uncle Fowle will sit down to a dinner of roast fowls! And if one or other of them were to find themselves in a foul humour —'

'Emma, it is cruel to speak of Aunt and Uncle Fowle so,' Anne replied.

'I expect it is, though it was meant only in jest.'

Footsteps in the hall were followed by a knock at the door. A maid entered with a message from Lady Forbes: Her Ladyship would receive them shortly, and should they require any small alteration to their gowns assistance was at hand.

'Thank you,' Emma replied. 'That will not be necessary. We are fit enough to be seen as we are.'

'Are you quite certain?' said Anne. 'Lady Forbes was very particular about dressing properly last time I stayed with her.'

'We have travelled a great distance and have not had a morsel to eat since the wedding breakfast. I am not inclined to make any great effort this evening for anyone.'

'But did you not hear talk of two further guests?' said Anne.

'Perhaps we are to be honoured by the famous Mrs F and her niece,' she replied.

The prospect of dining with two additional guests suddenly led to some anxiety on Emma's part. Could it be, thought she, that Captain Blake and his mother, due to some alteration to their travel arrangements, were expected? With somewhat less enthusiasm, Emma continued, 'What is done, is done. We must go down. You know that Lady Forbes does not like to be kept waiting.'

'Come! Come! Over here! Let me see the pair of you!' said Lady Forbes, as Emma and Anne entered to find each one of their parents already assembled. 'Emma, you are a little too brown. It does not suit you. Anne, I see you are much improved since last I saw you. A freckle or two does not signify but you must take care not to follow your cousin's example if you want to make yourself presentable for the wedding. When, I wonder, am I to have the pleasure of wishing Captain Blake joy in person? I suppose I shall see the good Captain at the wedding unless, of course, he cries off! I remember a young sea captain in seventy-six who left poor Miss White at the altar for a slight, mournful looking creature with five thousand pounds. I cannot think why, for Miss White was handsome enough and would have made him a tolerable wife. And so how do the Fowles go on?'

'I believe our sister is as happy as she can expect to be,' said Lady Osborne, looking to Mrs Musgrave to endorse her view of the matter.

'Penelope will find some pleasure and occupation in her new undertaking,' said Mrs Musgrave.

'Indeed,' Mr Musgrave replied. 'She has great plans for Mr Fowle.'

'And Brinshore. Though I rather think they are one and the same in your sister's estimation, my dear,' added Lord Osborne, with a look of amusement directed at his wife.

Lady Forbes was in a cheerful mood, heightened by those droll observations from 'dear Osborne' and 'dear Tom' to which she was, in former days, accustomed. 'We are quite full up this evening,' she continued. 'It puts me in mind of the old days when I had hardly a room to spare from one week's end to another. All those comings and goings over the years put a great strain on the staircase at Grosvenor Square. I was heartily glad to give up the place and let some unsuspecting purchaser have the bother of it. Fortunately, a retired colonel took it off my hands. He was perfectly satisfied with the stairs, though I suspect, given the state of his health, it is unlikely he will see out the year, and so, you see, he will not be troubled by the inconvenience of them much longer.'

A nod from one of Lady Forbes' footmen gave Her Ladyship warning that her two remaining guests were about to make their entrance and that dinner would shortly be served.

The astonishment of the entire party as the Dowager and Mrs Turner were announced afforded great merriment on the part of Lady Forbes and her old friends.

'What a sight to be seen! What a picture! What looks of bewilderment and confusion! Is this to be our welcome?' said the Dowager. 'No word of greeting? No salutation? No enquiry about the journey? Anyone might suppose you were not pleased to see us.'

'Our aim was Brinshore,' continued Mrs Turner, 'for we had a mind to attend the wedding, you see, more especially because Mrs Harding had expressly forbidden it.'

'No, my dear Mrs Turner. Mrs Harding meant only to prohibit you from attendance,' said the Dowager.

'That is by the by,' she replied. 'But once we were reunited with dear Lady Forbes, we gave up all thought of Brinshore, for we found that we had quite forgotten the delights of Brighton. It is enchanting, is it not?'

'And so you see, there was nothing to be done but yield to its charms,' the Dowager added.

'And how the landau was admired! Oh! We met with such looks of admiration and wonder!'

'Hats half raised, nods of approval, a smile here and there, even a wave from I do not know whom. No creature of our acquaintance I am sure!'

'Indeed we were vastly disappointed, were we not, my dear, to find that we had reached our destination quite so soon.'

'What? After six hours on the road?' said Lord Osborne.

'What is twenty miles of decent road?' his mother replied.

'It is forty miles at least from Delham!' said Tom Musgrave.

'Indeed it is,' Mrs Turner replied.

'Surely you did not expect Mrs Turner and I to manage the journey in a day?' said the Dowager.

'I had no expectations of either of you managing the journey at all. Indeed, I am astonished that you did not consult me first,' said Lord Osborne.

'Had we consulted you, my dear, every objection would have been placed in our path. And we were determined to attend the wedding, pay our respects to Brighton once again and visit our dear friend Lady Forbes whom, I should add, knew every detail of our plan,' said the Dowager.

'And immediately approved it,' added Mrs Turner.

'What is there left at our age to do but cause as great a nuisance as we possibly can to all our family!' said Lady Forbes. The three women of advanced years laughed heartily in much the same way they had done in their youth.

'Bravo Grandmamma! Bravo Aunt Turner! Bravo Lady Forbes!' said Emma, who shared the joke and laughed with them.

After tears of laughter had flowed in abundance, the three dried their eyes and endeavoured to compose themselves. But for Emma's enjoyment of the scene, the three women were met with looks of silent astonishment by the rest of their family.

'If you travelled but twenty miles, from what point did you begin your journey?' asked Lady Osborne.

'Crawley,' replied Mrs Turner.

'Crawley?' enquired His Lordship with a look of disbelief. 'Who do we know in Crawley?'

'No one, my dear. Mrs Turner and I are quite unconnected in Crawley. We put up at a coaching inn,' said the Dowager.

'A coaching inn?' said Lord Osborne, incredulous at the thought of two elderly women moving about with neither protection nor supervision. 'Gave you no thought to the danger — the recklessness of travelling alone and unprotected? Gave you no thought to your own safety, to the feelings and opinions of your family?'

'Indeed we gave a great deal of thought to it,' replied Mrs Turner. 'We had no wish to inconvenience you. And as fortune would have it, we had a famous time. Crawley was excessively diverting! We were introduced to a most charming gentleman by the name of Parker, and his good wife, fellow travellers on the road, but headed in quite the opposite direction. Bound for Reigate, said he. How fortuitous, said I, (for the Parkers, it appears, are not well acquainted with those parts). At first, you see, we suspected a Lowford connection, for whom else is there to speak of in Reigate. But no. Mr Parker was about the business of obtaining the services of a physician for a charming little place by the sea (having failed miserably at previous attempts of the same). Here comes the best part. Said I, of where do you speak? Where is this paradise to be found? Said he, Sanditon. Well, said I, what stroke of luck is this? For we are destined to pass through Sanditon tomorrow as sure as night follows day. Pass *through* Sanditon, Mrs Turner? Impossible! said he. You speak as though Sanditon is but a staging post on the road to Eastbourne or Hastings. I can tell you most unequivocally, my dear Mrs Turner, that Sanditon is the jewel of the south coast, and deemed as such by those privileged to reside within its environs, and by every visitor privileged to partake of the freshness of its air and the many beneficial properties of its sea water. I beg your pardon, sir, said I. This account of Sanditon is indeed encouraging, for when we last heard it spoken of it was not very promising. Poor Mr Parker! I do not know what possessed him, but he appeared to succumb to a sudden fit of apoplexy. At first I thought it might have been something I said, but Mrs Parker assured me that he often suffered in quite the same way. I expect that is why he is determined to obtain the services of a physician. And, I daresay, there is money to be made in Sanditon by any enterprising young man with a steady hand for stitches, a jar of leeches and a prodigious quantity of court plaster. The inhabitants of this paradise seem very ill indeed, said I. At length, Mrs Parker succeeded, by her good graces, in restoring her husband. So it came as a great surprise, when dinner was announced, that the Parkers were most insistent we sit at their table. They would hear of nothing else. And I must say, they paid handsomely for it.'

'Had we not the greatest good luck that it happened so?' said the Dowager. 'I should not have paid a farthing, for the cuisine was utterly inedible, much like the ingredients of Mrs Hedges' famous stews. It was, nevertheless, a timely distraction from what was to follow. For once the soup had been served, Mrs Parker proceeded to ask whether we had connections in Eastbourne.'

'Eastbourne? said I,' continued Mrs Turner. 'Why, we are bound for Brinshore. My niece is to wed there two days hence and though not, I may say, in the first flush of youth, she seems well pleased with her conquest. The gentleman in question — if one can describe him as such — goes by the name of Fowle. Said he, Mr Fowle you say? I did indeed sir, said I. But — and now comes the important part — said I, my dear Mr Parker, look no further in your quest for a physician, for I believe you have found him. Mr Fowle is the very man! He is the man you seek! Indeed, I have it on the best authority that Mr Fowle can do no wrong! His reputation goes before him, and though he is likely to reside in Brinshore for the foreseeable future, Sanditon is little more than half a morning's journey of good road. Brinshore's man will serve you well!'

'Never was there a more sincere nor well-intentioned word ever spoken. Therein was the solution to Mr Parker's predicament — and I can vouch for Mrs Turner, the assistance was kindly meant,' said the Dowager.

'Before I had time to draw breath, poor Mr Parker, the picture of dismay, choked on his soup with such violence that I thought he would expire there and then, thereby eliminating any need for the services of a physician, and saving himself a great deal of money,' continued Mrs Turner.

'But he did not, for Mrs Parker saw to it that the soup was removed from the table immediately. And not a moment too soon in my estimation,' said the Dowager.

Emma, who had listened with increasing amusement to the narrative, then spoke up. 'But Grandmamma, did you know nothing of the opposition raised in Sanditon to the plans for Brinshore's new spa, and Mr Fowle's part in it? Mr Parker is regarded as Sanditon's greatest advocate! Would it not have been prudent to stifle that which might add fuel to the flames? Mr Parker, as you must have surmised, is so intimately connected with the affairs of Sanditon, that he will not hear Brinshore spoken of in the same breath. I believe you and Aunt Turner knew what you were about, though I expect you have no intention of owning it.'

The Dowager and Mrs Turner made little effort to correct Emma's interpretation of the facts, and showed themselves to be more amused than affronted at the idea.

'Emma, my dear,' said Mrs Turner, effecting to smooth out the folds of her gown, 'what can you possibly mean? Surely you do not suspect your own family of artifice and subterfuge.'

'Not at all, Aunt,' Emma replied, 'but we are all capable from time to time of creating amusement for ourselves out of the foibles of others. Are we not, Grandmamma?'

'My dear,' replied the Dowager, 'I think you have stayed in Brinshore too long. The sea has affected your head! You sound like that poor clergyman who abandoned the godless of Surrey for the heathen of the East Indies.'

'Emma is quite right, Mama,' said Lady Osborne. 'What if poor Mr Parker had suffered a stroke or a heart attack? We do not know the state of his constitution.'

'Indeed we do,' said the Dowager, 'for he spoke of it without pause for some considerable time. There was nothing wrong with his appetite. You should have seen the sly way he had of helping himself to an additional portion of pie whenever his wife's attention was drawn elsewhere, and pretending it was the very same piece as before.'

'No harm came of it,' said Mrs Turner, conceding the point, 'and after all is said and done it was an opportunity too tempting to resist. We have heard all about Mr Parker from Mrs Blake, you see.'

'And we have been excessively diverted by all the goings on between Sanditon and Brinshore that a chance meeting with Mr Parker and his good wife was too tempting an opportunity to miss. It helped to pass an idle hour or two. Indeed, by the time we said our adieus, Mrs Turner and I had received a dozen invitations or more to visit Sanditon after the wedding.'

'Mr Parker,' added Mrs Turner, 'thought we might have need of respite and did not think we would tolerate Brinshore at all well. We left Crawley the best of friends.'

Said Lady Forbes, 'I should have enjoyed the scene above anything!'

'And I,' said Tom Musgrave, avoiding the reproachful look of his wife.

'You will be comforted to know that all ended happily,' said the Dowager, 'for Mrs Turner and I were able to be of service to Mr Parker.'

'In what way?' said Lady Osborne.

'We gave Mr Parker the name of Granby's nephew. He is perhaps a little young, but I believe he has a promising future as Sanditon's new physician.'

'Mr Fowle will have to look out,' said Emma.

'Indeed he will,' said Mrs Turner, 'for when Mr Parker has found his physician, his search for a spring with health-giving properties to rival Brinshore will occupy him in earnest.'

Lady Forbes glanced at the lateness of the hour. 'Shall we go in? I should not like the soup to spoil. I think we can do a little better than Crawley's fare.'

The dining room was furnished with every comfort, and on the table a fine array of dishes, hot and cold, was a happy sight for the weary travellers. Lady Forbes had paid particular attention to the seating of her guests, that they should not be too far apart, for she was determined to have her part in every conversation. She surveyed the room with the look of a general poised to rally his troops on the eve of a campaign.

'Anne, you have said not a word. I expect your thoughts are elsewhere,' said Lady Forbes.

'Oh, no indeed,' Anne replied. 'It is all so very entertaining. I have nothing of interest to say that could match so engaging a narrative.'

'Nonsense!' said Lady Forbes. 'You must tell us about the wedding.'

'The church was full and the wedding breakfast —'

'No, no, no!' Lady Forbes replied. 'I want to know about *your* wedding.'

Anne glanced awkwardly in Emma's direction. 'There is so little to tell.'

For Emma's sake, some among the party would have exercised greater discretion and allowed the subject of the wedding to subside. Mrs Turner, however, was not one of them. 'Anne must arrive at Wickstead in the landau,' said she, 'even though Captain Blake is most insistent that his own equipage be used once they are married. I expect he will have his own way, but I have always observed that entrances are of greater consequence than exits.'

Emma looked up to find Anne's eyes fixed on her as though awaiting an indication from her cousin that the wedding might be spoken of without discomfort or embarrassment.

'An excellent idea,' said Emma, smiling at Anne with uncommon diffidence. Surprised by Emma's reaction, Lord and Lady Osborne each met their daughter's eyes with looks of admiration and approval.

'And will the Howards and Mr Edwards be among the wedding party?' asked the Dowager.

'There was never any expectation of it,' said Mrs Musgrave. 'The journey is now beyond Mr Edwards' capability, and Mr Howard is in a critical state.'

'Then we had better hope Mr Howard has the good grace to linger until after the wedding, or the wedding may yet be postponed. Mr Howard had better not put Anne and his nephew to any inconvenience of the sort if he knows what is good for him,' said Mrs Turner.

'That may not be a bad thing,' said Anne. The party were astonished by her remark.

Lady Forbes put down her spoon and sat forward to give Anne her full attention. 'And why should that be? Do not tell me that you have a mind to cry off.'

'Do not let your mama be your guide. I recall how your mama led your papa a merry dance before they were wed,' said Mrs Turner. 'I hope you, my dear, are not inclined to do likewise.'

Mr and Mrs Musgrave exchanged amused glances. 'Well said, Mrs Turner! Never was a man so utterly ill-used as I!' said he. 'Is that not so, Lady Forbes?'

'My dear boy,' Lady Forbes replied, 'what a state you were in! I told you to go back to Delham at once and make Miss Watson marry you. I had a mind to go there myself, you know, and make her see sense.'

'Tom? You never told me this,' said his wife.

'Dear Tom was determined to give up Delham for good,' replied Lady Forbes. 'I shall never set foot in the place again, said he. Nonsense, said I. If you do not succeed, I shall succeed for you. I have never been one to brook opposition.'

Mrs Musgrave was astonished at Lady Forbes revelation and looked to her husband for an explanation. Mr Musgrave smiled and shrugged his shoulders. 'It was fortunate then that coercion was not required. For when I next came upon the impossible, but lovely, Miss Watson, she accepted me before my admonishment of her conduct was half complete. Take me now, said I, or I shall unleash Lady Forbes on —'

'You said nothing of the kind,' interrupted Mrs Musgrave.

Lady Forbes, Mrs Turner and the Dowager descended into fits of laughter as the younger among the party marvelled at their complete want of decorum.

But Mrs Musgrave was more anxious to comprehend the meaning of her daughter's earlier remark. 'Anne, my dear, why would you welcome a postponement?'

'Long engagements are never a good thing,' said Mrs Turner.

The Dowager disagreed. 'My dear, allow me to remind you that had you not rushed headfirst into matrimony a second time, you might have saved yourself the inconvenience of an infamous alliance.'

Anne, impatient to end the matter, said, 'I meant, simply, that a delay would increase the likelihood of Mr Fitzroy's attendance. It would please Captain Blake to have him there, for who else is there to represent his dear departed friend and fellow officer,' said Anne.

The Dowager replied, 'Has Captain Blake not fellow officers by the dozen? Surely they might be prevailed upon, though I doubt it will be necessary, for the promise of an excellent wedding breakfast is always —'

'Grandmamma! It is not the same thing,' interrupted Emma. 'Captain Blake and Captain Fitzroy fought together.'

'Indeed,' replied the Dowager. 'But did they alone defeat the French at Trafalgar?'

'Captain Fitzroy once saved Charles' life,' said Anne.

Emma was stunned by Anne's disclosure. It was a remarkable piece of information concerning Captain Blake of which she had been unaware. At one time, she might have been sorely wounded by the notion that Anne should have in her possession such knowledge while she was left ignorant of the matter; but the wound, though fresh, was quickly brought into check. This is how it will be, thought Emma: now, and forever. I must accept that over which I have no sway. Such precious details which once she was eager to garner and lay before the world, were now Anne's province. For some moments, she reproached herself inwardly for her failure to curb her curiosity about the concerns of Captain Blake. His business was no longer her business; his actions were no longer her concern; and his soul was not, nor had ever been, akin to hers.

'Well, my dear,' said Lady Forbes, in large part addressing herself to Anne, 'I should not hold out much hope of Mr Fitzroy attending the wedding. He is wholly occupied with other matters at present; and, I have it on good authority that he is likely to be much occupied in the future too.'

All eyes in the room were fixed on Lady Forbes. 'Lowford cannot keep a secret for long. He had it from his steward, who had it from his nephew who, as you know, is steward to the present Lord Allersham. I say "present" for it would appear that he is not long for this life.'

'That cannot be!' said Emma.

Lady Forbes replied, 'Given the life he leads, I should think he has done remarkably well to see his thirtieth year.'

'Is he expected to linger long?' asked the Dowager.

'Oh, my dear, I should think not,' replied Lady Forbes.

'And no offspring to care about. What an excellent thing!' said the Dowager.

'Why so, Grandmamma?' Emma replied. 'Mr Fitzroy will not think it an excellent thing. I am quite certain that he has no interest in succeeding him. His dearest wish is to enter the Church, not manage the crumbling estate at Allersham.'

'You have changed your tune, young lady,' said the Dowager. 'I remember a time when you were all for Mr Fitzroy making amends with his brother and furthering his own interests.'

'I did not know his character so well as I know it now,' said Emma.

'My dear Emma, you know perfectly well that Mr Fitzroy is not accorded the power of refusal,' her grandmother replied. 'He is his brother's heir, and that is the end of the matter.'

'He will be grieved indeed,' said Emma.

Emma was greatly vexed by her grandmother's remarks. As dinner drew to a close, Mr Fitzroy began to occupy Emma's thoughts in a manner that was at once pleasing and perplexing. At first, she had scorned both his desire to enter the Church, and his determination to marry Miss Barnes against the express wishes of his brother. When Miss Barnes saw fit to transfer her affections to another, the estrangement from his family might have been overcome had he chosen to abandon his deceased brother's wishes by bailing out the estate and consenting to marry a woman of Lord Allersham's choosing. But he would not. This, she had once supposed, was his greatest folly.

In that moment, Emma comprehended Mr Fitzroy's character more clearly, and in so doing, she began to understand herself better. The expectations, condescension and trappings of rank and privilege were of little consequence to a man, or woman, who valued liberty, whose mind and spirit were free. I pity Mr Fitzroy, thought she. For the sake of a line that would surely fall into extinction without him, Mr Fitzroy must now accept his fate.

Her grandmother's meaning could not have been clearer: the 'excellent thing' to which she alluded was the opportunity that Mr Fitzroy's timely elevation now provided for Emma; for her granddaughter to become the wife of a clergyman was unthinkable, but to be mistress of Allersham Park — a countess no less — was greatly to be desired.

A day ago, Emma would have wished Mr Fitzroy joy had he chosen to marry the daughter of a duke, another Miss Barnes or one of the fisherwomen of Brinshore. But as the realisation came to her that her interest in Mr Fitzroy's affairs was not as dispassionate as she had once supposed it to be, another more immediate consideration displaced it. Mr Fitzroy will never be more to me than a friend, nor I

239

to him, thought she. I may in future consider myself intimately acquainted with him should our mutual society with the Blakes continue to bring us together, but I could never marry him.

The following morning, Emma set out before breakfast for a walk on the Steine. Her mind was restless, and her body fatigued, for she had spent a wakeful night attempting to make sense of the thoughts and feelings that had become so perplexing to her. As she turned to walk towards the shore, she came upon her father who often enjoyed an early morning walk.

'Whatever are you doing at this early hour?' said he.

'The same as you, Papa. I am your daughter, after all. Do not you walk in order to think, as much as for the exercise it affords?' Emma replied.

'I do indeed,' said Lord Osborne. 'Shall we walk together?'

Emma took her father's arm; she had not spoken with him in private since their journey to Brinshore after little Frank's accident.

'How is Frank?' said she.

'Giving Nanny as much trouble as he can,' her father replied. 'Your grandmother is continually at pains to remind me that I was much the same at his age.'

Emma sighed. 'Have I given you much trouble, Papa?'

'Indeed you have,' he replied, 'and I wouldn't have had it otherwise.'

She sighed a second time.

Lord Osborne observed his daughter and asked, 'Are you troubled, my dear?'

'I hardly know, Papa.'

'Unless you have adopted a new habit of walking in the early morning, I can only assume that some matter weighs on your mind.'

'Do you not think Brighton is at its best at this time of day?' Emma replied.

'The world is at its best at this time of day,' said her father.

'Papa,' said Emma, some moments later. 'Why must Grandmamma always have her say? I wish she had not mentioned — Papa, will you ask Grandmamma to give up this absurd notion of hers. What she was about was as plain as day at dinner. No one was in doubt as to her meaning. She means to contrive a match for me with Mr Fitzroy now that he is likely to succeed his brother.'

'Give no heed to your grandmother,' her father replied. 'You must understand that she longs to see you settled while she still has breath. Try to overlook those imperfections in her behaviour that seem irksome to you, and strive to put all thought of Mr Fitzroy out of you head for the present. If his brother's days are numbered, there will be much to occupy our friend as the time draws near.'

'I expect he will be in mourning when next we meet,' said she. 'That will be my protection from Grandmamma's meddling, for she will be obliged to hold her tongue.'

'Do you dislike Mr Fitzroy?' her father asked, surprised by her remark. 'You defended him boldly at dinner. Were you often thrown together in Brinshore?'

'I see, Papa. You wish to draw me out too, to know my opinion of Mr Fitzroy,' said Emma. 'I do not dislike him.'

'So you like him,' her father replied.

'There was no particularity in any of our dealings in Brinshore.'

'You urged me to give him the living at Stanton.'

'For Anne's sake, Papa. I thought perhaps — but I was mistaken. And Mr Fitzroy did not take kindly to my interference.'

'As you do not take kindly to your grandmother's meddling.'

'There is a difference, Papa. My interference is guarded and prudent. Grandmamma observes no such constraints. You heard her pointed remarks at dinner. It was humiliating. If only Anne had not been there to hear them! Please tell Grandmamma that there can never be any understanding between me and Mr Fitzroy. It is quite out of the question. Mr Fitzroy would never marry a woman for the sake of convenience or advantage. And I could never marry Mr Fitzroy, Papa, because Grandmamma expressly desires it.'

'Ah,' said Lord Osborne, intrigued by his daughter's retort. 'I see. Well, that seems to settle the matter. There is nothing more to be said.'

'No, Papa. Nothing at all.'

'My dear Emma, we are so very alike, you and I,' her father said. 'If only your grandmother had had the good sense to forbid it.'

'Forbid what, Papa?'

CHAPTER TWENTY-EIGHT

On the morning of the first assembly of the season, Tuesday October the fifteenth, expectations were high that the Delham Assembly would be a good one, for it was understood that the Osbornes were to attend and bring with them a large party. The restoration of the assembly rooms, which had fallen into a dilapidated state during the latter years of the war, had been overseen by Lady Osborne and Mrs Musgrave. But for one enduring obstacle — the Dowager — the task had not been an onerous one, for the two women were of one mind, and strived only for those improvements that were considered essential and affordable. That the rooms were ready for the season's first assembly was little short of a miracle, for the Dowager had espoused grander ideas, and was not inclined to shrink from expressing them; and though unsolicited, the advice meted out had become something of a hindrance to the progress and completion of the work.

'I am shocked indeed that you did not use the upper rooms at Bath as your guide,' said she. 'The old rooms were serviceable enough, I suppose — the scene of countless intrigues and delights — but the upper rooms are a vast improvement — just the kind of thing Delham has need of.'

Lady Osborne was at pains to point out that Delham was not Bath and that such grandiose notions would appear incongruous in what amounted to little more than a village.

'I daresay, Mama, you will be better pleased with them than you imagine,' said Lady Osborne to her mother-in-law. 'Much thought has been given to the interior, and there has been much speculation in the neighbourhood about the new design. I expect the assembly will be well attended this evening for that reason alone. The Musgraves and the Blakes will attend, of course.'

'And how fares Mr Howard?' said the Dowager.

'Well, I believe. He is now quite out of danger,' she replied. 'And I have news that will surprise you. The Fowles are also expected to be among our party. They are due to arrive at three and —'

'— will likely be in no great hurry to return from whence they came,' added the Dowager. 'I understand my son has been worked on to give assistance to the Fowles. He will soon find that he has no finger left for his own pies, for he is wont to sink the fingers of both hands into too many other pies.'

'Osborne takes pleasure in employment of many kinds. If he should champion the cause of Brinshore, what harm is there in that?'

'He should leave Brinshore to the Fowles and make Osborne Park his preoccupation.'

'Dear Mama, you know your son as well as I,' said Lady Osborne. 'He will do exactly as he pleases. And we should be thankful that the matters he is pleased to uphold are generally of benefit to the many and not the few.'

Lady Osborne glanced at the portrait of her husband as a young boy which hung by the door.

'Frank has a look of his father,' said she. 'More so these last few weeks, I believe. He is happy now that his sister is come.'

'Emma will likely want for partners this evening,' replied the Dowager. 'Anne will be pleased to have Charles Blake to herself. But what is to become of Emma? The men of Delham are a dreary lot. There is no one of quality among them. My dear, you must take her to London for a season and let her see what she can do there.'

'I shall not press Emma to attend the assembly,' said Lady Osborne. 'It is enough that she has changed her mind and consented to be Anne's bridesmaid.'

'Has she?' The Dowager was genuinely surprised to hear it.

'I may take Emma to London in a week or two if Osborne is of the same view,' replied Lady Osborne. 'Shall we see you this evening?'

'Mrs Turner is determined to make an appearance. I myself may look in for five minutes, if only to please the neighbourhood and inspect the new shade of the walls.'

'You mistake my meaning. I am come to invite you to dine at the Castle, for we are to dine early and shall be a large party. The Musgraves, the Blakes and the Fowles are to dine with us.'

'Well,' replied the Dowager, 'I daresay I should pay my respects to Mrs Fowle. As to Mr Fowle, I am not in the habit of dining with physicians. I sincerely hope he leaves the particulars of his patients' insides outside the dining room. It is a great shame that Mr Parker and his good wife will not be present. I don't suppose you have extended an invitation to them. They were seen in Delham yesterday.

Indeed, I understand they have managed to snatch Mr Granby's nephew right from under our very noses!'

'That, I believe, was *your* doing, Mama,' said Lady Osborne.

'Be that as it may. Sanditon is to have its own physician at last. I daresay it is a good thing for Mr Fowle to have some competition. And Mr Granby's nephew must certainly be the handsomer and younger of the two.'

The Fowles arrived at the appointed hour, neither a minute too soon nor a minute too late, punctuality being a matter of the utmost importance to the physician who was at pains to recommend himself to those of greatest consequence among his bride's family. Twice on the road he had called for the coachman to drive faster; and when Osborne Park came into view at a quarter past two, Mr Fowle gave the order for the coach to slow to a snail's pace to avoid the inconvenience of an early arrival. Awed by the grounds and the stateliness of the Castle, Mr Fowle nervously adjusted his necktie. A succession of assurances extended by Mrs Fowle, that he was 'tolerably presentable', did little to quell his unease.

'You will do well enough,' said his wife. 'Have an eye to where you sit, for the dust was as thick as goose down when I last had cause to take a turn in the gallery.'

'I am to meet His Lordship in the library, my dear. I expect it is made better use of than the gallery.'

'Indeed it is not. I cannot count the times I have walked the gallery back and forth. But I have yet to spend five minutes complete in the library,' said Mrs Fowle.

'A library is as essential to life as the air we breathe! I hope, my dear, that you will strive to remedy your sorry neglect when Brinshore's circulating library opens its doors.'

'Have no fear on that score, for I shall be its foremost subscriber,' his wife replied. 'My dear, once your meeting is concluded, you may take a walk in the park if you will. I shall be engaged with my sister until it is time to dress.'

'Whatever you say, my dear,' said he.

The warmth of Lady Osborne's greeting for the new Mrs Fowle was tinged with apprehension and a desire to ascertain how well her sister had fared since the wedding.

'I see so little of Mr Fowle, it hardly signifies,' said she. 'He is much occupied with his patients. They call on him endlessly. And when he is not dispensing cures to invalids and neurotics, he is about the business of the spa. He means to go to Harrogate, you know, to see what they have done there. These treatments are all the fashion one minute and as ancient as the grave the next! Let them drink the waters. Is that not treatment enough? Is not our beloved Brinshore the greatest cure of all? My dear Mr Fowle, said I, if you promise cures for every ailment under the sun, the sick and the old will expect to live forever. Dr Harding was much of the same mind, you know, and was quite unwilling to give himself up to the grim reaper. Harrogate of all places! And in November! The ground will be three inches thick with snow, for you know what it is like in those northern towns. But Mr Fowle will not be moved. He will not. I told him plainly that nothing shall induce me to exchange Brinshore for Harrogate in November!'

'But you are content?' Lady Osborne replied.

'My dear sister, you must know that it is not in my character to court contentment. Mr Fowle is tolerable company. And it is, on balance, better to be married than to live the rest of one's days a widow,' said Mrs Fowle.

Before the sisters had time to exchange the news of the day, little Frank was brought into the drawing room to be seen by his Aunt Fowle, who observed that he had grown at least an inch since she last saw him. His look was one of apprehension on seeing his aunt, and when she reached out to ruffle his hair, he fled straight into the arms of his mother. No amount of coaxing succeeded in tearing him from her, and so before the half hour struck, little Frank was carried away by his nanny with the promise of a boiled egg and custard.

'I hear our own Mr Fitzroy is shortly to inherit Allersham. Emma must have a chance there, must she not?' said Mrs Fowle.

Lady Osborne sighed. 'Her grandmother takes the same view, but the very suggestion of it has set Emma utterly against the idea. Both Osborne and I suspect a growing partiality on both sides, but we are loath to intervene. We must tread carefully. Until Emma knows her own mind, no amount of persuasion is likely to bring her round.'

'She would be foolish to spurn a man of his prospects simply because her family *approve* the match! I hope for the sake of Brinshore that Lord Allersham does not drag his feet. May he not linger long,' said Mrs Fowle. 'Now, my dear, if you will excuse me, I shall rest my weary limbs, for I have no intention of missing dear Delham's first assembly of the season.'

Together with the occupants of the Castle — excepting little Frank — the Musgraves, the Blakes and the Fowles made up the Osborne set, and among them were the Dowager and Mrs Turner. As they entered the assembly room, the Dowager surveyed the scene before her.

'You must concede the point, my dear,' said Mrs Turner. 'The new arrangements are quite marvellous! The drapes look very well indeed. Are they not rather like the drapes in the green drawing room at the Castle?'

'They are. Indeed, they are one and the same!' said the Dowager, outraged by the discovery.

'At the Castle they appeared a little ordinary, even a little drab, as I recall, but here they can be seen to full advantage. What a remarkable difference they have made!' replied Mrs Turner.

Lady Osborne was pleased with her aunt's estimation of the improvements carried out, most especially her opinion of the new drapes. 'The drapes were Emma's idea. She has an excellent eye for such things.'

'I am shocked. Shocked and displeased,' said the Dowager. 'A perfectly serviceable complement of drapes, with another twenty years' wear in them at least! Given away without the blink of an eyelid!'

'Indeed,' said Lady Osborne. 'And there is another perfectly serviceable set in one of the old blanket chests to replace them. The drawing room will be just as well served by them.'

'Those old things? They are not fit to be seen! Does Osborne know of this?' the Dowager replied.

'Your son would have it no other way, Mama,' said Lady Osborne gently.

A vast improvement on their former state, the enhancements to the Delham assembly rooms were hailed a triumph. Airy, light and comfortable, the greater of the two was just large enough to accommodate the dancers. Card players were equally well satisfied with the stylish arrangements in the lesser room; and the addition of an elegant screen, carefully situated to give as little disturbance as

246

possible to their deliberations, was as welcome as the refreshments and the excellent plain cake served up in the tea room.

The absence of negus ensured the continued sobriety of all the guests throughout the evening, including the Fowles, who danced only two dances in the first half and two in the second.

Mrs Musgrave was at pains to conceal her disappointment that the waltz was not listed among the dances. 'Dear Tom was determined to waltz, but I should have been obliged to decline his request,' said she to Mrs Blake. 'He thinks nothing of causing a spectacle and would have had me on my feet if he could.'

Mrs Blake, though overjoyed at the prospect of having Anne Musgrave as a daughter-in-law, was greatly concerned about Emma. Several times she had observed Emma's countenance; in those unguarded moments, Emma, whether dancing or sitting down, had allowed her eyes to drift towards the engaged couple.

'Oh, my dear, dear child,' whispered Mrs Blake under her breath.

Lady Osborne took leave of her mother-in-law and soon found herself standing beside the happy couple.

'Dear Aunt,' said Anne, 'Charles tells me this is the very spot where first you met.'

'It is indeed,' said Lady Osborne, smiling. She turned to Charles and said, 'I recovered the glove you had lost. It was lying on the floor and I gave it back to you.'

Charles replied, 'A greater service you could not have rendered. I shall never forget it. Anne would not believe me when I told her that I was engaged to dance down every couple with Miss Osborne (as she was then). Do you recall? Colonel Beresford was not expected to attend, you see. But then, lo and behold, there he was. And I was left without a partner, for the good Colonel stole Miss Osborne from me! My disappointment lasted but moments, for I could not have found a better partner than Miss Emma Watson.'

'How the years have flown by!' said Lady Osborne. 'I recall vividly my first assembly in Delham as though it were yesterday.'

Charles replied, 'Would you do me the honour of dancing with me one last time before I am married?'

'Please do, Aunt,' insisted Anne.

'On one condition,' said Lady Osborne. 'That you take with you to your new home in Sanditon a rather fine stuffed fox and badger that presently reside in the long room at the Castle.'

Charles laughed heartily at the request; Anne was puzzled by it. 'I shall indeed if you desire it,' said he.

'I do desire it,' replied Lady Osborne. 'My dear Anne, when first we met, Charles insisted that I go with him to the Castle to view these exceptional creatures. Frank is a little too fascinated by them at present, and if they are to be placed in safe keeping at all, I know of no better place for them.'

Emma watched her mother dance with Captain Blake just as she had done some weeks earlier at the Brinshore Ball. So many changes have taken place since then, thought she, not least to my own expectations and situation. How I longed to dance with him then! To make him my own Captain Blake!

He had not slighted Emma, nor would he; early on he had come forward to request the honour of dancing the quadrille with her. The pleasure had been graciously declined, for Lowford's nephew had already secured Emma himself.

I am relieved that it should have happened so! thought she. The pleasure of dancing with Charles Blake can no longer be mine. How far I have come since the summer! That I should tolerate the sight of my cousin by his side! That I should wish them both joy and almost mean it!

Emma began to lament the absence of Mr Fitzroy. Their party seemed incomplete without him. She missed his wit, raillery, and astute observations most of all. I should have welcomed the opportunity to debate with him the merits of *Mansfield Park* over *Pride and Prejudice* or *Sense and Sensibility*. I expect he would have deemed *Pride and Prejudice* the inferior of the three for its portrayal of that silly clergyman, Mr Collins. Edmund Bertram, or indeed Edward Ferrars, would likely meet with his approval. Occasionally, as her eyes wandered around the room, she glimpsed in one or two of the young men present a similarity in bearing and countenance, but none among them had his expression or his natural style, nor even his handsome eyes.

Lord Osborne found his daughter quite alone standing by the window. 'You seem preoccupied, my dear. Are you in want of a partner?'

'No, Papa, I am in want of air,' she replied. 'I am not inclined to dance again for there is no one with whom I desire to stand up. Are we to leave shortly?'

'If you wish it,' said he.

'I do,' Emma replied.

CHAPTER TWENTY-NINE

The transformation of the Delham assembly rooms was hailed a triumph; even the Dowager, after finding fault with every alteration, sat down to whist for a full hour before partaking of a dish of tea and attributing the acclaimed improvements entirely to her own excellent taste and good judgement. There was general agreement that the success of the first assembly, having met with a universal chorus of approval, augured well for the second and every subsequent assembly of the season.

'You are to be congratulated, my dear,' said Lord Osborne to his wife.

'I could not have achieved it alone. Without my sister's assistance, I should have failed utterly,' she replied. 'Elizabeth understands the particulars of how to get things done. She is the best manager of mess and disorder in the world.'

Lady Osborne saw that her husband was deep in thought and carried on with her letter writing undisturbed by his presence. For some moments, he stood by the fireplace and watched her, as though intent on committing the scene to memory. At last, he moved closer to her writing desk and sat down. 'My dear, there is something you should know.'

The serious tone in his voice caused Lady Osborne to put her writing aside and give him her full attention.

'I have received a letter from my sister,' said he. 'It seems we are shortly to expect grave news and must prepare ourselves. Colonel Beresford has had a stroke. The physician who attends him does not expect him to survive the week.'

Lady Osborne reached for her husband's hand. 'I am grieved to hear it. Truly, I am,' said she. 'But, my dear, are we to wait for the express to receive confirmation, or should we make plans to travel directly? What must be done?'

'I confess, I'm inclined to leave directly, for my sister will require assistance with the management of things,' Lord Osborne replied.

Lady Osborne gave some thought to the matter. 'Forgive me, my dear. I wonder, should not I remain here? The journey is long, and the weather at this time of year will likely make travel more arduous. And you know that Frank does not travel well. There is nothing I should desire more than to be of assistance to Mrs Beresford at such a moment, but we must also think of little Frank, and of Mama and Aunt Turner.'

'It grieves me to say it, but I am of the same mind,' said he. 'You are right, my dear, though I shall miss you every second of every day.'

'And I you,' she replied. Lady Osborne kissed her husband's hand and held it to her cheek. 'Might you take Emma with you?'

Lord Osborne could imagine no better plan than this.

'Perhaps I should speak with Elizabeth first.'

'Why so?' said he.

'If Emma agrees to accompany you to Somerset, Anne will be left without a bridesmaid. And, having so graciously and unexpectedly given her word, I should not like Emma to be seen to break it lightly. I shall bear the responsibility myself, and I am sure my sister will understand when once the circumstances are made known to her,' said she.

'You shall not bear the responsibility alone,' he replied.

When explained in full, the Musgraves concurred entirely with the wisdom of the plan, and the matter was settled by the end of the day. While Emma had some misgivings about breaking her word to Anne, the prospect of going into Somerset, despite the grave purpose for doing so, was more appealing to her than she was willing to admit.

Before Emma bid her cousin farewell, Anne secured from her a promise that she would visit Sanditon at the earliest opportunity. 'We might call on the Fowles, you and I, and see how Brinshore's spa progresses.'

'And the famous circulating library. But let it be in the spring,' said Emma, 'when I am once again in my colours. Black does not suit me.'

'Perhaps the Colonel will rally,' said Anne hopefully.

'It does not seem likely,' Emma replied. 'Papa intends to bring Aunt Beresford back to Osborne Castle once the grim business is concluded. Poor Uncle Beresford.'

The arrangements for the journey into Somerset were accomplished in haste. But as Lord Osborne and his daughter were about to set out, an express arrived confirming the sad news: Colonel Beresford was at rest. The end came quickly — he did not suffer long — Mrs Beresford was at his bedside until he drew his last breath — the corpse looked peaceful.

'It will be some weeks, I know, before I shall see you again,' said Lady Osborne to her daughter. 'You shall be in my thoughts constantly while you are away. Take care of your father and comfort your aunt. My dear Emma, come back to me safely.'

'Have no fear, Mama.'

For some moments after the carriage disappeared from view, Lady Osborne, numbed by the suddenness of their departure, continued to gaze at the marks made by the carriage wheels that were imprinted on the ground. The chill in the air soon caused her to go inside; but instead of returning directly to her morning room, she went up to the nursery and spent the remainder of the morning with Frank, watching him ride upon his rocking horse.

The journey to Somerset was accomplished without difficulty; not a moment longer than necessary was spent on the road. By six o'clock the following evening, after leaving the Andover road, the carriage entered Somerset. The weather was calm and the road smooth; the gates of Whitcombe House came into view by a quarter past seven. Lord Osborne found his sister much as he had expected: consumed by grief at the loss of a husband with whom she had spent the happiest years of her life. Comforted by the unexpected and pleasing presence of her niece, Mrs Beresford rallied slightly and spent half an hour after dinner in quiet conversation giving an account of the Colonel's final hours, before bidding her guests 'goodnight'.

CHAPTER THIRTY

The practical affairs of the deceased, however unambiguous their bequests and intentions, must in the end be concluded by the living. Colonel Beresford was laid to rest on a cold October day in the churchyard at Whitcombe; according to the wishes of the deceased and overseen by Lord Osborne, principal among the mourners, the committal was a modest affair and was soon followed by the reading of the will. The Colonel's wishes yielded no surprises, and but for the matter of the estate, the legal undertakings were swiftly and satisfactorily accomplished. Colonel Beresford's worldly possessions, including Whitcombe, were left in their entirety to his widow.

Emma, who had spent almost every waking moment at her aunt's side, was persuaded of the view that Aunt Beresford was not likely to part with Whitcombe Park in a hurry; nor had she any immediate thought of returning to Delham and settling there.

'Papa, I desire it as keenly as you, but I do not think Aunt Beresford is yet ready to give up Whitcombe. This house holds too many memories. We must afford her time to grieve.'

Lord Osborne was less convinced of the practicalities of the plan. 'Your aunt is not accustomed to managing things for herself. The running of an estate like Whitcombe requires considerable time and effort.'

Both arguments were given due consideration by the person most affected by them; objections were raised, and solutions put forward. After much debate, Mrs Beresford was of the view that a tenant should be found for Whitcombe Park.

'One year, Osborne,' said she. 'I agree to one year only. And only if a suitable tenant should be found. I must have within my power the prospect of returning to my beloved Whitcombe. In time, perhaps, I shall view matters differently, but until then, I cannot give up my home entirely. My poor, dear husband! How shall I live now that he is gone?'

Emma comforted her aunt as best she could; she understood that the loss of a loved one, whatever form that grief might take, is not easily borne, conquered or forgotten. In the days that followed, when relieved of the business of sorting, wrapping and packing those treasured items of which her aunt could not do without, Emma sought solace in walking.

It was on one such afternoon in early November that she returned from her walk to find a parcel addressed to 'Miss Osborne'. On further enquiry, it appeared that the young man who had delivered it had received information that Lord Osborne and Miss Osborne were guests at Whitcombe House.

'He appeared to know something of the circumstances of your visit, for he would not be persuaded to stay. The young gentleman left his card, and his deepest condolences,' said Mrs Beresford. 'I thought that was very handsomely done. Of course, had Osborne been here to receive him, I should have urged him to await your return. Your father has gone into Frome to interview a prospective tenant. I should not have had the heart to do it myself. He is very good, as are you, my dear. Indeed, I should not have managed things at all well without you, for my dear Colonel managed everything for me, you see.'

'Dear Aunt, do not distress yourself. Come, sit here and let me mix the tea leaves,' Emma replied. 'Tell me how you first met my uncle. I should dearly like to know everything about him that I do not know already.'

'Should you, my dear?' said Mrs Beresford. 'I was reminded of our first meeting this afternoon when the parcel addressed to *Miss Osborne* was placed before me. I made my dear husband's acquaintance at one of your grandmamma's famous musical evenings. Your Uncle Tom introduced us. Miss Osborne, said he, may I present Colonel Beresford?'

'And what thought you of the Colonel when first you saw him?' said Emma.

'I thought I should not know a moment's happiness without — without —' Mrs Beresford wiped away a tear.

'You knew from the outset?'

'Not I alone.'

'Uncle Beresford too? You fell in love instantly?'

'We did,' said Mrs Beresford. 'I have never, nor could I, love another as I have loved your uncle.'

Mrs Beresford gazed at the parcel. 'I expect you long for a private moment in which to open it.'

'No, Aunt, I assure you. I have no secrets. Let me open it now.'

'Do you not wish to know the name of the person who delivered it?'

'The gentleman's surname must be Fitzroy? I recognise the hand.'

'Then you are more intimately acquainted with this young man than I had realised. Perhaps I should have pressed him to wait for you.'

'No indeed,' Emma replied. 'Mr Fitzroy is much occupied at present with his brother.'

'I expect you mean Lord Allersham? There is much speculation in the neighbourhood about the future of Allersham. Though we were never intimate with that family, the treatment of the youngest brother

253

of the three by the elder was widely known and denounced. Captain Fitzroy was thought to be a fine young man, and he had for some years been able to temper the Earl's excesses and exercise some measure of influence over him. Such regulation came to an end with his passing. I'm sorry to say it, but your Mr Fitzroy will be obliged to assume the almost insurmountable undertaking of saving Allersham.'

Her aunt was interested to learn more about the present Earl's brother; and, seeing how the distraction raised Mrs Beresford's spirits, Emma obliged and explained the degree of connection there had been between them during her stay in Brinshore.

'This is not at all what Mr Fitzroy had hoped for,' Emma replied. 'His greatest desire was to enter the Church.'

'If there follows no permanent improvement in his brother's state of health, he will be obliged to give up the idea entirely. But what you say surprises me greatly,' said Mrs Beresford. 'His father, the fourth Earl, was hardly seen. He was for many years too infirm for society. The present Earl, unlike his father, is cursed with those peculiar infirmities that advance through self-infliction.'

'If only Lord Allersham would rally.'

'Should you not like to be mistress of Allersham?' said Mrs Beresford. 'No. Of course you should not. Allersham will take years to put right.'

Emma replied, 'There is no understanding between myself and Mr Fitzroy, nor can there ever be, but I confess, I should be happy to renew our acquaintance.'

'Invite Mr Fitzroy to Whitcombe, Emma. I see no harm in it. Your papa may receive him as I cannot.'

Emma smiled. 'If you desire it, Aunt.'

'I should think you do,' said Mrs Beresford.

Her niece made no reply. Emma placed the parcel on her knee and untied the string. Inside was a novel. She opened the cover and read the title page: '*Emma*, a novel in three volumes by the author of *Pride and Prejudice*.'

CHAPTER THIRTY-ONE

Emma had glimpsed the woods adjoining Allersham Park from the brow of Whitcombe Hill. Several times she had walked there; several times she had imagined Mr Fitzroy making a tour of the Park while contemplating the destiny that fate had seen fit to place upon him. Obscured by its extensive grounds and the undulating landscape that encircled it, all that could be seen of Allersham Hall from the vantage point of Whitcombe Hill was its majestic dome rising imposingly above the grand central portico. The hall must be grand indeed, thought she; it must surely possess that fashionable and elegant air which Osborne Castle is quite without.

Perched comfortably on a rock atop Whitcombe Hill, Emma opened the volume at the page where she had left off. The narrative appeared promising; and while Emma endeavoured to give her attention wholly to the Weston's Christmas party, she found from time to time that her thoughts drifted beyond the gates of Randalls, towards the roof top of Allersham.

No! said she. He will not occupy my thoughts, not for a moment! I shall put him out of my head completely; I shall meet every foolish, absurd notion with the derision it deserves. It will be of no consequence to me when or whether we meet again; but, should our paths cross at some time in the future, near or far, I shall not be affected or disturbed. Indeed, how could I countenance a man such as he — a man to whom Grandmamma makes not the least objection!

Emma read on. Allersham, thought she, must be grander by far than Hartfield or Randalls and infinitely more stylish than Donwell Abbey! If only the author of the piece had had Allersham in view!

Lucky indeed for Miss Woodhouse that she had no cousin to thwart and wound her at every turn; unlucky for Miss Woodhouse that her papa should be old and sickly! Grandmamma, for one, would not approve of Mr Woodhouse eating gruel for supper.

But never was there a novel more perfect nor more fitting than *Emma*! Happy for Miss Woodhouse that she would soon meet Mr Churchill! Oh! But Poor Harriet! If only she had not been persuaded to transfer her affections from Mr Martin to that odious Mr Elton!

Never had such volumes as these been more welcome, nor more greatly treasured by their recipient. At least there can be no misunderstanding, thought she; *Emma* is quite the unlikeliest title for a book of sermons as there could ever be.

Until such a time, a little more than two months hence, when I might wear my colours again, *Emma* shall be my companion, thought she; the want of diversion and the absence of society will then not be so daunting a prospect as it seems now.

Emma reckoned up the hours until the moment she would see Mr Fitzroy. I expect he will receive my note after luncheon, she mused. Then he may likely be obliged to sit with his brother for an hour at least before attending to his own affairs. Oh! but if he should be called away on some business that cannot be put off — some arduous, time-consuming errand for his brother! If he should be engaged with his brother's steward, physician or attorney — or all three in one day! I cannot depend on the hour at which I should expect his reply. And if his brother should see fit to exit this world before luncheon is served, I may likely not hear from Mr Fitzroy at all except for a note, edged black, to announce the grave news. I shall *not* think of him. I *shall not* expect a reply — not for another full day at the very least.

Emma turned a page and read on. *The hair was curled, and the maid sent away, and Emma sat down to think and be miserable.* The presumption of that abominable clergyman! To imagine himself a suitor for Miss Woodhouse! Inconceivable! He must think himself very great indeed! But then, Mr Fitzroy once had hopes of entering the Church, and he is not abominable.

Disgusted by Mr Elton's unforeseen and imprudent declaration, and the likely consequences for poor dear Harriet, Emma read on with speed, eager for the appearance of Frank Churchill. I am determined to approve of Frank, indeed I am! How curious that he should bear the name of my brother! I hope he is not a clumsy fellow.

As the morning progressed, Emma found herself increasingly absorbed in the affairs of Highbury and Hartfield. In the distance a figure began to climb Whitcombe Hill but remained hidden from view until footsteps belonging to the same became audible. Emma had thought little for her own safety until then; alone and unprotected, she stood up and looked about her in anxious anticipation.

The meeting she had wished for had come sooner than expected; there, before her, several paces away from the summit, was Mr Fitzroy.

'How came you to climb Whitcombe Hill?' said she.

256

'I suppose I climbed Whitcombe Hill in much the same way as you — one foot in front of the other,' he replied.

'What a curious coincidence,' she replied.

'It is no coincidence for I came in search of you as soon as I received your note. Your father said I might find you here.'

'You find me reading *Emma*, Mr Fitzroy.'

'I hope the novel meets with your approval.'

'*Emma* is quite delightful, though I doubt the narrative is to your taste, for poor Mr Elton is not what one hopes for in a clergyman. I do not get on with him at all. Mr Churchill promises to be quite the most charming man of the piece. He is already a favourite with me. If only his aunt would release him so that he may pay a visit to Randalls. He is certainly an intriguing young man, is he not? Emma is bound to fall in love with him.'

Mr Fitzroy smiled. 'Intriguing? Perhaps. But it is not the most dependable quality.'

Emma closed the volume and said, 'I once heard you, Mr Fitzroy, described as intriguing.'

'I am sorry to hear it,' said he.

'I believe it was meant as a commendation and not a criticism,' Emma replied.

'Was it indeed?' said he. 'Then I am sorely grieved.'

Emma looked about her, lost for something to say.

'I am sorry for your loss,' said he gently.

'Thank you,' Emma replied. 'Colonel Beresford was a dear man. My aunt will miss him dreadfully. But how came you to hear of it?'

Mr Fitzroy hesitated.

'Captain Blake. Of course,' said she.

'Charles wrote to me, but I had not the pleasure of receiving the information contained in his letter until my return from Delham, and by then I knew it all.'

'You were in Delham?'

'My brother rallied unexpectedly. I attended the wedding, you see.'

'Oh,' said Emma.

'I must say, I was surprised not to find you there.'

'How did the bride appear?'

'As any bride appears. In a pale gown — lace, I believe — and in the best of health,' said he. 'You were missed.'

When Mr Fitzroy next spoke, it was of Stanton.

'I happened to pass through the village of Stanton on my return.'

'Then you must have seen the parsonage. Did you observe the church porch? It is where Papa proposed to Mama, and where Grandpapa —'

'Yes,' he replied.

'It was the living I thought — you might — one day have — the living in Papa's gift.'

Mr Fitzroy followed Emma's line of vision to the dome atop Allersham Hall. 'What plan had you in mind when first you proposed it?'

Agitated by his question, Emma looked away. 'If I had any plan at all, Mr Fitzroy, you can hardly expect me to own it. Indeed, should a plan of some kind ever have been in my sights — theoretically speaking — the purpose no longer exists.'

'Because Mrs Blake is now happily settled in Waterloo Terrace?'

'Is Mrs Blake gone to Sanditon again? I had understood that she intended to remain in Delham,' Emma replied.

'I was referring to Mrs Charles Blake.'

'Of course you were. How stupid of me.' Emma looked down at the volume in her hands. She began to finger it nervously.

'Forgive me,' said he. 'I did not mean to cause you pain.'

'The cause of my pain, Mr Fitzroy, is entirely of my own making. You must think me devoid of good sense, full of guile and mischief. Tell me, did you refuse Stanton because you suspected my motive in putting you forward?'

'I should not have accepted it on such terms, nor I doubt, would your father have offered it had you placed before him your reasons for proposing it. But I believe it was kindly meant.'

'In part. I confess, I thought mainly of the advantage to myself,' said Emma. 'May I ask, Mr Fitzroy, when you first suspected an understanding between my cousin and Captain Blake?'

'When we first sat down to dinner together in Waterloo Terrace,' said he.

'Even then?' said she, shocked by his disclosure. 'Was I so blinded by my own desires and expectations that I did not see that which you perceived the instant you saw them together?'

'I was but an observer and had no desires of my own to obscure my perception. Perhaps I should have put you on your guard.'

'I should not have heeded your warning had you attempted to do so,' she replied. 'I can lay the blame for my suffering at no one but myself.'

'*Time, my dearest Emma, time will heal the wound.*'

'What?'

'Mr Knightley comforts Emma Woodhouse with those very words,' said he.

'Mr Knightley? That cannot be! What wound? Surely you do not mean Mr Churchill?'

'Who else?'

'Mr Fitzroy, how could you reveal the ending?'

'Have I?'

'Indeed you have! Mr Knightley must be the man, and not Frank Churchill! You might as well own it now that you have removed completely that element of surprise that a novel must depend on. I shall read on, of course, to discover how he secures her in the end.'

'Forgive me, Miss Osborne, but one need read no further than the first few pages, for it is as clear as day that Emma must marry Mr Knightley. That she should have imagined herself in love with Frank Churchill is but a detail that must be consigned to history, a mere transient obstacle in the way of their happiness. Tell me, Miss Osborne, do you comprehend my meaning, or should I speak plainer?'

Emma smiled, 'I believe I comprehend your meaning, but I should like you to speak with your usual candour nevertheless.'

'Very well,' said he. 'When first I made your acquaintance —'

'When you splashed my dress with mud —'

'I did not think you too promising.'

'Nor I you,' she replied.

'Of that, I was in no doubt,' said he. 'But as I stood by and watched you endure the agonies of disappointed love, I watched in wonder and admiration as you succeeded in putting aside your own desires for the sake of another couple's happiness, in the knowledge that their union would be a perpetual reminder of your own thwarted hopes and dreams. You are deserving of the profoundest love. And if I thought I might — if I thought you would find a moment's happiness as my partner in life, I should offer you my heart, my hand, here and now.'

Perplexed by the manner of his declaration, Emma was in doubt as to whether Mr Fitzroy had made her an offer at all.

'What am I to say?' said she. 'Do not suppose me capricious, flighty or inconstant when I say that I should welcome your address. I did not know it until the day we parted — for we have not met since Michaelmas — but it is you whom I have grown to esteem and love. Was it not you on whom I relied and with whom I was most at ease? Was it not you with whom I could own my blunders and imperfections without fear of censure? Mr Fitzroy, so much has occurred since we last met in Brinshore. I shall always hold Charles Blake in the highest esteem as a cousin and a friend, but I can say hand on heart that I do not love him as I thought.'

'My dearest Emma, it is so? Truly?'

'Yes,' she replied. 'I am beset by neither doubt nor indecision. I know myself as I did not know myself before.'

'I did not dare to hope.'

'It *is* true.'

'You know that my future is as uncertain as any future can be. My brother may yet be restored to his former health. It is not unknown for such a reversal to occur.'

'I *pray* that he may rally! I pray that you may be spared the burden of Allersham, for I know that in your heart you have never desired it. Do not forget, I am the granddaughter of a clergyman. It may surprise you to find that, after all, I find I have no objections to becoming the wife of one.'

'Nevertheless, I am surprised.'

'Please do not imagine that I transferred my affections for more material considerations. The prospect of a fine house and extensive grounds is all very well, but I may live my days at Osborne Castle just as easily and benefit from the same there.'

'In return, do not imagine my object to be a suitable alliance.'

'No one could accuse you of fortune hunting, Mr Fitzroy, with your history.'

'Henry.'

'Henry.'

'Even so, my dearest Emma, allow me to set before you the facts. Allersham Hall has fallen into a state of disrepair and is not so very fine, though the grounds, I grant you, are extensive. There are considerable debts, the extent of which I am still uncertain.'

'Yes, I know.'

'And still you have no doubts?'

'None,' she replied. 'Shall you speak to Papa?'

'I have done so already.'

'Oh,' said she. 'What said he?'

'Your father gave his blessing.'

'Dear Papa! I knew he would,' said Emma. 'And your brother? Shall I win his approval?'

CHAPTER THIRTY-TWO

Long engagements are never greatly to be desired, less so prolonged periods of mourning. Lord Allersham passed away peacefully and at an early hour on the morning of the nineteenth day of November; at his bedside was his brother with whom he had seen fit to make his peace before breathing his last.

The expectation of the event did little to lessen the shock; on that fateful day, Mr Henry Fitzroy stood in silent disbelief as Allersham's chaplain, in accordance with his dying brother's wishes, administered the last rites.

The estate, being in a sorry state of disrepair, delayed the business of matrimony beyond the normal period in which the customary duties and obligations incumbent on the heir of the deceased are ordinarily discharged.

In the intervening year, the future Countess of Allersham spent her time moving between Osborne Castle, Whitcombe House and Trafalgar Terrace. Aunt Beresford did not give up Whitcombe; the decision was welcomed by her niece and the new Lord Allersham who, on the recommendation of his fiancée, sought her aunt's advice on the replacement of the drapes and the painting of the walls at Allersham Hall.

And when the foundations for the spa at Brinshore were complete and required Lord Allersham's presence, Emma was just as pleased to visit her Aunt and Uncle Fowle. It was on a visit to Brinshore, in the spring of seventeen, that Emma visited Sanditon and called upon Captain and Mrs Blake at Waterloo Terrace; she was pleased to find them in excellent health and expecting the birth of their first child at Michaelmas. The reception she received could not have been warmer or more sincere, and all three parted on the best of terms.

Lord and Lady Osborne were as delighted as the Dowager and Mrs Turner at the news of their daughter's engagement; and neither occupant of the Dower House gave the least heed to their own advancing mortality; indeed, both were determined to see Emma a countess first, and meddle as much as possible in the preparations for the longed-for event.

Frank adored his brother-in-law to whom he looked up to as an uncle; and when Lord Allersham presented the boy with a cocker spaniel pup, he could not have bestowed on Frank a more treasured gift.

In time, Brinshore was pleased to boast its own spa. Visitors flocked to seek cures for every ailment of mind and body by partaking of the waters, internally and externally, under the careful direction of Mr Fowle. His wife was never better satisfied than when she was afforded the pleasure of boasting that a great number of ladies and gentlemen of the highest circles had taken the waters and recommended Brinshore above every other watering place in England. Never had she found one single instance of its inefficacy, even among those parties previously bereft of every other hope of relief. Fevers, cholic, flatulence, nervous disorders, sickness, vomiting, weakness peculiar to the female sex, gouty spasms, hysteria, low spirits, hypochondriacal affections and loss of appetite — all these maladies, and more besides — were certain to find a cure in Brinshore.

Emma never neglected to visit her two young friends on every return to Trafalgar Terrace. Within a small and private educational establishment, under the kindly protection of a Mr and Mrs Worth, a couple of maturing years, the children displayed before their friend the fruits of their labours. Brinshore Buns and asses' milk, gifts from their patroness, were sent in liberal quantities to the establishment every Sunday throughout the year.

A little more than a year after the engagement of Emma Osborne and Henry Fitzroy was first announced, the notice of a marriage appeared in the London and Bath newspapers. On Saturday December 20th 1817, the Dowager took up the *Morning Post* and read: 'On the 16th instant at Stanton Parish Church, the Right Honourable the Earl of Allersham, of the County of Somerset, to the Honourable Emma Osborne, only daughter of the Right Honourable Viscount Osborne of Osborne Castle in the County of Surrey.'

'My granddaughter a countess!' said she. 'It is all just as I had planned. And now I have only to await the arrival of Lady Forbes' fine pianoforte.'

'Lady Forbes' pianoforte?' replied Lady Osborne.

'Yes, my dear. I should have been loath indeed to give up the Meissen.'

'Lady Forbes will be most put out for she treasures that fine instrument!' said Mrs Turner, attempting to make herself comfortable in the Dowager's armchair. 'Indeed, I am not best pleased myself.'

The new seating arrangements had not gone unnoticed by Lady Osborne; the room had been rearranged, and her aunt and mother-in-law were now seated in each other's armchairs.

'Mama, tell me, you did not enter into a wager involving your own granddaughter.'

The Dowager rearranged her shawl.

'There was no doubt in my mind that my granddaughter would one day wear a coronet. Emma a countess! What a clever creature she is!'

'You once thought her head full of emptiness,' said Lady Osborne.

'Not I, my dear,' the Dowager replied, 'for Emma takes after me. She bears no resemblance whatsoever to your Aunt Turner!'

Books by Ann Mychal in the
Watson Novels series:

Emma and Elizabeth

Laura Place